Apocalypse Law 5

Liberty or Tyranny

John Grit

This book is a work of fiction. Names, characters, and events are either the product of the author's imagination or are used fictitiously. Any resemblance to actual events, locales, or persons, living or dead, is entirely coincidental.

Copyright ©2014 by John Grit

Manufactured in the United States of America.
Cover photo © 2014 Bigstock by Delion

Chapter 1

The middle-aged woman lay on the floor. Her dead eyes stared up at the ceiling. Nate Williams looked down at the dried puddle of blood and tried to ignore the sickening metallic smell in his nostrils. The cold weather helped, but the smell still made him wish he could walk outside and get some fresh air. He couldn't do that. As acting sheriff of the county, he had to find the killer. It didn't matter that once he arrested him there was no court system to try him and no prison system to take the killer off his hands. In the end, justice would most likely be in the form of a bullet, little different from the murder that started the manhunt in the first place. In this post-apocalyptic world, right and wrong had become a matter of a person's conscience, not of law.

Second-guessing his conscience consumed too many sleepless nights. Being a man of short temper with little tolerance for people abusing others, he had long ago taught himself to control that temper and seldom acted without first thinking things through. It had saved his life many times through the years. It didn't, however, spare him sleepless nights.

Nate avoided looking at the woman's face and wouldn't allow himself to wonder what kind of person she was. There was a time before the plague when most Americans were never a part of violence, unless they served in the military or were in law enforcement or were first responders of another sort. Those days died along with most of the world's human population. Killed by the plague. Societal infrastructure collapsed for want of manpower, and violent panic spread like a wildfire across every modern city around the world. The thin veneer of civilization that had taken humankind thousands of years to build had been stripped away, laying bare the ugliest of man's nature. The eyes of everyone left living had witnessed many horrors. Their nostrils had smelled death in most every home and in every street, their souls tortured by the tragedy.

Early morning sunrays slanted in through the open front door of the small, two-bedroom home and caused the bloody shoeprints that led outside to glisten. Nate shivered in the cold and followed the tracks – never a complete shoeprint but only a dab or smear of dried blood here and there – down the drive and onto the street. He took note that the steps were short. Perhaps the killer was small, or perhaps he was carrying a heavy load. The house had been ransacked and it appeared items had been taken, so he leaned toward the heavy load premise. The blood trail faded, and it became more difficult to see the partial tracks on the rough asphalt, but Nate was able to follow the trail to the house next door. He hadn't been able to determine the killer's size, but the tracks did tell him where he went. Was he still in the house?

The body had been found by a hungry neighbor who wanted to ask the woman if she could spare some food. She found the front door ajar and looked in. When she saw the body, she ran screaming for home. Her seventeen-year-old son went for help. That was just after sunrise. The victim had been dead for at least two hours. No one had heard the gunshot.

Atticus and Tyrone kept watch for danger, one armed with a shotgun, the other a rifle, while Nate rushed to a tree in the front yard. A shot rang out, and bark flew from the oak near Nate's head. He dropped to a knee, keeping behind the thick trunk. *Well, this case isn't going to take much detective work. Damn fool.*

A woman yelled from the house through the same window the shot had come from. "Go away!"

Nate stayed behind the tree. "We can't do that. A woman has been murdered. Shooting at us is just going to get you killed. Being arrested is better than getting shot."

"I have children in here." With her victim lying dead, she had little reason not to kill again. "You shoot and you'll be shooting at innocent kids."

Nate fumed. *You get the mother of the year award.* "Then come out with your hands empty before they get hurt. You're not going anywhere. You might as well give up now. I'm not certain what the outcome will be, but you'll get some kind of a trial. Maybe the Army will take you off our hands."

While he was yelling at the woman in the house, Sergeant Deni Heath drove up in a Humvee and jumped out wearing full body armor, topped off with a Kevlar helmet. She had learned of the murder from a citizen. Deni had made up her mind she would spend the last two weeks before leaving the military helping Nate stay alive, while he kept his promise to a friend to act as sheriff until they could get married and return to Nate's farm with his teenage son. She heard the shot from three blocks away. Her face revealed relief when she saw Nate was unharmed.

With her M4 carbine held at the low ready, she ran and took position behind a thick tree in a yard across the street. A shot rang out. There was no evidence where the bullet went. Perhaps it went high and plowed into the roof of the home behind her.

Nate took the time to make sure she had not been hit, momentarily directing his attention away from the house the shooter was in. He felt safer knowing she was backing him. *Just stay behind that tree.*

Tyrone, who had been a deputy before the plague and the only real lawman among them, tried to rush for the backyard, so he could stop the murderer from escaping out the back of the house, but a shot forced him to take cover behind the engine block of a disabled small car in the murdered woman's drive. He was in a dangerous position. A rifle bullet could go through the thin metal of the car and kill him. He got up and ran for the front door of the house. Sometimes being a large man had its drawbacks, and he struggled to move fast. A volley of shots rang out, answered by Atticus's shotgun and Nate's rifle. Forced to take cover, the murderer stopped shooting before she managed to get a bullet into Tyrone, who disappeared into the victim's home.

Deni bided her time, exposing only one side of her head enough to see past the tree she used for cover. She searched for movement in the windows facing the front of the home the shooter was in. The woman shot at Nate again. The resulting muzzle flash in the dark living room illuminated the woman's face for a split second. Deni fired. Her three quick shots were followed by a promising silence. Was it over?

Nate's radio squelched and Tyrone's voice emitted from the speaker. "I'm in position to storm the backdoor. It's closed and probably locked, but it looks like I can go through it pretty quick."

Nate put the radio to his mouth. "Hold off on that. Wait for Atticus. You'll need him to back you with his shotgun. Also, Donovan gave me a flash-bang grenade the other day. When I throw it through a front window, you go in through the back door."

Tyrone agreed. "Just make sure you cover Atticus while he makes his way back here."

"Deni's across the street. Between the two of us, we'll keep the shooter's head down."

The plan seemed simple enough, but if the shooter was still alive, it could all go to hell at the speed of a bullet. Nate hand signaled Atticus to make his way to Tyrone.

For an old man, Atticus moved fast, but age and past injuries slowed him, and he took twice as long to get to the victim's front door as Tyrone had. Nate and Deni were ready to provide cover fire, but no one shot. Nate fired into the windows a few times anyway, to interrupt the woman's aim. He began to think Deni in all probability had killed the shooter.

Tyrone's voice came over the radio. "We're ready."

Nate pulled the grenade from a jacket pocket and readied himself. He jumped up and ran until he was so close he knew he couldn't miss the window, threw the grenade, and swerved to his right, jumping behind a small cedar that was nowhere near thick enough to provide cover from rifle fire, but it was all the cover he had.

The grenade went off. A flash of bright red flame lit the interior of the room the woman was in and smoke billowed out of the broken windows.

Despite the cold, Nate and Deni sweated in their clothes and held their rifles to their shoulders, looking over the sights, ready to fire at a second's notice.

Silence.

Tyrone's breathless voice blared from Nate's radio. "It's over. She's dead and she was the only one in the house. No children."

What they found inside was as unpleasant as the scene in the victim's home.

Nate glanced down and saw the body, then turned, blocking the front door. "Deni, will you stay out front to keep the gawking neighbors away?"

She stopped in her tracks and stared at him. "So it was my bullet that got her."

"Maybe." Nate motioned down the street. "There's the woman who found the body, and several people are with her. You would be helping more by learning what you can from them and keeping them out of our way."

She double checked the safety on her rifle. "Must be a gruesome sight. It's not like you to coddle me."

Nate cast his eyes down for a second. "It's no worse than anything else you've seen, not as bad, really. But what's the point of you having the image burned into your memory?"

She shrugged. "Okay. If it makes you feel better to be the big man who shields his woman from the world." She turned and walked away.

Nate unloaded a load from his lungs, certain he had just pissed her off, but glad she wasn't going to see what her bullet had done to the woman's head.

Atticus appeared from the kitchen. "Looks like what we were told by the neighbors was accurate. They said someone must have killed the woman for her food, because some of her supplies were missing." He jabbed a thumb over his shoulder. "There are canned goods and other food piled everywhere. She must've made several trips after killing the victim."

Tyrone added, "The victim had a reputation as a survivalist or what they call a prepper. She had a lot of supplies stored in her home and had been handing food and other supplies out to the neighbors until a few weeks back, when she said she could spare no more, having little left for herself. Some of the neighbors, who had grown accustomed to getting at least a little something from her just by showing up at her door and asking, grew angry, saying she was being selfish and was lying about being out of extra supplies."

Atticus shook his head. "I guess it's kind of a miracle it didn't happen months ago. She should never have let anyone know she had the stuff. This one decided she would just go over and kill the woman and take what she could haul off." He had found a sheet in a back room. Speaking as he spread it over the woman's upper body, he said, "Neighbors say both were widowed by the plague. It seems one was killed for being too kind, the other for being a vicious murderer. Uh, that and shooting at us." He looked at the other men. "I guess God will sort it out now."

Tyrone wiped his forehead with the sleeve of his jacket. "I don't like speaking ill of the dead, but neither one was too bright."

Nate stepped out onto the front porch and watched Deni talk to the growing crowd of a dozen or more neighbors, who spoke in subdued tones, their breaths misting in the cold. He joined them, standing beside Deni. "It appears she killed her neighbor for her food. Are the people around here that hungry? The warehouse food will not run out for months, so why would she be so desperate?"

A mother holding her baby in her arms spoke. "Yes, we're hungry. The warehouse handouts have been cut in half. The Army says it must last until that farm people are working on starts producing more, and no one knows how long that'll be."

Her husband added, "We need food now, not six months from now. Starvation rations will just prolong the agony. People keep asking why I don't help on the farm. But how can I work when I'm so weak from lack of food?"

Atticus had followed Nate to the street. He stood beside him and stared the man down. "No one's gaining weight, but most of us are pitching in and doing what we can. If you represent even ten percent of the people in this county, we're all going to starve. Everyone must do their part if we're going to pull through this."

The man glared at him. "Yeah, right. All you do is carry a gun."

"Oh, shut up, Larry," a woman standing nearby said. "I'm sure they'll give you their job, if you like getting shot at and being forced to kill people. I offered several times to advise you on how to grow vegetables in your backyard and give you some seed, but you always said you had other things to do."

Atticus snorted. "Job? A paycheck usually comes with a job. None of us are paid a thing. And the last two months, all

I've had to eat is beans and rice. Once, I had eggs for breakfast."

Tyrone walked up, glanced at Atticus, the man who raised him as his son, and then faced the crowd. "Atticus is a little short-tempered at the moment, since we just had to kill a woman who tried her best to kill us. That aside, we'll ask Colonel Donovan about the rations. If he's reduced them, there must be a reason."

Nate's patience ran thin. "For now, we could use some help with the bodies. I understand the victim's name was Wilma Thresher. Maybe some of you who have enjoyed her generosity could see to it she receives a decent burial and contact Reverend McKnight. He may be willing to attend and say some words over her." His stare wilted those in the crowd who had a conscience. "That is, if any of you think she deserves such consideration."

"What about the food the killer took?" Larry wanted to know. "She won't need it."

Ignoring him, Nate continued. "If either of the women had relatives or friends in town, I would appreciate it if one of you would inform them of their deaths." He walked away, shaking his head.

Deni caught up with Nate. "Don't be too hard on them. They're just people."

He stopped and looked up at the sky. "Cold front's coming in tonight. We're going to have another long, cold winter." He stepped close and touched her face. "I wasn't coddling you. I just didn't think there was any reason for you to see what your bullet did."

She tried to smile. "I think you're homesick. This fast life in the big city doesn't suit you."

He grunted. "What I'm sick of is the feeling of being overwhelmed by things I can't change. I tell you this: When the two weeks are up and you're out of the Army, I'm heading back to my little farm, and you're going to have to run to keep up with me."

Deni seemed relieved. "You promise?" She examined his face for a second. "Oh, that's right; you did promise you would fill in as sheriff for only two weeks."

Nate looked away at nothing in particular. "Yeah. As if you'd forgotten. I expected you to hold me to that promise when I made it."

"You bet. This town is trouble, and when government officials in Washington decide to come down here and throw their weight around, it'll be this town they come to, not some little farm in the sticks. And Donovan isn't going to be able to stop them. In fact, he'll be the one they expect to carry out their orders."

"I don't want to be in his shoes." He held her for a second and let her go before she had time to respond. "He made sure you got out of the Army in time. We owe him. But there's nothing more we can do to help him or these people. Whatever is going to happen will happen whether we're here in the middle of it or not. We can't change a bit of it. If Washington wants to get rough, there's nothing to stop them."

She looked at him as if she were trying to read past his words. "You're right, but you can't help yourself. You'll still do what you can, no matter how helpless it all is. I just wish you'd listen to your own words and get out of here. Marry me and take Brian and Kendell and Mel and Caroline – if they want to come – and get away before the shitstorm hits."

Nate felt the cold wind on his face. "The other side of the coin is we'll be easily outgunned at the farm, and there are still plenty of troublemakers around. The government isn't our only worries." His face was expressionless. "And I wouldn't bet on the government not coming after little farmers. Remember the photos of private gardens they used drones and satellites to get?"

Deni changed the subject. "We could get married sometime before I'm officially released from the Army. It'll save time, and we could leave the afternoon they let me go."

For a moment, Deni was the only person on his mind. "If that's what you want. The wedding is certainly not going to be as fancy as what you deserve."

"We all deserve better than the life we've been living. The human race has had a bad year, but there's always next year. I'll be satisfied with us standing in front of a preacher and saying 'I do.'" Her eyes lit up. "If you want something fancier, you'll have to pay for it yourself. I don't have a rich father willing to pay for his daughter's royal wedding."

He smiled, but then a thought came to him and the smile vanished.

She noticed. "What?"

"There is someone I need to talk to before we leave town, and it might as well be today. Would you give me a ride?"

Puzzled, she answered, "Sure."

"Just let me talk to Tyrone and Atticus first." He ran to the house, where neighborhood men were helping Tyrone and Atticus carry the covered bodies to the pickup Nate had driven to the scene. He conversed with them for less than a minute and ran back to her. "Let's go. Head for downtown."

~~~

They came to the old house the mother of the little boy Nate had accidently run over a few months back lived in. "Pull over here," he said.

Deni stopped the Humvee. "So this is who you need to speak to." She turned in the seat to face him more squarely. "It wasn't your fault."

"I just want to apologize."

"This might be a mistake. I doubt she's the kind to accept your apology with grace."

"I owe her that."

"You don't owe her a chance to attack you and call you a murderer again. It was an accident. It would've happened no matter who was driving. The little boy ran out from between two cars and there was no way anyone could've seen him from behind the wheel of that big truck. Brian told me the only reason he saw the boy was because he was on the passenger side and happened to be looking that way when he ran out into the road. If Kendell or Brian had been driving, they would never have seen the little boy either. They're both a lot shorter than you and would've seen even less."

Nate rubbed his forehead and looked inward. "I wasn't thinking straight that day."

"Yeah, you were recovering from a head wound. But if one of the boys was driving it would have changed nothing. The mother should have never let her little boy play in the street."

"I guess it may do more harm than good." He looked at the house, half excepting the mother to come charging out the front door with a shotgun in her hands, screaming about how he had murdered her child.

"That's certainly possible," Deni said. "Especially if she goes into a rage on you. That would do neither of you any good."

"I just don't want her to think I've forgotten her little boy, like I just ran over a squirrel or something."

"I don't know what she thinks. I do know it's time for you to let it go."

His thoughts struggling with his conscience, Nate sat there in silence. He looked down the street, his eyes focusing on nothing in particular. "It's not something you just let go." Turning to look at the house one more time, he said, "But you've talked me out of bothering her. Take me to Donovan, so I can tell him about the murder and ask why food rations have been cut."

Deni put the Humvee in gear. "It was nothing more than an accident. If you didn't feel bad about it, you wouldn't be you. But it was still an accident."

He nodded. "Let's go. It can't be undone and there are other tragedies to avert – if possible."

~~~~

Deni pulled up to the entrance of the Army FOB (Forward Operations Base) in the middle of what was the county fairground, just outside of the downtown area. Two-ton concrete blocks and anything else that would prevent car bombs and other vehicles from getting within 300 yards of the inner fence had been lined along the outer perimeter. Soldiers armed with M4s kept watch from behind sandbagged guard posts. Every tenth soldier was armed with a squad automatic weapon. The downtown area was looking more like a war zone every day. Most civilians believed it was a sensible response to the many months of lawlessness and the various radical groups that had emerged recently, but a few were becoming more and more uneasy with the Army and what they were learning about the new government in Washington.

Lieutenant Colonel Mike Donovan met them at the security gate. He appeared more harassed than the last time they spoke to him. He motioned with his left arm. "Come on to my office. We need to talk."

"That's what we're here for," Nate said.

Donovan spoke over his shoulder as he stepped into a small building his men had hastily assembled from portable storage containers lifted in by helicopter. The meager bullet-stopping ability of the thin sheet metal had been reinforced with sandbags.

"Your new accommodations aren't as comfortable as the last place," Nate observed.

"The threat level has increased." Donovan sat behind his desk. "The Army and Guard both have been under attack in Miami, Orlando, Atlanta – all over the country." He motioned to steel folding chairs in front of his desk. "Some of it is radical groups, but in the cities most of it is mob anger at everything government. They just can't understand why things haven't gotten better by now." He leaned forward and rubbed his eyes with the palms of his hands. "They're hungry. I guess you can't blame people for not thinking straight after all they've been through, but killing soldiers will not be tolerated." He looked up at them with tired eyes. "To make matters worse, Washington and the Pentagon have become institutions for the insane."

"Weren't they always?" Deni quipped.

Nate noticed Donovan's freckled face was nearly as red as his hair and he appeared to be angry as much as exhausted. "You look like I feel. Except I'm dealing with local idiots."

Donovan raised an eyebrow. "Yeah, well. Uh." He looked up at the ceiling for a second, perhaps to get a better grasp on his temper. "The powers that be have stepped up their demands for results and cut food rations to soldiers in the field. I guess they think if we soldiers are hungry we'll be more willing to get rough with the people and demand they give up 'their fair share' of any crops they have raised." He slumped in his chair. "We're in the middle of another freakishly cold and long winter and these idiots want me to take what little food the local people have. Doesn't Washington realize that if people are forced to choose between starving and dying from lead poisoning they'll choose the latter? What do they want, a damn civil war?"

"I expect that's exactly what they're afraid of," Nate answered. "I bet people have been starving in the cities since not long after the plague hit. Food production and shipments came to a halt surprisingly fast, and city people are a lot less self-sufficient than rural people. I remember the early news reports, before the power went out. All of the stores were empty in less than a week. The level of violence is certainly much higher in the cities, also."

Deni added, "As all of us have witnessed over the last year, desperate people do desperate things."

"Well, they're about to get more desperate around here." Donovan looked at Deni as he talked. He had something on his mind.

"What?" Deni asked.

He smiled. "Get lost, that's what. You two get married and get out of town. Head for the sticks. It's about to hit the fan around here, and there's no reason for you to be around when it does. You have no official duties, anyway. To hell with the formalities. Turn in the rest of your gear and get out of town before it gets bad."

"Wow." Deni's eyes flashed to Nate and back to Donovan. "They must really be putting pressure on you to send food, no matter how rough you have to get with the locals."

Donovan grew grim. "Don't tell me you two haven't talked about getting out before your two weeks are up. Go ahead. I'll okay it."

Deni sat up straight in her chair. "Well, before you get rid of us, tell us what's going on."

Donovan rubbed the back of his neck. "Everything I feared Washington would do over the next few months is already in play." He shook his head. "They just promoted me and already they're threatening to relieve me of my command if I can't gather up at least five truckloads of produce and meat within a week." He threw his arms into the air. "What the hell are a few truckloads of food going to do for the country? The country needs more people willing to get off their ass and work the fields. Forcibly taking food from those who work will discourage others from following their lead. Why bother if you're going to go hungry anyway?"

"How are they going to get semis up the interstate highways?" Nate asked. "Have they been cleared of all those abandoned vehicles?"

Donovan's face lightened up a bit. "They tell me the highways will be cleared soon. I doubt it, but that's what they claim. The Army did get fuel tankers through a while back, but only by using bulldozers to push everything out of the way, clearing one south-bound lane. And that was only between here and Fort Benning. It took months."

Nate had an idea. "Did they specify what kind of meat and produce?"

Donovan crossed his arms and leaned back in his chair. "What do you have in mind?"

"We might be able to buy you some time. They're having problems at the new farm with wild hogs tearing the fields up. Some of the men have built traps and are harvesting a dozen or more hogs a night. They've been butchering them and handing out the meat, but I think we can talk them into giving you a few dozen of the older, less palatable boars. The meat is really gamey, but it will fill stomachs. They could also spare some trash fish. It's edible, but not tasty. As for produce, there's 500 acres of potatoes being harvested 12 miles east of town. I'm sure you could make a trade with the farmer. Maybe some diesel fuel or something. Also, there are some greenhouse-grown tomatoes, green beans, cabbage, and other stuff, but people will be reluctant to let that go. Production capacity is limited in small greenhouses and this extreme winter cold has limited open field production drastically. An overnight freeze can wipe out a whole crop. Even so, some people have been producing onions in decent amounts. You might get a little of that without resorting to taking it at gunpoint."

Donovan scribbled on a notepad. "That would help, but it will not hold them for long."

The expression on Nate's face changed. "I just remembered the beet farmer southwest of town. Beets are something people will be willing to part with by the truckload, and there's plenty of it. Beets are easy to grow. You should be able to get several semi loads for a little fuel or something else the family needs."

Donovan added to his notes. "A few truckloads of beets and hogs may satisfy them well enough I might not have to bother with the other produce much. I might be able to convince them the extreme weather has prevented most other crops from surviving long enough to be harvested. That would be the unfortunate truth, anyway." Donovan's face hardened. "But no matter how much time this buys, sooner or later the order to use force will come down." He shook his head. "I will not order soldiers to rob Americans of food they toiled in the fields for, and I will not order soldiers to fire on peaceful civilians."

"I'm sorry you're in this terrible position," Nate said. "You're doing the best you can, but someday soon your conscience is going to get you in trouble."

Donovan shrugged. "No one alive today is without his problems, including those in Washington."

Nate nodded. "And the way they're trying to solve one problem is just going to cause a hundred more. There's still no government at the local and state level, at least in our part of the country, and Washington's control of things is tenuous at best. They need to think before they go too far and lose what control they have over what's left of the American population. If that happens, there may not be a United States of America. A few years from now, when the survivors have organized locally and regionally, we may have five or six countries, instead of one."

"Anything's possible," Donovan agreed. "If our enemies abroad were not in worse shape than we are, we might be facing an invasion already. We finally managed to deal with Mexico and their claims on the Southwest. It was a bloody job, but we beat – rather shot – them back to Mexico. Certainly, America hasn't been this weak and vulnerable to military attack since our earliest days as a young nation." He got up from his chair. "But right now, starvation is the most immediate danger." Showing them to the door, he said, "You two should really think about leaving town as soon as possible. I could be relieved of command any day, and my replacement might be as crazy as the man I replaced. Get out while you can."

Nate stopped before reaching the door. "We wanted to tell you about the murder of a woman that took place this morning. We were forced to kill the suspect in a gunfight."

"I have someone on scene talking to witnesses." Donovan spoke to a soldier waiting outside the storage container that was his office. "Escort them to the gate."

Nate stopped in front of Donovan. They shook hands. "I have a feeling we might not see you again."

Donovan tried to smile. "You're probably right – if all goes well and you follow my advice. But *I'm* not going anywhere. Not until they send someone to get me."

Deni blinked tears. "I feel like I'm deserting you."

Donovan shook his head. "Don't. You're a civilian now. Go be a civilian. Hell, don't bother with turning in your gear. Keep it. Go find a place to wait out the storm." He turned and closed the door behind him.

Nate and Deni got into the Humvee. As she drove away, she started to speak several times but stopped.

"I know," Nate said. "Donovan's a good man caught between a rock and a hard place. The fact is, though, his problems with higher-ups in the Pentagon and Washington are his fight, not ours."

Deni clenched her jaw. "You're right. There's nothing we can do to help him or the people here."

Nate looked out his window. "That's what I keep telling myself."

She glanced his way and back to the road ahead. "What about leaving town tonight?"

He turned and gave her his full attention. "We're not married yet. Also, I would like to see Chesty buried before we leave. We should talk to a preacher tomorrow, though. Certainly, we need to be ready to leave this town behind us soon."

"Yeah. How do you feel about that?" she asked.

"Terrible. I don't like leaving Donovan with this mess, and I don't like abandoning the people here. But I usually let my mind do my thinking, not my feelings. My mind tells me there is nothing the two of us can do to change whatever is going to become of Donovan and the people of this little town. My main goal from the beginning has been to keep Brian alive. Lately, I've gotten off course. Some things have changed. You for example. But keeping Brian – and you – alive is still my main goal." He thought of a black teen he had taken under his wing and friends he had met over the last year. "I doubt Kendell will be willing to leave the orphaned kids at Mrs. MacKay's farm for any length of time, so he'll probably decide to stay there with the children. I don't know about Caroline. She may want to stay at the farm too. Whether they come with us or not, my days of trying to help everyone I come across are over. I can't save the world."

She looked straight ahead and gripped the steering wheel tight. "I agree, but have my doubts you'll be able to live by those words."

Nate jerked his head around and stared at her for several seconds. He started to speak of how seeing Brian close to death had cured him of getting involved with others' troubles, but stopped himself.

Chapter 2

That night, a cold front charged down from the north, blown in by powerful winds. Heavy rain pounded on a window on the other end of the bedroom, and cold penetrated the thin wool blanket Nate had over him. He lay there shivering and looked around the dark room. But it wasn't the cold that had awakened him. Thunder? Or was it gunfire?

It was then he realized for the first time he had already reached for the Kimber 1911 that he kept on the nightstand beside the bed. It was in his right hand, his thumb on the safety and muzzle pointed at the window.

His sleeping bag was tied to his backpack in the closet. It offered warmth the thin blanket couldn't, so he tossed the blanket aside and sat up in bed.

Thinking of his son Brian and Kendell, he got up to search the house for more blankets to bring to them. Kendell was in another bedroom. Brian had insisted on sleeping on the living room floor behind a couch, his rifle beside him, saying something about how the terrorists, who for some crazy reason feared the rebuilding of society and were willing to kill to stop it, wouldn't expect anyone to be sleeping on the floor. Considering the fact a close friend had just been murdered in bed, Nate couldn't argue against his son's precaution. In some ways, things were getting better, but they still lived in a deadly, lawless world. He would never argue against putting safety first. Sleeping on the floor wouldn't hurt him, and forgoing the comfort of a bed for added safety made sense.

Nate found Brian already awake in his sleeping bag, unzipped so he could get out fast and grab his rifle that lay next to him. He sat up. "What? Did you hear something?"

"I'm getting a blanket for Kendell," Nate whispered. He went on to the room Kendell slept in and found him looking up, his rifle in his hands.

"Trouble?" Kendell asked.

"No." Nate dropped two blankets beside him. "I brought you these. Go back to sleep. There's nobody around, as near as I can tell."

Kendell ignored the blankets. "I thought I heard a shot a few minutes ago."

Nate hesitated for a moment. "I think it was thunder." He left the room and checked the front and back doors, peering out into the rainy night through every window, one at a time, his pistol in his hand. Then he went back to bed and slept fitfully, wishing Deni had not insisted on staying at the Army base one more night to learn what she could about what the Army was up to.

When dawn broke, he got up to put his boots on, first putting on the thickest wool socks he had. He glanced at his dead friend Chesty's badge on the nightstand, just before slipping it into his jacket pocket. The thought came to him that he should not bother carrying it. Why pretend he was something he wasn't? He was no lawman. He was a vigilante, plain and simple. Tyrone was the only one in town who had been a real lawman (a deputy) before the plague killed most of the human population around the world. Chesty had been town marshal before everything went to hell, but he was dead.

The void Chesty had left behind – the town people's need for law and protection – had to be filled by someone. Nate knew that it wasn't him. He had planned to do what he could until Deni got out of the Army, but he was becoming ever more convinced they needed to get out of town soon and not wait. Donovan gave her permission to leave as soon as possible, and he felt she should not turn down the offer. The people would have to find another sheriff. Tyrone was certainly the man for the job, the only man. He would need help, but it was time for others to step up and carry some of the load. He still remembered the look on Deni's face the night he agreed to carry Chesty's badge. At that moment, he had decided that two weeks was all they were going to get of him. No matter what might happen, he was going to marry Deni and they were going back to the farm. "Sorry," he said to no one, "but even two weeks is too long."

Nate wore his .44 magnum revolver under his jacket in a shoulder holster a former gunsmith had given him only the day before and had the 1911 .45 on his right side for fast access. He carried two speed loaders for the revolver and four magazines for the pistol. If someone killed him, it wouldn't be for lack of shooting back. The thought he should put on his poncho lived and died in less than a second. He would rather get wet and cold than not be able to get to his handguns if needed. Besides, the courthouse was only two blocks away, and it wasn't raining all that hard at the moment. His clothes might not even be soaked through by the time he got there.

After slipping into his load bearing harness that held six magazines for his M14, he put on his boonie hat, grabbed the rifle, and quietly walked into the living room to wake Brian. He didn't want both of the boys sleeping while he was gone. Someone needed to be awake and guarding the house, in case trouble showed up.

Brian sat up and took a drink from his canteen. "I'm awake. Don't worry about us."

Nate stepped out the front door, locking it behind him.

Out on the sidewalk, he kept his eyes busy, looking for signs of trouble. The wind-blown rain hit him in the face, feeling like hot needles, a strange contradiction, since the rain was ice cold. He turned a corner and headed for the courthouse. The first item on his mind was to check his dead friend's desk and maybe find a note or something that might lead him to Chesty's murderer. The young man who'd killed Chesty Johnson while he lay in bed had himself been killed by his victim. They had shot at the same moment, each killing the other. But the assassin had been sent by someone, and Nate wanted to know who. He told himself once again that it was about protecting the townspeople from a terrorist group. It didn't matter. He could lie to himself a thousand times, but he knew it was personal. What's more, he knew Deni knew. Hell, his friends Tyrone, Mel, the National Guardsman, and old Atticus knew. They had the same mind-set. Trouble was he had little time to find the killer.

Running most of the way, the wind driving rain at his left side and soaking him, Nate made it to the courthouse in less than three minutes. To anyone who might have been hiding in ambush, it may have appeared he wasn't all that aware of his surroundings as he ran, but he had seen the man watching from a window on the other side of the street and was ready to jump for cover if he had seen any hint of a rifle in the man's hands. He also knew Mel was watching from his own sniper's nest, somewhere on his side of the street. Mel was a good shot, but it wasn't the National Guard that had taught him the finer points of accurate shooting. It was his late father. Still, Nate rushed through the courthouse door and had it closed behind him as fast as he could manage it.

The lobby was empty and dark, nearly as cold as outside, but a lot less wet and windy. There was no power in the building, of course. The only buildings with electricity were those the Army had taken over, including the clinic that had been turned into a small hospital, complete with three emergency rooms. Nate went through what had been the security guard station. A metal detector that people once had to walk through before getting past the security guards stood useless. Being a small town in a rural county, the courthouse wasn't as large as most in the state of Florida. Still, it was three stories and contained many rooms. He headed down a dark hall and turned right, where he opened a door and stepped into the room that was being used as the temporary sheriff's office.

Sitting behind a desk in the dim glow of a kerosene lantern, Tyrone looked up and reached for a shotgun at the same time, not relaxing until he saw who had just barged in. His intense eyes appearing very white in his black face as he looked across the room at Nate, he was obviously ready to kill if need be. Recognizing Nate took only a fraction of a second, and he put the shotgun back on the desk without ever having actually aimed it at him.

Ignoring his friend's precaution and noticing that Tyrone was in the process of going through Chesty's desk, Nate asked, "Find anything? I woke early to go through his desk for anything that might lead us to any others involved with his murder, but I see you beat me to it." He took his hat off and slipped out of his load-bearing harness, then shed his wet jacket, hanging all on a hat rack standing near the entrance. The cold in the unheated room immediately penetrated his thin shirt.

Leaning back in the seat, Tyrone took a few seconds to answer, "Nothing so far. I haven't been here long."

Nate rubbed as much water from his face as possible with his bare hands and wiped them on the driest side of his jacket. "We have a few hours. The funeral's not until 9 AM. I sure would like to know for certain if his murder was related to the terrorists or if it was something else entirely." He walked across the room and stood beside the desk.

Tyrone pulled a stack of papers out of the top right desk drawer and handed it to Nate. "Well, start with this pile. Maybe one of us will get lucky and find something. I don't hold out much hope, though. We knew as much about the terrorists as he did, and if he was working on something he would've let me in on it. The fact is anyone could've killed Chesty and for any reason, sane or not."

"Yeah," Nate said. "But it's the first place to look, since we have nothing at all to go on." He found a chair and went to work, scanning his dead friend's notes. He spoke while he read. "You're the only one here with law enforcement training and experience, and I fully understand that." He looked up from the notes. "You and I both know you're the boss here. I'm just trying to help out. Also, I may not wait two weeks before heading back to my farm. I'm sorry about deserting you, but that's the way it is."

"I figured that." Tyrone didn't even look up. "I just hope I can find two or three good people before you leave."

Nate regarded Tyrone. "You don't hold it against me?"

He shook his head and looked up. "No. You said two weeks, but things have changed."

The two exchanged glances.

"Something I don't know about?" Nate asked.

"No. Donovan has told me the same thing he told you. Said he has given Deni permission to leave anytime she wants. I guess he was warning me I'm going to be short on help soon." He tossed a pile of papers aside. "A lot can happen between now and the time you leave. I hope what *does* happen is we get every SOB that was involved in Chesty's murder. And I hope that's *all* that happens. Deni's not going to be too happy with me if you get shot."

~~~

Two hours later, the men had found nothing in Chesty's desk that produced any useful information.

"That's the last of it." Nate set a stack of paper on the desk. "Nothing there that could help us. It was mostly ideas on how to build a new sheriff department someday and how the deputies could patrol at least part of the county on horseback, if fresh supplies of fuel for vehicles never materialize. It appeared to me most of the ideas came from you." He walked across the room to the hat rack and grabbed his load-bearing harness. "I don't have a watch, but I expect it's about time for me to go get my son and a few others, then head for the cemetery."

Tyrone's chest heaved. He rubbed his eyes with the palms of his hands. "Yeah. It's time to bury one of the best men I ever knew."

They stepped outside onto the sidewalk together. The cold rain had slacked off, but the wind had strengthened considerably, and the temperature, if anything, was colder.

Nate pulled his boonie hat down tighter on his head and scanned the street in both directions. He took note that Tyrone had also taken a rifle with him, an M4. They walked to the next intersection, where Nate looked up at a third-story window and pointed at his left wrist, as if he were wearing a watch. He caught formless movement back from the window in the shadows of the room and knew Mel would be appearing at the ground floor door in a minute or two.

"I wonder if he saw anything suspicious while he was up there keeping watch," Tyrone said, thinking out loud.

Nate kept his eyes busy, scanning the streets and peering into windows. "He can give you a full report if you ask. Soldiers are trained to observe everything while on post."

"Just the important stuff. That's all I'm interested in."

An office door with a broken lock swung open and Mel stepped up to them. He spoke before the other men had a chance. "Two hours before sunup, two skinny young guys wearing black hoodies came ambling along, trying to appear nonchalant. The fact they were out at night in this miserable weather tells me they weren't out for a stroll. They kept their hands in their sweatshirt pockets, but they were damn sure casing the area. Seemed to be really interested in the courthouse."

Nate ignored his freezing ears in the howling wind. "I would suggest we move our little office to the Army base, or at least find a building that's more secure. They could plant a bomb while we're at Chesty's funeral and set it off when we come back."

"Yeah." Tyrone glanced down the street at the courthouse. "What we need most are more men. Several people to keep 24/7 watch on our base of operations."

Mel tilted his head in a futile attempt to get more wind protection from his helmet. "What you guys need is a real squad of deputies, not untrained civilian volunteers. There must be more cops who survived the plague, perhaps in surrounding counties. We just have to find them."

"Right now we have a friend to bury." Tyrone walked away.

~~~

Almost everyone who attended Chesty's funeral was armed, despite the Army sending a squad to provide security. Many teens attended, but no small children. The cold and damp was too much for mothers to risk their children getting sick. Weather or no, the crowd of adults was large. There were not many in the town of Glenwood who didn't feel indebted to Chesty.

Deni had come with the squad. She wore her best uniform, worn but clean. It was all she had. She stood between Nate and Brian, her arms hooked in theirs. Kendell stood off to the side, looking around at the crowd for any sign of trouble. Mel roamed through the crowd, searching for two thin young men in black hoodies. Tyrone and Atticus stood by the grave, both crying unashamedly.

Nate expected Lieutenant Colonel Mike Donovan to attend. Chesty and Donovan hadn't known each other long, but they had worked closely together from the day the Army arrived in town until the night Chesty was killed, and they had grown to respect each other. The fact Donovan wasn't there made Nate nervous. There could be something serious going on that had kept Donovan away.

The preacher spoke of a life of service to others and years of dedication selflessly given. Then he read from the Bible. Nate didn't hear much of his words. He thought of all the good people he had met and lost to both the plague and violence. Weariness seeped into his bones and chilled him more than the wind. He wished to God there was someplace he could take those closest to him, some place where they would be safe. But he knew there was no such place on earth.

Deni gave his arm a squeeze, as if she had read his mind.

Chesty's closest friends grabbed a shovel and went to work. The crowd thinned as people quietly walked away. Nate and Brian had to finish the job when Tyrone and Atticus turned their faces into the cold wind and stood in quiet grief, their shovels forgotten.

Brian handed his shovel to the man who had brought them, then turned to his father. "We seem to always be burying someone."

Nate put a heavy hand on his son's shoulder. "I know I've been saying this for over a year now, but someday it'll get better."

"It's not like it's your fault." Something behind Nate caught Brian's attention. He nodded. "Soldiers. I think they're looking for Tyrone or you."

Nate turned to look. "Yeah. There must be a reason why Donovan didn't show. Something's up."

Deni said, "My thoughts too. Never a dull moment around here."

Fifty yards away, a young private talked to Mel, who pointed toward Tyrone and Atticus. The soldier walked briskly up to Tyrone. "Sir, Col. Donovan requests that you come with me to his office to discuss an important matter."

Atticus had his shotgun slung across his back, out of the way. He soon had it in his hands. "Terrorists again?"

Tyrone nodded toward Nate. "He's the acting sheriff. You should be talking to him."

The soldier glanced Nate's way. "Nate Williams is to come too. And Sergeant Heath."

"Did he say anything about a senile old man?" Atticus asked.

The question seemed to throw the young soldier off his stride.

"Uh," Tyrone said, "we'll follow you in our vehicles."

Nate, Deni, Brian, Kendell, and Mel hopped in one pickup. Tyrone and Atticus scrambled into a dirty white sheriff cruiser Tyrone had scrounged up. The soldier led the little convoy in a Humvee. The downtown streets had been cleared of nearly all abandoned vehicles and other debris, one of Donovan's directives. This included only the downtown area, though, and just three miles out the streets were navigable only by threading a vehicle around many obstacles.

~~~

Donovan watched from the window of his office as a Black Hawk helicopter lifted off, carrying a team of soldiers, armored up and loaded for battle. It was obvious they were heading to a trouble spot somewhere. Donovan turned to the others. "Sorry I couldn't attend Chesty's funeral. We've found the rest of that gang of punks you ran out of town a while back. My soldiers are... uh... pacifying them. Unfortunately, most of them are too stupid to just give up. It's gotten bloody."

"They're a bunch of idiots, alright," Atticus said. "Real dead-end losers. I bet they've been giving people trouble wherever they've gone."

"Where did you find them, on the interstate near the Florida/Georgia line?" Nate asked.

Donovan seemed surprised. "Yeah. How did you know?"

"Just a guess. Are there many women and children with them?"

Donovan tilted his head. He appeared to be wondering what Nate had on his mind. "Some. It complicates matters."

Nate nodded. "Yeah. At least it does for anyone with a conscience. It wouldn't be near a big truck stop, would it?"

The corners of Donovan's mouth turned upward as he just nodded in silence.

Nate continued. "The women and children with them wouldn't be part of the terrorist group we've been dealing with lately, would they?"

"Ha! I was wondering when you would get to that." Donovan crossed his thick arms. "But I bet you haven't figured it all out, though you may think you have."

Nate coughed and shook his head. "No, I do not presume to think I've figured it all out. The fact is Chesty's murder has kept my mind busy lately. Besides, we're dealing with people who aren't thinking straight. It's not easy to understand people like that."

Tyrone couldn't contain himself any longer. "Figured what out?"

"Yeah," Atticus broke in, "How about letting us in on the mystery."

Brian and Kendell were all ears and eyes, as they looked around the room at the adults.

Deni finally spoke up. "I'll wager that no one here knows as much as he thinks he does." She folded her arms. "But I would like to learn what has you two looking so smug."

"I had no idea that I *was* looking smug," Nate protested. "Certainly, I have no life-changing revelation that I'm keeping to myself. I just connected the semis the terrorists have been using with interstate truck stops. They could've gotten stranded trucks at rest stops anywhere along the interstate, where they were abandoned when the traffic jams and massive pileups took place during the early panics. I also believe the terrorists and the youth gang we ran out of town are connected in some way."

Donovan sat on the front edge of his desk. "It's no big mystery, when you think about it. Some of you have already touched on the problem, days, weeks back." He looked around the room at the others. "People have been forced to adjust to living without government, with no rule of law whatsoever and no government services, no so-called safety nets. They had to adjust or die, and by adjust I mean they had to toughen up and kill or be killed. The free-for-all that's lasted over a year now has culled most of the weak, leaving behind the most vicious predators and the toughest survivors. The remaining predators will have to be dealt with, the survivors who kill only when they have no choice and do not take from others but work to survive and come by their food and other needs honestly are an asset, exactly what the human race needs to rebuild."

Donovan waited for a helicopter to lift off and fly away, so the noise would fade enough he could be heard without yelling. "There is another group of survivors who are almost as dangerous as the predators. They have grown accustomed to living without any rule of law and do not want any government to tell them what they can and can't do. For over a year, they've been living in the wilderness, or the Wild West, so to speak, and they've grown to like their newfound freedom, despite its danger and hardship. They've managed to learn how to provide for themselves and they don't think they need a government anymore, so they want their Wild West to remain untamed."

"That's crazy," Brian blurted out. "If we don't rebuild the economy and government, we will run out of things that are already hard to come by, like medicine and fuel. Do they want to continue to see people die of sickness and injuries that could've been easily taken care of in a modern hospital? Do they want to live in a war zone the rest of their lives, forced to carry a rifle while plowing their fields behind a mule? Don't they want life to be better for their children and the next generation? Why purposely go backwards?"

"They're not thinking like that," Donovan answered. "The horrors of the plague and its aftermath have twisted their minds."

Deni said, "It's only natural that some would blame the government for the plague and the lack of help for the people after. And it's a given that some would blame technology, since there's suspicion our own government manufactured the disease in a laboratory, or some other government did."

"On the question of where the plague came from, do you have any info on that?" Nate asked Donovan.

"No. It started in countries that are U.S. allies. That looks like terrorism. But then it spread around the world. If someone wanted to attack us, it backfired on them and killed their own people. Of course, it could've been a doomsday thing and they wanted to die along with everyone else." He shrugged. "If Washington and the Pentagon know something, they haven't told me. Either way, knowing how, who, and why the plague started isn't going to solve our problems."

Steering the conversation back on course, Donovan continued. "Hatred of government authority is growing all across the country. Americans have been and are still killing one another for little or no reason. I've been getting warnings from down the chain of command about warlords popping up and people forming their own little governments. Even some military officers have… Colonel Hewitt isn't the only officer to go nuts. Societal degeneration is still a problem in many areas."

"So this little community is actually doing better than some," Tyrone said.

"Better than most." Donovan crossed his arms. "Soldiers have found pockets of children who were left to fend for themselves." He looked down. "It was like Lord of the Flies. Sure, people are getting their act together in some areas, but in other areas they've devolved back to medieval times. Some in Washington have deluded themselves into believing we're well on our way to recovery. We're not."

"How about other countries," Nate asked.

"I've been told that Americans are actually faring better than most." Donovan moved to a map on the wall and pointed at the American South and West. "Those two areas are doing much better than the rest of the country and the rest of the world. We 'ugly Americans' have proven ourselves to be civilized compared to most of Europe. Jolly old England isn't so jolly nowadays."

Nate glanced at Deni and then directed his attention to Donovan. "Expect Washington to react harshly as soon as they have the means. As the people harden their attitudes toward troublemakers, so will government. The innocent will suffer along with the guilty."

"I don't think there's any way to tell how things will go," Deni countered. "Yeah, it may get worse before it gets better, but there's no real reason why the government or the people should drag us backward. If enough people all over and in Washington fight for not only law and order but human rights at the same time, we should be able to stay on course. After all, most people are basically good."

Brian looked worried. "I remember reading The Diary of a Young Girl, by Anne Frank in school. She wrote something like that even though her and her family were arrested and taken to concentration camps to die."

Chapter 3

President Russell Capinos sat at a large English oak table. Vice President Piers Trant sat on the opposite side, and the Secretary of the Department of Homeland Security, Shirley Montobon, sat to his left. Soon, her position would be obsolete, as the president planned to have the military take over most federal law enforcement and national security duties. Capinos hadn't told her yet, but it was a done deal. Many federal agencies were going to be merged or shut down completely. Outside threats were considered to be nonexistent. It was hungry, lawless Americans Washington feared and needed to control. He still hadn't decided whether to cut the NSA to a bare minimum or just close it down completely. There just wasn't any Internet, phone, or anything else in the way of electronic surveillance to be done. Only fears enemies abroad might restart their most sophisticated technologies sooner than anticipated caused him to hesitate to close the agency down completely. They certainly didn't need a massive NSA just to listen in on HAM operators conversing among the many small groups of survivors. Yeah, the government wanted to watch them closely, but a much smaller NSA could handle that easily.

President Capinos was forced to lean over to reach the table, as his prodigious belly kept him too far back. He and his family were among the few Americans who had not missed a meal over the last year, or lost a child to the plague. He wasn't president when the plague hit, had never held any office before, and had never ran for as much as mayor of a small town. Until the plague, he had never needed to hold office to yield power. Satisfied to stay out of the limelight and keep his anonymity, using his wealth to control government officials as tools for his own plans, he had never needed or wanted direct political power. Indirect power had been much safer and in many ways less trouble, since he didn't have to waste time running for and holding office and keeping up a charade for the public. Not an ideologue, he didn't give a damn if the country moved to the left or to the right. He found political debate boring and inconsequential. No matter what way the political winds blew, he could buy anything he wanted, from a county commissioner to a president. Who gave a damn if the person you kept in your back pocket belonged to this or that party?

There had been many just like him, but then came the plague, changing everything. Wealth suddenly became almost meaningless in the post-plague world. When he saw others like him maneuvering to take political power directly by demanding special elections and then preparing to run for office, he knew he had no choice but to play the same game, but on the highest level, and he knew he had to win.

He and those like him had made certain there was a presidential election right on schedule, even though 95% of the American population had been lost to the plague. They made it a matter of pride in Washington that not even the Civil War had delayed an American national election, and they swore the plague would not delay this one. Since there were so many vacancies in Congress created by the high mortality rate of the plague, many special elections had been held to replace them. The result was an entirely new U.S. Government, one that had no resemblance to the old one, in organization or values.

During the elections, there had been little to no pretense of following the Constitution or rule of law. No one in Washington cared what the rest of the country outside of the Northeast thought. Very few outside of Washington even knew of the elections. The actual number of Americans who voted had been minuscule. Fewer voters decided who would be a congressman or senator than had voted for a local sheriff in normal times, and none of the voters actually lived in the state the congressmen and senators supposedly represented. It took only a quarter million votes (all from the Northeast only) to put Russell Capinos in the White House. By all reason, he should have been called President of the Northeastern States, not President of the United States. Nevertheless, once in power, he immediately decreed the already existing state of emergency permanent and removed what few constitutional protections the former government in Washington had left in place.

Because of the plague's tendency to kill the elderly at a higher rate than the young, the Supreme Court Capinos inherited had exactly two sitting justices. He had no trouble convincing the new Senate to fill every vacancy on the bench by the end of the first month. They were all handpicked men and women who had little to no respect for the idea of constitutionally limited governmental power. For the first time in Capinos' life, he would be pulling the strings with his own hands, instead of paying others to pull the strings for him, and he worked every day to consolidate his power. Power became his new drug, replacing wealth. His addiction grew stronger by the hour. So far, he had been able to hide its effects on his psyche, but he worried about the day it became obvious to those around him. Would they join him, or revolt and become his worst enemies? He had to choose his allies carefully. Until the day people began to see what he was up to, he would keep his demeanor as business-like as possible, portraying himself as a level-headed businessman turned political leader doing his best to help the American people and get the country back on its feet. Those times when he asked for more power – more exemptions from constitutional restraints – he would present a logical argument and make them see the necessity for such actions. After all, didn't everyone want the same thing? Didn't they all want to see America recover and the American people return to at least tolerable living conditions?

Fortunately for most survivors of the plague, Washington had not been able to reach into their lives as of yet. Government just didn't have the resources or the manpower. Most people had not even seen a soldier or Guardsman since the plague, and certainly no federal law enforcement.

In modern America, most people lived in cities and had little idea where food came from. All they knew was you went to the store and bought it. The plague ended that. The stores had no food to sell in as little as three days in some cities and closed soon after. It hadn't taken Capinos long to learn that food was power and he used it to keep a lid on a dozen of the largest Northeastern cities, though the pot did boil over on occasion and the streets were not exactly peaceful on the 'quiet' days. Trouble was, in recent months he had less and less food to hand out, and withholding food was the hammer he held over the people's head to keep them in line. The other half of the equation – rewarding people with just enough food to keep them alive for being compliant – would soon be impossible. Threatening execution didn't work. Starving people considered a bullet in the head to be a mercy, a painless way out of a slow, agonizing death.

Born into a family of means, Capinos was a man who had experienced the thrill of massive wealth his whole life, and wealth had become passé to him. As he grew older, he had turned to a new drug called power. Before the plague, the two came hand in hand, but wealth had not only lost its luster in his own mind, money had become almost useless in a society that was in survival mode. Addicted to power, Capinos wanted more, and that meant he needed more units of wealth called food. For the time being, food was more valuable than all the gold in the world. He needed more food, and he was going to get it. Given the choice of freedom or food, people would choose food.

The rural areas were doing a better job of feeding themselves and therefore were less of a drain on Washington's resources, but they were also the least controllable. Control was what concerned Capinos. Reports from afield informed him millions of people had returned to subsistence farming and were just beginning to produce crops. Rural survivors of the plague and the violence that came after were enjoying the fullest stomachs, as many already knew how to produce food and had most of the equipment and fertile land. They also were the ones forming their own little governments and had the least respect for outside authority, especially from Washington. To make things worse, they tended to be much better armed than city people and were more likely to know how to use those guns. The rural South was infested with veterans.

Experimentation with new (and old) forms of government had become a challenge to Washington's authority. Something had to be done. Yes, the old Constitution and form of government was dead, but it would be Washington that decided just what the new government would be, not little warlords and farming communities out in the far reaches of the country, deep in the backwoods and small-town streets of Jerkwater, U.S.A. But how to control them?

Withholding food wouldn't work on people who fed themselves. Damn independent people who provided for themselves, anyway. The only answer was to take most of their crops by force. Use the military for something useful for a change. The military would be the new IRS, collecting food instead of taxes. This would give the government food to hand out in the cities – or withhold until they behaved – and reduce the hicks' food supplies at the same time, thereby increasing their dependency on Washington and forcing them to be somewhat more pliant, too. And if soldiers and Marines took some of the best food for themselves, so be it. Washington needed their loyalty, and food would work as well on them as the civilians. Normal military supplies were running out. Everyone must eat, and hunger pangs could be a great motivator.

"Let's get to work," President Capinos said, leaning on his elbows that were propped up on the table.

The unwashed bodies of heads of government agencies, many newly created, added to the smell of cold sweat in the air. The men and women in the room had been washing themselves from a bucket carried into their apartments for over a year, and they were hesitant to endure the cold water in the dead of DC's coldest winter. Even so, they were lucky to have clean water and toilets that flushed by pouring water in from the same buckets. They even had people to carry the buckets of water in for them. Most in the city had no such luxuries. The smell from backed-up sewage systems was overpowering at times.

The White House was one of the few buildings in Washington that had fuel for generators and thus had power. The city water system had been shut down since early in the plague and had yet to be restarted. There were not enough workers left alive who knew how to operate municipal utilities, and there was no power for the same reason. Every city across America, indeed the world, had the same problem. The economy collapsed soon after the plague hit and then all the normal supply lines shut down for lack of manpower. Within days, there was no food, no fuel, no power, and no water. Then there was no police or fire protection and no law but the law of survival. Those early days were bad in the Northeast, but in many ways things had gotten worse in recent months, not better. Violent, feral teens, who had lost their parents and had not been to school or witnessed a working society for over a year, prowled the streets, killing, raping, and robbing people of what little food they had. Murder victims, or those who died of starvation or natural causes, were left to rot where they lay, threatening to bring another plague to the land.

Most of the men and women at the table lived in a compound protected by Marines. Washington was not safe, and they needed all the protection they could get. Twice, angry mobs tried to storm the White House. Capinos ordered machine guns used to sweep the streets of anyone standing, mowing down over two hundred rioters. The second time it happened seemed to have discouraged further such disturbances, near the White House at least.

There was an obvious look of worry on the face of everyone sitting around the table. No one spoke. Instead, they waited for Capinos to ask a question.

Capinos gave them all a cold stare, one at a time. "Well. Someone tell me what's going on out there among the useless eaters, something I don't already know."

Army General Carl Strovenov, Chairman of the Joint Chiefs of Staff, sat next to the Secretary of Defense Martin Hackleman. He waited for Hackleman to speak, but when he didn't seem to have anything to say, Strovenov started his situation report.

A barrel-chested tall man of calm demeanor and a thinning flat buzz cut, Strovenov's voice carried well, even in a hurricane. He didn't need a megaphone. In fact, he had to tone down the volume to prevent bursting eardrums in a room like he was sitting in. "Over the past six days, we've been receiving reports of a rapidly growing insurrection. Military outposts have been attacked and ransacked, supplies taken, and soldiers killed."

"Do we know who's behind it?" President Capinos asked. "This seems to be separate and apart from what we've come to think of as normal violence. I mean, actually taking on the military is something entirely different."

The General nodded. "The attacks appear to be uncoordinated and lacking any kind of central authority or command structure. Based on what we know, it's more of a widespread civil uprising than an organized rebellion. And, of course, much of the senseless violence among the civilians themselves is more about robbing for food, guns, ammunition, and other needful items. They're hungry and desperate, and that makes them dangerous."

Capinos pressed it. "But this is different, right? My question is: Are we seeing the beginnings of a rebellion of some sort?"

"It could be the early stages of one. We've talked about the threat of a Balkanization of America before. This is a sign it's happening. At the moment, though, it's more about people blaming government for the hell they've been through. From the start, rumors the plague was the result of a weaponized disease designed by our government or at least some other nation's government, was on the minds, if not the lips, of millions. Certainly, many blame government for the hell they've been through. In short, there's a lot of anger against government out there. People used to social safety nets and a relatively easy life suddenly finding themselves on their own in a hell that seems to have no end aren't likely to be in a good mood."

While Capinos took a sip of water, Secretary of Defense Hackleman took the opportunity to speak. "This violent anger against the military and government in general is a result of the lack of food, water, electricity, and police protection. The thing is, there's little we can do we haven't already been doing."

Capinos looked across the table. "There is one thing we can give them: Law and order. But we'll have to stop coddling them and strike fear into anyone who even thinks of stepping out of line."

General Strovenov couldn't contain himself. "Mr. President, I wouldn't say the American people have been coddled. I consider it my duty to inform you of the danger of a revolt in the military itself, if orders are given to fire indiscriminately on civilians. We are not at war with our own people. Not yet, anyway."

Capinos fumed inside, but held his temper. He needed General Strovenov's help if he had any chance to implement his plans, and he didn't have time to look for a qualified replacement. "That's not what I was suggesting. We have a violent, criminal element to deal with. Those are the ones I was suggesting we get tough on." Regaining his full composure, he went on. "The American people deserve to feel safe in their own homes, and we're going to see to it they are. Before we can get power, water, and medical services restored, much less an economy, we must restore law and order, so people will be safe."

General Strovenov stared straight ahead. "Yes sir, I agree."

President Capinos turned to the Director of Homeland Security. "Director Montobon, do you have anything to add?"

She swallowed. "Yes, Mr. President." She seemed close to tears. "I think it's too late."

Capinos flinched. "What's too late?"

"All of it. Everything. It's been more than a year since the plague, and millions more have died from starvation and other diseases since the initial pandemic killed most of the human population. Then there was the violence that continues to this day. Most of the developed world is just as bad off or worse. The third world that had been depending on the U.S. and a few other more prosperous countries to feed their starving hordes has suffered even higher mortality rates."

"Are you saying the human race is in danger of dying out?" Capinos frowned. "I don't believe that. We still have a population of at least fifteen million, and that's just the U.S."

"No." She shook her head. "I'm not saying that at all. What I *am* saying is we don't have a country anymore. Someday maybe, but not at this time." She ignored the strange stares she was getting from around the table. "And we won't have a country for many years to come. Just getting the power grid back up for a few cities will take years. Getting municipal water systems going in even a small number of major cities will take even longer, as we need power to do that." She looked around the table. "The American people are on their own. What food stores there were is running out. They'll either learn to feed themselves, or they will starve. They'll either learn to defend themselves, or succumb to the lawless element. We can do very little for them from here in Washington. In fact, we in the upper echelons of government are not completely safe from hunger or the violence that's just outside the gates." Several around the table cleared their throats and looked down, obviously thinking she had lost it. She continued, despite the discomfort and disagreement with what she was saying. "Don't delude yourselves into thinking that months or a year from now, we won't all be as susceptible to starvation and violence as we were to the plague. The plague didn't care if you were high and mighty or low and weak, sickening and killing almost everyone. The dangers and many hells our people are going through now are no different. Those dangers and many hells aren't just outside the gate and roaming the streets, they are with us, right here in this room. We just can't see the truth before our eyes. Things are not going to get better, not for a long time."

Capinos snorted. "Stop that! We don't need your defeatist BS."

General Strovenov spoke up, not so much for her defense, but to try once more to instill a little reality in the president's mind. "Mr. President, I know you have grand plans, but–"

Capinos interrupted him. "I don't like your tone, General. You are treading close to insubordination. I expect respect from my inferiors!"

"You misunderstood, sir. I meant no disrespect. I only wanted to warn–"

"Warn?" Capinos jabbed his finger at him. "You don't warn, you answer questions when I ask them. You advise, but you never warn the President of the United States! Is that clear?"

"Yes sir. Again, you misunderstood–"

"My 'grand plans'?" Capinos glared at everyone at the table. "This meeting is over. I suggest all of you work on serving the people and getting this country back on its feet. That's what we're here for, and never forget it."

No one wasted any time getting out of the room.

Capinos spoke to his secretary. "Send in General Clark."

As General Strovenov walked down the hall, he nodded to General Frank Clark, Chief, National Guard Bureau. "Watch yourself. He's in one of his moods."

Clark's eyes revealed respect. "Thanks for the heads-up." Just as they passed, he whispered, "We need to talk."

Strovenov whispered, "Yes, we do." The two kept walking.

Chapter 4

Just before sundown, on the same day they buried Chesty, Nate and Deni stood before a pastor and said their vows. The afternoon had grown colder, but the rain had stopped hours before, and the wind died to less than three miles per hour. The clear western sky lit up in bright red, just above the setting sun. It was a simple ceremony that lasted only a few minutes. A small crowd gathered to witness the event. There was no celebration afterward. People just offered their congratulations and went on their way, leaving the two newlyweds with Brian, Kendell, and a few friends.

Donovan opened a bottle of bourbon he had been hoarding. "This calls for at least one drink."

Atticus wet his lips and thrust a WWII surplus canteen cup out. "Hit me on the heavy side. I have a feeling our two lovebirds aren't going to be hanging around much longer, and I need something to help me not think about what it's going to be like without them around."

"I second that thought." Tyrone held an empty coffee cup out. "I miss them already."

Donovan poured drinks for everyone but Brian and Kendell. He poured a short drink for himself and held it up. "To good friends."

"Always a rarity, but never more so than now," Tyrone added.

Deni took a drink. "Winter soldiers and apocalypse friends, the only kind worth dying for."

Mel emptied his canteen cup before saying anything. "I have an announcement. Col. Donovan called me to the base today, and I had a little chat with my CO over the radio. It seems I'll be leaving for my old unit tomorrow, just after daylight. They're sending a chopper to get me."

"Sorry to hear that," Nate said. "The fact I expected you to be called away a long time ago doesn't relieve my regrets one bit. We'll miss you."

"Yes," Deni said. "I hope we see you again soon."

Everyone there seconded that thought.

Brian had been staying back from the adults with Kendell. He moved closer to Mel. "Do you think they'll let you out of the Guard soon, so you can move back to your retreat?"

Mel's answer didn't please Brian. "I doubt it. They need every soldier they have. I don't have to tell you how bad it is out there."

Disappointment shadowed Brian's face. "They can't keep you forever."

Mel smiled. "Ah, no, but they're not letting me go anytime soon."

Brian remained silent for a second, before saying, "Well, be careful and come back as soon as you can."

"I plan to. I plan to do just that."

A soldier rushed from a Humvee parked in the lot, not fifty yards from the church, stopping in front of Donovan. "Colonel, there's shooting at the courthouse, and the building has been firebombed."

Nate rushed to the pickup and his weapons, Deni not far behind. He slipped into his load-bearing harness and froze when he saw the look on Deni's face. "Just this last thing before we go. This is bound to have something to do with Chesty's murder."

She reached behind the cab to grab her rifle and helmet. There was no time to put on all of her armor. "It's a good thing I'm not wearing a silly wedding dress."

Nate stood there looking at her.

"Well, let's go," she said. "You didn't think I was going to stay here and pout while you had all the fun, did you?"

They jumped in the front. Not far behind, Mel jumped in the back behind the cab.

He slapped the roof. "Good to go."

Nate yelled out his window at Brian and Kendell. "You two arm yourselves and get in the church. Stay there until we get back. Keep your eyes open and your brains working."

The two boys grabbed their rifles from the truck, along with extra ammunition.

Donovan and his soldiers were already tearing down the street. Nate hit the gas and struggled to catch up. Tyrone and Atticus followed in the sheriff's cruiser.

Deni held on and yelled above the roar of the engine. "This could be a trap. Firebombing the sheriff's office might be bait to lure us in. We shouldn't barge in like this."

Nate held the wheel with both hands and smoked the tires, as he slid around a corner. "I agree, but the Army may have the scene stabilized already for all we know. I doubt Donovan will blunder into an ambush, but we'll stay back a little when we get close."

Deni kept her M4 pointed up and chambered a round. "Anywhere between here and the courthouse could be an ambush site."

They hit Main Street and turned left. The windshield shattered. Nate stomped it and made a beeline for an alleyway between two three-story buildings. One had been rented for a bridal store before the plague, the other a musical instrument shop.

Mel held on for life until the truck halted, and then jumped down, taking cover at the corner of a building. He fired rapid rounds at a second-story window. "I saw the bastard. He's across the street, two stories up, third window on the right."

Nate and Deni bailed. Staying low, they ran to the front of the truck, then made their way to Mel's side of the alleyway and eased up to the corner of the building.

Deni bit her lower lip and strained to catch a target, scanning the building Mel warned them about and the street itself. "They let the Humvee go by."

Tyrone and Atticus had veered to the left, ending up on the far side of a fast food restaurant. They quickly vacated the cruiser and took up positions, looking for attackers and ready to back up the others.

"Yeah," Mel agreed. "What's that about?"

As he spoke, Donovan's Humvee reversed for over a hundred yards and stopped sideways in the road three blocks down. The machine gunner on top charged the weapon and waited for orders.

Donovan and four soldiers piled out, rifles in hand, and took up positions, while Donovan spoke on the radio, calling in help.

Nate scanned the building across the street with binoculars and tried to see into the dark rooms. After taking a quick look, he jerked his head back behind cover. A bullet sent shards of concrete flying off the corner of the building, prompting a quick response from the machine gunner and several others. The rattle of automatic fire echoed down the street. As the echo faded, silence was drowned out by ringing in Nate's ears.

~~~

Brian glanced around the church, sighed in boredom, and sat in one of the empty pews. He reached down and ran his hand over the smooth varnished pinewood, wondering if he should call Deni Mother, since she was married to his father.

Kendell walked from window to window, looking out. The windows were stained glass and difficult to see through. "We need to be alert, Brian. There ain't no time for prayin'."

Brian almost rolled his eyes. "I'm not. I'm keeping an eye on the back door while you watch the front. I have my rifle in my hand. I wish I had more ammo with me, though."

"Best to see 'em comin' before they get to the door." Kendell moved to another window and checked the front parking lot. "Most likely, there won't be no trouble, but you never can tell. It seems like trouble is like one of them mythical monsters that sprouts two more heads every time you cut one off."

Brian scratched the back of his neck. "I doubt there's any danger, but like I said, I'm ready if there is. Dad, Deni, and the others are the one's I'm worried about." He saw the door knob move and instantly had his rifle shouldered and the safety off, aiming loosely at the doorway. "We have company," he whispered.

Kendell didn't hear him. He was watching two armed men in hoodies creep up to the front of the church.

Brian kept his attention on the back door. He watched as the door swung open and a man in his mid-twenties rushed in with a rifle shouldered. Brian fired just as the man saw him and swung the barrel to aim. As the man fell, Brian's rifle spoke again, the three quick shots reverberating in the confines of the church, temporarily rendering both boys deaf. The dead man lay in an expanding puddle of blood, his rifle next to him. Brian held his rifle on him and watched the door at the same time.

Kendell checked on Brian and to see what he was shooting at. As he turned back to the window, his face took shards of glass, and something hot slammed into his shoulder, turning him to his left and nearly knocking him off his feet.

Brian heard the impact of a bullet hitting flesh and knew Kendell had been hit. He fired at the open back door several times to hold anyone outside off and ran for Kendell. Bullets came through the front double doors. Brian and Kendell both fired back blindly, further splintering the wood.

Kendell saw something through a clear section of a stained glass window. His eyes grew wide. "Run!" He turned and tackled Brian, shoving him over the back of a row of pews. Brian hit his head on the floor and saw stars for a second. He heard window glass shattering. Struggling to free himself from between two pews where he was wedged, he looked over and saw a wall of flame boil up around Kendell. Roaring filled his ears. A wave of searing heat burned bare skin instantly. Kendell emerged from the inferno as a human ball of flaming fire, screaming and running for the front door, away from Brian.

In shock over the sight he was witnessing, Brian froze for a full two seconds. Recovering, he jumped up screaming. He circled around the spreading, gasoline-fueled fire near the broken window and charged the double doors Kendell had just disappeared through. They would expect it. It was a dangerous thing to do, but he didn't care.

Outside, Kendell managed to get a shot off with his bolt-action rifle before collapsing in the parking lot, hitting a thin young man in a hoodie in the stomach just as he reared back to throw another Molotov cocktail of gasoline. He doubled over and collapsed, the bottle and its flaming wick, ripped from an old T-shirt, clattered on the asphalt, but didn't break.

Brian fired two more shots into him and frantically scanned the lot with enraged eyes. "Come on, you bastards!" He swung his rifle, searching for someone to take his rage out on. Finding no one, he looked over at Kendell's charred body and fell to his knees, crying. "You bastards!"

The fire behind him snapped and crackled, growing in size and fury, consuming the church. A column of pitch-black smoke rose into the sky, along with red-glowing embers. Pushing grief and horror aside, he tried to stand, but his legs lacked strength, so he crawled to Kendell, dragging his rifle with him, tears running down his face. He frantically snatched a canteen from his belt and poured it over Kendell's head. It was only half full, but the water steamed on contact. He dropped the empty canteen and set his rifle down. The smell of burnt flesh made him want to retch. His whole body racked, as he held his shaking open hands up in anguish, not knowing what to do.

He had been through many fights and had experienced the terror and horror and felt his stomach knot up so tight he couldn't breathe and the pain so strong it felt as if he had already been shot, but he had also experienced the relief when it was over and everyone he cared about was alive and unharmed. Knowing that he and those he cared for were still alive and it could possibly be weeks or months before the next fight lifted his spirit and untied the knot in his stomach almost instantly. The fact he had killed human beings didn't even bother him much anymore. He could even sleep without having too many nightmares, and he had hope that someday they would go away completely. The first time he saw his father kill – it was the day he was shot in the leg – the boy he used to be couldn't believe his eyes. He had no idea his father was so ruthless, the world so cruel. That was a lifetime ago, when he was more than a year younger. Sometime between then and this day, he had stopped resisting it and had relinquished himself to the violent new world and had become a killer. He had read that a man was never more alive than when being hunted by or when hunting another man. He found that to be insane. It was after the fight and everyone he cared about was safe that he felt most alive. The best of all breathing. The best feeling in the world. So strong and deep, it even overpowered the horror of it all for a while. This time, there would be no relief, not even for a little while. This time, there was just the horror, the pain, and the loss of a good friend. This time, the nightmares would never go away.

He didn't hear the gunshots in the street or the yelling men and women. A crowd came up and formed a semicircle around the boy and the charred body. The church continued to burn.

A middle-aged man put his hand on Brian's shoulders. "People heard the shots and came running. Others saw the smoke and knew the church was on fire." He knelt down beside Brian. "I'm sorry, son, he's gone."

Brian kept his eyes on Kendell and grieved in shocked silence.

A man in his early thirties rushed up. Catching his breath, he said, "We killed one of 'em. Two others we caught alive."

Hate overcoming grief, Brian grabbed his rifle and pushed up off the asphalt. He straightened and stood. His short stature notwithstanding, he looked the man in the eye and asked, "Where are they?"

The man pointed.

Brian rushed through the crowd. The look on his face seemed to generate an invisible force that pushed them aside and created a lane for him to pass through. He found them on the sidewalk, being shoved along at rifle point by four angry men. Their hands were tied behind their backs. They appeared to be in their early twenties. Before the crowd closed the lane Brian had just passed through, the prisoners were able to see across the parking lot, where Kendell lay. One looked over at Kendell's smoking body and gave a feral sneer.

When Brian got within ten yards of the men, he raised his rifle. Sensing the danger, everyone pulled back out of the way. The two men had just enough time to understand what was about to happen. The sneers vanished just before Brian shot twice, hitting both between the eyes and killing them before they hit the ground. Without a word or a glance at the others, he turned back to Kendell. The opening once again formed ahead of him like the bow of a ship parting waves. He kneeled down and took his jacket off, placing it over the charred remains.

The world had changed Brian, but it had changed those in the crowd, too. No one said a word of protest. After they had time to think, a murmur rose up. People in the crowd near the two dead men argued, fingers pointed, and hands flailed the air. After a few minutes, they came to an agreement. Someone untied the dead men's hands. On by one, they fired a shot into each of the two bodies. There were over thirty men and women in the crowd, and by the time they were through, the men had been shot to pieces.

Brian watched in half-interest for a few seconds and then turned back to Kendell's still smoking body. Tears washed two trails down his smoke-blackened face, as he sat on his heels, appearing to be in shock. Finally, he said, "You saved my life. You could've saved yourself."

~~~

Nate scanned the building across the street with binoculars. No one had fired for ten minutes, giving soldiers in the area time to arrive. As Nate watched, soldiers stormed the building the sniper had fired from.

"He's gone," Mel said, not waiting for the soldiers to complete clearing the building. "I bet this was all about luring us here for some reason."

"Well, there's still a fight going on downtown." Deni moved from her position to stand beside Nate. Gunfire could be heard in the distance. "They didn't want us helping the others."

"And what was the point of burning the sheriff's office?" Mel asked. "I think all of this was about luring us here and away from someplace else."

Nate put his binoculars down, letting them hang from his neck. "We were at a church getting married. What, now there's a cult or political movement that's against marriage?"

Deni smiled. "I guess we shouldn't be surprised by anything. There are a lot of messed-up people out there. The plague and its aftermath left all of us scarred."

They watched soldiers spill from the building, obviously not finding the sniper inside. They rushed out in an expanding circle, trying to find him before he got out of the area. A Black Hawk circled above, providing eyes in the sky and directing men on the ground. The beating of its blades and roar of its engine reverberated off the buildings.

After ten more minutes, the all-clear was sounded. Mel was the first out in the street, followed by Nate and Deni. Donovan's Humvee raced up and he yelled out the front passenger-side window. "We're going on to the courthouse." He pointed at the black column of smoke rising in the sky. "I got a report the church we were just at is on fire. Go check that out."

Ten yards down the street, Tyrone took one look at the black smoke and ran for the cruiser. Atticus turned and ran, struggling to keep up, his shotgun in his hands.

Nate, Deni, and Mel jumped in the truck and took off behind them.

A thought suddenly came over Deni. She held her hand over her mouth. "Brian and Kendell!" She looked at Nate with terror in her eyes.

Nate responded by driving faster, passing Tyrone and Atticus on a straight stretch of road at 100 miles per hour.

Slamming on the brakes in the middle of the street in front of the burning church, Nate exploded out of the truck, followed by Deni and Mel. They pushed through the large crowd, searching for the boys. A woman pointed. The three turned and simultaneously gasped at the sight of Kendell's charred body and Brian's devastated smoke-smeared face.

Tyrone and Atticus jumped out of the cruiser. They were directed to the two dead men before they had a chance to see Kendell and Brian.

Atticus looked down at the bodies. "Uh, I think they're dead. They're the most shot-up bastards I've ever seen."

Tyrone noticed the odd position the two bodies were in. He stepped around the wide circle of blood and bent down to examine their wrists. "I see ligature marks. These men were tied up when they were shot."

Atticus took note of the crowd's reaction and saw an immediate hardening of their faces. "Tyrone... let's go check on the boys."

Tyrone looked up and saw what Atticus was seeing. He stood and walked toward the burning church without a word. It was then they saw the tragedy that had taken place. They rushed to the others, but when they reached them all they could do was stand there and look sick and helpless.

Deni and Nate both held Brian. "I'm sorry," they said. "I'm sorry."

Nate reached out and touched Kendell with his left hand. Tears emptied from him.

His reaction to the sight of Kendell compelled Brian to forget his own grief. He held his father. "It would've been me, but he pushed me out of the way."

Atticus said, "Damn it." He turned pale.

It was one of the few times in his life Mel had nothing to say.

Tyrone stood over Kendell and held his hand over his mouth and nose to fight off the overpowering smell of burnt flesh. He heard a noise and looked up in time to see the burning cross fall from the steeple and crash to the ground. Bending down, he whispered something in Nate's ear.

Nate seemed to stop breathing for several seconds, then he looked at his son's smoke-blackened face. "Brian..."

Brian wouldn't look back, casting his eyes away.

Instinctively understanding, Deni pulled Brian closer. "Don't," she said. "Leave him alone. It can wait."

Nate held them both for several minutes. It took all of his strength to stand. He didn't notice the rivulets running down his face. With the weight of the world on his shoulders, he made his way through the packed crowd and saw for himself what Tyrone was talking about. "Who shot them?" he demanded, looking around at the crowd. No one answered. He rushed back to Brian.

Brian struggled to stand. Deni helped him.

Brian croaked, "I–"

A chorus of male and female voices rose up. "I shot them. I did. I did. We all shot them."

Nate scanned the crowd, his eyes narrow and hard. Realization washed over him and drained the last of his strength. He dropped his rifle and staggered to Brian. Silently, he held his son and walked with him to the truck.

Deni followed, her face streaming.

Mel picked up Nate's rifle and walked through a sea of sadness. "Don't back down on this," he warned. "It wasn't their fight, but they stayed and helped."

A bald man in his fifties, wearing dirty overalls, pulled his shoulders back and stepped forward. "I shot them. I'll say that until the day I die, because it's true. My bullets are in both of them."

Brian sat in the truck and stared blankly though the windshield. "They burned my best friend alive."

"I know," Nate said, his voice uncharacteristically soft. He got in beside him. "It's my fault. I shouldn't have left you alone."

Deni, already on the driver side and about to get behind the wheel, nearly screamed, "No it's not! We all know whose fault it is. Brian didn't do anything wrong and neither did you."

Mel handed Nate's rifle to him through the open passenger door. "They think they can kill kids? To hell with them. Brian, you didn't do a damn thing I wouldn't have done." He started to walk away, then stopped. "I'll stay here and take care of... everything. Tyrone and Atticus can help me make the arrangements."

"Thank you," Nate said. "We'll bury him in the morning."

Deni cranked the motor and drove away.

Chapter 5

Brian insisted on starting the grave himself. The morning broke colder than the day before, and the first inch of soil was frozen hard. He tried pushing the shovel in but was forced to stand on the back of the blade to penetrate the frost. As he dug, people began to converge on the cemetery and gather around, their faces solemn. They were coming early, before the grave had been finished.

A mule-drawn wagon came slowly down the street, driven by a worn-out-looking raggedly old man, so thin, his clothes hung loose and limp on his frame. The mule's shod hooves clattered and the wheels rattled on the hard pavement.

The sun seemed to catch in one place, just past the edge of the eastern horizon, fixed and still as the clear sky itself, out of sight and offering no promise for a brighter, warmer day. Brian dug for 30 minutes. The sun finally relented to the earth's turning. Its upper edge inched reluctantly above the horizon. As he continued to dig, the sky brightened a little, but remained as cold as before, colder. Brian stopped to rest for a moment and looked to the east. There was no warmth to the dawn, just a red ball that hung there, suspended and immovable, it seemed. Its slanting rays reflected off a sheet of crystalline frost that sheathed everything not human or animal. There was no wind, just penetrating cold.

The mule plodded along in its slow, steady gait, neither hurried nor hesitant, oblivious to the mood of humans.

Donovan had seen to it soldiers were present in numbers designed to discourage attack and handle it if an attack came anyway. Nevertheless, everyone there was armed. Their faces revealed more than sadness. Most showed anger, defiance, and an expression that said, "If you want a fight, we're ready to give you one."

Brian went back to work and dug faster, as if the gathering crowd was pushing him on or he wanted to finish before the mule arrived with its cargo in the back of the wagon.

Nate finally spoke. "Take a rest. He was my friend, too."

Brian pushed the shovel in and lifted more of the dark earth, throwing it aside. "It should've been me. He could've gotten out of the way, but he pushed me and let the gas get on him instead."

Nate grabbed the handle. "Then I owe him my son's life." Brian relented and stepped back, his face wet again. *Damn it,* Nate thought. *It seems I can't protect him from anything. Should've left this miserable town sooner.*

He felt something tugging at his insides, telling him a job he had started wasn't finished. Some group of crazy assholes had murdered a friend, burned a good boy alive, and tried to kill his son. Was he just going to let it go and act like he had become some kind of a pacifist? There was more to these radical groups than what appeared on the surface. For one thing, they were becoming more sophisticated in their planning of attacks. There was a hidden purpose to them. They seemed like a bunch of nuts at first glance, but there was something else going on. He had no idea what, but something. Did they have a new leader, one with a little training?

The driver swung around the crowd and backed his wagon to the fresh grave, giving gentle commands to the mule. He jumped down and waited for someone to help him carry the simple plywood coffin, standing there in baggy stained overalls and wearing a straw hat. In combination with the old, weather-worn wagon and the malnourished mule, he could have been from the Depression era. "My truck wouldn't start," he explained, "so I hooked up the old mule."

The mule waited too, standing there already drowsy, ears drooping, back steaming in the still cold of the morning, after its two-mile pull down the streets of a dying town still haunted by ghosts of the dead and inhabited by the few remaining survivors of the biggest holocaust in human history.

Mel took a corner of the coffin, as did Tyron and Nate. They carefully lowered it into the grave. Brian stood by the pile of fresh dark earth that had little smell to it because of the cold, wiping his face with his jacket sleeve.

Deni moved closer and stood by him. "Do you want to say a word before the preacher does?"

Brian nodded and stepped closer to the grave. Looking down at his friend, he swallowed. Then he began to speak in a voice much older than his years, sounding more like his father than the boy he was the day before. "He knew the firebomb was coming, but he didn't think of getting away, he thought of me, pushing me to safety. It cost him his life." He looked up at the sky. "I read that if a person knows his next breath will be his last it becomes the sweetest breath of his life. Kendell was denied even that, dying in a burning ball of fire. But he lived long enough to kill the one who killed him. He died as he lived, thinking of others and fighting for justice. He was my friend. I will never forget him."

The preacher began to speak, but Nate didn't hear him. He couldn't take his eyes off his son. He realized that two boys had died the day before, and one man was born. He had witnessed it over the last year, but Kendell's death had completed the process. *Death of life and other things often come out of season,* he thought. Sadness filled his heart, tempered by pride.

~~~

Brian said little more than three words all the next day. He cleaned his rifle and then washed his spare clothes – what little he had – and his spare socks, hanging them all over the bathtub to drip and dry. Then he rubbed his boots with leather soap from a small container Atticus had given him and checked the strings. Emptying his pack, he set everything out on the floor and did an inventory. That's when he looked at his worried father and spoke his three words of the day. "Need more ammo." After repacking everything, he promptly went to work sharpening his five-inch hunting knife.

When Deni gave Nate a worried look, he silently went to work on his own weapons. She sighed and left the room.

~~~

Several hours before daylight, Nate and Deni were woken by a low noise coming from the living room. They armed themselves and crept down the hall, finding Brian sharpening his knife again, tears running down his face as he stood in the dark, looking out a window at the moonlit front yard and street. It had spit snow for hours, leaving everything sheathed in a light covering of white. Nothing moved outside in the still cold.

Without a word, they turned and went back to bed, not sleeping for more than an hour, just lying there in their sleeping bags, worrying about Brian.

It was still dark when Nate woke. The room was almost as cold as the outdoors. They didn't have any way to heat even one bedroom. He felt exhausted. A heavy weight pressed on his shoulders. Some of the townspeople had stood up for Brian, and he couldn't forget that. Chesty and Kendell's murder was yet to be fully investigated and those involved brought to some kind of justice. A duty to stay and do what he could gnawed at his gut. Yet, he feared for the safety of Brian and Deni and felt so tired of the fighting and killing and dying. His first responsibility was to his family. He knew that. Yet...

Deni woke soon after, in the mood to argue. Sitting at the dining table, she stated flatly, "We should leave town as soon as possible."

Nate didn't want a fight with her, thinking she had taken it all so well, considering the simple wedding and no honeymoon, yet no complaints about any of it.

"Wasn't Kendell enough?" she asked.

His silence seemed to anger her more than if he had told her he wasn't leaving town until he was ready.

Then Brian walked in and stated he was staying in town until he had hunted down every last one involved in Kendell's death. "You two go on to the farm. I'll stay here and help Tyrone and Atticus find out who sent Chesty and Kendell's killers."

She waited exactly ten seconds for Nate to tell him he *was* coming with them and *not* staying in town, before exploding. "Damn it, Nate, hold your temper and start thinking straight. I know you're pissed. So am I."

"It's not that," Nate said. "It's what they did for Brian after Kendell's murder. It makes me think some of them are worth fighting for."

She lost her momentum for a second. "I can't argue with that."

"I know what you're thinking," Nate said. "I already wish I'd taken you, Brian, and Kendell away from this place. Kendell would still be alive."

She tilted her head and looked at him, determined. "There's still the three of us. We're not dead yet."

Brian threw himself on a couch. "Will it really be all that much safer at the farm? Is any place safe anymore?"

She crossed her arms. "You're making too much sense, Brian, shut up."

"There are advantages and disadvantages to going back to the farm," Nate said. "One disadvantage is we'll be isolated and easily outnumbered if attacked by raiders again."

"Or the terrorists, or whatever the hell they are," Brian added. "This world isn't going to get any better by itself. Someone has to stand up and make it happen. Kendell did his part."

Deni leaned back and looked up at the ceiling. "I see I'm outvoted. If we're going to stay, we need to be more careful than we've been in the past. Staying in a regular house like this is too dangerous. Maybe Col. Donovan will let us stay at the base."

Nate thought for a moment. "Maybe not the base, but you're right about finding a defendable place to use for our headquarters."

Deni sat up straight. "You don't trust Donovan?"

"Yes," Nate answered. "But I don't trust his superiors or those in Washington. We have no idea what kind of government we have now. We know we have a new president and many new congressmen, but did you or I or Tyrone or anyone else we know vote since the plague? How can that be legit?" He grew grim. "Understand something, both of you. I'm declaring war on everyone involved in these terrorist attacks, and I don't care who they are. Kendell and Chesty didn't die for nothing. Someone is going to pay."

"I knew you were as pissed as me." Brian reached for his rifle. "Mel has to go back to the Guard, but with Tyrone, Atticus, and the three of us, we have a rifle team, anyway."

"Hold on, soldier," Deni warned. "That's a good start, but we need more help."

"Yes we do." Nate stood. "But for now let's pack up and touch base with Tyron and Atticus, let them know we're staying."

Brian started for his bedroom to get his partially dry clothes that were still hanging over the tub. "And ask them if they know of any bunkers in the area we can use for an HQ."

Deni and Nate's eyes met. They both laughed.

Deni became serious. "You sure about this? Risking Brian's life for these people again?"

"Risking your life too, Deni." He rubbed his face with callused hands. "It scares the hell out of me. If something happens to either one of you…"

They held each other. "And if you don't do anything about Kendell and Chesty's murder, you'll have to live with that."

Nate held her tighter. "I think I would lose Brian if I didn't do something. He's really upset about Kendell. Up until a few minutes ago I was afraid I would lose you if I did stay and fight."

"Bullshit. That would be the day. Hell, we just got married. I'll give you at least a few months to straighten up and fly right before giving up on you."

Brian walked in, holding his pack by one shoulder strap. "Uh, I thought we were leaving."

~~~

The Williams family found Tyrone and Atticus at the burned-out courthouse, trying to salvage what they could. They were both relieved to learn the three were going to stay.

"We can sure use your help." Atticus looked them over. "I don't blame you for being pissed. Hell, *I'm* pissed. We have to make this community a decent place to live."

Tyrone nodded toward the parking lot at a group of men working on a sheriff cruiser. "We have three volunteers so far, but people are reluctant. Some are not willing to risk their life, and many have families to feed. They're busy preparing for spring planting."

Mel walked up, looking as if he had just been out for a stroll, though he had actually been patrolling the area, looking for someone that needed killing, hoping some idiot would start something. What they did to Kendell had his blood boiling. He didn't say anything, just stood there and listened. He did seem a little surprised to learn Nate and family were staying in town.

Nate nodded, and Mel took the opening. "Well guys, I have a helicopter to catch and have only a few minutes to get to the Army base." He raised his eyebrows. "And just when it looks like things are going to get interesting around here. It doesn't take a prophet to see what's coming. Someone's going to get their ass kicked. I would love to stay and help, but I have to go kick ass with the Guard."

"I'll drive you," Nate offered.

Mel nodded toward a Humvee pulling into the drive. "Col. Donovan sent a ride."

Nate glanced at the Humvee. "In that case, this is it." The two shook hands. "Do the people of this county a favor and talk the ear off every officer you can buttonhole. The more people with some power who understand what's happing here, the better."

"It's all in my report, but you can bet I'll spread the word." Mel scratched his newly shaven chin. He spent the early morning hour cleaning up in preparation for reporting to his commanding officer. "The thing is, more than likely it's pretty much the same story everywhere, except worse."

Atticus thrust his hand out. "Good luck to you and come back as soon as you can."

Tyrone added, "I knew that any friend of Nate's had to be a reliable man." The two shook.

Brian stayed back, not speaking.

Mel turned to Deni. They held each other for a second.

"Take care," Deni said.

"Yep. You take care of those two. Keep 'em out of trouble, if you can."

"That's a tall order," Deni quipped.

Mel looked at Brian. "I'll be back here someday. In the mean time, the bunker and all that's in it are yours."

Brian blinked and looked away. "Just come back. I'm tired of losing friends."

Mel shrugged his shoulders. "The fickle finger of fate, Brian. When Death points his finger at you, you can't run fast enough. All we can do is the best we can. In some ways, I've already lived more than men who die old." He shook his head and smiled. "Don't feel sorry for me, friend, no matter what happens." He grabbed his pack and rifle, then headed for the Humvee.

Chapter 6

A man named Jarrod Ashton came to Tyrone and Atticus one morning and told them about a convoy of big tractor-trucks that had been speeding by his home every night, first heading south around 10PM and heading north around 4AM. He lived on NE 228 Ave, twenty miles outside of the township limits of Glenwood. Having previously heard of the terrorists using tractor-trucks, he was worried they might raid his home and harm his wife. He made the trip on horseback, having run out of diesel fuel for his pickup long ago. He figured it would be safer to travel at night, so he could see headlights coming soon enough to give him time to turn the horse into the woods and hide while they went by.

Tyrone wanted to get the Army involved.

Nate shook his head. "We'll do this alone. No telling what we find out."

"What do you mean?" Atticus squinted in the sunlight.

"I'm just saying we should wait until we learn what we can before getting anyone else involved, especially the Army."

Everyone there seemed puzzled by Nate's words, but all remained quiet and let it go. Deni did have a question. "How can we be sure they're part of the terrorist group? It's possible others have scrounged up a semi to use for transportation."

"Yeah," Tyrone agreed, "but not likely. Those things drink fuel fast and are about the worst choice for simple transportation you could come up with. Still, we need to go easy if they let us. Don't want to hurt innocents."

"They're with the terrorist assholes alright." Brian seemed to have no doubt. "Mr. Ashton said there are a lot of semis going by his home, not just one or two, and they go by every night."

"Yeah." Deni put her helmet on. "Still, we better not go in with guns blazing, just in case we're wrong."

Nate scrounged up a horse trailer and hitched it to a truck, so he could give the man a ride back to his home. Deni and Brian prepared for a fight, going heavy on ammunition supplied by Donovan, and scrambled into the cab. Tyrone and Atticus followed in the sheriff cruiser.

The farther out of town they got, the fewer abandoned cars they came to in the road, and that allowed them to make better time. The two-lane country road was so overgrown on both sides, with brush overhanging, it appeared to them they were driving down a woods path paved with cracked asphalt. They had their windows down, and the brush made a swishing sound as they sped by.

They went on after dropping off Mr. Ashton at his home, leaving the horse trailer there.

"Look," Nate said. "There's another abandoned vehicle that's been pushed off the road out of the way. Someone's cleared this road."

"Yeah." Brian pointed. "That tree had fallen across the road but someone pushed it out of the way."

"It took heavy equipment to do that," Deni said. "They used a bulldozer or something. Otherwise, they would have had to cut it up into manageable pieces if they used only manpower." She glanced at Nate. "This is getting curiouser and curiouser."

Nate drove by another abandoned car. "As far as I know, the Army hasn't been out here clearing this road and no one else has either."

"And the Guard damn sure didn't do it," Deni added. "They haven't been back in months."

"Well, someone went through the effort and expense of fuel and labor to clear this little road for a reason," Nate said. "Look for a big tall tree we can cut down across the road. We need to set up an ambush spot as soon as possible. We damn sure don't want to be driving down this road when they show up. No telling what they'll do."

"They'll try to kill us. That's why they'll do," Brian said. They crested a hill, and Brian pointed. "Look at that tall healthy pine. It'll do the job."

Nate slowed down. "It's as good a spot as any." He found a Jeep trail and pulled off the road, hiding the truck behind thick woods after turning around, so they could drive straight out and leave in a hurry. They all jumped out and gathered at the tailgate. Nate lifted a two-man crosscut saw out of the truck. "Let's get that tree down as fast as possible. Bring your entire load with you. We might get into a fight before we're ready and have to abandon the vehicles."

Tyrone drove past the truck, squeezing between it and trees, turned around, spinning in the sand, and pulled in behind them with the cruiser. He got out. "I guess you guys have noticed someone's cleared the road."

"Yep." Deni nodded. "We've been discussing it for miles."

"What do you make of it?" Atticus wanted to know.

Nate carried the saw past them, heading for the pine tree. "Maybe we'll learn something tonight."

Everyone put on their packs and grabbed their rifles, scrambling to catch up with Nate.

Atticus and Deni kept watch while Nate and Tyrone sawed. Brian climbed an oak tree, so he could see trouble coming from farther away and give them an earlier warning.

When they were halfway through the tree, Deni yelled, "Trucks coming! Get down!"

They left the saw by the tree and did as she said. Four military trucks, deuce and a halfs, barreled by at high speed, going south toward town. Their canvas tops prevented them from seeing what kind of load they were hauling, if any.

Nate leaned his rifle against a tree. "So, the military *is* using this road."

"Does that change anything?" Brian asked. "I mean, should we still block the road?"

Nate didn't answer his question directly. "We'll wait until dark, when those semi drivers are supposed to show up."

Deni remained quiet, but it was obvious she had something on her mind that bothered her.

"What?" Nate wanted to know.

"What the hell is going on? That's what." She looked down the road. "Is there a connection between the trailer-less semis and the Army? And if so, is there a connection between the Army and the terrorists who drive those semis?"

Brian pulled his boonie hat off and mopped his forehead with it. Despite the cold weather, everyone was sweating. "Why would the Army be using semis that aren't hauling anything?"

Nate pulled binoculars out from under his jacket, where they hung from his neck. "Maybe we'll get some answers tonight. All of you take a nap while I keep watch for a couple hours. You're not likely to get any sleep the rest of the night and maybe tomorrow, too."

Scanning with binoculars, Nate took the time to memorize every tree and rock, every swell and dip in the terrain, and estimated the range of every prominent feature he could see from his position. He also got out a topographic chart and memorized every important feature of the area, in case they had to flee on foot. With only four adults and one teen, it wouldn't take much to outgun them. They needed to be ready and able to retreat, if necessary.

He watched the dying afternoon view fade from bright green to dim gray and the blue sky darken to purple twilight. The wind had picked up, and he was worried the partially sawed tree might fall before they were ready, but as the sun fell below the horizon, the wind calmed.

Deni woke. Before she was on her feet, Brian was also awake. The first thing he did was grab his rifle, even before he looked around.

"How long has it been dark?" Brian asked in a whisper.

Nate's answer was: "Time to cut the tree. If you two need to take a leak or anything, do it now. The fun may start at any time. Wake the others." He took three steps and grabbed one end of the saw. In less than five minutes, the tree fell with a crash, frightening a buck and two does that were feeding on grass beside the road, only 70 yards away.

"I guess cutting that smaller tree down on the other side of the road would be too obvious," Brian commented.

"Yeah." Nate put the saw behind a tree, out of the way. "There's a 99% chance they'll be suspicious anyway. That means they'll not likely stop right at the tree. Brian and Atticus, you watch to the south, while the rest of us watch to the north. Mr. Ashton said they usually come in from the north late in the evening and head back from the south early in the morning. As soon as we see headlights, we're going to have to get into position. We'll spread out 50 yards apart. They'll probably stop as soon as they see the log and think on what to do next, while they look around for trouble. During that minute or so, Tyrone and I'll rush them from their blind spot and get the drop on them. The rest of you will be staying behind cover and overwatching everything, including down the road in both directions. Since they may be associated with the Army, there's a good chance they'll have night vision devices. We've got to be careful here. If they're associated with the Army, they're probably not regular legs, because whatever they're doing is definitely a covert operation."

"Legs? What does that mean?" Brian asked.

"It means they may be Special Forces," Deni answered in a worried tone of voice.

"Legs?" Brian asked.

"Infantry soldiers." Deni answered. "Special Forces are always airborne qualified, thus they're not 'legs.'"

"Oh. Dad never talked about the Army much."

Nate's terse voice came from out of the dark, "Less talk, more looking and listening."

Nate and Tyrone agreed it would be best to position as if the trucks were most likely to come in from the north side, so they decided to set up the ambush with that in mind.

Nate considered the situation. "If they're the usual punks we've been dealing with, they just might drive up to the log, but if they're associated with the military or civilian government, they're going to stop as soon as they see it and not go anywhere near until they're sure it's not an ambush. So right off the bat, we'll know whether or not we're dealing with anarchist idiots."

Deni added, "If they're Army, they might come in with their lights off, using night vision instead."

"Yeah," Nate agreed. "That'll be another clue early in the game."

That was the last of their conversation. Deni, Atticus, and Brian lined up along the edge of the woods, separated by 50 yards, with Nate and Tyrone at the northern end of the kill zone, everyone on the same side of the road. Tyrone would come around the back of the semi and take on the passenger, while Nate approached the truck on the driver side. They hoped to take at least one prisoner alive.

At 10:15, Nate heard the wine of a truck's big tires coming in from the north. He checked his Aimpoint electronic sight, shouldering his M14 and looking through it. The red dot glowed too brightly in the dark, obscuring the tree he used for a test target behind it, so he reduced its brilliance. When the truck crested a distant hill, he noticed right away they were running with no lights. *Shit! This is going to be dicey.*

The driver slammed on the brakes. Tires smoked and screamed. When he locked them up, the back tires bounced on the asphalt, as the truck slid sideways in the middle of the road.

Nate and Tyrone exploded from the dark woods and charged the truck. Approaching the driver's side, Nate screamed "Sheriff's Department. Hands up! Get your hands up or I will shoot!"

The shocked driver turned his head and looked at Nate with the latest military night vision device. The muzzle of Nate's rifle convinced him. He immediately raised his open hands.

Tyrone tried the same tactic on the passenger side but had less luck. "You're under arrest. Don't move! I'll shoot!" He was forced to shoot the man in the head when he snatched an MP5 machine pistol off his lap and tried to bring it up to fire. Some of the contents of the man's head splattered on the driver. He yelled, "Don't shoot! Don't shoot!"

"Tyrone," Nate yelled, "Come around on this side and open the door while I hold my rifle on him."

Tyrone did as directed, swinging the door wide open and staying back out of the way.

"Get your ass out of there and put your belly on the asphalt," Nate demanded.

"Okay, okay. Don't shoot." The man followed Nate's instructions explicitly.

Tyrone cuffed his hands behind his back and yanked the night vision goggles off his head. He stood up and looked down the road. "I think I hear another one coming." He grabbed their prisoner by an arm and yanked him to his feet.

"Move it." Snatching the tall, thin man along, Tyrone got him in the woods before the truck crested a distant hill to the north.

Nate climbed into the cab and took a quick look around, finding nothing of interest. He jumped down and climbed onto the back, where the trailer would usually be hitched, and found ten military-style boxes four feet long, two feet wide, and two feet high strapped onto a makeshift platform, all colored olive drab. He could see no markings on the outside, but they were certainly military looking. A hand radio on the seat squelched twice and a man's voice came from the speaker, using military call signs and protocol. Obviously, those in the other truck were trying to find out what was going on. There was no time to look any closer, so he jumped down and ran for the woods. He saw Tyrone and turned to his right, slowing his gait.

Tyrone had the prisoner on his belly and his big right boot planted between his shoulder blades to make sure he stayed there. "What now?"

Nate answered, "Depends on what the people in that truck do. If they drive away, I'll go back out there and take a look at what the hell is in those boxes and then we'll take this one someplace between here and town and interrogate him."

They watched as the truck backed up and disappeared over the crest of the hill.

"They're not gone," Tyrone said.

"No they are not." Nate pulled his binoculars out and scanned the horizon in the direction of the hill. A half-moon was out, and he could see well enough with the light-gathering ability of his high-quality binoculars. "The price of going out there to find out what's in those boxes is likely to be high."

Tyrone pressed down with his right boot, driving it into the man's back. "Why don't we ask this bastard?"

"We will," Nate said. "First, let's get the hell out of here."

Tyrone snatched the man to his feet. "You're under arrest for terrorism and conspiracy to commit murder."

"Whaat?" The man laughed. "Just take me to Col. Donovan."

Nate grabbed the man by his shoulder and spun him around. "Are you working under Donovan's orders?"

The man's answer was, "I'll only talk to Col. Donovan."

Nate fumed at the thought Donovan could be involved, but all he said was, "Let's get the hell out of here right now."

They stayed hidden in the woods back from the road, forcing the man along with them, as they headed south for the others.

When they were close enough Deni could see, she commented, "You got one."

"Did you see the other truck?" Nate asked.

Confused, Deni answered, "No, I didn't see anything but that one."

"Must've been too far for you to see in the moonlight. They saw their friends in trouble and backed up behind the hill," Nate said. "I'm sure they're waiting up there for a chance to put a bullet into one of us."

"I'll get Brian and Atticus. You guys go to the vehicles." Deni rushed ahead, pushing through the brush in the dark.

Approaching the truck and sheriff's cruiser, Nate threw his pack in the back of the truck and barked orders. "Everyone load up. Deni drive the truck. Atticus drive the cruiser. Tyrone, watch the prisoner. Keep in mind if he's what we think he may be he's dangerous as hell. Watch him closely. Don't rely on the cuffs to render him harmless. He won't be harmless until he's dead."

Tyrone shoved the man headfirst into the back seat of the cruiser and sat on him. "Don't worry. I got him."

"Start the engines and be ready to take off when I come back." Nate ran down the Jeep trail toward the road. He heard footsteps behind him and turned to see Brian following close behind. He stopped. "Whoa! I meant for you to get into the truck with Deni. These guys know more about night fighting than both of us put together. Go on back to the truck."

Brian didn't move. "What are you going to do?"

"Just take a look down the road and see what they're up to."

"In that case I might as well come with you."

"No. Go back like I told you."

"Shit." Brian turned and ran back toward the truck.

Nate slowed down when he got near the road and eased up to the edge of the brush where it ended and the asphalt started. Dropping to his knees while still hidden in the tall brush, he crawled close enough he could see down the road with his binoculars. They were out there, up on the hill with rifles. The dim moonlight wasn't enough to allow him to see that far, but he knew they were up there. He back-crawled from the road ten feet and then ran for the others.

He ran past the truck and stopped at Atticus's driver-side window. "Leave your lights off until we're way down the road. Don't step on the brakes; it'll light up your taillights. They're up there waiting to get a shot, and they'll probably see us with night vision devices when we leave, so we're going to come out of the woods like a bat out of hell and take off down the road as fast as we can. Expect to take a bullet or two in the back of the car, so stay down as low as you can."

"You bet," Atticus said.

Nate ran to the truck and opened the passenger side door. "Brian, sit down on the floorboard. I know it's tight, but squeeze yourself in down there and stay low." He ran around to the driver side and opened the door. Speaking to Deni, he said, "I'll drive. Scoot over and lay down in the seat with your feet in my lap. I want you as low as possible. If I get hit, I'll slow down and turn into the woods on the left side of the road. You bail out and hit the woods, both of you."

Deni frowned in the dark. "Yeah right. Bullshit." She did as he said, despite the fact it was obvious she wasn't going to bail out and leave him if he were wounded.

Nate waved his left hand out the window to signal Atticus. There was no need to floor it and throw dirt on the cruiser's windshield. Nate took off fast but without spinning the rear tires. By the time he made it to the hard road, he was going as fast as he could and still navigate the sharp turn to the left. The rear of the truck skidded around and he had it straight in the road when he floored it, tires squealing and smoking. The cruiser was faster, and Atticus had no trouble staying right on his rear bumper. The rear of the cruiser took two bullets, one going through the rear window. In ten seconds, they were behind a six-foot swell. Fifteen seconds longer, and they disappeared around a curve.

Nate didn't let up on the gas until they came to a side road. He slowed and turned off to the right.

"Now what?" Deni asked.

"If they're Army, they've already called in air support – if they have any available. We have to stay off of that road and get out of the area."

"Can I get up now?" Brian asked. "It's cramped as hell here."

Deni maneuvered herself over by Nate and made room for Brian. "Go ahead. If we get shot at from the air, staying low won't do you any good."

Nate drove a few miles farther and stopped. He opened his door. "I'll go check on the others. One of them may have taken a bullet."

Atticus stuck his head out of the window of the cruiser. "Not a scratch here. You guys all right?"

Nate bent down and saw the bullet hole in the back. "Yeah. We need to get to town a different way. I'm afraid they've called in air support."

Tyrone still sat on their prisoner. "Maybe we should hold out somewhere till daylight."

"Well, we'll need a barn or something to hide these vehicles in. Do either of you know the area?"

Tyrone spoke up. "I used to patrol this part of the county. There's a little hamlet about six miles down the road. It's got a junkyard. The guy that owned it is probably dead but I don't know for sure. Anyway, he had a big metal building he used for a work shop. We might could break into that and park of our vehicles in there."

"Sounds like our best bet. You get in front and lead the way." Nate ran back to the truck.

"Where are we going?" Brian asked.

Atticus sped by.

"Junkyard." Nate put the truck in gear and took off.

Deni had a thought. "If they asked for air support, it would've been here already. Col. Donovan's choppers are not that far away."

"I hear you," Nate said. "Chances are Donovan knows nothing about any of this. These guys are covert. They may be taking their orders straight from the Pentagon and someone there might be taking his orders straight from the president. This is probably political bullshit. And I'm starting to think the so-called anarchists are also bullshit. Oh, the young punks are real enough, and they're true believers – but someone has put anarchy nonsense in their heads."

Brian narrowed his eyes and looked at his father. "I don't understand. What you're saying is just as crazy as what we've been thinking was going on before now. People have died because of this."

Nate's voice grew sharp and cold. "People die because of politics all the time, Brian. War is politics by another means. The number of people murdered in the last hundred years by their own government is higher than the number killed in warfare. And wars are started and waged by governments. That's not to say I'm against government. Government is a necessary evil, as our Founding Fathers stated many times. But it must be kept small, weak, and inexpensive."

"I agree," Deni said. "But a small, weak, inexpensive government is exactly what we have now."

"But is it really a representative republic?" Nate kept his eyes on the road. "It seems most of those in power in Washington were elected only by voters in the northeastern states, and only a small number of voters at that."

Deni tried to get comfortable in the seat, which wasn't easy while wearing her heavy body armor and spare ammunition. "We're not even certain those guys are Special Forces. But assuming they are, what's the point of causing trouble around here and getting people killed?"

"That's what I'm hoping our prisoner will tell us." Nate saw the little community ahead and slowed, putting a little more distance between them and the cruiser.

They parked in a dirt and gravel driveway at the entrance to the junkyard, which was fenced off with old roofing tin, so people couldn't see the junked and crumpled cars, as they drove by. The fence of rusty metal roofing certainly didn't spare anyone's eyes any unpleasant sights. Flattened cars were stacked 30 feet high in places and they could be seen over the ratty-looking fence.

Someone yelled from out of the dark, "Who are you and what the hell do you want?"

Tyrone yelled back, "We're with the Sheriff's Department or what's left of it. We need to park our vehicles in your workshop until daylight. We're not here to arrest anyone or cause any trouble."

"Tyrone, is that you?" The hard edge in the man's voice disappeared. "It's Sam Broker. I guess you didn't think I survived the plague or the aftermath. But I'm still here. Let me unlock the gate and I'll let you in."

Chains rattled. A few seconds later, someone pushed the gate aside on its rollers. A skinny old man in dirty jeans and a brown T-shirt waved them on through. "Come on in. Don't linger out there. Someone might take a shot at you. Lots of folks around here need the parts I have to keep their vehicles running. That is if they have any fuel for them. We've had trouble with people wanting to take what they want and not trade food or fuel for it."

They drove both vehicles into the junkyard and stopped in front of the closed door of the metal building. The man pulled the gate closed and padlocked the chain.

Tyrone walked up to him with a big smile on his face and they shook hands. "Damn glad to see you're still alive, Sam."

"Same here. You're the best deputy this county ever had." Sam glanced at the others. "What's this all about?"

"Too complicated to explain now. We need to get these vehicles in your building as soon as possible. Choppers might be looking for us."

Sam produced a ring of keys from his pocket and moved as fast as he could to the wide double doors of the shop. "Okay, but I want a better explanation than that as soon as you're parked inside."

Inside the shop, Nate and Tyrone manhandled their prisoner, pulling him feet first out of the cruiser.

Sam lit a kerosene lantern. "Who's he?"

"That's just one of many things we're going to find out." Nate answered.

Atticus deftly moved in to distract Sam. "I'm Atticus, Tyrone's father. And before you ask, yes, he's adopted."

Sam laughed and shook his hand. "I wasn't going to ask."

Nate and Tyrone jerked their prisoner along until they came to a support post to tie him to.

Nate gave their prisoner a hard stare. "We're going to be here a while. That'll give us plenty of time to get to know each other. The best thing for you is to answer my questions without forcing me to resort to persuasion. There are plenty of tools, vices, and welding torches around here I can use along those lines. But I would rather not. We're both Americans. We're both human beings. Problem is I'm pissed off. I've seen a lot of good people die recently. And I think maybe you had something to do with it."

The man swallowed. "I haven't killed anyone lately. I've never killed anyone in this area. And the only time I *have* ever killed anyone, I was following orders." He looked straight into Nate's eyes. "Whose orders are you following?"

Nate stared back, cold and hard. "Following orders? I don't have that crutch to lean on. And I'm restricted only by my own conscience. Right now, I'm just pissed enough that I'm listening to another side of me and keeping my conscience boxed up somewhere dark and so far back inside of me I couldn't hear it if it was screaming."

After introducing herself and Brian to Sam, Deni asked, "Is there anyone else around? If there is, you need to inform them we're here. We don't want any unfortunate mistakes that result in someone getting hurt."

"Yeah," Sam answered. "I've got two families living with me and my wife. Eight people, including the children. We help each other survive. I'll let them know you're here. Just don't go outside the building until I come back and tell you it's okay." He went out a standard-sized side door and closed it.

Nate looked his prisoner up and down, noting that he didn't have an ounce of fat on him. It wasn't thinness from malnutrition; it was evidence of a high level of physical conditioning. Everything about the man, his physical appearance, his calm demeanor, his fresh haircut at a time when there wasn't an open barbershop in the entire state, and his hunter's eyes told Nate he was an operator. "What's your name?"

The man spoke without hesitation, "I would rather not say. Knowing my name will do you no good anyway."

"Okay. It's not important. I'm not interested in hunting your family down. All I want to know is what you're doing in this area."

"Why?" the man asked.

Nate sighed, losing patience. "I was hoping to avoid crippling you, but if you answer another question with a question, you'll regret it."

"I was delivering the boxes strapped to the back of that semi."

"And what was in those boxes?"

"HE, small arms ammunition, a little food, and propaganda leaflets."

"Who were you going to deliver them to?"

"Pawns."

Nate lowered his head slightly and stared at him. "Explain that."

"People naïve enough to be led by the nose and persuaded to cause trouble here locally. My job was to give them a cause and rile them up enough they would get violent. It's not exactly a difficult thing to do. People have seen the inner circle of hell and are under severe mental stress. Probably three out of ten of those who survived the plague and its aftermath are basically nuts. Plant a seed of hate in their heads – this or that group caused all their problems – or the government did it – and they go out looking for someone to kill. It worked okay for Hitler."

Tyrone broke in. "Are you saying the government has ordered you to artificially drum up antigovernment movements in the area? What the hell for?"

"More terrorist attacks," the man answered. "It gives Washington an excuse to clamp down on people's freedom. They're just trying to protect you from the terrorists, don't you know. And to do that, they need more control over your life. Our new president is power-hungry, and he needs an excuse to burn what's left of the Constitution." The man shook his head slightly. "And believe me, there's very little of it left already. The guy used to be a corporate mogul – richer than six feet up a bull." The man shrugged. "Now he's president. Money's no good anymore, so his new drug is power."

Nate glared at him. "Didn't you swear the same oath I did?"

"Hey, they feed us and provide my family with healthcare. I still have my wife and daughter. My son died in the plague. Survival: it's the name of the game."

Brian looked around. "I wonder if there's some gas or kerosene around here. Some of your pawns burned my friend alive the other day. I think it's eye for an eye time."

The man pulled against his ropes. "I didn't burn your friend."

"You just admitted you put them up to it." Brian spit his words out, burning with rage.

Nate broke in. "As long as he's telling us what we need to know, we have no excuse to get barbaric." He glared at the soldier. "But the minute he stops talking or starts telling us what we think are lies, we'll light a welding torch and go to work."

Brian took a rusty gallon can off a shelf. "Paint thinner. It'll burn slower than gas. Take longer to kill him. He'll scream longer that way."

Deni's head swiveled from Brian to Nate. She kept her concerns to herself, but it was obvious she was uncomfortable with the conversation.

Nate noticed her reaction but said nothing. "Why the hell are you using semis? And why are the terrorists who call themselves anarchists using semis?"

The soldier lifted both shoulders slightly. "The government's short on resources the same as everyone else. There's a big truck stop just north of the Florida-Georgia line and a few others between here and there. We just found some trucks that were still usable and filled the tanks. Then we made them available to the indigenous halfwits. We use them ourselves, mostly because military vehicles would be too obvious and they're great for pushing stalled vehicles out of the road."

"We saw two deuce and a halfs go by earlier."

"I don't know anything about that."

"So the Army is using this road too?" Nate asked. "I mean besides you operators."

The soldier shrugged again. "I guess so. They weren't our trucks. We've been using the silly semis all along."

It was growing colder in the metal building, and Tyrone zipped up his leather jacket. "What's our new president's name? I damn sure didn't vote for him. What party is he in?"

The soldier looked as if he didn't want to talk about it. "Russell Capinos. There is no political party anymore. The old pre-plague government's gone. What we have now has no connection to the old government. It's as different as the pre-plague America was to today's America."

"Russell Capinos," Tyrone said. "Never heard of him."

"All I know is he was some kind of a corporate big shot and one of the wealthiest assholes in the world before the plague. Now he's residing in the White House and pulling the strings. Almost everyone in Congress is one of his cronies, put there by him. Same goes for almost every justice on the Supreme Court." The soldier gave everyone a grim look. "Capinos has this country by the short hairs. He issues executive orders every day. It's a Simon says government now, and he's Simon. So far, what's left of the high brass in the Pentagon has followed his orders as if he's completely legit. It looks like they'll continue to do so, for the present time anyway. They still refuse to go against the prime directive of staying subservient to civilian government."

"Well, Washington and the Pentagon are both out of our hands." Nate rubbed the stubble on his chin. "The question now is what to do with you. You've seen our faces. You're a trained killer and part of a team of trained killers, all well equipped by our wonderful new government. It won't take you long to learn who we are and almost everything about us, just by asking around. You admit you're more than willing to follow orders from a corrupt government, even when those orders are unconstitutional, illegal, and immoral. I have a strong feeling if I let you go it'll be the worst mistake of my life."

The soldier looked away but said nothing. Finally, he turned his head and looked at Nate. "I'm not going to beg you not to kill me. I do ask that you treat me like a soldier and execute me with a bullet to the head rather than kill me slow." He looked at Brian. "I'm sorry about your friend. But I didn't burn anyone, and I didn't tell anyone to burn anyone."

"Well," Brian said, "that makes it all okay then. I'll go to his grave and tell him you didn't really mean it."

Chapter 7

Mr. Broker entered through the side door. He hesitated for a moment before walking over to the others and entering the dim glow from the lantern. He seemed to be relieved when he saw that the soldier had not been beaten or injured in some horrible way. "Everybody knows you're here now, so you can walk outside without getting shot if you want."

"Good," Nate said. "We'll do just that." He turned back to the others. "Atticus, will you watch our guest while the rest of us have a conversation outside?"

Atticus nodded. "Sure. If you hear my shotgun going off it'll be him dying."

Nate glared at their prisoner. "I know what you're thinking. Yeah, he's old, and you may be a high-speed operator, but you're not that fast." He checked the handcuffs and rope. "He'll kill you. And you'll have died for nothing."

The soldier raised an eyebrow but remained silent. Nate was certain he had caught the true connotation of his last sentence: They still had not decided they were going to kill him, or at least Nate had not decided yet.

Standing outside the building in the dark with Deni, Tyrone, and Brian, Nate turned to them and asked, "Well, have we fallen so far that we're willing to kill this man in cold blood?"

Deni didn't hesitate. "My answer is no. I believe most of what he has told us. And I don't think he directly killed anyone in this county."

"But he put them up to it," Brian protested, raising his voice higher than necessary. "What about Kendell?"

"I know how you feel." Deni but her hand on Brian's shoulder. "But the fact is those directly involved with that horrible crime are already dead. I doubt very seriously that this man actually put it in their mind to go out and burn a church with two teen boys in it and burn one of them alive."

Tyrone spoke up. "I can't pull the trigger myself. And I won't be a part of consenting to anyone else doing it. The church killings were different. I would've done the same thing if I hadn't gotten there after it was all over. But I do not want to live the rest of my life knowing I was part of executing a man who may be an asshole but didn't really deserve to be killed."

Before Nate gave his opinion, he asked Brian, "Do you think killing this man is the right thing to do?"

"Uh. I…" He exhaled forcefully. "No."

Nate nodded his head slightly in the dark. "Okay then. The next question is what do we do with him?"

Brian let his rifle dangle across his chest from its sling and threw his hands up in the air in frustration. "Hell, if we aren't going to kill him, we have to let him go. What else can we do with him?"

"Take him to Col. Donovan," Nate answered. "It'll get him off of our hands, and we can study Donovan's reaction when we bring him in and ask him if he knows anything about the Army clearing a little two-lane country road of abandoned vehicles and using it every day to haul truckloads of stuff either to the little town of Glenwood or out of the town, heading north. I would also like to ask him, and watch his reaction closely when I do, about the covert operations our prisoner just told us about."

"Yeah," Tyrone muttered, rubbing his chin.

Deni said, "I trust Col. Donovan. But I don't see anything wrong with your plan. We have to either let this guy go or give him to the Army, so giving him to Donovan sounds like a plan to me."

Nate opened the door to the metal building, and a shaft of dim lantern light shot out from the opening. "Let's go inside and tell Atticus and our guest what we have decided."

~~~

Atticus pulled on his white beard and stared at the soldier. "You guys sure about this? If we let him go, we're all going to have to leave town and go into hiding. Washington will not want us talking. The best way to shut us up is kill us."

The soldier spoke up. "That won't be necessary. I'll tell them I didn't see anyone's face or hear anyone speak a name and have no idea who you are."

Atticus snorted. "Yeah, like we can believe you. No. To be safe, we'll have to leave town if we let this guy go."

"And who is going to protect the townspeople?" Tyrone asked. "They need some kind of law. The Army will not stay long."

"Sorry," Atticus answered. "The fact is if we let him go we have to leave town and go into hiding. There ain't no two ways about it. Someone else is going to have to step up and take over where you and friends left off."

Tyrone rubbed the back of his neck and glared at the soldier. "That's a hell of a price for the townspeople to pay. I wonder if this asshole's worth it."

The soldier pulled against his ropes, obviously growing more concerned about his fate. "All I have to do is tell them you wore masks at first and later kept me blindfolded. Blindfold me before you turn me in to the Army. They'll get nothing out of me that could lead them to you."

Deni collapsed onto a dirty old stool and stood her rifle on her knee. "Atticus is right. We can't take any chances. If we let him go, we'll all have to leave town immediately afterward. It's that simple."

Brian pointed at the soldier. "It's his damn fault! Assholes like him are always forcing us to do things we don't want to do. They back us against a wall and give us two choices: either we let them kill us, or we let them force us to become killers like they are. They're turning us into animals. Every day, they force us to become more like them. Every day they steal a little more of our humanity." He shouldered his rifle and aimed at the soldier. "Tyrone asked if he was worth it. No he's not. He's not. The people of that town will not have any protection other than the Army. And how long will they stay? How long before the Army leaves and they have no protection at all? Just because we don't want to kill this one asshole. How many others will die so he can live?"

Nate rushed over and forced the muzzle of Brian's rifle up. He knew Brian was just upset enough to pull the trigger.

Brian didn't struggle. He let his father take the rifle from his hands. He just stood there with his head hanging low and his face dripping.

Nate pulled his son to him. "I know. I know. Go ahead. There's no shame in it. I know it eats at you. It eats at me too. Watching you go through it is the worst."

Deni held them both. "We're going to let him go. It's the right thing to do. Sometimes doing the right thing is expensive."

Nate leaned Brian's rifle against a toolbox. He searched around until he found a five-gallon bucket to sit on and carried it closer to the lantern so he could see. From a jacket pocket, he produced a folded map to study the back roads. He certainly wasn't about to use the same road they had ambushed the soldiers on. No, he would find another route back to town. "Most of you guys might as well relax and get some rest. We're going to stay here a few hours before heading back."

Brian walked over and picked up his rifle. "I can watch him while everyone takes a nap. I promise I won't kill him unless he gets loose."

~~~

Nate managed to sleep two hours before they all scrambled into the truck and sheriff cruiser, thanking Sam for his help before opening the double doors and backing out of the metal building.

Tyrone took the soldier up on his idea of blindfolding him. He couldn't possibly have seen much while lying in the back seat of the cruiser with Tyrone sitting on him in the dark, and Tyrone didn't want him to see anything on the way into town and maybe bring trouble to the little community around the junkyard, not to mention Sam and his friends. Best he knew as little as possible about where he had been taken. Other than the cruiser getting stuck in a sandy Jeep trail, they had no trouble making it back to Glenwood.

At the Army base in town, Nate presented his prisoner to Col. Donovan and had him repeat what he told the others at the junkyard the night before. Donovan grew more angry as the soldier spoke, appearing to be struggling not to strike the man. "Do you have any idea how many people in the area have been killed and injured because of you? You son of a bitch!"

"You can always have him executed," Brian commented dryly.

Deni nudged him with an elbow.

Donovan's eyes flashed around his office, but it was obvious he was looking inside himself. "I'm serving a lunatic sham president, who was never really elected. I don't know what his game is, but he damn sure doesn't care about the American people."

"And a Congress that was never really elected," Atticus added. "I know of no one who has voted since before the plague. Last night was the first time I had even heard of this new President Capinos."

Donovan glared at the Special Forces soldier. "Who's your commanding officer?"

Still in Tyrone's handcuffs, the soldier stood erect and looked straight ahead. "Sir, I respectfully refuse to answer any questions. If you contact the Pentagon and explain the situation, someone will come and get me. But it is very unlikely you will receive any answers to any of your questions."

Nate raised an eyebrow and stared at him. "You answered our questions freely last night. We didn't have to lay a hand on you."

The soldier continued to look straight ahead and stand erect. "The threat was there. I knew you meant it when you said you would use torture if you had to. In the end, I would have talked anyway. No human being can stand up to torture. It would've been all for nothing. So I talked, and I told you the truth. Now I'm through talking. I doubt very seriously the colonel will allow any torture committed by anyone under his command. I know his reputation."

Col. Donovan shrugged and sat down behind his desk. "You're not my prisoner. You have been arrested by civilian authorities for the crimes of terrorism and accessory to murder, among many others. What makes you think you're my prisoner?" Speaking to Nate and Tyrone, he said, "You can take him to your jail now. I expect there'll be some kind of a trial, conviction, and execution. It'll probably all be over by nightfall. Any of the townspeople serving on the jury is not likely to need any persuasion that the son of a bitch is guilty of the crimes he's accused of. Bring his body back and I'll see to it he gets a full military burial. Of course, we will not be able to notify his family, since he refuses to give us his name."

Tyrone grabbed him with both hands and jerked him toward the door. "He'll be dead in less than an hour."

Brian added, "He should die the way Kendell did."

The soldier's eyes flashed to Brian and saw hate staring back. "Okay, Colonel, I'll answer your questions. It's all bullshit anyway. America died along with most of the population. What's left is just crazy bullshit, from the White House on down to the local fake sheriff. It's not like I'm betraying my country. There is no America anymore."

Nate helped Tyrone sit him down in front of Donovan's desk. "I don't think we're America's enemy, so how could you be betraying the country?"

The soldier leaned forward in his chair to avoid pressing against the cuffs and cutting off circulation to his hands. "First Sergeant Henry Kramer."

Donovan pressed the start button on a recorder sitting on his desk. "Okay Top, who is your CO?"

Thirty minutes later, Donovan stopped the recorder. "You will be held until I receive orders from my superiors." He called in soldiers standing outside his office to take Sergeant Kramer away.

"Now what?" Nate asked. "You're between a rock and a hard place. Where are your allegiances going to be? The people or a fake government in Washington?"

Donovan swallowed. "I have no idea what I'm going to do."

"Do you know anything about the military trucks we saw heading south?" Nate asked. "Our prisoner said they aren't his outfit's trucks. He claims they've been using the semis all along."

Donovan leaned back in his chair. "The Army has cleared a shortcut from town to the interstate. Starting four days ago, we've had an open route all the way to the Georgia line. I managed to get some of that wild hog meat shipped north in refrigerated trailers using the cleared roads. Supplies for the base arrived last night in fact. They must've been the trucks you saw."

Nate decided to let it go for the time being. "Well," he said, "it's been a long time since any of us had any sleep. We're going to find a place to crash and get some rest."

Donovan seemed to be lost in his own thoughts. "Yeah, you do that." For some reason, he stood and shook Nate's hand.

It was then that Nate realized Donovan knew he and the others were leaving town.

"Good luck to you." Donovan looked at the others. "Good luck to all of you."

Deni looked sick. "I'm sorry we caused all of this."

Donovan shook his head. "Don't. You did the right thing. Never be sorry for that. Now I have to finish it."

They filed out of the office in silence, looking like they had just lost a friend.

In the parking lot, Deni leaned against the truck and folded her arms. "I think we just said good-bye to Col. Donovan."

Nate said, "Yes we did."

"What's he going to do now?" Brian asked.

"I'm not sure," Nate answered truthfully. "Whatever he does, he's powerless to stop those in Washington or the Pentagon. He's just a colonel and follows orders. He's not much different from our friend Sergeant Kramer."

Deni looked in the direction of Donovan's office, a collection of metal storage buildings, reinforced with sandbags. "We may have just handed Colonel Donovan a death sentence. Either way, his career is over. His life is over." She looked up at the sky. "Damn it. We should've just killed the bastard."

Brian agreed. "Yep, every time we let an asshole live, someone else suffers for it. I think I had the right idea last night. I don't know as we would feel any worse than we do right now, if we had killed him."

Atticus looked around the base. Soldiers scurried here and there performing their duties, paying them no attention. Many stood guard, weapons in hand, ready to repel attackers. "Folks, I think it's time to pack our shit and get out of Dodge while we can. Sometime soon, all these soldiers around us are going to be issued new orders, and we'll no longer be welcome here."

Tyrone's chest deflated. "Atticus is right. There are a few things I would like to pack. Let's all meet at the lumber yard on the south side of town in an hour."

"We're already packed," Nate said. "There's not much point in taking any more than you can carry in a backpack. We're going to be on foot soon anyway. When the fuel we have in our tank runs out, that's it."

"We might as well go with them, instead of rendezvousing at the lumber yard," Deni suggested.

"Okay, let's get out of here." Nate slid behind the wheel of the truck.

~~~

When they stopped in Tyrone's driveway, a home he hadn't been back to in many days, Nate once again implored them to take only what they could carry in a backpack and a little extra food they could throw in the truck and live on for a few days. By that time, they would be out of gas and on foot. For that reason, it didn't take Tyrone long to grab a few things and emerge from his home, ready to go.

They rushed to Atticus's home, which was in the direction they needed to go. While they were inside, Nate siphoned gas from the cruiser into a five-gallon can, then transferred it to the truck's tank. He managed to get an extra eight gallons.

Atticus and Tyrone emerged five minutes later. After throwing what would soon be all they had on this earth into the truck, they turned and looked at the house. For Atticus, it was the home he and his late wife raised a son in. For Tyrone, it was the home he grew up in.

Nate noticed their faces. "Sorry, guys. I wish I had never gotten you involved in this mess."

Atticus waved him off. "Not your fault. None of us had any idea where the investigation would lead to."

The father and adopted son climbed into the back of Nate's truck, leaving the cruiser in the driveway. Thirty minutes later, they left the little town of Glenwood behind, heading for Mrs. MacKay's horse farm.

Chapter 8

The pickup rattled along at 15 mph down the pothole-pocked dirt road. They were about five miles from Mrs. MacKay's horse farm. Deni looked over from behind the wheel and noticed it appeared something was on Nate's mind. "What?" she asked.

"It's possible trouble could be waiting for us at the farm. I think we should abandon the truck and hide it in the woods back from the road a ways. We'll travel by foot from now on. I'll leave you guys in a safe place and go take a careful look at the farm to make sure everything's okay there before coming back to get you."

Deni had no arguments against his idea. "Yell when you want me to pull over."

Six minutes later, Nate said, "Pull over here on the right side. There's enough of an opening in the woods between the trees we can get back a ways and hide the truck."

Deni did as he directed. The drainage ditch on the side of the road wasn't that deep there, and the ground was fairly firm. She had no trouble with the tires spinning and left little in the way of tire marks in the soil, but the crushed weeds she ran over would not be difficult for anyone passing by to see. There was really nothing that could be done about that. Chances were they would never come back for the truck anyway. They were about to be hunted, wanted by the federal government, their only crime discovering a government conspiracy.

Tyrone got up from where he sat behind the cab and jumped down. "I guess we're going to walk from now on."

"Yep," Nate answered. "We're asking for trouble, if we go any farther by truck." He let the tailgate down, so Atticus could get out of the truck easier.

Atticus walked to the back, and Tyrone and Nate helped him down.

"Thanks," Atticus said. "I can walk just fine, but I ain't fast. You guys remember I'm an old man. Don't run off and leave me."

"If we didn't think you would be an asset, we would've left you in town," Nate said.

Brian reached into the truck and handed Deni her backpack. After handing everyone their packs, he slipped his on and grabbed his rifle off the seat. He rolled the window up and closed the door as silently as he could. "It's those at the farm I'm worried about. Everyone in town knows we're their friends. Anyone who comes after us is certain to visit the farm, and there's no telling how rough they'll get when they do."

Atticus adjusted his pack's shoulder straps, while Tyrone held his shotgun for him. "We really stepped into it when we decided to investigate those damn semis. The trouble we have caused is spreading all over this county."

Nate pulled a compass from under his shirt, where it hung from a string around his neck. "It can't be undone. We'll have to live or die with it now. And, yes, it's a damn shame others are going to pay for our actions." He took three steps and stopped. "Brian, behind me. Deni, watch our six. Everybody, 10 foot spacing. Try to walk as quietly as possible and no talking. Keep your eyes and ears open and your mind concentrating on staying alive."

~~~

An hour later, Nate raised his hand and stopped. When the others caught up, he whispered, "I'll go the rest of the way by myself. Should be back just about dark." He looked at the faces around him. "Deni knows more than the rest of you about woods fighting. Your best chance is to listen to her. Consider her in charge while I'm gone." He studied the reaction of Tyrone and Atticus. "I don't mean to be bossy. But Deni can keep you alive. Even Brian knows more about woods fighting than you two city guys. He's had a lot of experience lately. You're not lawmen anymore; you're guerrilla fighters and your cause is survival."

Atticus snorted. "Glenwood ain't exactly New York City. But I get your point. We don't mind taking orders from you or from Deni."

Tyrone added, "Especially if she can keep us alive."

Nate took one last look at Brian and Deni, then turned and walked away.

After paralleling the road for miles and staying back from it several hundred yards, he turned left and made a beeline straight for it. He wanted to cross before he got near the farm, in case anyone was watching. He planned to come in on the north side of the farm and observe with binoculars before moving on in and searching out one of the more distant guards near the front gate. He didn't want to be misidentified as a threat and get shot.

Approaching the clay road, Nate readied his binoculars. He wanted to scan every inch of the road in both directions for any sign of danger and needed to find a dip in the road or at least a hill that would limit how far he could be seen in one direction. One direction was about all he could hope for. The sound of motors roaring and vehicles rattling from the north caught his attention. He turned his binoculars on the road where it crested over a hill. He froze for a second. *I'm too late.* He stayed hid in the woods and watched a convoy of military vehicles – mostly Humvees with .50-caliber Browning machine guns mounted on top – race by. It was obvious they were looking for a fight.

His mind raced. *How in the hell did they react so fast? The high brass in Washington must've already known about our association with MacKay and others at the farm.* He started his return to Deni, Brian, and friends, deep in thought. *Maybe they're not looking for us. It could be a coincidence, a normal patrol.* He shook his head. *No. The Army has never been out this far before. Why would they come out here now?* He worried about those at the farm.

Atticus almost jumped when he saw Nate appear, materialize from the wall of green, without any indication that he was anywhere near until he was standing only 10 feet away.

Brian stepped out of thick brush, where he too was standing watch. He motioned with his head to Deni. "He's back," he whispered.

Deni jumped to her feet in surprise. "Already?" She saw the worry on Nate's face. "What?"

Tyrone and Atticus stepped closer to the other three, so they could speak in low tones and not make much noise.

Nate swallowed. His face grim, he explained, "I never got across the road. A convoy of soldiers went by, heading for the farm. That would be my guess anyway. What the hell else is out here? And the bridge is out, so they're not going long distance to another part of the county. No, they're going to raid the farm. Looking for us."

Deni's jaw dropped. "Already? How? What the hell's going on?"

Nate just shook his head.

"We have to help them," Brian said. "This is our fault."

"There's nothing we can do." Nate gave him a stern look. "Don't argue with me about it or give me any trouble. I don't like this any more than you. But the fact is all we can do is pray the soldiers were not given orders to get rough with him. Hopefully, they'll just search the farm, and once they see we're not there they'll leave without harming anyone."

"Damn it!" Brian kicked a pine tree. "The whole world went to hell all at once. No. It had already done that. Now it's gone insane."

Atticus coughed. "You got that right."

"What now?" Tyrone asked.

"Well," Nate scratched the back of his neck. "I'm worried it might not be safe to go to Mel's bunker. They may already know about it. Certainly, a few in the Guard do. We can't go back to my place, either. I think we should wait until tomorrow, and then I'll recon MacKay's farm and try to learn what's going on. I'm hoping the soldiers will be gone by then, moved on in their hunt for us."

"Nice," Brian said. "Real damn nice." He sat down on a three-foot-wide limestone rock. "The kids; Caroline; René and her father; all the others. All we can do is wait and hope the soldiers have a little humanity and don't kill them."

"I think that would be a safe bet." Nate slipped out of his pack. "They appeared to be regular soldiers, not some kind of special unit of goons. Even the Special Ops guy we took prisoner couldn't be described as some kind of crazed killer or Nazi. It's worrisome, but I doubt we're going to find the aftermath of a massacre tomorrow morning. All we can do is stay here and wait. Until then, get some rest."

~~~

Ramiro, Mrs. MacKay's foreman, rushed to a large red brick building that contained the horse stalls. Alarm on his face, he swung the three-foot-wide side door with its barred windows open and stuck his head in. "We just received a radio message from Colonel Donovan: evacuate immediately." He stepped back outside and slammed the door shut, then ran to the front of the building and entered through double doors that allowed the horses to enter and exit the building. "Radio message: evacuate immediately."

Mrs. MacKay was busy showing Caroline how to properly saddle a horse. On hearing Ramiro's voice, she stiffened and her eyes widened. "Get the horses out into the pasture." She worked feverishly to get the saddle off.

Ramiro ran inside, to be met by Caroline, who was leading two horses out of the building. "Did you hear me?" he demanded.

"Yes. We're releasing the horses into the pasture. Help the others. We'll be there in a minute or two." Caroline pushed past him.

Mrs. MacKay led the still-bridled horse to Ramiro. "Make sure you take the bridle off before releasing it in the pasture." She moved as fast as her advanced age would allow and yelled over her shoulder, "I'm going to the house to remind everyone to stick to the plan. We don't know how long we have, so we'd better get out of here as soon as possible."

Ramiro nodded, but said nothing. He led the horse out of the building.

The big two-story house was alive with activity, as were the smaller outbuildings where most of the men slept. Children were loaded into trucks, both standard pickup trucks and larger flatbeds. On other trucks, boxes and bags of supplies were loaded as quickly as possible. In less than ten minutes, over four dozen adults and children were loaded up and ready to go. Mrs. MacKay and Ramiro rushed through the house to be sure no one was left inside. Others checked their assigned buildings, in an all-out effort to be sure not to leave anyone behind.

Twenty minutes after Ramiro received the warning over HAM radio, a convoy of trucks and other assorted vehicles headed out the gate, stopping only long enough to pick up the guards, who ran and climbed on the back of vehicles. Those with children or other family searched the vehicles for their loved ones and climbed in beside them. Two men jumped from the vehicle they were on and climbed onto another one to make room for those who wanted to be next to their children. The convoy picked up speed, rattling down the rough clay road, heading south, the direction of Nate's farm.

But long before they got to Nate's farm, they pulled off onto a Jeep trail, traveling over four miles before parking the vehicles under trees and rushing on foot into the woods to a pre-designated hiding place, dragging or carrying their supplies along with them. No one had any idea how long they would be there or if they would ever be able to come back to the farm. Seeing the worry on their parents' faces, many of the smaller children cried. Adults kept rifle and shotgun barrels pointing outward. All they knew was danger was coming and they had to be prepared for it. Their first plan was to flee and hide, but if forced they would fight. While most of the group hid in the woods, a few men stayed with the vehicles and cut brush to camouflage them with.

~~~

Less than ten minutes after the farm was evacuated, a military convoy turned into the drive and rushed through the open gate. The captain in charge wondered if the open gate might be an invitation to an ambush. Had they been warned somehow? Captain Cleef had no intention of being a part of any massacre, but feared the potential for such a disaster was there. So many civilians in one place, and all armed, was a boiling kettle of shit about to be kicked over. He hated assignments like this. His orders were to arrest five people, including one teenage boy. Intel was they might be hiding on this farm. The red light for him was the fact the farm was full of civilians who were not wanted for anything. There was no information at all as to what the five were suspected of. His orders were to find and arrest them at all costs. *Bullshit. All costs? What the hell does that mean? The lives of all his men? The lives of dozens of civilians? Or both? So many bullshit orders recently. I've had enough of it.*

~~~

Ramiro supervised the hiding of the trucks under trees, making sure they were spread out over many acres. Camouflage nets were spread over the vehicles in an attempt to hide them from aircraft, but he knew, as did most of the other adults there, the heat of the engines would give them away. It would take only one helicopter to fly over with heat detection equipment, and they would be discovered. They could only hope no aircraft came along until after the engines cooled, but the metal of the vehicles would hold heat and still might be detected by infrared devices.

Three miles from the trucks, tents were erected under trees and the children made as comfortable as possible. They carried some of the supplies they had taken with him but not all, leaving the rest near the trucks, hidden in the woods.

Ramiro approached Mrs. MacKay. "Do you think we should dig up some of the pre-placed supplies now?"

Mrs. MacKay did not hesitate. "No. We brought enough with us for a few days. As soon as we get the radio set up, we should hear more from Glenwood. When we do, we'll have a better idea of how long we'll be staying here."

Ramiro looked around at the busy people, already setting up a defense perimeter. Selected men and women were just then heading out to man observation posts that would afford them an early warning if attacked. Each team carried a two-way radio, so they could communicate with the base camp. The radios had been scrounged up by Colonel Donovan. Proud of their people's efficiency, he said, "We have come a long way since the last time this happened."

MacKay nodded. "Yes, thanks to Nate, Mel, Deni, Colonel Donovan, and many others in Glenwood."

"Still," Ramiro said, "if the soldiers find us, we'll be at their mercy. All of this is for other threats. As before, if the soldiers come, we must surrender. Their weapons are too strong for us to fight."

MacKay raised her voice, "They must not find us this time. Watch them. Make sure everyone stays under the cover of trees. I have a bad feeling about this one. I fear that if they find us, we'll lose more people than last time."

Ramiro turned grim. He had lost his wife during a military raid on the farm. That raid had been ordered by an insane Army officer. "The man on the radio said someone in Washington was out for blood. He said, 'Run like hell.'"

She looked around, near-panic in her eyes. "Maybe half a dozen adults should take the children deeper into the woods. This time they may not need an excuse before they open fire on us."

Caroline was checking her M4 when she heard. "Maybe we should spread out in groups of ten and rendezvous back here in a couple days."

"I hate to do that." MacKay rubbed her hands together. Her face lined with worry and doubt as to what course to take. "But it seems like it may be the best thing to do."

Ramiro agreed. "The radio message was very ominous. I think Caroline's idea is a good one. It will be much more difficult for them to find all of us if we are spread out."

"Let's do it," MacKay said. "We will need time to make camp before dark, and if we are to spread out far enough to do any good we will need time to travel."

~~~

Captain Cleef pulled off the dirt drive just inside the gate and let the other Humvees go on by. Colonel Donovan was on the radio warning Captain Cleef not to harm any innocents. "I'm almost certain the individuals you are after are not at that farm. If you allow any unnecessary killing of civilians, you will answer to me. And I don't give a damn what Washington or the Pentagon says."

Cleef grew indignant. "Colonel, I have never allowed the murder of civilians. My men have strict orders to fire only when fired upon."

"Good. Stay on your toes and make sure they follow those orders."

"Yes Sir. Colonel, we have just arrived, and I will give you a report in 10 or 15 minutes."

"Fine. You do that."

Ten minutes later, Captain Cleef's voice came over the radio speaker in Donovan's office. "Colonel, the farm has been evacuated. It's obvious someone tipped them off. I have men out searching the area at this moment. But so far, we have found no sign of large groups of people having traveled through the woods and the surrounding area recently. There are only a few vehicles on the compound and those seem to be disabled. That tells me they left by motor vehicle. I request at least one Black Hawk to search for them."

"We have one in the area already," Donovan answered. "Load up and be ready to move out at a moment's notice." He did not mention that his sincerest hope was the pilot would come up empty. It would be dark soon, and if those being hunted were careful enough to stay under a thick canopy of cover, their chances of not being found were better than even.

Chapter 9

Something woke Nate. He scrambled out of his sleeping bag and sat up, listening. He looked over and saw Brian sitting up also, his rifle in his hands. It was then he realized that he too had his rifle sitting on his lap. The sound of a distant helicopter faded away.

Deni was on watch. She heard the commotion when Nate woke and stepped closer. "They've been searching for hours. South of us."

"What terrible criminals we are," Brian said. "That they should burn so much fuel looking for us." He lay back down and got comfortable in his sleeping bag. Still several hours before dawn, the temperature was in the 30s. His breath misted as he turned on his side and propped his head up with a rolled jacket. "I'm going back to sleep. Wake me when the war starts."

Deni dropped to one knee beside Nate. Speaking in a whisper, she said, "You go back to sleep also. It'll be Tyrone's turn to pull security in about 30 minutes."

"Wake him now, and get some shuteye. I want you to come with me to check out the farm. The others will stay here again."

Relieved to learn he wasn't going alone, she didn't argue. "Okay."

~~~

The dark night woods gradually lightened to gunmetal gray and revealed the world around Nate and Deni a little at a time, until they could see well enough to leave the others and head for the farm.

Brian watched them sink into the cold mist that hung only feet above the forest floor and disappear into the towering gloom of the wilderness, swallowed by the forest, its obscurity offering at least some refuge from a modern army. The temperature had dropped below 30 and he didn't really want to leave his warm sleeping bag, but he knew Tyrone was tired and it was time for him to pull security and let Tyrone get warm in his bag and catch a few hours of sleep. Atticus was ten feet away, snoring peacefully. *At his age, things are going to get really rough for him out here in the woods,* Brian thought. *Let him sleep. He can pull security during the middle of the day when it's warm and he's rested.*

~~~

Approaching the farm with extreme caution, Nate and Deni bounded from cover to cover, one overwatching with rifle shouldered, while the other moved forward, leapfrogging past each other. As soon as they were close enough to see through the brush, Nate used his binoculars to scan the north side of the farm.

"The horses are in the pasture. There's not a single human out there visible to me." After lowering the binoculars, he said "Let's move around to another angle. I want to take a look at the front of the house."

Ten minutes later, Deni caught a glimpse of the front porch and door. "Front door's smashed. Porch furniture is overturned. They've been there all right. Question is, did the people get out before the soldiers arrived?"

Nate scanned the porch with binoculars. "I think the helicopters last night answered that question for us. They were searching for Mrs. MacKay's people."

"Could've been searching for us."

"Yep." After scanning the front yard, he put his binoculars away. "But if they had taken prisoners from the farm, they would've learned we hadn't been in the area in a long time. In that case, they probably would've been searching at our farm, perhaps Mel's bunker. No, they were searching for Mrs. MacKay's people. Besides, most of the vehicles are gone. I'd say they left before the soldiers got here."

"So," Deni said, "it's probably safe to assume everyone on the farm got away, at least for now."

Nate nodded. "Either way, it's too late to warn them."

A reassuring thought lit Deni's face. "It's almost a sure thing they were warned. And if they were it must have been Colonel Donovan." She appeared to be in a better mood than she should be under the circumstances. "Nice to know you can still trust a friend. Doing the right thing may cost him."

Nate nodded. "Yeah."

Something on his face prompted Deni to ask, "What?"

"Donovan can only go so far. Once he does, his usefulness to us or anyone else will be over. This may be the last time he can help us. In fact, he may be already relieved of duty and under arrest. Those in power aren't completely stupid. They've already figured out that someone warned Mrs. MacKay's people."

Keeping low, they backed away from the farm and started their journey to return to the others.

~~~

Colonel Donovan had not left his office all night. The only sleep he managed was two hours of lying on a blanket on the cold hard floor. He paced back and forth in the small room, waiting for the next report from Captain Cleef and praying his soldiers would not find the civilians they were looking for. *This entire operation is bullshit. Nate and the others have committed no crimes.* He stopped pacing his office. *They get them, I'm next. All to keep corrupt politics undercover. How many more people are going to die?*

Realizing his predicament, he collapsed into the chair behind his desk. He was willing to die for the people of Glenwood and his friends, but he had no idea how he could help them. He feared what little power he had to change things would soon be taken away. He felt cornered. And when a man like him is cornered, he becomes dangerous.

Send a protest up the chain of command? He cast his eyes around the room, but he was looking inward. *What good will that do? The orders came straight from the Pentagon. And they got their orders straight from the president.* A thought came to him that lived and died within the span of a millisecond. *Stage some kind of a revolt? How many soldiers will follow me?* He shook his head. *Don't go crazy. We have enough bat shit blowing in the wind as it is.*

Capt. Cleef's voice came over the radio speaker. "We found six of them, all adults. They refuse to tell us where the others are. They did tell us they haven't seen our fugitives in weeks. They say the last they heard, the ones we are hunting were still in Glenwood."

Donovan's face turned white. His last hope, the small chance that they would not find any of Mrs. MacKay's people, just vanished into thin air. "Do not harm any of them. They're not wanted for anything. They're American citizens."

Capt. Cleef responded, "Yes, sir. We've been through that already. None of them have been harmed. They surrendered peacefully."

"Keep it that way. Remember, it's their right not to talk to us."

"Yes sir. We will hold them and continue to search for the others."

The two Army officers signed off.

Sergeant First Class (SFC) Quint Bartow could hear the conversation from his desk outside. Agitated by what he heard, he entered the office. "Excuse my bluntness, but what the hell is going on, sir? This looks like déjà vu all over again."

Donovan raised an eyebrow and looked across his desk at Bartow. "It is, but this time the nut's in the White House, and he's more crazy like a fox than anything else. It's a long story, but the gist of it is the president wants total control. Right now food is power, and that means he wants control over all food supplies in the country. He's obviously worried about the large farm the people of Glenwood have been working on. He doesn't want anyone to be able to feed themselves. He wants them reliant on government. The idea is to keep them hungry, while maintaining control of all food production, so he can hand it out a little at a time and keep the people compliant. Most people don't even know we have a new president, because they didn't elect him. In fact, most people outside of the Northeast don't even know we had an election. His tenure in power is tenuous and bound to come to a screeching halt as soon as the rest of the country understands what's happened and demands a real election. One that includes all 50 states and every eligible voter. If he doesn't consolidate his power soon, he'll be kicked out of office before the end of the year. He's desperate. And a desperate tyrant is the most dangerous kind."

Bartow stood erect; though it was obvious Donovan didn't expect him to be so formal. "You mean the president is a ruthless son of a bitch politician willing to do anything to gain more power, sir."

A light flashed behind Donovan's eyes. "Yes, that's exactly what I mean. It's possible more civilian innocents are going to be harmed before nightfall today. A team of Black Ops types flew in last night and immediately joined the search. They wouldn't talk to me, directing all questions to the Pentagon. Other than giving me a little deference to my rank, they pretty much told me to go play with myself. I suspect they're CIA. Whatever they are, they're spooks and not regular military. We can't allow them to get their hands on those civilians. If they do, there's no telling how far they'll go to get information."

Bartow swallowed. His face grew grim. "Sir, my allegiance is to the American people and the Constitution of the United States of America. And I don't give a damn about some fake tinhorn would-be dictator in Washington." He cleared his throat. "In case you didn't already know what side I'm on. Because it looks like things are going to get bloody in this country and people are going to have to decide what kind of Americans they are. I know you, Colonel, and I know what side you're on. Now you know what side I'm on." He saluted and left the office.

Surprised but not shocked, Donovan's mind raced. At that moment, he began to rethink his entire life. A cold realization of what he and the American people faced settled into his stomach and weighed him down. *A civil war? Oh God, how much more do the people have to suffer?* He resolved to do what he could to head off the looming tragedy and prayed there were people in much higher positions than him already working on the problem. But he could not wait on others to help Mrs. MacKay and her little group of survivors. The local problem had to be dealt with immediately, and as for the bigger problem of Washington, he would need help from people with a lot more power than him. But who could he trust? He could be executed for treason if things went bad.

~~~

General Carl Strovenov watched the scene of apocalyptic atrocities race by the window of his armored limousine. Even after so many months, over a year, he found it almost impossible to believe that Washington DC, the capital of America, could appear as squalid, violent, and lawless as any third-world country, worse in fact. His vehicle was the third in a convoy of five. The other vehicles were all armored-up Humvees except for the leading vehicle, which was an armored personnel carrier. The APC was armed with two .50 caliber Browning machine guns on the top, mounted in tandem and electrically controlled. Sweeping the streets of Washington with machine-gun fire had become a necessary and frequent event. There were times government officials couldn't get from their office to the White House without resorting to such drastic measures. As they raced down the streets, the more peaceful citizens held up crudely hand-painted signs that said things like 'We're starving Mister President. Where is the food?'

The entire city smelled of sewage. The system hadn't worked since the first wave of death came, brought by the plague from across the sea. Rotting bodies swarming with flies littered the sidewalks and even the streets, flattened by government vehicles like road-killed stray dogs. Most government officials had become almost complacent to the horrors, but not the smell.

The worst of it was he knew that every major city in America was in just as bad a condition, if not worse. *It didn't have to be so bad. Damn it.* He shook his head. *Not this long. We should be much further down the road to recovery by now.*

Thinking back on the plague, he shuddered. The first responders were wiped out almost immediately, leaving America with almost no law enforcement officers, very few firefighters and paramedics. And then the nurses and doctors began to fall to the disease. He shuddered again. The damn plague almost wiped out the entire medical profession. Imagine, if every doctor, nurse, pathologist, pharmacist, and everyone else trained in the field of medicine had died! That was close. Damn close. It would've taken 20 years to train medical professionals. No, who would train them? What schools of medicine would they go to, and who would train the trainers? As bad as it was, it could have been worse. What few medical professionals were left alive were worth 10 times their weight in gold to the American people and the country. Just about every other technical field also clung to a thin thread, dangling over a black void, the know-how and technology on the verge of being lost for a generation, if not forever.

But the aftermath, all of this time wasted, all of those who died in the violence and famine; that is on those in governmental positions of power and responsibility. He swallowed and looked inward. *We in the military are not without blame. We let Washington handle things and make most of the decisions. We turned a blind eye to what we knew was happening. We saw the takeover, the fake elections, the dismantling of constitutional limitations on federal government, and we stepped aside and let it happen. Like good military officers, we stayed in our place and took our orders from the civilian government. Fear of violating our oath as military officers by stepping in and interfering with civilian governance of the United States of America meant that we violated our oath to support and defend the Constitution of the United States. In the end, we are just as guilty as if we had violated our oath in the first place, and if we had, hundreds of thousands of Americans would still be alive today. We are damned for not acting. And if we had acted, we would still be damned.*

In the back of his mind that same constant ache ate at him, because he knew if the military had acted it may have saved a lot of lives and brought America much further down the road to recovery, but on the other hand he also knew that military coups seldom if ever resulted in more freedom and stability. You just could not trust one general or a group of generals with absolute power. The trouble was, they had a new president who was reaching *his* goal of absolute power, and the results were likely to be even worse than a military coup. For this man had no honor, no compassion, no humanity.

The APC slowed and hooked a right turn, where the driver was confronted with an instant decision of whether to drive on and run over a group of men in the middle of the road or stop.

Six or seven skinny, filthy young men from 15 to 25 years of age were in the process of raping an equally emaciated and filthy teenage girl. In most cases, the driver would have just run them over, but he knew the general would be angry, so this time he swerved around to the right and passed them.

As the limo went by, the general saw what was happening. He yelled to his driver to radio the APC to stop. He reached for an M4 and opened the door of the limo. Immediately, the driver and his bodyguards protested loudly. He did not hear them. Already out of the limo, he aimed and released a 10-round burst. Two rapists remained unscathed and tried to run, but he cut them down before they got 10 yards. The girl lay on the asphalt crying, looking at him in dismay.

Carl Strovenov, General of the Army and Chairman of the Joint Chiefs of Staff, reached inside to his seat and grabbed a bag that was going to be his next meal. Soldiers swarmed around him, their weapons trained outward, scanning the area for danger, as he walked up to the girl and handed her the bag. "Here is some food. I'm sorry I can't do more for you." He gritted his teeth and walked back to the limo, sliding in and closing the door behind him.

The girl took the bag and ran down the street.

Carl Strovenov put the smoking M4 down on the seat beside him and wiped his face. He kept his head down and refused to look out the window all the way to the White House. *We could've had law and order by now. We could've had them fed by now. Fed two or three times a day, 365 days a year. So much time wasted. So many lives wasted. If only the government itself had survived the plague somewhat intact, if the president and a few more Senators and Congressmen had survived, things would've been different.* He shook his head and closed his eyes, pressing moisture from them, causing a rivulet to flow down each side of his weathered and strained face. *And this faux president. The SOB's evil. He hides it, but his actions reveal his true heart. People are expendable to him. He loves only power.*

He reached into a pocket and produced a photo of his late wife and two sons. Both sons were in their 20s and in uniform at the time the photo was taken, recent graduates of West Point. Other than memories, the photo was all he had left of his family.

Chapter 10

On entering the White House, General Strovenov was searched way beyond normal procedures, in fact he was nearly disrobed. *I know the president doesn't trust me. You bastards don't have to light up a neon sign.* "Are you through?"

"Yes we are, General," the Secret Service agent answered. "Sorry for the inconvenience." He waved him on past the security station.

An aide to the president escorted the general to the Oval Office, where the president waited behind his desk.

President Capinos stood. "Thank you for coming so quickly, Carl. There is a situation down in Florida that I think you should be brought up to date on."

Strovenov sat down, laying his thin folder on his lap. It contained information he had gathered and wanted to show the president. For months, he had been trying to persuade Capinos to concentrate on two things: providing protection for the citizens from the criminal element, and helping the people produce their own food. He believed that all they needed was technical know-how, some equipment, and if allowed to farm fertile land close enough to their homes that they could walk there without any need of motorized vehicles, they could learn to feed themselves. This would allow them to not only farm the land but to get the produce to the people who needed it, and all without burning any more scarce fuel than needed for the farming equipment.

So far, his efforts had been in vain. In fact, the president had grown ever more angry whenever the general brought the subject up. He intended to try harder this time, even if he had to throw out protocol and insist, even be rude, more than that, dare to accuse the president of actually wanting the American people to starve and be at the mercy of violent criminals in the streets. Yes, such a thing would be insane, but he was more convinced each day that the president wasn't playing with a full deck of cards. Certainly, you would find more humanity in a block of marble stone.

Capinos immediately threw a monkey wrench into the general's plans.

"Carl, we have a lieutenant colonel in North Florida who is giving us problems. He's reluctant to follow orders and continuously restrains his men from performing their duties. I want him relieved of command and put up on charges."

Though Strovenov tried to conceal his reaction, he was not entirely successful. "I don't believe I've ever heard of a president being directly involved in the discipline of Army officers below the rank of general. If there is a problem with any officer, it will be dealt with. I'll look into it."

Capinos leaned over his desk and glared at the general. "Not good enough, Carl. I want action today."

The general stared back. "So far, all you've given me are vague statements and accusations. Reluctance to follow orders? What orders? Was the order immoral or illegal, such as to slaughter half of a town? I have to look into this and see what the hell is going on before I have any officer relieved of duty and charged with a crime. You say put him up on charges, what charges? Anything I can think of, just to get rid of him?" His face turned red. "I don't work that way. I refuse to ruin a man's life without good cause. Exactly what crime has he committed?"

Capinos looked him up and down, disgust in his eyes. "For one thing, I have reason to believe he tipped off enemies of the state. He told them they were about to be arrested, and gave them a chance to get away. We're searching for them now. But that would not have been necessary if he had not tipped them off."

The general coughed. "This sounds like another one of your witch hunts to me. I'll have this investigated." He tried to relax in his chair and regain control of his emotions. His stomach felt like a boiling bowl of acidic bile, and a severe case of heartburn was adding to his burning fuse that was growing shorter by the second. "Exactly what do you mean when you say he's overly restraining his soldiers?"

"He coddles the indigenous people of the area and insists his soldiers do the same."

Strovenov's eyes flashed something undecipherable for a millisecond. "Must you insist on vagueness and indirect, meaningless answers when I ask you a question? I cannot charge him with coddling the American people. There is no such crime. I cannot charge him with instructing his soldiers not to commit atrocities, if that is what you're referring to. Again, there is no such crime. On the contrary, if he had instructed his soldiers to murder American citizens or abuse them in any way, he *would* be guilty of a crime. Even if he had simply looked the other way and allowed it tacitly and without any spoken or written orders given, he would be guilty of a crime. But you seem to be complaining that he has done exactly what he was supposed to do. So far, it sounds to me that we have a good officer down there. As to the other charge of tipping off fugitives – some group of people you call enemies of the state – as I said, I'll look into that."

Capinos jumped to his feet. "You're treading close to insubordination yourself!"

You have no idea, Strovenov didn't say. "Mister President, I have simply asked you to be more specific. I still do not know what crimes this man has committed other than the one charge of tipping off what you call enemies of the state. And I have already said I'll look into that. The coddling of civilians is so silly there is nothing I can do to respond to it. As I have stated, it's not a crime. This is why I have asked you to elaborate and be more specific as to what the problem is."

Regaining his composure, Capinos sat down and spoke with measured words and in a calm tone of voice. "For now, I will be satisfied to see your report on my desk by 10 PM tonight detailing the results of your investigation of this officer's crime of warning criminals and giving them enough time to get away before my men arrived. If you find anything at all on him, I want him relieved of duty and under arrest."

General Strovenov raised an eyebrow. "That's not much time. It won't be much of an investigation. The colonel is in Florida. I'm here in Washington. But I'll do what I can." He stood. "Now, with your permission, I must communicate with my subordinates in order to get this investigation rolling."

"Yes, by all means." Capinos exhibited a cold smile. "I look forward to your report at 10 PM tonight."

~~~

Brian heard something in the brush 20 yards to his left. He slowly shouldered his rifle and clicked the safety off, waiting to be sure of his target. It was about time for his father and Deni to be back, but to assume it was them before laying eyes on one of them could prove to be a fatal mistake. Well hidden in thick brush and camouflaged with his boonie hat and olive drab jacket on, he remained perfectly still, moving only his eyes.

Two minutes passed, and he caught a slight movement in the shadow of tall pines. And then he saw four square inches of Deni's face and recognized her. Turning his head slightly to his right, he witnessed his father emerge from the wall of green, materialize. One second he was not visible, the next he was, standing there looking at Brian.

Nate hand-signaled him to remain quiet and worked his way slowly over, while Deni stayed back and overwatched.

The silent question on Brian's face could not have been spoken louder with words.

Nate answered, "It looks like they got away before the soldiers arrived. Someone warned them."

Brian's eyes lit up. "Colonel Donovan."

Nate nodded. "Or he had someone else do it for him."

Deni stood beside them. "Anything happen while we were gone?"

Shaking his head, Brian answered, "Nope. We managed to get a little rest in between worrying about you and the people at the farm."

Tyrone and Atticus heard them talking. They walked up with their packs strapped on and ready to travel.

"Good news it seems." Atticus scratched the back of his ear. "We haven't had much of that lately."

"You two want to rest a while before we head out?" Tyrone leaned forward slightly to counterweight his heavy pack and held his rifle in both hands. He still was not used to carrying a heavy load. "Glad to hear they got away. Probably we should be making tracks ourselves."

Everyone agreed. Brian took just long enough to grab his pack and strap it on before they headed deeper into the woods, downhill, to the wet lowlands and the river valley.

~~~

Nate chose a spot just on the edge of dry land but not far from the river. It had been way too cold for mosquitoes the last four months. In fact Nate felt mosquito season would be so late in the year they would not arrive in great numbers until summer was finally well set in. Tyrone and Atticus mostly stayed out of the way and stood watch, while the other three worked to set up camp. In less than 30 minutes, they had a lean-to set up, using a nylon tarp and covering it with freshly cut pine boughs. They cut palmetto fronds and laid them on the floor to provide some waterproofing from the moist soil. On top of that, they added six inches of the driest leaves they could find to provide insulation from the cold ground at night. So far, winter had showed no signs of relinquishing its hold on the weather and allowing spring to arrive, and they had no idea how long they would be there, since going back to the farm or even Mel's bunker was out of the question for the time being.

Next on Nate's agenda was a reliable source of drinkable water. Both he and Brian had water filters in their packs, and Deni had chemical water purification tablets. But Nate preferred to boil the water to make it potable. And he preferred the cleanest water possible for boiling. With that in mind, he and Brian left the others in camp and headed for the river to look for a spring or at least a sand boil on the river's edge.

The sand in Florida sand boils was usually granulated limestone and could be filtered out with cloth from a shirt or some other apparel. Sand boils were small, weak springs, and the water clean, straight from the aquifer. Even so, Nate always boiled or purified it with chemicals or filters before drinking spring water just to be safe.

This was where Nate and Brian's knowledge of the area came in to play. Though they were many miles from Mel's bunker and even farther from their farm, they both had intimate knowledge of every inch of the river for 25 miles or more in either direction from where they stood. As a boy, Nate had spent many days exploring the river valley, searching out the springs along the river. Some of the springs were fairly large and in the bottom of the river itself or on the edge, while others were anywhere from a few yards to hundreds of yards back from the river and in the swamp. Most of the larger springs were known by fishermen and other people who frequented the area, but the smaller ones were known only to Nate and Brian. If not for the danger of the largest springs being known by others and therefore an attraction that could result in unwanted visitors, Nate would've brought the group to a very large spring eight miles away. Not only would it have been a source for clean cool drinking water, the spring held enough water in its basin to hold many fish and would've been a convenient source of food. The spring's run also held fish that they could've trapped or caught with hook and line. Unfortunately, such a large spring would be well known by the locals and serious fishermen, hunters, and backpackers from other parts of the state. He knew of one spring 20 miles south of him that canoe trip guides brought tourists to before the plague ended normal life. Such a spring would be so well known he wouldn't be surprised to learn there were three or four families living near it, trying to ride out the storm.

Nearing the river, Brian moved close enough to Nate he could whisper. "If I remember correctly, there's a sand boil or two downstream a ways, where the river gets a lot deeper."

Nate nodded, keeping his eyes busy scanning the woods for trouble. "Yeah, and uphill from that about 100 yards from the river into the swamp, there's a pool of clean spring water that comes up out of the ground. The little pool is about five feet wide with a white sandy bottom. I suspect it's from the same underground stream that the sand boils come from. Just a little ways farther, the ground slopes up fast, gaining over 50 feet in elevation. I guess the underground spring runs under that hill and the pressure causes it to boil up at this place I'm looking for."

"Why didn't we set up camp at the spring?" Brian kept his voice low and his eyes busy.

"Even though it's a small spring, we might not be the only ones who know about it. I didn't want to take the chance on us stumbling onto a nasty group and get into a shootout, just because we were unwanted quests." Nate grinned. "Besides, I don't remember exactly where it is after all these years. It's better to have a camp set up until I find the damn thing."

Brian's eyes lit up. "Oh." He looked around. "I guess we've been lucky to have all these woods around our farm and Mel's bunker. These woods have given us a place to hide many times when we needed it."

Nate agreed. "And it's acted as a buffer. The remoteness of our farm and all this state and federal forest land around us has kept a lot of undesirables away." He glanced at his son and grinned. "Even though it hasn't seemed that way at times, especially when that gang was trying to get across the bridge. It's the reason Mel bought that land close to our farm in the first place. He was looking for a remote area with lots of woods, few roads and few people."

"I hope Mel makes it back here someday."

"So do I. Let's find that spring. We're wasting time."

They headed uphill in silence. Despite everything, they were both in a good mood, simply because they knew their friends at the horse farm had managed to escape before the soldiers arrived. Even so, there were plenty of dark clouds hanging over not only their heads but everyone they knew and cared about.

Brian talked as he moved along behind his father. "You know, that old guy is going to have a hard time out here. How long are we going to have to hide in these woods?"

Nate froze for a second. "There are plenty of empty homes and hunting cabins in the area. It won't be too long before we find better accommodations than sleeping on the ground." He thought it best not to tell his son the whole truth. Chances were, they would be fugitives from the law until Washington was cleaned out, and no one had any idea how long that would be – if ever.

<u>Chapter 11</u>

Lieutenant Nelson Herzing called Capt. Cleef over. "Sir, some CIA spook is on the radio and claims to have direct orders from the president himself." He grimaced.

"What? Out with it, LT," Capt. Cleef growled.

"He says they're taking over the operation and we're to assist."

Capt. Cleef bellowed, "Bullshit! My CO is Colonel Donovan and I take my orders from him." He rushed over to the radio. Talking to the radio telephone operator, or RTO, he said, "Get me that damn spook." He scratched his chin. "Forget that. To hell with the spooks. Get Colonel Donovan."

SFC Bartow found Colonel Donovan sleeping on a couch someone had carried into his office, so he would not have to sleep on the floor. "Colonel. Colonel, we have a problem."

Instantly awake, Donovan sat up. "What is it?"

"That team of spooks has contacted Captain Cleef, and their leader is demanding to take over the operation. Cleef is on the radio now asking instructions from you."

Without hesitation, Donovan rushed to the radio. He dispensed with all the normal radio procedures and protocol and went straight to the point. "Captain Cleef, I order you to let the civilians go and tell them to run like hell and hide. Give them back their weapons and other personal property."

Cleef's confused voice came back and resonated in the office. "Yes Sir."

"And Captain Cleef," Donovan added, "abort the search for the rest of the civilians. Leave those people alone. If the spooks give you any trouble, tell them to kiss your ass. Tell them you take your orders directly from your CO, not the CIA."

"Yes Sir." Capt. Cleef signed off.

Donovan's face turned a shade redder than normal. "Someone raise that damn spook team. I want to talk to the SOB who is harassing my officers."

SFC Bartow grinned. "Yes Sir." His grin vanished with a thought. "Sir, you know calling off the search for the civilians without orders is crossing the Rubicon. If you weren't in trouble already, you will be shortly."

With a perfect deadpan face, Donovan said, "I didn't think of that."

Bartow didn't smile, instead, his brow knotted with concern. "Do you have an end game? This could get nasty."

Donovan answered, "There is no end game. At least not one that finishes well. Nasty isn't the word. More like deadly."

Bartow nodded and swallowed. "I'll get the spooks on the horn for you."

After cussing out the CIA team and telling them to stay away from his soldiers, Donovan spoke to Brigadier General Bernard Myers in Fort Benning, Georgia by satellite phone. "Sir, none of the civilians I've been ordered to hunt down have done anything wrong. Six of them were investigating terrorism in the county and stumbled onto some kind of a Black Ops nightmare ordered by the president himself. The six are all associated with the local Sheriff's Department here and were doing their best to protect the people of the county. When they realized what they stumbled onto, they ran for it, knowing Washington would want to shut them up. The other civilians at the horse farm have nothing to do with any of this. They just happen to be friends of the six local law enforcement volunteers. They most likely still know nothing about the Black Ops BS."

"I see," the general said. "This is a spook matter and you do not have the clearance to even be discussing it." He hesitated for a second. "Hell, if I'm going to look into this mess, I need to know what you know. What exactly is this spook operation?"

"It's worse than just bullshit politics, sir. It appears the president wants more social and political instability, as if we don't already have enough. I think he's also worried about the big farm the locals have been working on here. He's been using food to control the people and he doesn't want the citizens here or anywhere else to be able to actually feed themselves. Never mind the fact Washington doesn't have the ability to feed everyone and has allowed starvation to spread over the country. He has spooks drumming up antigovernment sentiment in the area – and who knows where else, maybe all across the country

– and terrorist activity has increased here as a result. People have died. With the psychological condition that most of the people are in after the trauma they've been through over the last year and a half, it's not exactly hard to push them over the edge."

The general sounded like he blew a gasket, but he said nothing.

"Sir, I believe the order to hunt down innocent civilians and hold them for questioning, perhaps to be tortured by CIA operatives, and to arrest the local law enforcement personnel here is unlawful and immoral. I hereby inform you that I respectfully refuse to follow this order. If you wish, I will resign my commission immediately."

"Well." The general sighed audibly over the satellite phone. "When you decide to dump a shitload on me, you don't play around. This conversation alone could get both of us in hot water. Give me some time to digest all of this, will you?"

"Sir, the American people are drowning in deep shit from the bottom up, and they do not need this fake president and his own private Congress in Washington doing all they can to make it rain shit on their heads from the top down."

"I hear you. Well, try to hold the fort until tomorrow. In the meantime I'll find a replacement for you, just in case you do wind up having to resign. Just keep in mind one thing, I believe in civilian control over the military. I believe it is a basic concept of America's system of government, and I will not support any kind of revolt or coup."

"Yes sir, I understand that. And I have not mentioned any such thing. I have simply informed you I refuse to follow unlawful and immoral orders and have offered my resignation. What happens after I'm gone is a matter for others to decide."

"Just sit tight, Colonel, and wait until I get back to you. In the meantime, do not speak to anyone about this matter."

~~~

It was Brian who stumbled onto the spring. He hand-signaled his father the way he had been taught. While waiting for Nate to ease through the brush and close the 35 yards that stood between them, Brian examined the water's edge and saw many tracks. He noticed deer, wild hogs, raccoons, possums, even foxes and coyotes frequented the spring for water. He knew other predators were probably attracted to the area also, to prey on those animals that came for a drink and the raccoons that came to catch fish and whatever else they could find in the water.

When his father came close enough, Brian whispered, "No human tracks."

"Good." Noticing Brian's interest in the tracks, Nate observed, "Even though the spring's not that far from the river and other sources of water, it's still a natural watering hole."

Brian nodded in silence. He slid out of his pack and prepared to fill his canteen, along with Deni's. "This would be a good place to set up snares, since there are no people around, just a lot of thirsty animals."

Nate followed suit, slipping out of his pack. "Hold on a second and watch how I do it." He took a two-quart canteen, leaving the lid tight, and thrust it down into the clear, roiling water, holding it in front of the spring opening, which was only three or four inches in diameter and lined by limestone rock. With his other hand, he unscrewed the lid, letting the air escape as the water rushed in. He didn't bother to filter it with a shirt or some other cloth because the spring wasn't a sand boil, and the water was clear. When the canteen was full, he screwed the lid tight, lifted it out of the water, and handed it to Brian, taking an empty one from him at the same time. "This water is cold." He stood knee-deep in it, and already his lower legs felt like ice.

"Maybe you should've taken your boots off first," Brian suggested.

"Too late now. Give me another canteen." Exchanging a full canteen for an empty one from Brian, Nate said, "This'll be a good place to sit and soak during the heat of summer."

"Yeah, but it's not summer now. And I doubt your boots, socks, and pant legs will be completely dry by tonight when the temperature's down in the 30s."

"I have extras, except for the boots."

Standing on the edge of the water and leaning over, Brian handed him another empty canteen. "We can't chance a warming fire at night, can we?"

Nate filled the last canteen. "No. And we'll have to be careful about cooking and boiling water. We'll dig a small hole to build a fire in with a narrow ventilation tunnel off to the side. Burning only the driest wood will help keep the smoke down, and using a fire only large enough to do the job will reduce the heat signature as much as possible. Still, a fire of any kind is a risk. Modern technology has made it much harder to hide, even in the woods. I've read many accounts of Che Guevara being tracked by U.S. satellites, which led to his execution. Supposedly, they were able to track him by satellite as he made his way through the jungle, because he stopped every night and built a fire for tea. Personally, I think he would have been building a fire for coffee. Anyway, he was traveling along a river, building fires every night, so the CIA only had to tell the soldiers where to wait in ambush. He was captured alive and then executed. One rumor has it at least one finger was removed, in case Washington wanted to get fingerprints for verification. An entire hand was sent to Castro."

"Wow. I didn't know our government did things like that."

Nate waded out of the water. "Every government does much worse than that, or at least has in the near past. The reality is I don't know exactly what happened. I've read so many different accounts, all being a little different, or in some cases a lot different from the one I just told you, there's no way to ferret out the truth from the rumors. Other accounts say a local villager tipped soldiers off to the location of Guevara's guerrilla fighters. It does seem to be established that his hands were cut off and sent to Castro so Castro couldn't claim he wasn't dead."

While they were stowing the canteens in their packs, Brian asked, "What about our body heat?"

"Satellites can't tell human body heat from animals, and these woods have a lot of deer, bears etc. roaming around. Aircraft, on the other hand, is a risk. But they pretty much have the same problem, unless they're close enough and catch one of us in the open, where they can make out the outline of our heat signature, telling them we're humans walking on two legs. So it's a risk, but if we stay under a thick canopy of treetops and they don't fly directly over us, we should be okay. After all, people get lost in the woods all the time, and they're trying to be found."

Brian slipped into his pack and grabbed his rifle. He had been listening intently, learning as much as he could from his father. He pulled a compass from under his shirt where it hung from his neck on a string. "I want to see if I can find camp on my own." He glanced up at his father. "But if I'm getting off course, let me know. We have no time to waste."

"Good idea." Nate looked up and located the sun shining through the swamp canopy to judge the time. "Think it would be easier if we headed for the river and then went downstream before turning and heading for camp?"

Brian nodded. "Yeah, you always said to aim for a big target and you won't get lost."

"We can't miss the river."

"And we'll know when to head east again, because it's just a little south of that sharp bend in the river."

Nate nodded. "Let's go." He let his son take a couple steps before speaking again. "Are you factoring in declination? Decades ago, it was tiny in Florida, but it has grown over time and it's now enough it should be factored in. Remember what the declination is for this area from the last time you looked at a topographical chart?"

Brian stopped for a second and did some calculations in his head, then checked his compass and went on.

~~~

Back at the camp, Tyrone and Atticus learned why the others preferred stainless steel canteens. While they could've boiled water in a plastic canteen by being careful, it was much easier and faster when not being forced to worry about melting the container.

Since it was late in the day by the time they were through purifying their water, everyone enjoyed an early supper and rested. Though they felt relatively safe, as far in the woods as they were, at least one person was on guard duty at all times, standing back from the others and staying hidden in thick brush. They wanted an early start in the morning, because setting up a new camp near the spring would take time. Nate also planned to do a little fishing at the river. What little food they had in their packs would not last long unless they supplemented it with food taken from the woods.

~~~

Brigadier General Bernard Myers wished Colonel Donovan hadn't dropped such a hot turd in his lap, but he couldn't ignore it now that it had come to his attention. He also wished the military's computer network had been maintained properly over the last year and a half. He wished a lot of damn things. Hell, in a few months the military's (and America's civilian) satellite constellations would probably be useless. They simply didn't have enough trained technicians left after the plague to keep the systems properly maintained and in proper orbit around the Earth. Everyone's fervent hope was that their enemies were in even worse shape than them. The thought they could be blind, while their enemies still had eyes in space looking down on everything on Earth, was the stuff of nightmares. Already, the U.S. Global Positioning System was acting wonky and becoming less and less reliable. Soon, their most advanced missiles would have no guidance systems and pilots would be forced to resort to navigation techniques left behind generations ago, such as celestial navigation. Ditto for Navy navigators.

He contacted General Carl Strovenov by Sat-Com: another system that many feared was near collapse from lack of maintenance. "Carl, I just heard from a lieutenant colonel down in Florida who is threatening to resign over what he considers to be immoral and illegal orders." He spent the next five minutes explaining the situation. "Colonel Donovan is a good man, one of the best officers I have ever known. He knows the people in his area of operations and he knows the situation down there. I believe what he has told me is true."

General Strovenov's immediate reply was surprising. "I agree with you. Colonel Donovan has assessed the situation accurately. The president and his puppet Congress are the most immediate threat to the American people at this moment. The problem is what do we do about it?"

General Myers was momentarily at a loss for words.

Strovenov laughed. "Where did you go, Bernard? You know me to be a blunt, truthful man that doesn't play politics. I know that is contradictory for an officer who has made it to the top like I have. But none of that matters now. I'm on the president's not-so-short shit list already. He knows I'm not with him; I'm with the American people. I expect to be replaced soon."

Myers took a few seconds to regain his thoughts. "That still leaves us with the question as to what to do about the problem down in Florida and our wayward colonel."

"No," Strovenov said, "Florida is a symptom of the disease. The cancer is in Washington. What to do about Washington is the real question."

"Uh, I don't like where this is going."

"You mean you don't like where America has already gone." Strovenov insisted. "I think the situation in Florida may be an opportunity. I've talked it over with the Joint Chiefs of Staff, and everyone agrees. We've already started to ask other generals what they think about the situation. And I believe we have a majority of general officers on our side. While I'm in contact with you, I might as well bring you into the fold with the others."

Myers broke in, "Carl, I'm afraid you may have misjudged me. I agree the Washington situation is a disaster. We have a faux president and Congress, which means we have a fake federal government at the moment. But I have every faith that the American people will correct this in the months ahead and demand real elections."

"No, no," Strovenov insisted. "You misunderstand me. We have a letter of protest and I'm inviting you to sign it along with almost every general officer in the military. We are simply petitioning the president to abide by the Constitution of the United States of America and to put the American people's welfare in the forefront of everything he does, instead of this mad power grab he's been on since he took office."

Instead of being relieved, Myers was shocked. "He'll be thoroughly pissed. There's no telling what he'll do."

"Well," Strovenov said in a calm voice, "he can't have every high-ranking officer in all branches of the military executed or imprisoned." He laughed under his breath, revealing a little nervousness. "Though he just might have everyone on the Joint Chiefs of Staff executed as an example. But I'm willing to take that risk and so are the others."

General Myers came back five seconds later with, "Okay, I'm in. I still would like advice from you on how to handle the Florida situation and Colonel Donovan."

"Good. I'm glad you decided to come along for the ride. This reminds me of what the fat bald guy said during the signing of the Declaration of Independence. Something about everyone hanging together in a desperate attempt to avoid being hanged separately."

"Sorry. I'm not in a laughing mood. But I get your point."

"I understand," Strovenov said. "Tell the Colonel to hold tight and try not to get into too much trouble over the next 24 hours or so. Sometime tomorrow, I'll talk with the president about the Florida situation first, and then lower the boom when I lay our little petition on his desk for him to read. I'll get back with you as soon as I can. That is if I'm not immediately arrested."

Chapter 12

In the fading hours of the day, the wind began to build and dark clouds scudded across the darkening sky. Even before the sun sank behind the horizon, a chill blew in from the north. It only got colder as the night wore on.

Knowing he would need the sleep, Brian crawled into his bag not long after sundown. He woke an hour later to the sound of rain pelting the lean-to inches above his head. A lightning bolt flashed, momentarily lighting the surrounding woods, and he saw violent motion all around him as the treetops swayed and bent under the force of the storm, momentarily reminding him of the storm of worry in his mind. A moment or two was all it took for him to check on the others sleeping beside him in the lean-to. He knew Tyrone was out there in the rain standing guard. Somehow, that was sufficient to ease his worries. His eyes soon grew heavy and he fell back to sleep.

When Nate woke him at 3 AM the rain had stopped and the wind had slacked off almost completely, but as soon as he threw his sleeping bag open the chill hit him. He was in for a miserable night. Brian buttoned his jacket and pulled the collar up around his neck. He had volunteered to stand guard from 3 to 6, the coldest hours. His main reason for volunteering to stand watch over the early morning hours was to allow Atticus a chance to stay warm in his sleeping bag when it would do him the most good.

Though it had stopped raining, the woods were still dripping wet, so he slipped his poncho over him before finding a good place just outside of camp to hide in brush and under the shade of the pines where it would be darker and render him harder to see.

He stood there for two hours, scanning the woods and listening, thinking that this must have been the coldest night of his life. And it didn't matter that it was so late in the year. Everything else in the world was screwed up, so why not the weather? He was cold. He didn't shiver, his whole body shook, causing the frozen poncho to crackle and shed its thin layer of ice. If he had eaten lately, there might have been enough fire in his belly to thaw him a little, but he had not eaten lately, and there was no fire in his belly. The cold seemed to condense and crystallize the air until the dripping woods could drip no more, sheathed in ice. A north wind gathered strength and spit snow in his face. A turn to the east allowed him to use his boonie hat and the poncho's hood as a windbreak, protecting his face to some degree. He unbuttoned the poncho on his side and kept his right hand in his coat pocket. The trigger finger must work if the time came on his watch. Other than the violent shaking, he barely moved, his eyes working back and forth, scanning the woods for danger, seeing little but indistinct forms of gray, black, and darker black. It was motion he was searching for and not so much the full form of a man. The wind made his task more difficult, but he would have no chance at all of seeing danger approach if he did not look. So look he did, into the dark woods, constantly scanning, constantly listening. All the while, he resisted the urge to stomp his freezing feet, his only movement, that uncontrollable shaking.

During the last hour of his watch, a directionless shot rang out. It could have been near or far, but it was impossible to tell in the freezing blackness of the night woods. Before the first one had faded, another shot hung in the air, afloat in the atmosphere, lingering, living on long enough that it was still reverberating among the unseen towering trees when still another shot assaulted the night. The last shot was punctuated by a burst of full automatic fire, and Brian finally thought he had an idea from which direction the shooting was coming from. But he still had no idea how far away it was, except that it was not close. The motion in the camp behind him gave evidence that the others were awake. In seconds, Nate was standing 20 yards away, looking for him. "Over here," Brian whispered.

Soon, everyone was standing by Brian, a white-knuckle grip on their rifles and Atticus his shotgun, their nervous breaths misting in the cold.

"I guess someone just died," Brian stated flatly, speaking in a low tone of voice calculated to be heard only by those near him. "I hope it wasn't anyone we knew."

"I couldn't tell how far," Deni said.

For the first time in over two hours, Brian shifted his weight from foot to foot in an effort to get circulation in them. "I couldn't tell either. They did seem to be coming from the direction of the road."

As they spoke, the wind ceased and a deathly still descended onto the woods around them. They all knew that meant it would grow even colder before sunrise.

"Who else but the people from the horse farm would be out here?" Tyrone observed, not really asking a question. "And who but soldiers would be shooting at them with full auto weapons?"

As if on cue, a distant throbbing buzz drifted to their ears.

"Chopper," Deni whispered. "Has Donovan let us down after all?"

Brian looked at his father, though he couldn't see much in the dark. "Maybe we should forget about that spring and cross the river. If we retreat into the big swamp over there, we'll be harder to find. At least we'll be further away from the roads."

Nate considered Brian's idea for a second. "Before we leave, we need to hide evidence of our camp here as much as possible. We'll need some daylight to do that. Everyone go back to sleep and get some rest. I'll stand watch until dawn, then wake you."

"It's still my watch," Brian protested. "No one here is any less tired than I am, including you." He added, "It looks like making ourselves comfortable here was a mistake. We probably should worry more about being tracked by leaving sign behind us from now on and less about comfort."

Deni and Nate smiled, though they couldn't see each other in the dark.

Nate cleared his throat. "It does seem we're not as safe out here as we thought we were. Someone has gotten serious about wanting us, and they're not afraid to expend resources to get what they want."

"Yeah, we're big terrorists or something now," Brian hissed. "We know too much."

Atticus laughed under his breath. "And that makes us dangerous to somebody. Well, screw them, whoever the hell they are."

Everyone but Brian and Nate went back to their sleeping bags to catch what little sleep they could before false dawn. "With danger so close, I'm doubling the strength of our security," Nate explained.

~~~

Nate stood as still as a statue and watched the silent woods turn from dark black to dark gray and then lighter gray. There was no chirping of the birds or quarreling of squirrels in the trees. It was too cold even for creatures that lived all their lives exposed to the elements, and so they waited longer than usual for the sun to warm their world before coming to life. The prior evening's moisture laden sky and dripping woods had turned much drier over the hours, allowing the air to shed warmth and the temperature to drop. There was no fog, too dry for that, despite yesterday's rain. Dew did not drip from the towering trees above and bombard the understory below, as was the norm for a Southern morning in the woods.

The return of the sun awakened a slight breeze, and the trees swayed, creating a clinking sound as ice-covered branches slapped into each other. Short icicles of one to three inches length broke off 30 feet above Nate, bombarding his head and shoulders, the light chunks of ice barely indented his boonie hat, but made it difficult to hear if someone was sneaking up on them in the woods.

It's time. We can see well enough to work now. Nate eased over to Brian, 50 yards away. "I'll wake the others and we'll get to work breaking camp," he whispered. "Stay alert and keep your eyes and ears working."

Brian nodded.

Thirty minutes later, they had dismantled the lean-to and covered the cut saplings with leaves and then sprinkled more pine needles over the camp area, including the refilled fire hole they had dug.

No one said a word as they worked. When Brian saw them slipping into their packs, he silently walked over and put his pack on. Nate led the way deeper into the obscurity of their freezing, gray world. Their only chance stealth, every step they took was calculated to be as silent as possible, knowing that if they were discovered their chances of surviving a gun battle with soldiers were slim to none.

A look of dread washed over everyone's face when they came to the river's edge. They all knew what was coming next.

Brian moved closer to his father and whispered, "Are you sure we should abandon our friends and just run and hide?"

Nate laid his hand on his son's shoulder. "I know how you feel, but there's only so much this little motley crew can take on. The fact is there's nothing we can do for them, not as far as taking on the Army goes. It's why we fled into the woods in the first place and it's why they too fled into the woods instead of staying at the farm and fighting. There's just nothing we can do to help them. We'll be lucky if we get out of this area ourselves."

Brian swallowed. Two seconds later, he nodded.

~~~

As ordered by the president, General Strovenov had delivered his report the night before. He was 30 minutes late, only because of the ridiculously thorough search at the security entrance. It was obvious the president was worried his top general might be a danger to him. He added a lot of filler to pad the report and to force the president to take longer to read it than the sparse substantive information it contained would have; an obvious ploy to prevent him from reading it while the general waited in the office. It bought him a few hours of time.

At exactly 6 the next morning, General Strovenov was summoned to the White House again. He was still rearranging his uniform after the rather intimate search he just endured when he walked into the Oval Office.

President Capinos slammed the report on his desk. "This is bullshit, General."

Strovenov did not flinch. "What exactly about my report is bullshit, Mister President?"

"You say you have no idea who tipped the people at the horse farm off and allowed them time to escape before the soldiers arrived. That, General, is bullshit. We both know Colonel Donovan, or someone working under his direction, warned them."

"I didn't exactly have much time to have my people conduct a thorough investigation. I told you that the last time we spoke. Either way, the fact is there is no proof that Colonel Donovan warned anyone."

Capinos pivoted to another subject, temporarily letting his disapproval of the report go. "We have another more serious problem with the good Colonel Donovan down in Florida. It seems he is refusing to cooperate with a CIA team that was sent down there on a very important mission. I am told he had six suspects in custody but ordered them released and has ordered his soldiers to refuse to cooperate with the CIA." Capinos turned red as he stood and slapped his desk with an open hand. "I will not tolerate insubordination in the military. This officer must be relieved of duty immediately."

General Strovenov responded, "Yes Mister President. You do understand, though, how it is. You see, soldiers and CIA spooks don't always get along. I am told they were rude to the colonel and every other officer and noncom when they arrived on scene. Interagency rivalry sometimes rears its ugly head and clogs up the machinery. Might be that's what happened here."

Capinos waved him off. "I don't give a damn about any of that. The colonel let six suspects go. People I believe were involved with antigovernment activity."

"My investigation so far does not bear that out. The people at the farm are just people, American citizens. Evidently you want them because they are associates of the six Sheriff's Department volunteers who stumbled onto some kind of asinine Black Ops operation. There is no evidence that the people at the farm know anything about your clandestine operation or the whereabouts of the six law enforcement volunteers you are after. I happen to agree with the colonel. We're wasting time bothering these people at the horse farm. For God sakes, Americans are living under lawless anarchy and starving, while we waste time and resources hunting down innocent people for no apparent logical reason."

Capinos tapped General Strovenov's report with a finger. "So. There's more to your investigation than you included in this vacuous report."

"The pertinent facts I just spoke of are included."

Capinos glared at him from across the desk. "I'm speaking of your conclusions. Conclusions you just mentioned but failed to include here." He pointed at the folder and then threw his hands up in disgust. "It's obvious to me now that you're just as guilty of insubordination as the wayward colonel in Florida is. You have decided that I just do not know what I'm doing. General, you have overstepped your pay grade. MacArthur made that same mistake. And we all know how fast Truman fired his ass."

Strovenov sat erect in his chair. "Mister President, I serve at your pleasure. If you wish to see my resignation on your desk later today or early tomorrow, just say the word." He set a folder on the desk. "In the meantime, I have a petition here I would like you to read. It has been signed by almost every general officer in the Army. We are in the process of getting more signatures from all branches. That will take time, but I expect the number of signatures will be impressive." He slid it closer to the president. "If this doesn't get your attention, nothing will."

Capinos glanced down at the folder as if it were a coiled diamondback rattlesnake and then looked back up at Strovenov, fear lined his eyes. He stood and backed away from his desk one step, his mouth half open, glaring at the general.

General Strovenov continued, "Mister President, it's time the American people had an opportunity to elect a real Congress and a real president. It's time America returns to the Constitution that so many American people have fought, killed, suffered, and died for."

It took a full 30 seconds for Capinos to regain his composure, but once he did he sat down and read the petition, taking five minutes to do so. As he read, he grew more and more uncomfortable. His efforts to hide his rage and his fear failed.

General Strovenov said nothing and showed no sign of noticing it.

After taking note that the first names on the long list of signatures included everyone on the Joint Chiefs of Staff, Capinos looked up at Strovenov, keeping his composure. "I've always said that my service to the nation as president was temporary and that I would step down as soon as we got things back in order and the nation back on its feet. I have no objection to national elections. But you do understand that it'll take at least six months perhaps a year before we could even think of doing that. The country is in just too bad a shape at the moment. How could we have a nationwide election when we do not even have the roads cleared and there is no nationwide communication? What kind of a campaign could the candidates run without newspapers, TV and radio reporters, hell, without TV, without radios, without power? It would look like something out of there early 1800s."

Strovenov spoke in a subdued voice, "If our forefathers could make it work, I'm sure we can."

"But you have to be reasonable. Certainly you and the others understand we can't have elections right now. Everything's too chaotic."

The general's face turned expressionless. "At the rate we've been going, things will still be chaotic 20 years from now. Mister President, the people need a democratically elected government, and they deserve one, and they deserve a government that puts life-and-death priorities first. We must provide them with protection, law and order. We must help them feed themselves. The lawlessness and the hunger must end ASAP. We could've accomplished this already. It's a crime that we haven't."

Capinos jumped out of his chair. "There it is. So you blame me. I've worked day and night to better the people's lives." He adjusted the black-tie on his white shirt, which suddenly seemed too tight. "Taking everything into consideration, I believe I've done the people a great service and the country has made great strides since I took office."

General Strovenov looked sick. "We could've done much better. We *should* have done much better. This isn't about blaming you or anyone else; it's about doing the right thing."

Something flashed behind Capinos' eyes. "You're patronizing me, General." He sat back in his chair, his mind racing. "I could be hard-assed about this, but I'm trying to be reasonable." He rubbed his cleanly shaven chin. "I believe we can come to a gentleman's agreement. One that you can take back to the other generals, consider it, and then give me an answer tomorrow. Normally I wouldn't do this, but these are unusual times, and I fully admit that I was not elected by all of the people. There simply was no way for that to happen under the circumstances at the time. I don't believe it can happen even now or a year from now. But I'll agree to a special series of national elections for both my office and all of Congress, both houses, if you generals agree to serve under me and pledge your allegiance to my presidency until the elections take place."

"Those elections need to be soon, Mister President," Strovenov insisted.

Capinos gave him an unreadable expression. "We have to look into whether or not it's even feasible. And, as I said before, I don't think it is possible. Not today, not six months from now, perhaps not even a year from now."

"We can make it work. The question is, do you want to make it work? After all, almost everything you've done since you took office was about consolidating power and concentrating it not only in Washington in general but in your office in particular. With all due respect, Mister President, I don't believe you will give up on your dreams of a dictatorship so easily." He leaned forward in his chair. "And let's stop playing games here. You and I both know what you've been up to. The colonel down in Florida knows, every general who signed that petition knows. Killing those six local law enforcement volunteers will not keep it quiet. You can't undo the damage. It's time to call off your cloak and dagger show down there and leave those people alone."

Capinos fumed. "Now you're going too far. Haven't I been reasonable with you? I've agreed to elections sometime in the future. I thought we were having a civilized conversation here and coming to a gentleman's agreement. But now you seem to think you're my boss. The coup hasn't taken place yet, General. It hasn't even started, and you're acting as if the military has already won and is in control." He shook his head. "You're delusional. Don't mistake my reasonableness as weakness."

Losing patience, Strovenov raised his voice. "There has been no talk of a military coup, here or among officers. The petition is an attempt to, as you say, come to a gentleman's agreement. Everyone who signed the petition, including me, believes in the Constitution and in civilian control of the military. We all know that military coups have a long history of making things worse, not better. America may have taken a great fall, but we're still not a banana republic. No one who signed the petition is interested in any kind of military coup. We will, however, continue to insist that national elections take place as soon as possible and constitutional government is reinstated. We have all sworn an oath to support and defend the Constitution against all enemies foreign and domestic, and we intend to fulfill that oath." He glared at Capinos. "And we will not tolerate any more human rights violations."

Capinos turned red again. "Damn you! You talk as if I'm some kind of a Hitler. This country is in much better condition than it would've been without me. I stepped up and I served. And this is the thanks I get for it."

Strovenov said in a calm voice, "This isn't about you. It's about the American people. Your ego isn't worth the lives of any more Americans. So please, let's get back to the issue at hand."

His jaw dropping, Capinos glared at him, incredulous that someone would say such a thing. After he simmered for 30 seconds, he spoke again. "I agree that we need to have nationwide elections as soon as possible. I thought I had already told you that. I'll appoint a committee to look into it and have Congress start a committee for the same purpose. I suggest that you in the military do the same thing. Certainly, we'll have to coordinate our efforts to make it happen." He raised his open palms in the air. "But as I've already stated, I have my doubts we can get this done within six months. Be that as it may, you do your investigation into the viability of the whole thing, and I'll have people look into it on the civilian side." He sat back in his chair, looking exhausted. "For now, I think we have said all that can be said about it." His jaw set as he looked across the desk at Strovenov. "Now get out of here and don't bother me again until I call you."

Strovenov didn't move. "There is still the Florida situation. Are you going to call off that CIA team?"

Capinos ground his teeth and glared at the general. "I can't make any promises on that. But I will tell them to stay out of your soldiers' way down there."

"It's too late, you know," Strovenov stated flatly. "Too many people know about the operation. I guess you would call it a PSYOP. Whatever the hell you want to call it, it's bullshit. I suggest you call off your team now, and the whole thing will just die down naturally."

"That operation is above your pay grade. I'll look into the matter," Capinos spat. "Now get out of my office."

Chapter 13

General Strovenov's mind raced as he walked to the waiting armored-up Humvee. He turned and looked back at the White House. *The son of a bitch is buying time. In some ways that was too easy, despite all his pissing and moaning. No telling what he'll do. The crazy bastard just might be planning a purge. Everyone who signed that petition may be dead in a few days. The best we can hope for is that he hasn't made a decision yet, since he has at least six months before the elections and will probably stretch it out a year. There's no telling how much damage he could do between now and then.* He felt sick. *One thing for sure, he'll do everything he can to hold onto power, and that means he'll never allow any elections.* He grasped the Humvee's door handle, but not to open it – for support.

A soldier standing at attention next to him spoke. "Sir, I'll open the door for you."

Strovenov seemed to not hear. His eyes stared 1000 yards into oblivion. Suddenly he jerked his head and faced the soldier. Stepping out of the way, he said "Thank you."

The soldier opened the door and stood at attention. "It weighs 600 pounds and can smash your fingers easily."

Six hundred pounds? Strovenov thought. *I wish the load on my shoulders was so light. Six hundred pounds of cold, lifeless steel that doesn't feel pain or hunger or anguish over the loss of loved ones or terror over what tomorrow may bring would be as light as a feather on my shoulders.*

~~~

Nate and the others traveled all day, heading deeper into the swamp. For all they knew, soldiers or CIA operatives could be in the area, so they had to be as quiet and careful as possible. Necessary precautions such as staying under the cover of trees in case aircraft or drones were searching for them also slowed them down. Still, they managed to travel almost 12 miles before it became too dark to go any farther. Their camp consisted of only unrolling their sleeping bags on the driest ground they could find and stretching a tarpaulin on a rope between two trees. One good thing about the cold was it meant no mosquitoes and they didn't need to bother with netting.

They ate their meals cold, not chancing a fire. Deni had a pack full of MREs, and everyone ate one for the energy and to fill their stomachs, if not for the taste.

While the others slept, Nate, Brian, and Deni sat on a log and spoke softly.

"I'm starting to wish the government had just stayed the hell out of this county," Brian complained. "Here we are hiding in a damn swamp, and we don't know what's going on with our friends in town or the horse farm."

Nate waited a few seconds before saying anything to give himself a chance to listen for any unnatural sounds in the woods that might warn him someone was approaching. "I guess we have to take the bad with the good. As I recall, the Army saved your life with modern medicine."

"As I see it," Deni said, "we have two immediate problems. One of them, Brian just mentioned. The other is that we can stay out here only so long before running out of supplies. Sooner or later we're going to have to go to Mel's bunker, or the horse farm, or back to town to get supplies."

"We have caches of supplies buried near the farm. Remember?" Nate reminded Deni. "They are far enough back in the woods we could probably sneak in there and dig one of them up without getting caught, even if soldiers are watching the farm." He cupped his left ear in an effort to listen for distant aircraft. "We'll wait a few days before we try that, though. Hopefully things will be settled down a little by then."

Brian asked, "You think we might be able to sneak into the bunker and use the radio? I mean if it doesn't look too dangerous to try it."

Nate seemed doubtful. "Uh. We'll see. I might try it alone, providing we haven't seen any sign of soldiers in the area over the next several days. First we'll have to get more supplies."

"Just don't broadcast," Deni warned. "The Army will damn sure be listening in. Worse, those spooks will be waiting for just such a mistake. If they don't already know about the bunker, they will when they triangulate the source of your transmission and send an assault team to the area."

Nate nodded in the dark. "Yep."

"Radio's the easiest way to learn something about what's going on," Brian noted. "After all that shooting we heard, I'm worried we may have lost more friends."

"I know," Deni said. "Me too."

~~~

Caroline clasped her hand over Samantha's mouth to prevent her from screaming and turned her face away so she couldn't see. They hid in the brush and watched a CIA operative kick Ramiro in the stomach as he lay on the ground. His hands were bound behind his back with zip ties.

Bo Lyndson, an ex-FBI HRT (hostage rescue team) member and CIA operative the last four years, appeared to be boiling over with rage. When he was about to be fired from the FBI for beating a nineteen-year-old boy until he revealed where his father was hiding out after killing a Bureau of Alcohol, Tobacco, Firearms and Explosives agent, Lyndson jumped at a job offer with the CIA. He was promised there would be no such constitutional restraints to deal with at his new job. The lean, six-foot-tall man of around thirty-five years of age grabbed Ramiro by his thick black hair and pulled his head back. "Where are the others?"

Ramiro spit blood. "I told you. I do not know. Causing me pain will not change that. I cannot tell you what I do not know."

Lyndson pulled his fighting knife and held the point less than a quarter of an inch from Ramiro's left eye. "Do you think you're some kind of a badass? Believe me, you're not."

"It is not courage that stops me from speaking." Ramiro swallowed. His chest heaved. "I cannot tell you what I do not know."

"Damn you!" Mrs. MacKay screamed. "None of us know where they are. We separated into small groups and fled into the woods. Leave him alone. He has done nothing, committed no crime." Tied to a tree, she pulled at her bindings. "Is this how you serve the American people?"

For a moment, rage overtook Caroline's thoughts. If she had not had Samantha to worry about, she would have started shooting at that moment. Instead, she carefully retreated back into the woods taking Samantha away from danger. She couldn't save the others, but she might be able to save one little girl.

A shot rang out. Caroline froze for a second, tears running down her face. She looked down at Samantha and saw that she was crying too. "Come on, little friend. We must be very quiet."

Ramiro looked up from the ground, his eyes wide with fear. Lying on his back, all he could hear was a ringing in his head. His ears useless. The CIA operative had fired his pistol only inches from his left ear, but had not aimed to kill.

Several parents tried to calm their screaming children, who had just witnessed the beating and the faux execution.

One man on the CIA team mopped sweat from his forehead with his jacket sleeve and nervously looked over at the screaming children. "This is bullshit."

The man who had just shot glanced over at him and glared. "What?"

Ken Rittleman, a former Green Beret sergeant, answered, "I said this is bullshit. Are you really willing to do this in front of children?"

MacKay saw more than ten adults and children she had grown to think of as family struggling at their bindings, terror on their faces. Her anger rising, she yelled at the two operatives standing before her. "You already have innocent blood on your hands. Exactly what crimes have we committed to deserve this?"

Lyndson rushed up to her, his knife in his hand. "I want to know where the other insurgents are."

MacKay held her chin up and glared at him. "Insurgents? From where I'm standing you're the insurgents. As I told you, when we left the farm we broke up into small groups and separated before fleeing into the woods. I have no idea where the others are. I do know they have committed no crimes and are not insurgents."

"Damn you, you old hag," Lyndson hissed. "I'm talking about those pretend Sheriff's deputies from Glenwood. Nate Williams, Brian Williams, Deni Heath, ex-Army Sergeant and supposedly now married to Nate Williams. And last but not least, Tyrone Hayes and an old man by the name of Atticus."

She shook her head in dismay. "Why, I know even less of their whereabouts than I do the people who were with me on my farm. The last I heard, they were still in Glenwood. We haven't heard from them in weeks."

Lyndson raised the knife. His eyes turned to slits and he spit his words through his teeth. "I've seen how you live around here. I don't want any part of it. And the thing is you have it easy compared to the major cities where it looks like a medieval world, with everyone walking around looking like skeletons, starving, dying a little every day." He ran the blade down her left arm to her elbow, cutting one quarter of an inch deep. Blood ran down her arm and dripped from her fingertips, splashing on a bed of pine needles at her feet.

MacKay tried to jerk her arm away, but the ropes had her bound to the tree so tight she could barely move. She clenched her jaw, not making a sound. "Young man, you don't live as long as I have without becoming intimately familiar with pain. Have you been kicked by a horse? I won't ask if you've given birth."

He leaned over, bringing his mouth closer to her ear. "My wife is dead, but I have a son and a daughter. The thing is, they are fed three squares a day and so am I. So that my children can eat, I will do what I am told." He cut her left arm again, deeper this time. "My orders are to hunt down, capture, or kill the people I just named. If I don't accomplish my mission, my children may not eat tomorrow. They may not ever eat again. That's what motivates me. It's what I think of whenever I have an unpleasant task." He slashed her face from her ear to the corner of her mouth. The others had not been able to see him cut her left arm, because he was blocking their view. But they all saw him cut her face. The children screamed and cried, and the adults screamed obscenities at Lyndson. He either paid them no attention or did not hear. "I'm willing to do whatever I must to please Washington so my children will continue to eat. You need to tell me what you know before I stop playing around."

MacKay moaned slightly and caught her breath. "It'll do you no good. I have already told you the truth."

Ramiro struggled to his knees, rage on his face. As he tried to stand, Lyndson turned and knocked him down by striking the side of his head with the butt of his knife. "I've wasted enough time here. Where are they? If I have to ask again, someone's going to die."

Stunned, Ramiro lay there on the forest floor blinking. After catching his breath, he said, "If I knew, I would've told you already."

"Damn it, you know where they are." In a fit of rage, Lyndson kicked Ramiro again. He glared down at him in frustration, pulling his pistol and firing a round into his chest. Ramiro's eyes grew wide, as he coughed and gasped. Lyndson watched him struggle to catch his breath while he drowned in his own blood. Ramiro's gasps grew faster and shallower. Finally, his eyes rolled back and life ebbed away.

Shock-induced silence ended when pandemonium erupted among the captives.

Rittleman turned as white as a sheet and threw his hands over his head, letting his M4 hang from its combat sling across his chest. He appeared to be sick.

Another operative, who had been standing watch on the eastern side of the perimeter, came running, ready for trouble. When he saw Ramiro dead and MacKay, blood dripping from her, he surmised the situation instantly. First Sergeant Henry Kramer, the CIA operative who had been captured by Nate and the others, yelled, "Are you insane? If word gets out about this, there's going to be hell to pay."

Lyndson yelled at the screaming captives. "Shut up!" His eyes swept them, looking like tandem guns on a turret, dangerous, full of hate. "Shut the hell up!" He turned to Kramer. "Word isn't going to get out."

Kramer looked at him, his mouth slightly open and his head tilted. "You can get that shit of your head right now. No one else is going to die. These aren't the people we're after. I know what they look like, and they're not here. I wasn't able to stop the killing of that other group, but that's not happening here."

"But they know where they are." Lyndson jabbed an accusing finger at MacKay. "She knows. She's their leader."

Kramer swept his left arm over the group of terrified captives. "I'm standing between you and them. Your call. Take it or leave it. You want them; you come through me."

Lyndson glared at Kramer. "We'll see about that." He took his pack off and produced a satellite telephone from it. After making contact with someone, he spoke into the receiver, "We have indigenous personnel who refuse to cooperate and tell us where the insurgents are. Do we have authority to go as far as necessary to make them talk?" He listened for a few seconds. The scowl on his face softened somewhat. "I need you to repeat that to my number two man." He motioned for Kramer to come and take the phone from him.

Kramer held it to his ear. "What are my orders?" He listened for several seconds, his face turning whiter as he held the phone to his ear. "Yes sir. No sir, I have no questions." He handed the phone back to Lyndson.

"Now you have it," Lyndson said. "Straight from the president himself."

Kramer clicked the safety off on his M4. "It doesn't matter. It's still an illegal order."

Lyndson laughed. "Why didn't you tell him that?"

Kramer stared him down. "Why argue with a madman?"

Lyndson flinched. "Mad or not, he gives the orders. In case you haven't kept up on current events, the world has gone to hell."

Kramer braced himself, his M4 ready. "He's not the only crazy son of a bitch giving illegal orders."

"Oh shit, Henry." Lyndson reared back, incredulous. "Most of these people will be dead in a few months from starvation, anyway."

Growing more angry by the moment, Kramer spit his words. "That's not for you to decide. These people survived a year and a half. If they can survive that long they'll probably make it."

Lyndson threw his hands up. "Whatever. The government feeds my children and feeds me. For that I follow orders. And I don't give a damn if the president is building himself a dictatorship or not. Nor do I give a damn if he was actually elected or not. Look at the sorry bastards America elected before the plague. Who's to say the next one they elect won't be worse than Capinos?"

Kramer shifted his M4, raising the muzzle a few inches. "Again, that's not for you to decide."

Lyndson's eyes narrowed. A shadow fell over his face. "Okay. Where did you get the idea you can decide which orders you follow and which ones you don't?" His posture changed, and he appeared to look more relaxed and less confrontational. He lowered his M4 and took his left hand off of the weapon, holding it by his shooting hand only, muzzle down. He looked past Kramer with a smile on his face and nodded. "I wasn't going to hurt any of them." In a blur of motion, he raised his weapon and squeezed off a short burst. Most of the rounds were stopped by Kramer's ballistic vest, but he wasn't wearing full body armor, and his shoulders were exposed. One round went through his left arm, near the shoulder. The impact spun him around, but he managed to raise his own weapon and fire single-handed, hitting Lyndson in the forehead and killing him instantly.

Shock slowed Rittleman's reaction, giving Kramer enough time to aim with one hand. "How about it, Ken?" He held his M4 on him. "Am I going to have to kill you too?"

Rittleman swallowed and shook his head slowly. "I guess I should've done something sooner. But…" He looked down.

"Well," Kramer said, "in that case, cut these people loose and help me with my arm."

Rittleman jolted and then ran to MacKay. In a few minutes, he had everyone free of their bindings. He got out his medical supplies and cut Kramer's jacket sleeve away. "What about Capinos? The bastard's going to be pissed."

"Let him." Kramer's eyes wandered over to his dead team member. "He was convinced that if he didn't do what Capinos said, his kids would starve."

"He went too far." Rittleman examined the wound. "No major blood vessels hit and nowhere near the bone. If you can avoid infection, you'll be okay."

Kramer looked at the people gathering around him while Rittleman wrapped his arm in gauze. "I apologize to you people for what happened. We'll do what we can for the wounded and then you're free to go." He swallowed. "I have no idea if it'll be safe for you to return to your farm. There's no telling how the president will react to this."

A man working to staunch the bleeding of MacKay's wounds glanced over at them and said, "Maybe you should be worried about how the people react to this." His anger boiling over, he added, "There are still enough combat vets left alive to give Washington a guerrilla war they'll never forget. They better back off and they better do it while they still can."

MacKay ignored her pain as she reached to touch Ramiro's shoulder. "My dear old friend." She blinked tears. "I will never forget you.

~~~

Capinos greeted CIA Director William Shekel at the door to the Oval Office. "What's so important you needed to speak to me immediately, Bill?"

Director Shekel closed the door behind him before speaking. "We've lost contact with two of our men in Florida and found another one dead."

Capinos froze for a second. "What? Communications problems?"

Shekel shook his head. "We don't think so. Their equipment was working fine earlier today. They're not answering. We sent a nearby team to check on their last known position and we found one of our men dead. Shot. The other two must've been taken prisoner."

Capinos sat on the front edge of his desk. "I had direct contact with two operatives only hours ago. They wanted authority to use enhanced interrogation techniques on insurgents. Was there any other sign of a struggle, more bodies? Of insurgents I mean. Those guys aren't that easy to get the better of. I can't believe local yokels were able to sneak up on them or outfight them."

"They found one grave. A Hispanic man was in it. They also found blood that must've come from another person, maybe two – no body. There were spent casings from military style weapons, but no sign of any other type of weapons being fired." Shekel adjusted his suit. "Uh, I think I should mention at this time there has been a killing a few miles from where we found the grave and dead operative. Another one of our teams killed over a dozen civilian adults. The civilians refused to drop their weapons, so our men shot them all."

Capinos waved him away. "That's not pertinent to the lost team we're talking about." He hardened his expression. "They're not related, are they?"

"No way to tell. Could be our lost team was attacked by locals out of retaliation for the killing of the civilians. They may have taken the two missing operatives captive or we just haven't found the bodies yet."

Capinos shook his head. "No. There wasn't time for word to spread about the killing of those few locals." He rubbed his chin. "Could be we have a mutiny. Operators against operators. I got the impression from my last communication with them that one on the team was being pigheaded about harming civilians."

Shekel blinked and swallowed. "That could be bad."

Capinos glared at him. "Of course it is! No doubt about it."

"What I meant to say is if that's what happened, it could be the start of something much larger. I've been getting reports of growing discord in the military. Many high-ranking officers are losing patience with your administration."

Capinos snorted. "Yeah, tell me about it. Damn near every general officer just stabbed me in the back. They signed a petition demanding national elections as soon as possible." He clenched his jaw. "Can you believe that shit? They're saying my presidency isn't legit and they will not follow my orders much longer." He moved to his chair and collapsed in it. "I'm not sure how to respond. I'm afraid if I get tough with them, it'll be counterproductive. On the other hand, if I show weakness, it'll encourage them to demand more, maybe my resignation." He looked out into empty space, focusing on his thoughts and not the Oval Office or Shekel. "They say things could've been much better by now, but my leadership has been lacking, hindering the recovery of the country." He shuttered. "They're full of shit. I've helped this country through its darkest hour. Why, if not for me…" He noticed a strange look on Shekel's face and his voice trailed off into thin air. "Oh, to hell with all of them."

Shekel had to speak fast. He didn't want Capinos to realize what he was thinking. "I have an idea. But first I need to find our lost men. We might be able to blame them for the killing of civilians. Rogue CIA agents or something." He tried to gauge Capinos' reaction to his next words. "But I think you should back off in Florida for now. Until all of this simmers down. Those Southerners can be hotheads, and we don't need locals down there riled up. On top of that, your trouble with the military makes matters worse. It's no time to get tough on the people in Florida. The whole idea was to keep your operation quiet. If we go in with guns a-blazing, there won't be anything quiet about that. In fact it'll be all over the country in no time. What's the point of it now? Best to handle this more delicately."

"Our operation," Capinos interjected.

Shekel nodded. "Our operation. Sacrificing two men to defuse this ticking bomb is well worth it. We need time. The military wants results. If we can give them results over the next few months, they'll be pacified. They don't give a damn if a chimpanzee in diapers is in the White House. What they don't like is the American people suffering unnecessarily, and they believe we in Washington have failed them. You're the president, so you take most of the blame." He clicked his tongue and smiled, pretending he just thought of it. "I've an idea. Lift that blame off your shoulders and dump it in the military's lap! Give them a free hand, both as far as law and order goes and the food relief efforts too."

Capinos almost yelled, "What?"

"Think about it. Those jarheads in the military are only good at war and then they pour tax money out on the ground like so much water. When it all goes to hell, and it will, you step in and take over, telling them they had their chance."

Capinos frowned. His eyes turned to slits. Anger rushed to his head, turning his face red.

Shekel braced himself, believing he had failed. *He just will not give up an ounce of power, even to save himself and his presidency. And of course to hell with the American people and the country.*

Then the president's frown turned into a smile. "They'll not dare try any kind of a coup after they've failed to handle the country *with* the government's help. They'll damn sure not be in a hurry to try it on their own." He jumped up and paced the room, punching his open left hand with his right fist. "I'll give them three months."

Shekel quickly spoke up. "That's not long enough for them to get themselves into trouble deep enough. You must give them enough rope to hang themselves with."

"Six months then," Capinos said.

Shekel tried again. "I would think nine or ten."

"No. Six months." Capinos seemed firm on the matter. "They'll be wanting elections by then and I must have their tail feathers trimmed and their ass singed before they start insisting."

Shekel relented. "Six months then." He appraised the president's face, trying to read him. Making a snap decision, he moved in to finish it. "We both know your election was a farce, as was the election of most of those in Congress and as a consequence the appointment of every new justice on the Supreme Court. The generals have that to hang over your head and use as an excuse for their insubordination. My guess is all they want is results. I've been keeping an eye on this little revolt of theirs. And I can tell you not a single one of them is interested in a coup. Nor is a single one of them wanting to take your place or hungering for power. It's the American people they're worried about. If you want to hold on to your office, you're going to have to do a much better job than you've done so far."

Capinos suddenly became afflicted with a tic in the form of his left eye blinking uncontrollably. "Whose side are you on? We've been friends since Harvard."

Shekel continued. "Sorry friend, but that's the way I see it. I'm trying to help you get past that six months we've been talking about. Once the military tries and fails, concentrate on production of food and providing the people with law and order. And by that, I mean protection from the criminal element, and not through oppression from government." He looked Capinos in the eye. "You want to stay in power? You want to be known by historians as the man who led America through its darkest hour? Then do it. Lead them through this darkest hour. The path you've taken so far is the path to hell. Give them six or eight months of stability, safety, protection from violent criminals, six or eight months without hunger, without fear, without needless suffering and death, and you'll win that special election in a landslide."

Capinos had a strange, half-smile on his face. He tilted his head and looked at Shekel as if he thought he were insane. "I had no idea you thought I was that damn stupid. Did you really think you could just pat me on the head and tell me I really could be a good little boy if I would just try?" He bit his upper lip and thought for ten seconds longer. "What you suggest would certainly buy me some time. That much I agree with. Go ahead and do what has to be done to blame the so-called atrocities in Florida on our wayward operatives. I'll get with my cabinet and start doing some of the other things you suggested. If I can win an election six months from now, that'll put me in a strong position to implement my other programs and solidify my power here in Washington. I'm sure that's not what you really meant, but I still think it's a good idea." He rubbed his hands together and frowned, staring off into space. "Of course, it just may be the last election America ever has."

Shekel's face became a blank slate. He nodded. "I think if you help the people feed themselves, provide them with protection, and respect the Constitution while you're doing it, you will win that election." He took two steps back from the president's desk. "I've got work to do. The thing in Florida must be handled delicately and will require more resources. I'll give you a report tomorrow evening on the progress."

"Good. You do that," Capinos said. He sat behind his desk, leaned back, and stared at the ceiling, in deep thought.

Shekel closed the door behind him and leaned against a wall. *Maybe the country just took a step forward. Maybe. Six months. A lot of food can be produced and a lot of people can be fed in six months. After that, well, we'll see.*

Chapter 14

Kramer and Rittleman knew they would soon be hunted men. It didn't dawn on them the charges would be massacring civilians and not disobeying orders and killing CIA operative Bo Lyndson. Lyndson was touted as the hero who tried to stop *them* from murdering civilians and was murdered by the crazed Kramer and Rittleman for his humanitarian efforts. They left the civilians and headed west, hoping to make it to the Gulf and catch a ride on a boat to Texas, where they both were from. In the back of their minds, they thought stealing a boat and enough fuel to get there was the most likely scenario, but there was a small chance they just might catch a ride on a sailing yacht. Whatever. They needed to get the hell out of the area.

~~~

Brian smiled when he saw the limb shaking. Another big fish on the line. He had set a dozen brush hooks along a creek just before dark. Sunrise found him checking the lines, and he already had enough on his stringer to feed the crew for the day. A thought came to him that not long before, when he was only a boy, back a year or so ago, he would've enjoyed this fishing trip a lot more. But that was before the world became a dangerous place, where men hunted each other.

He bent over to reach for the line when a sound in the woods alerted him. Squatting behind a cypress tree for several seconds, he scanned the wall of green. His ears had picked up something unnatural, but he had yet to decide exactly what or where it was. Dropping to one knee, he shouldered his carbine and waited. Ten yards past the far bank of the creek, a heavy boot crushed dry leaves. Clicking the safety off his carbine sounded loud to his ears, but he told himself no one could have heard it more than a few feet away. His heart rate jumped, and he struggled to control his breathing. *Anyone walking that quiet out here is probably a soldier.*

For some reason, the eight-pound catfish decided to come to the surface and splash around while struggling against the hook and line. *Shit!* Brian pulled his head down lower and tried to stay as still as possible.

The splashing of the fish grew louder. The woods became quiet, and Brian knew whoever was out there had heard the struggling fish and had stopped moving. Someone was doing the same thing he was: waiting and listening. He wished his father was there.

The day's catch, still on a stringer he had dropped only four feet away, flopped around on dry leaves. One three-pound channel cat seemed to be trying to make it to the creek's edge but wasn't about to drag all the others tied on the same string with it. The noise it was making was about to get Brian killed.

Then Brian saw him, or at least his face. Like Brian, he wore a boonie hat. He could see part of the man's right shoulder and could tell he was wearing a soldier's uniform and had an M4 aimed in his general direction and ready to fire. He also knew the man had only an idea of where he was but had not seen him yet. Looking through the Aimpoint sight, it was an easy shot. But he couldn't squeeze the trigger. He wasn't sure yet. No matter how afraid he was, he wasn't sure if he should kill this man. At that moment, the weight of all the men he had killed in the last year weighed on his shoulders and he couldn't pull the trigger.

Motion to his left and farther back from the creek caught his attention for a moment. Finding nothing, he turned his attention back to the man he had his sights on. He was gone. Something inside him turned up the volume on all of his senses. At that moment, he found himself more alive than he had ever been in his life, and he knew he was only seconds away from death.

~~~

Standing guard over the camp, a sudden chill came over Deni. She looked downstream where she knew Brian was and wondered what was keeping him. Atticus and Tyrone were boiling water. They were running low from drinking so much with the evening meal the night before. She glanced over in their direction, but she was looking for Nate. When she finally saw him, he was on the edge of her vision and mostly obscured by brush. He had his load-bearing harness on, which contained most of his spare ammunition. In his hands, was his M14. She saw him nervously scanning the woods downstream.

Without warning, a rifle shot cracked the cold air. Nate rushed to the fire and stamped it out. In a low voice, he warned

Atticus and Tyrone, "Prepare to defend your life. I'm going after Brian."

The two men scrambled to their weapons in silence.

Nate hand-signaled to Deni that he was going downstream to look for Brian.

She nodded, her face ashen. Assuming he wanted her to come with him, she ran to catch up.

After running 50 yards, Nate heard her running behind him and stopped. He started to tell her to stay with Atticus and Tyrone but changed his mind. The two men were friends, but Brian was his son. Being a trained soldier, Deni might make the difference between Brian living and dying. If it wasn't already too late.

Nate hand signaled for her to slow down and stay ten yards behind him. As much as he wanted to rush to help Brian, his training would not allow him to blunder into an ambush. Before they traveled another 50 yards, a second shot rang out and echoed in the trees. They pushed on, keeping low and staying as quiet as possible.

A man's clear voice came from back in the trees on the other side of the creek. "Stop shooting, boy. We mean you no harm."

Another rifle shot rang out.

"Damn it. I told you we mean you no harm. Stop shooting and we'll go our separate ways."

Nate moved in close enough he could see Brian taking refuge behind cover between two large cypress trees and aiming his rifle at something or someone on the other side of the creek. He had also heard the man's voice, which allowed him to locate his approximate position. What he didn't know was how many men were out there and what their intentions were. The 40 seconds it took Nate to get Brian's attention and signal for him to lay flat on the ground were long and torturous. After Brian's two shots, chances were almost 100% that anyone out there in the woods knew just about exactly where Brian was, and Nate wanted him to get down as low as possible before he got shot.

Deni directed most of her attention to the other side of the creek, where it seemed the danger was coming from. Bare aluminum on the soldier's M4s where the finish had worn off caught a glint of sunlight, and she focused on that. Ten seconds later, her eyes had made out the partial form of a soldier, dressed and equipped for combat. The only part of the man she could see clearly was his left shoulder. She made that her target and aimed. Another ounce of trigger pull and the sear would release.

The man she was aiming at yelled out, "Look damn it, don't make us kill you. We're not here to do you any harm. We're just passing through this way."

Deni and Nate both recognized the voice immediately. It was Henry Kramer, the CIA operative.

Nate yelled out, "If you're not here to kill us, show yourself. Come out and stand in the open. We won't shoot."

Brian lifted his head up to try to see. Nate yelled, "Get down!"

A shot rang out. A bullet plowed into one of the trees Brian was hiding behind. Nate and Deni both noticed the shot didn't come from Kramer.

"To hell with this," Deni muttered under her breath. She tightened her aim on Kramer's shoulder and squeezed the trigger. When Kramer spun around and landed on his back, disappearing behind brush, she knew she had hit him.

Someone opened up on full auto, and the swamp roared with gunfire. Brian hugged the muddy ground and flattened himself as low as possible. Bullets flew over his head and chewed up the trees around him.

Nate dropped to the rice paddy squat and fired three quick shots. He saw all three bullets connect, center mass on the man's chest. Before the echo of gunfire rolled down the river swamp and faded out of hearing range, Nate had belly crawled to another position and was already aiming across the creek, searching for another target while looking over his sights. He had no idea what they were up against, but expected there to be a platoon of the soldiers out there. He had little hope they would survive the next five minutes.

Five minutes passed in silence. No gunfire. No movement in the woods. Not a sound.

Nate signaled for Deni to cover him. After getting Brian's attention, he motioned for him to make his way back from the creek by staying as low to the ground as possible and behind cover at all times.

Brian nodded and crawled away, inching along the ground.

Nate and Deni covered him until he was 50 yards back and had enough trees between him and danger to stop any bullet and prevent those on the other side of the creek from seeing him.

The three spent the next 15 minutes retreating quietly and making their way back to camp. They found Tyrone and Atticus had already packed everything and were ready to leave.

Nate noticed Atticus and Tyrone both immediately looked for any sign of injuries on the three of them and seemed relieved when they found none. The relief was temporary, though, and they were obviously eager to get the hell out of Dodge. With Nate in the lead, they did just that.

It was over an hour later when they stopped and formed a defense perimeter while taking a rest and a badly needed drink that Deni spoke up and told him that one of the men they had shot was the CIA operative Henry Kramer. "I know I hit him," she said. "I saw him spin around and fall. The left shoulder was the only target I had available, so I doubt I killed him."

Brian's face hardened. "Should've killed the bastard while we had the chance."

Nate removed the magazine from his rifle and pressed loose rounds into it to top it off. "Well, the other one's dead for sure. As far as I can tell there were only two of them. But even a CIA team should be working with a reconnaissance team of three to six men. At any rate, we were lucky it wasn't a platoon of regular soldiers."

Deni nodded. "They didn't seem to be looking for trouble. The whole thing was strange. Remember what Kramer said to Brian?"

Brian flinched. "I didn't believe him. And if I'd recognized his voice I would've believed him even less. It's not like I shot at them for fun." He looked down, his breath coming in gasps. "How the hell am I supposed to know when a man comes at you with a gun, sneaking up on you in the woods, if he means to use it or not? Besides, Kramer was an asshole. We know people have suffered, probably died, because we let him go. We were weak. We were weak, and people died because of it."

Nate raised his voice, "Okay. Okay, damn it. No one here is blaming you for what happened. You did the right thing. Now stop blaming yourself. Don't lose a moment of sleep over it. We're the ones who shot them, not you." Anger flared up on his face. "It's what we have to live with right now, Brian. We're all alive and unhurt. That's all that matters in the end. The rest is a luxury only those who live in a civilized world can afford. The fact that it bothered you is proof you're not becoming what you fear. Now let it go and forget it."

Deni pushed her boonie hat off her head and ran her fingers through top of her hair. "I agree with all of that. But if there were only two of them, Kramer's back there wounded and alone. The question now is what do we do about that?"

Atticus and Tyrone stopped scanning the woods for danger for a second and looked at the others.

Brian cleared his throat. "It's awful damn dangerous."

Nate looked up at the canopy of trees above them for a second. "Yes it is."

"It would be a damn stupid thing to do," Brian added.

Nate nodded and looked back in the direction they came from.

"I'll go." Brian pressed loose rounds into his rifle magazine.

Deni and Nate glanced at each other and smiled.

Nate thought for a second. His chest rose and fell several times. The look on his face hardened and took on the sharp, cold edge of stone. "No. No one's going back. Kramer knew what he was getting into when he signed up for his job. He's probably already radioed for help. I go back there; I'll be walking into a death trap. Hell, we don't even know if there were only two of them. There could've been a dozen more moving in on us before we got the hell out of there. We may be a lot luckier than we even know. Just because only two of them shot and we only saw those two, doesn't mean they were alone. I'm sure at first they thought Brian was alone, until Deni and I started shooting. Maybe they wanted to take him alive."

Brian reinserted his now full magazine. "Yeah. It's not worth the risk. But I thought if someone was going to go it might as well be me. After all, I caused all of it."

"It just happened to be you who saw them first. You didn't cause anything." Deni put her canteen away and prepared to hit the trail again. "I think it's time to start walking, guys."

Nate stood. "Yep. Let's put miles under our feet before dark."

With everyone on edge, the slightest sound, a squirrel scurrying up a tree, or a tree branch falling on the leaf-carpeted swamp floor, resulted in everyone bracing to dive for cover, shouldering their weapons, scanning the woods for danger. Adding to their worries was the danger of death from the sky. All they could do was move as fast as possible through the woods without blundering into an ambush. At nightfall, they stopped to rest. Half stood guard while the others ate and then tried to get some sleep.

~~~

Brigadier General Bernard Myers expected a call from his friend General Strovenov, so he wasn't surprised when a call came in by Sat-Com. He pushed a button and leaned back in his chair before saying, "General Myers here."

"You won't believe this," Strovenov said, more than a hint of glee in his voice. "For some unexplainable reason, the president has gotten an entirely new bug up his ass and has decided to give us a free hand in dealing with the famine and lawlessness. He promises Washington will be hands-off for six months."

General Myers sat up in his chair, a look of disbelief on his face. "What?"

"He didn't explain a damn thing, just handed me a letter giving all branches of the military, including the Guard and Coast Guard, full authority over the task of providing security for American civilians and ending the famine. We also have authority to take over oil wells and refineries during the six months period and any farmland we deem necessary to feed the people. Nothing in his letter or his spoken words in the Oval Office said a damn thing about what to do with those oil wells and refineries after the six months period is over or who to hand them over to." He laughed. "But to hell with that. We have six months to feed millions of people and to protect them from the violent criminals that are now prowling the streets and countryside of this nation of ours. Thank God Almighty."

"Thank God is right," Myers agreed. "Too damn late for tens of millions of Americans, but thank God nonetheless. Must've been that petition all the general officers signed."

Strovenov remained quiet for a few seconds. "I'm not sure why he did it. All I know is we have a hell of a lot of work to do and we need to get it done yesterday. The Joint Chiefs of Staff will be sending out a flurry of policy changes down the chain of command sometime tonight, and the resulting stream of orders from COs will probably continue on for days. You can tell the colonel in Florida his ass is off the hook for now. Tell him to roll up his sleeves and get busy serving the American people. That little CIA manhunt down there is off. Hunting season is closed. Tell him to expend his resources hunting down real criminals and leave the innocent civilians alone."

Meyers smiled. "Yes Sir! Unless there is something else, I would like to cut this conversation off now and get to work."

"I understand. We have a long night ahead of us up here in Washington too. I'll get back with you as soon as possible."

~~~

General Myers got back on the satellite phone and explained the new developments to Col. Donovan. "I have no idea what precipitated the sudden 180-degree turn in Washington. I have theories but won't mention them now. Anyway, we'll forget the matter of your objection to illegal orders and offering your resignation. You have new orders now, and I expect you to carry them out. Remember, we only have six months to show results. I'm hoping that conditions will be so improved that the president will extend those six months to a year."

Donovan kept his surging emotions under control. "Yes sir."

"Good. Unless something drastic comes up again, I expect your reports to go up the normal chain of command from now on. I'm glad you'll be staying with us."

Donovan smiled as they ended their conversation. He stepped out of this office and rushed to the communications room. "Call all patrols in. They are ordered to convey their apologies to any civilian they meet along the way for violating their constitutional rights and explain to them that it was all a mistake and that it is safe for them to go back to their homes. No soldiers will bother them." He turned to several sergeants who had overheard. "I want every off-duty noncom and officer standing in front of HQ at 1800 hours to receive new orders."

Sergeant Quint Bartow walked in. Smiling, he asked, "Does that mean your ass is out of the sling?"

Donovan answered, "I guess so, since we've been ordered to stop terrorizing the innocent people of this county and start feeding and protecting them. The Williams family and the other two are no longer wanted in Washington."

"Great." Bartow raised both eyebrows. "Now how do we get word to them? They may be in Georgia before they even know they're not wanted anymore. And the thing is the people here need some kind of local law enforcement besides the heavy hand of the Army. Those guys were damn sure better than nothing, even the kid."

"Good question," Donovan said. "But I don't have an answer." He rushed outside to look when he heard a Black Hawk coming in to land. He yelled for Bartow to join him outside.

Donovan watched soldiers spill out of the helicopter, running bent over, carrying their heavy combat loads. Though the Black Hawk was over 100 yards away, he had to yell above the noise. "I've been told the spooks were called off hours ago. I don't believe it. Not yet. Pass the word. Tell all the patrols heading out to check for any sign the CIA is still working the area. I want to know the minute there is anything new."

Bartow yelled above the noise, "Yes sir."

Donovan thought for a moment, then spoke again. "Radio Lieutenant Herzing at the farm on the lake and tell him he'll be getting more manpower and equipment sometime tomorrow. This long winter has to end sometime. The civilians need to be ready to plant every inch of that land as soon as they deem it safe to do so. There can't be too many more freezing nights left for this year. If there is, we must be entering another Ice Age."

"Yes sir. I doubt that." He raised an eyebrow. "If that's the case, it would probably finish off the human race."

Ignoring the sergeant's last comment, Donovan added, "Get a few teams to reach out to other farmers in the area and see what we can do for them. I know they need more fuel, but what else can we do? Whenever soldiers have contact with civilians, I want them to ask about criminal activity and what their most pressing needs are. If they say they need protection, we'll have to give it to them by placing a team on location until the troublemakers are IDed and apprehended. That's it for now."

"Do you want me to wait until the officers are given your orders at 1800 hours?"

Donovan shook his head. "No. Get on it right now. We can't wait until then. Just fill them in on your activities after the meeting, so they'll know what you've accomplished so far and not duplicate your efforts. If any officer gets on your case before then, just tell them you're following my orders and they'll be filled in at the meeting."

"Yes sir." Bartow rushed into HQ to begin his many tasks.

~~~

Two weeks later.

Nate looked at the measly small pile of food sitting on a log: a small bag of rice and another of beans. "Well people, that's all we have left." He looked at the others who were all sitting in a circle looking at him. He half smiled. "Unless one of you is holding out."

Only Brian had anything to say. "Nope."

"That settles it," Deni said. "One or two of us will have to risk going to Mel's retreat or the farm. We have no choice."

Atticus scratched at his gray beard. "I'd just the same die of lead poisoning as starve."

"I vote with Atticus," Tyrone said. "Except I think we might as well all go together, instead of just Nate and Deni." He looked at Deni. "I'm sure that's what you meant when you said one or two of us. But I think we should all go."

"Yeah," Brian said. "That is if I get a vote." He looked at Nate.

Nate stood and turned his back to all of them, looking out into the swamp. He rested his hand on his holstered pistol, thinking. A few seconds later, he faced them and said, "We haven't heard any aircraft lately, no gunfire, not a single soldier or even a boot track. There's no sign that they're hunting us anymore."

"I think you've already made your decision," Deni said. "But will it be just the two of us or everyone?"

"We'll all go," Nate answered. "But you and I'll leave the others several miles back and go in slow and easy. We'll check on Mel's bunker and cave first. If we find no sign the soldiers have been there, you and I'll go on to the farm and check it out, moving in slow and easy. We see so much as a boot track we'll turn around and get the hell out of there. The food at Mel's place will get us by for a while."

"I sure wish we could move back home," Brian said. "Looks like it's starting to warm up now. We could get a good crop in if we get seeds in the ground soon."

"You're not the only one that's homesick, Brian." Tyrone glanced at Atticus. "This living in the woods shit is hard on me and Atticus both."

"Yeah, I'm too old for this." Atticus had a gleam in his eye as he looked at the others. "But I'm not complaining. I can take it if you kids can."

"That settles it then." Nate snatched up his rifle where it leaned against a nearby tree. "I'll check the squirrel snares and gather them up. Hopefully we'll have a few squirrels to eat before we go."

Brian sighed. "Damn. I sure hope this is the last time we have to eat game meat. Right now I feel like it would be worth taking on the whole damn U.S. Army to get a little decent food."

Atticus chuckled quietly, sure not to make too much noise. "I think you'll change your mind if there really are soldiers waiting for us there."

"Maybe." Brian pulled his pack close to him and started putting lighter items in the bottom of the main compartment. "Let's get packed while Dad's gone. I don't hold out much hope for his snares. He's likely to come back with no squirrels at all."

Tyrone stood and checked the safety on his rifle. "Go ahead and pack. Someone should be standing guard, even if we haven't seen any soldiers lately."

~~~

Casper Tanner, 72 years old and showing every year of it, stood next to his tractor, waiting for the sunrise to bring enough light he could see well enough to start plowing 200 acres of the massive 1200-acre field. Looking to the east over the newly plowed field of black peat, rich in nutrients and waiting to grow many kinds of vegetables, his chest swelled with pride over his part in the building of this farm. A 28,000 acre stretch of land was a state wilderness preserve next to Lake Jackson. The farm had come to be known as Lake Jackson Farm, or just the Lake Farm. It was the third such farm built in North Florida with the help of the U.S. Army and National Guard, as well as local citizens. The last two were modeled after the first one that Nate and Second Lieutenant Colby Jacobson, among many others, had designed and built and was already producing food for hungry people.

Lieutenant Jacobson walked up and stood beside him. "No frost. That makes ten mornings in a row." He looked at the old farmer. "What do you think, Cap?"

Casper's face wrinkled even more. He spoke without looking at the lieutenant. "I think we should've started planting several weeks ago. It'll take a while for the seeds to sprout, so even if we get another frost or two, it probably won't hurt nothin'. A little cold'll harden the sprouts some. But then again, a hard freeze'll kill 'em." He took his straw hat off and scratched his bald head. "Once we get the seeds in the ground, we got to keep them moist, and that ain't goin' to be easy without pumps and a real irrigation system. This here primitive system that works by gravity feed from the lake is better than nothin', but we really do need to have some kind of sprinkler system and pumps to pressurize it. If we can't keep the seeds moist, they ain't comin' up and those that do'll be stunted and produce little to nothin'."

Jacobson smiled at the farmer's backcountry accent. "We're working on it. Got a couple big pumps coming in soon. But we're going to be short on diesel fuel for a while. Remember, there's other farms besides this one."

"Oh, I ain't forgot that," Cap said. "Ain't the first time I had to make do when I didn't have much to work with. Come hell or high water, we'll feed some people. I can promise that. Can't promise much else. But I can promise that. No way am I goin' to let that Nate Williams guy down south of here outdo me. Get back out of my way. It's time for me to crawl up on this rig and get to work."

Lieutenant Jacobson smiled and rushed back to the little building made of scrap plywood that was his office, headquarters, radio room, and home away from home. A large olive drab canvas tent stood 50 yards behind the building. The men who served under him slept there. Its duplicate stood 50 yards further back. It served as the mess hall. Surrounding the plywood building and tents were six sandbagged machine gun nests. More soldiers patrolled the perimeter of the entire farm, and at least two guards were kept at the gate 24 hours a day. They hadn't had any trouble with terrorists lately, but they couldn't afford to take the chance with lax security.

~~~

The American people's rage over recent revelations stood ready to boil over. It had become common knowledge that President Capinos and the CIA were responsible for drumming up trouble in an effort to destabilize the country further and give Capinos an excuse to grab more power and remove more constitutional limits to government. A tidal wave of demand for a real national election had grown to a fever pitch, and almost everyone knew that if that election didn't take place soon, there was going to be trouble. The fieriest rhetoric usually came out of the mouths of those who believed the military was with the people. Those who were not so sure, were more restrained out of concern for their safety, but were just as determined to see real national elections by the end of the year.

Reestablishing law and order was still a long way off, and brigands roamed the land almost at will. Occasionally, though, they ran afoul of armed civilians, the National Guard, or the Army. Someone in Washington had decided that the Marines would operate mostly west of the Mississippi, and the Navy and Air Force would concentrate on defending the country from outside threats. The rest of the country was the Army and National Guard's responsibility. The Coast Guard did what it could wherever it could, especially in Alaska. Hawaii had been left nearly devoid of human life. Early in the onslaught of the plague, world-traveling tourists brought the deadly disease to the islands, and it devastated the population there even more than on the continent of North America. No federal official had dared even set foot on Puerto Rico in over a year. A fly-over told them it was nearly devoid of life. A few Americans thought it would be the place to flee from the plague, not realizing tourists had brought the deadly disease there early on. With business and pleasure travelers jetting around the world, there was no refuge from the plague, except the most remote areas, where there were no airports and no roads. Alaskans living in the bush stopped coming into town for supplies and had to rely completely on hunting and fishing. Their already rugged lives became a constant struggle to survive.

Mexico, south to Costa Rica, were hit hard by the plague, leaving few alive. Only those who lived deep in the jungles of South America, away from any contact with the outside world, had been spared. They too, had been forced to isolate themselves even more and live off the land completely, the same as those in the Alaskan bush.

No one in government seemed to have any idea if the plague had been a product of nature or if it had been a doomsday weapon produced in some laboratory. Opinions and guesses were plentiful, but solid information was impossible to find. Not only had the U.S. Government not yet come to any conclusion on the source of the plague, other than the fact it started in Israel, the UK, France, Germany, and other allies of the U.S., Washington had nothing to say on the subject. Rumors were plentiful, and varied from reasonable to fantasies from the Twilight Zone. If it had been a terrorist attack with intentions of harming only the U.S. and its allies, their plan had backfired, killing almost everyone on the face of the earth. But then, that too could have been their intention. A doomsday weapon. A weaponized disease designed to wipe out the human race. After all, there were people just that crazy. Speculation abounded, but facts were few.

Chapter 15

Nate purposely led the group into the rougher country north of Mel's bunker. Mel's cave wasn't the only one in the area, and he knew exactly where one was that would be perfect for the others to hide in while Deni and he went on to scout the area around Mel's bunker for any sign of danger. Caves were generally not a good place to hide, as there was no exit in most cases. If an enemy discovered you, the cave would become a grave. But Nate was most worried about aircraft equipped with forward looking infrared, or FLIR. Their heat signature would not be detected in a cave.

"Take your time. Don't rush it," Brian admonished his father. "If they have a trap set, it might not be so easy to see on first glance."

"That's good advice," Nate said, his rough voice echoing in the cave. "Everyone stay back from the entrance while we're gone and be as quiet as possible."

Deni hid any worries she might have had behind a smile. "If everything goes well, we'll be back by nightfall with our packs full of food."

"Just be careful, and you'll be all right," Brian said.

Tyrone and Atticus wished them both luck, as they slipped out of the cave entrance.

With their packs empty of everything but a little water and ammunition, Nate and Deni slipped into the woods light on their feet. Unlike most of Florida, this area was hilly and marred by deep ravines that slowed their progress. Sinkholes and springs were also common, as were limestone outcroppings that had to be climbed over or skirted around. While keeping their eyes and ears on full alert for danger in the woods, they also listened for aircraft in the sky. Their enemy had all the advantages. Their only shield was stealth.

The two stayed back in the shade of tall pines as they navigated around a large sinkhole. Both scrutinized the mud at the water's edge for any boot tracks. To their relief, they found none. Nate noticed something in the clear water. A stone in a peculiar shape. His mind wasn't really on the puzzle it presented, since he was more concerned with walking into an ambush than such trivial matters, but it flashed in his mind that he had just seen a fossilized mastodon tooth. He didn't bother mentioning it to Deni. They had more important things to worry about. He hoped that some day in the future during more pleasant times, he would mention what he saw in the clear water and perhaps make a joke about it. At the moment, his main concern was living long enough to experience those more pleasant times.

Because of the necessity of stealth, their progress was slow, and morning grew into afternoon before they were within half a mile of Mel's bunker. Nate motioned for Deni to come closer. He whispered, "Stay back ten yards. We're going to be moving extremely slow from now on."

Deni nodded. "Slow it is. We've got nothing but time."

As they made their timorous progress, the tree shadows all around them grew longer and the warmth of the afternoon faded along with the light. The dying sunless afternoon found the couple peering through brush and out into the small clearing around Mel's bunker. They had yet to find any sign that a human being had been in the area lately, not a single boot track. Still, they didn't let their guard down and stayed in the darkening shadows of the tall forest, skirting around the clearing and heading for the cave.

The tree Nate and Brian had planted so long ago was still alive and had grown to a height of five feet, completely hiding the entrance. Anyone walking by would never have noticed the olive drab painted steel door behind it.

Though it appeared safe, they did not move in and approach the cave entrance until they had circled around the entire area and found no sign of danger.

Keeping his voice low, Nate said, "You overwatch while I go on in. I don't want to expose myself in the clearing until I'm over by that big pine." He pointed. "When I come out of the cave, I'll head over in the other direction towards that big rock and enter the woods that way. There's no point in me coming straight to you and focusing their attention on your position."

"Okay," Deni said. "There's no harm in being extra careful, even though we're pretty sure there's no one out here."

Nate touched her face lightly, as if he were thanking her for not giving him any grief for keeping her out of danger as much as possible while exposing himself to any sniper who might be waiting for him to walk into the clearing. "If all goes well, I'll take your pack and return to the cave for another load."

"Any shooting starts while you're out there in the open, just dive for cover. Shouldn't take me long to find him and take him out. The clearing's not very large, so he couldn't be far away. Just stay down so he can't get a bullet into you."

Nate smiled. "Listen to us. We're 99.9% sure there's no one out there." Before Deni could respond, he stood and walked away, slipping into the wall of flora and sinking into the darkening gray woods.

She swallowed and said to no one, "Can't be too careful."

An outcropping of trees that protruded into the clearing more than ten feet afforded Nate a little more concealment and cover before he was forced to bolt out into the open and rush to the entrance to the cave. He squeezed past the tree he and Brian had planted, and pressed in behind it to get at the entrance to Mel's cave. He had to fish around in his pockets for the key. Reaching around behind a limestone boulder, he withdrew several hidden bolts that prevented the door from opening even when unlocked. The hinges were rusty and protested when he pulled it open, taking most of his strength to do so. The door probably weighed over 200 pounds, since it was made of cold rolled steel.

Even with the door swung wide open, little light entered the cave because of the tree growing in front of the entrance. He lit a match and used the light from it to help him find a kerosene lantern sitting on a small table. The same match lit the lantern, but he did burn his fingers a little while doing so.

Nate stepped past the five gallon buckets of wheat, rice, and dried beans and headed for the cans of freeze-dried food and quickly stuffed his pack full of a variety of meals. In less than five minutes he was out of the cave and rushing toward the tree line near the large limestone rock he'd told Deni he was going to head for.

He slipped into the shadows, ten feet back from the edge of the clearing, and caught his breath, relieved that no one had taken a shot at him while he was in the open. Moving on to Deni, he dropped to one knee and grabbed her pack. The two exchanged glances, but neither said a word. He stood up and moved to a different location before darting across the clearing again and disappearing into the cave. A few minutes later, he came out with her pack bulging with more freeze-dried food. Before emerging from behind the tree, he took the time to lock the cave door and reinsert the hidden bolts.

This time Deni saw him coming. She grabbed his pack and walked the last 20 yards to him. Together, they slipped farther back from the edge of the clearing and carefully snuck out of the area. An hour and a half later, they were with the others and enjoying their first real meal in days.

"Don't eat too much, guys," Deni warned. "We're going to be hitting the trail again in a few minutes, and full stomachs will weigh you down."

Brian swallowed his last spoon full of lasagna. "So you two have decided it's safe to check out the farm now?"

Nate folded the can opener on his Swiss pocketknife and put it in his pocket. "We'll ease back down into the low country on the edge of the river valley and then make our way south until we get within a few miles of the farm. Then Deni and I'll leave you three and go on in the rest of the way alone. Won't be time to do all that before dark, so we'll be camping out in the woods again tonight."

"And if there's trouble at the farm, then what?" Atticus asked. "Are we going to be living out here in these woods for the next ten years?"

Tyrone stopped chewing, but didn't say anything. He looked at Atticus in a way that revealed he was worried about him.

"If there are soldiers at the farm, there's no point in picking a fight with them," Nate answered. "They won't be there forever. In a week or two, they'll be called away. They might burn down my house and barn before they leave. But they're not likely to find our caches buried out in the woods nearby.

It's those caches we need at the moment. We can always go to one of the many hunting shacks out here in the woods and stay there a few months. But we need supplies to do that. We already know Mel's place is safe at the moment. So we can go back there and get more food before leaving the area and looking for one of those hunting shacks to stay in for a while. Either way, we won't be sleeping on the ground out in the woods for much longer."

Deni tried to encourage Atticus. "You've been standing up to all of this well so far. It looks like it might be over soon, or at least the worst part of it." She put on a brave face and rubbed her stomach. "My spirits are a lot brighter now than they were when I woke up this morning. A full stomach will do that for you."

Atticus laughed quietly, keeping his voice low. "Yeah, I know what you mean. But there ain't any of us likely to be gaining weight anytime soon." He glanced at Tyrone. "Don't worry, I haven't given up yet."

Adding to Deni's efforts, Nate added, "There's a good chance there won't be anyone at the farm."

Brian blew dust off the lens of his Aimpoint sight and adjusted the brightness of the red dot while aiming his rifle at a tree. "That don't mean we can just move back home though. We're still being hunted by the government."

Atticus sighed and pretended to be devastated. "Shit, Brian. Don't you know Deni and Nate were trying to cheer me up? You just spoiled all their efforts." He shook with laughter and scratched at his grizzled beard.

Nervous release soon had everyone rolling on the ground laughing.

"Might as well laugh as cry," Atticus said.

It was Nate who put an end to it. "Okay guys, quiet. We *are* still being hunted." He slipped into his pack and grabbed his rifle. "You have a minute to make sure you don't leave anything behind. Then we're moving out."

Deni cleared her throat. "He's worried. We've had people hunt us before, but when it's the government after you, you're basically at war."

"We've had the Army after us before," Brian reminded her. "And he's been in a real war."

She put her hand on Brian's shoulder. "I know," she said softly. "We've all been in a kind of war since the plague, and it's wearing us down. Before we got ourselves into this last jam, he was hoping we could go back to the farm and find some peace, at least for a while. Everyone here has lost friends and family, so I don't have to tell you how he feels."

~~~

Nate purposely chose a route that provided them the best cover from the air. Highflying drones could not be seen or heard, and newer attack helicopters could spot targets on the ground from over the horizon, long before their targets knew they were in danger. They moved silently through a heavily forested area, staying in the shadows as much as possible and always undercover, skirting any clear area they came across.

By nightfall they were where they wanted to be and set up a simple bivouac camp.

Nate quickly ate and grabbed his rifle. "Deni and I'll take first watch. That way we'll get plenty of sleep before leaving early in the morning."

Deni wiped her hands on her dirty pants and stood. "Just so you know. Nate and I have decided that if we run into trouble at the farm, we're not heading back this way. We'll lead anyone hunting us in the other direction. So we'll be heading south."

Atticus and Tyrone exchanged furtive glances.

Brian started to protest. "That's bullshit."

Nate had walked away from the others, but he turned and came back. "Just sit tight, keep your eyes and ears open. Don't make any noise. Don't build any fires. Stay right here and wait for us, unless you know danger is coming close and you have to leave. If that happens, move upriver and wait it out. When you think it's safe, go back to Mel's cave and get more food." He handed a ring of keys to Brian. "Don't come looking for us. If we don't make it back here in a couple days, it means you can't do a thing for us."

Brian fumed, but remained quiet. Finally, he looked at Deni and Nate and said, "Just come back."

Deni tried to smile. "We will."

~~~

False dawn turned the dark and brooding forest gray. Though winter had finally released its cold grip on the land, the early morning hours still brought with it a cold that seeped through a jacket and left anyone standing watch shivering. Atticus felt the cold the most, but even the youngest one among them was not immune to it at this early hour.

Thankful to be able to move again and get his blood circulating, Brian emerged from heavy brush where he had been hiding while on watch and stepped over to Nate where he slept beside Deni. He reached down and shook his father's shoulder and quickly stepped back while calling to him in a low voice just loud enough he knew Nate could hear. "Time to wake up." Past experience had taught him it could be dangerous to wake his father from deep sleep. "Combat veterans are like that," his late mother had told him when he was five. She went on to explain that she always woke Nate by poking him with a broom handle. That put her at a safe distance, or at least out of reach. By the time the plague hit, Nate's demons had nearly gone away, or at least that's what those closest to him had thought, but Brian and Deni both had noticed a change in him over the last few months. He had come close to losing Brian and Deni too many times, and the stress was starting to show. The horrible death of Kendell had affected him as much as Brian. His mood, words, and actions told Brian especially that something had changed within him. Nate's old saying that if you keep kicking at rattlesnakes, sooner or later you'll get bit was his way of saying that he was becoming ever more worried their luck was running out. Yes, they had lost friends, close friends, but Nate was still fighting on only because he still had Brian and Deni. If he lost them, he might lose the will to go on. Mentally and physically exhausted himself, Brian understood the feeling.

The first thing Nate did was grab his rifle.

"Time to wake up," Brian said again, just to be sure.

Nate sat up and looked around. "Yeah," he said, in a whisper barely audible to Brian only a few feet away.

Deni woke up on her own.

Nate whispered to her, "Time to go."

She coughed. "This will either turn out to be a really good day, or a really really bad one."

"As long as we make it back here alive and unhurt," Nate muttered. He quickly rolled his sleeping bag up and stuffed it in the top of his backpack. "We'll eat a little something before we go, but we better make it quick."

"No fire and no hot coffee, I presume," Deni quipped.

"No eggs, bacon, grits, and biscuits, either," Nate whispered.

Deni made a face. "I can't stand grits. Must be a Southern thing."

"I can take them or leave them myself," Nate responded. "Brian hates them. I guess this is when I say something about painting with a broad brush or something."

Deni fished for some freeze-dried food in her pack. "Yeah, you remember that the next time you two or one of our friends start in on Yankees."

Brian smiled in the fast-brightening woods. "You guys must be married. Be careful today. I'm going back on watch." He slipped into the shadows and found a place to hide.

Nate and Deni had nothing else to say while eating their meager meal and listening to Atticus snore. In less than ten minutes, they grabbed their packs and rifles and disappeared into the gray, brooding forest.

Traveling quiet meant traveling slow. With less than four miles to the farm, they were in no hurry. Rushing through the woods could get them killed. Veterans themselves, they knew how well soldiers were trained to ambush, and they took every precaution. The closer they got to the farm, the slower they traveled and the more they used their eyes and ears, constantly scanning, searching for any sign of danger. Their senses on high alert and turned to full volume, the two felt ever more alive as they crept ever closer to what could be their death. Each had total confidence and trust in the other. Past experience had given them that more than the fact they loved each other. They had both seen the elephant many times and proven themselves.

In between overworking their eyes and ears in a desperate attempt to see and hear their enemy before their enemy saw them, they examined any bare ground they came across for boot prints. Not finding any was of little relief.

They approached the fields on the west side of the farm and stayed as far back from the tree line as they could and still see anything. Nate scanned what little he could see with his binoculars. "The field has grown up so much I can't see more than the roof of the house and barn from here. Where I last grew tomatoes, the weeds are as tall as a man in places."

"We'll have to circle around and get closer to the house." Sweat trickled from under Deni's helmet and down her right temple. The day had grown warmer as the sun had climbed in the sky. "We might even go a little further and check out the driveway for sign anyone's been down it lately."

Nate slipped his binoculars under his jacket and let it hang from his neck. "Good idea. We'll do that first and then come back to the house and have a look from a distance."

Thirty minutes later, they were both relieved somewhat, but still nervous. There was evidence the driveway had been used within a week or two, but only once. Tall weeds had grown up in the driveway and some of them had been flattened by a vehicle. Nate surmised it was probably a Humvee. Soldiers had come looking for them. Finding nothing, they left without burning the house or barn.

Deni kept low behind a pine tree. "They may have booby-trapped the place. I'm not so sure they refrained from burning the house and barn out of kindness. They could've left the buildings as bait for a trap."

Nate nodded. "Yep." He motioned with his head and eased away from the driveway and deeper into the woods, circling around so they could get a look at the house and barn.

The hardpan around the house and barn hadn't grown up so much with weeds, and Nate could scan both buildings and the surrounding area with his binoculars from his position 20 feet back from the edge of the clearing and well hidden in the woods. He lowered his binoculars and bit his lower lip. Glancing at Deni, he shook his head. "I don't see anything," he whispered. "But I'm still nervous." He considered the situation for about ten seconds, and then motioned for her to follow.

They retreated into the woods until Nate stopped and waited for her to catch up. He rubbed the salt-and-pepper stubble on his chin and appeared to still be considering what to do next. "I think we should go on to the road and see what's going on there. There's a hill about half a mile north of the drive. We'll take advantage of it and have a good look-see with the binoculars."

Squatting low next to him, she raised an eyebrow and regarded his face, as if she were trying to read his mind. "Okay. We can't be too careful. An hour of time is certainly worth trading for all the hours of the rest of our lives."

Nate started to move on.

"Wait." Deni touched his arm as he went by.

He stopped and looked at her, his face a question mark.

"I'm mentioning this now, so you'll have time to mull it over in your head over the next hour or so." She tapped her military armor with her left forefinger and then her helmet. "I should be the one that goes out there in the open when the time comes. I've got this armor and you've got a better sniper rifle than me."

He shook his head and started to speak.

"Don't answer now. You've got plenty of time to think about it. Decide after we get back here. I think you'll agree that I'm right."

His chest rose and fell in silence. He swallowed and then moved on without a word.

They stayed 50 yards back from the road until they reached the tall hill. Easing up on all fours, they got close enough to see what kind of prevailing brush grew along the side of the road at their exact location. Both of them covered their faces up to their eyes with olive drab mosquito netting and cut brush to add to their camouflage, helping each other diffuse the outline of their head and shoulders, attaching a few strategically placed leafy limbs to their backpacks. They wanted to be as difficult to spot as possible and weren't going to bet their lives on anything less than their best effort. Snipers were trained to be expert at spotting enemy hiding in brush from long distance, and they both knew it.

Nate scanned every inch of both the left and right side of the road as far as he could see from his angle. He also looked for tire tracks and boot prints both in the road and along the edge of the woods line, lingering long in the area where his driveway connected with the road. The driveway was too far for him to see any tracks or boot prints, but he examined it as closely as he could anyway. There just might be something that could warn him of danger. Perhaps a dark place in the clay where someone had dug and buried something like a landmine or even a motion sensor. He handed the binoculars over to Deni. "Have a look. You might catch something I missed."

She spent 30 minutes examining every inch of the road and woods line. "Nothing," she whispered, and handed the binoculars back to Nate.

They backed away from the road 30 yards, and then made their way to the other side of the hill's crest, so they could have a look in the opposite direction. The results were the same. They found nothing suspicious. No sign of danger anywhere that they could see.

"Well," Nate said, "let's head back to the house."

They came in from a different angle and scanned the scene with binoculars again. Still not satisfied, Nate tapped her on the shoulder and they backed off from the edge of the clearing. Fifty yards into the woods, they stopped to have a short conversation.

Nate removed his boonie hat and used it to mop his forehead. "In the interest of staying alive, I think we should head down to the river, cross to the south side of the farm, and then work our way up the hill and do the same thing all over again from the south side."

Deni had a different idea. "Why not across the driveway and make our way around from the east? We can check out the road to the south a little better, also."

Nate put his boonie hat back on. "It's six of one, half a dozen of another. Your idea may actually turn out to be better. I just wanted to check out the river landing. They could have a boatload of soldiers down there waiting. Also, I have caches buried in the area to the south. On the other hand, they may have a platoon of soldiers waiting on the blind side of that curve south of the farm. If they do, we'll be sorry if we don't check it out."

Deni coughed. "Yeah. They have all the advantages. They can hit and miss. We can't miss once."

"One mistake and it's over," Nate agreed. "However, we have to be back with the others by nightfall or they'll be worried. We don't have time to do everything possible and make it back to them before dark."

"Might as well swing down by the river," Deni said. "I have no objections."

Nate half smiled. "If we get killed, you can blame it all on me."

She coughed but didn't smile back.

Easing their way down slope, into the wetter lands, they took their time, turning south just before reaching the river.

There was no boat at the landing, no soldiers. They came across no boot prints and found no sign anyone had been in the area lately. Still, they refused to let their guard down. As far as they knew they were still being hunted, and they were not taking any chances. The farm was an obvious place for a trap. Nate was homesick and wanted to return to a somewhat normal life, even if he never admitted it. Even so, he was risking Deni and his life only because they needed the supplies buried in several caches around the farm. His interest in the house and barn was more out of homesickness than anything else. It prompted him to move in once more and take another look from a different angle. What they would find changed everything.

Nate scanned the front of the house through his binoculars. For the first time, he had a good look at the front door and windows. The first thing he noticed was everything was intact. The door hadn't been knocked down or the window shutters broken. The second thing he noticed was something white on the door. He checked the barn and found no evidence anyone had bothered it.

"Take a look at the door for me, will you?" He handed Deni the binoculars. "You have younger eyes."

She examined the door for several seconds and lowered the binoculars. "Looks like someone nailed or stapled a sign to the door. It's too far for me to read."

Nate raised an eyebrow, a look of surprise on his face. "I guess I'll have to move in and get close enough I can read it with the binoculars. Might be Mrs. MacKay's people asking for help or something."

"So you haven't even considered our discussion?" Deni stared at him.

He knew what she was referring to. "Okay damn it. But take your time and be as careful as possible. Don't get any closer than you need to to read the damn sign."

Her eyes lit up. "You did say I have younger eyes. That means I won't have to get as close."

"I hope it doesn't say if you can read this you're dead."

She looked out across the clearing for a second and then back at him. "My, you're cheerful this afternoon."

"I'm really going to be pissed if you get shot."

"That'll ruin my day too." Deni hung the binoculars around her neck and slipped them under her jacket so they wouldn't be hanging down and snagging on brush while she crawled to the nearest cover out in the clearing. "Someone takes a shot at me; just make sure it's his last. My armor might save me."

"He'll be wearing armor too, if he's a soldier. The armor they have now can withstand what I'm shooting."

"That's good to know. I'm wearing the same armor." She looked back and smiled at him while on her stomach. "Aim for his face. I'll keep my head and butt so low about the only thing they'll see is my pack mysteriously moving across the ground in the tall grass over there."

Nate almost smiled. "Move slow enough and they won't even notice that. Just take your time, Deni. We have all afternoon. And don't get any closer than you need to to read the sign."

"I promise." Deni slithered on her belly a few feet and stopped to look back. "I'm going to swing around to the left some. The grass and weeds are taller there."

Nate nodded. "Keep an eye out for rattlers. It's been warming up lately and they'll be out crawling. You get bit in the upper body by a big one, you probably won't make it."

She shook her head. "So cheerful today."

"Just be careful and make it back here in one piece. I'll be full of cheer. Might even smile once."

~~~

Deni continued her slow progress, dragging her body along on her belly, staying as low as possible. Occasionally, she would sweep the weeds in front of her with the rifle barrel. Perhaps that would scare off any diamondback rattlers or at least prompt it to rattle and give her a warning.

One problem she immediately noticed was that her attempt to stay well hidden in the tall grass and weeds prevented her from actually seeing the house, and she was soon less and less sure of her exact position and exactly where the front door was. She could see the roof of the barn and used that as a guide until dead reckoning told her she was close to where she wanted to be. Turning to her right and heading directly toward the house, she hoped to move just close enough to the edge of the tall weeds and grass that she could see the sign and read it through Nate's binoculars.

She stopped five feet from the edge of the taller grass and pulled the binoculars out of her jacket. Propping herself up a little higher on her elbows, she steadied the binoculars as she looked through them. The lettering on the sign was too small for her to read. She strained and tried to focus on the message but couldn't see it well enough to read what it said.

Damn it. She slowly inched closer. When she ran out of tall grass and still couldn't read the words, she realized she would have to expose herself to anyone waiting along the tree line with a rifle if she was actually going to read the message. *Looks like I failed this mission.*

Just as she was about to turn back and give up, movement along the tree line behind and to the left of the house caught her attention. She trained the binoculars on that area and saw nothing at first. Then someone moved into a beam of sunlight that had slanted into the tree-shaded sniper's hide and illuminated the person's face. She focused on it for a second and recognized Caroline. *What?* The features were familiar, but the face was somehow different, harried, rigid with tension. Even at that distance, their eyes seemed to connect for a second through the glass of the binoculars. That was when she saw death staring back at her. She shivered and lowered the binoculars and her head. Instinctively, she knew that if Caroline saw her hiding out there at that moment she would kill her before she had a chance to see who she was. Nate had told her Caroline had been through seven kinds of hell, but seemed to be better as time passed. The short glimpse Deni had just seen of her was more than enough to tell her Caroline was in a killing mood.

Deni backed deeper into the tall grass, lying flat and moving as slow as she possibly could. Her life depended on Caroline not seeing her out there, and she knew it. Following the same route she had taken before, she pulled herself along on her belly until she was within hearing distance of Nate. "You won't believe it."

"Keep coming until you're back in the tree line again," Nate said, seemingly ignoring her words.

It took her several minutes to get far enough back in the tree line that she felt safe enough to stop sliding along her belly. "Caroline's out there hiding behind and to the left of the house."

"What?" Nate closed the distance between them by crawling on his hands and knees.

Exhausted from her long crawl, Deni caught her breath and mopped her forehead with a jacket sleeve. "Only saw her for a second. But I can tell you she's dangerous at the moment. Even from that distance and through the binoculars, looking into her eyes sent chills down my spine."

Nate frowned. "Oh shit. Something's happened to her. You're right. She could be dangerous." He looked toward the house. "Was she alone?"

"Only saw her for a second and no one else." Deni took a long swallow from a canteen. "Scared me more than if I'd seen a Special Forces sniper out there."

"Yeah, I've seen that look before. Though it's men she hates. And for good reason."

Deni put her canteen away. "What're we going to do?"

Nate raised an eyebrow. "It would be wrong to just leave her out here. It's obvious something's happened. She needs our help. The problem is helping her without getting shot."

"Well," Deni said, "I'm sure she can recognize our voices. Should be safe enough for us to get close and yell her name and identify ourselves. We can do all that while behind cover."

"Okay." Nate glanced toward the house. "I would feel better if you stayed here and I did it alone. But like I said, she hates men, and hearing your voice might make the difference."

She looked up at the sky for a second. "Nice of you to give me permission to come along."

Nate had a strange look on his face for a second. "This isn't about me being a chauvinist pig. We're discussing the best way to stay alive. Someday when we're not fighting for survival, I promise I won't boss you around at all. You can do whatever you want while I work the farm. I won't care if you sleep all day, never cook a meal, or wash a dish, or help in the field. You can go back to college, get a job – if that's possible again someday – whatever. I don't care. Just be alive and healthy and happy and live to be one hundred. In the meantime, I won't be apologizing for doing everything possible to keep you alive until the day comes we can put our rifles away except for target practice and hunting."

She laughed. "Wow. I wasn't expecting a speech."

"At least you didn't call it a rant." Nate wanted to change the subject. "Since she didn't take a shot at you, I'm guessing you're pretty sure she never saw you."

"Oh, I'm certain she never saw me. If she had I would be dead. I'm telling you, she looks like she wants to kill somebody."

"Well," Nate said, "let's go. We'll make our way around to the back of the house. Slow and easy like."

"We'll just pretend we don't want to get shot," Deni added.

~~~

Forty-five minutes later, Nate and Deni hid behind thick pine trees ten yards apart, still searching for Caroline.

Nate signaled for Deni to yell out Caroline's name.

Deni yelled out, "Caroline! It's Deni."

Nate scanned the woods for any sign of danger.

No answer.

Deni yelled out Caroline's name and identified herself again.

Finally, Caroline's voice came back to them and echoed in the forest. "Are you alone?"

"Nate is with me," Deni answered.

"Have you seen any soldiers?"

"Not lately. We've been hiding from them," Deni answered. "We came to check out the farm and were worried it was a trap. While we were looking for any sign of soldiers hiding in the woods, we saw you." When no answer came back, Deni asked, "Are you okay?"

"I'm unharmed. Soldiers killed a lot of people, but Samantha and I escaped."

Nate had not seen her, but her voice had allowed him to locate her approximate position. "Is it okay for us to come on in? You're an old friend, and we don't want to just leave you here alone. We have food and other supplies with us."

Samantha spoke for the first time. "Deni, I think Caroline is sick. She's afraid of everything."

"She has no reason to be afraid of us." Deni changed her voice to a softer tone. "Have you eaten lately, Samantha? We have plenty of food."

"She won't let me go to you."

Nate broke in. "Caroline. If I step out from behind this tree, are you going to shoot me? You know Deni and I are friends and we mean you no harm."

Caroline's response was incongruous. "Last thing I saw, they were torturing the old horse woman, MacKay."

"Who?" Nate asked. "Soldiers?"

"They killed Ramiro." Caroline stepped out of the shadows and emerged into a small clearing, holding Samantha's hand at her side. "They also killed more than a dozen others from the horse farm."

Nate lowered his rifle and stepped from behind the tree. "You'll be safer with us."

"Not if you two keep yelling and talking so loud," Caroline said. "If there are any soldiers in this part of the county, they know we're here now."

Nate smiled. "First things first. We didn't want to get shot by you." The fact Caroline had her right hand occupied by holding Samantha's relieved his worries to some degree. He stepped closer. "You two look like you've been through it."

"Yeah," Deni said.

Samantha rushed to Deni. Deni dropped to her knees and held the little girl. "Are you hurt?" Deni asked.

Pent-up emotion poured out onto Samantha's face. "No. Caroline took care of me. She protected me from those mean men. They were hurting people wherever we went. We saw dead people in the woods. One of them cut Mrs. MacKay with a knife."

Deni held her again. "Oh God. Did we cause all of this?"

Nate glanced at Deni for a second and then kept his eyes on Caroline. "Somebody's been here. They left a sign on the front door of the house."

"Yeah," Caroline said, with a strange look on her face. "Soldiers. They came and looked around a little a few days ago. Then they put that sign on the door and left. But I don't believe them."

Nate raised an eyebrow. "Don't believe what?"

"What the sign says."

Nate asked, "What did the sign say?"

Caroline didn't answer.

Deni stood. "I never got a chance to read it. Never got that close."

"I did," Caroline said. "It says the soldiers are no longer looking for Nate Williams; Deni Williams; Brian Williams; Atticus Hayes, and Tyrone Hayes. It also says you can stop hiding and come back to your farm now. It's signed by Colonel Donovan."

Deni and Nate both stared at Caroline in amazement.

Caroline looked at them like they were crazy. "You don't believe that bullshit, do you?"

Nate checked the position of the sun in the sky. "Right now we need to get back to the others. They'll be worried if we don't make it back by dark."

Deni wasn't ready to let the subject go. "What about the idea we're not being hunted anymore?"

Nate looked at her and Caroline. He inhaled deeply, a question mark on his face. "Who knows? Maybe Donovan called the assholes in Washington off some way. Right now we have to get back to the others."

Chapter 16

Brian peered into the darkening woods and gripped his rifle tighter. He thought he had heard something a moment before, but thought it might have been a squirrel late to its nest and in a hurry to get to its bed before it got dark. Tyrone and Atticus were in camp 30 yards behind him, conversing quietly about what to do if the others didn't show up before dark.

Worry heightened his senses, and he heard Samantha's cough from 35 yards deep into the darkness, though he didn't know at the time it was Samantha.

Something scraped against a palmetto frond to his left. He turned his whole body in that direction; ready to raise his rifle and fire.

Nate's voice came from out of nowhere. "It's your father. Don't shoot." Nate's indistinct form emerged from the darkness only five yards away. "We have Caroline and a little girl with us."

"Caroline?" Brian hesitated only for a second out of surprise. "Come on in. Any trouble?"

Deni suddenly appeared beside Nate. "No trouble. But things may have changed for the better."

Brian turned. "Well, come on to the camp. We'll prepare something for you to eat." He led them to where Atticus and Tyrone were waiting. They had heard them talking.

"There must be a story behind all of this." Brian couldn't see faces in the dark. "Who is the little girl?"

"Samantha," Caroline answered, while Samantha clung to her, holding her hand. "I'm happy to see you're still alive and kicking," she added.

"Same here," Brian said. "You and little Samantha both. Uh. We lost Kendell, though."

Caroline froze in the dark for a second. "Damn it! He was a good young man. He fought like hell when the terrorists attacked the horse farm, and later he backed me all the way when I killed that weasel child killer."

"He was my best friend," Brian almost whispered. "He saved my life. I'll never forget him."

~~~

It was too dark to see, so Nate chanced a small fire to provide light and to warm their freeze-dried food.

Brian watched his father work. "You always said no fires while we're being hunted."

Nate looked up from cooking. "It's a small risk. We'll put it out as soon as we're through eating."

After the four new arrivals had eaten, Brian dug around in his pack and came up with some cocoa powder. He heated water on the fire to make a cup of cocoa for Samantha. "You probably haven't had anything sweet for a while." He handed her the cup.

Samantha silently took it and sipped the contents. Never far from Caroline, she sat next to her and seemed to be more at ease as she got used to the strangers.

Atticus and Tyrone had been standing guard while Brian helped the others prepare a meal and eat. After 30 minutes, Tyrone came back to camp, leaving Atticus on security duty. "Earlier, Deni said things have changed for the better. What's that about?"

Nate answered, "There's a sign on the front door of the house signed by Colonel Donovan. It says we're not being hunted anymore and we can go home now."

"You believe that?" Tyrone asked.

"Not completely. Not yet," Nate answered. "If it's true, it means those at Mrs. MacKay's horse farm can also go back home. We'll head that away tomorrow morning and take a careful look sometime in the next day or two."

Caroline spoke up. "I can tell you that not all of them will be going home. Some of them are dead, killed by the Army or CIA. I don't know. They were not wearing regular military uniforms. But they acted and talked like soldiers."

"Spooks," Nate commented.

"Like the bastard we let go," Brian added. "I wonder how many people we killed by being too weak to do what we knew was the best thing."

Nate moved closer to Brian. He spoke in a low voice, "We're all feeling the same thing. And we're all just as confused. What's the right thing to do? Sometimes the answer doesn't come so easily. I do know that human beings caught between a rock and a hard place naturally become hard themselves. The better side of us resists that and clings to our humanity. Some people resist it more than others. Some people are cold and cruel only when they have to be. A conscience can be a terrible thing at times. But it's what separates us from animals."

"But that's what we're becoming," Brian insisted. "This is worse than war. We're not just following orders and relying on others to decide who dies and who is let go and what's the best thing to do for the greater good. It's all on us."

"Yes it is," Nate said. "And we're going to make mistakes. You almost died because I made an enemy of Slim when I broke his jaw. I should've either left him alone or killed him. He nearly killed you because of my actions."

"Well, it can't be undone now." Brian sat down. "Don't worry about me. I'm just pissed that people were hurt and killed."

Nate stomped the small fire out. "Someday we'll look back on this time in our lives and thank God we managed to struggle through it all so we could enjoy the better years. The wild card now is what Washington has in store for America. There's no way to know if we face freedom or tyranny."

Tyrone cleared his throat. "It's not looking good. We damn sure don't want to risk coming out of hiding just because someone left a sign on a door."

"Yeah," Nate agreed, "we need to talk to people we can trust. We'll start for MacKay's place as soon as daylight comes."

"So you're thinking we can't trust Col. Donovan anymore?" Deni asked.

Nate thought for a moment. "I don't know."

~~~

Just past 2 AM, a thunderstorm came rolling in. No one had predicted rain, and they had not bothered to put up a tarp. One was quickly stretched over a rope between two trees, and everyone but Deni, who was on guard duty, was soon back asleep.

Nate pulled security the last two hours before false dawn. When the dark woods faded to slightly lighter gray, he walked over and woke Brian and Deni up. The others heard them preparing a quick breakfast of cold reconstituted freeze-dried beef stroganoff. They woke up and joined them. Everyone was in a hurry to get moving, except Samantha, who was still sleepy.

It took them all of 15 minutes to eat and pack up. They pushed through the weeping woods as quietly as possible, but no one wasted time lingering. They needed answers to questions that hung over their heads like a guillotine. Impatience urged them on.

A buck and two does burst out of a palmetto patch and gave everyone a fright. Caroline looked down at Samantha. "Just deer. I see their white tails bouncing as they run."

The little girl stood on her toes and tried to see over the weeds but was too late.

A dim sun appeared through fog and cloud, burning away some of the moisture in the heavy air. They moved on. Noon came and went. They agreed not to waste time. They would eat when they made camp that night. Samantha ate during a ten-minute rest, but the adults just drank water.

Mid afternoon found them working their way through a tangled mess of thorny blackberry brush and windfalls from a past hurricane. Caroline had difficulty lifting her artificial leg over the logs and fell twice. Once they were through the wait-a-minute thorns and windfalls, she had no trouble keeping up.

Samantha grew more tired as the day wore on. Nate noticed it and insisted they stop every 30 minutes to let her rest. "We're not going to make it to the farm today, no matter how fast we travel."

"I was going to say something," Caroline said, "but…"

"Never worry about speaking up," Nate assured her. "The only reason we're in a hurry is because we have questions we want answers to. There's no tactical reason why we can't slow down. The slower we travel, the less likely we are to walk into an ambush, anyway."

~~~

That night, Nate and Deni stood first watch. Deni edged over his way so they could have a quiet conversation. "I didn't want to say anything in front of the others, especially Brian, but from what Caroline was saying it's possible that Mrs. MacKay is dead. Hell, they could all be dead."

Keeping his voice down, Nate said, "It does seem like things have really gotten out of control. It could be the beginning of a whole new nightmare. If it is, we could be spending the rest of our lives hiding in these woods and living like animals. The last thing I want to do is drag you and Brian into a civil war. The chances of any of us surviving that are so small and the chances of us making any difference are so tiny, it just doesn't make sense to be a part of it. I'm more worried for our future at this moment than I ever was in the middle of a gunfight. Battles end. The nightmare we're facing now has no ending."

Deni slung her rifle out of the way across her back and held him. "It's obvious some people have decided to take advantage of the chaos and seize control of this country. The people's welfare is the last thing on their mind. I do not believe this is just spooks and soldiers getting out of hand. They have orders. Orders straight from the top."

Nate put his left arm around her and pulled her to him. "This is too big for us to stop. Either the military will follow Washington's orders and become an instrument of oppression, or they will execute a military coup. Both of those scenarios scare the hell out of me. If there is a coup, power will be handed back to civilian government and constitutional law restored only if the officer corps of every branch is populated with living saints. I wouldn't bet my life on that. George Washington was given several chances to become King of America and turned it down every time. There are not many men born in one hundred generations who would turn down a chance to yield absolute power."

"Now you're really scaring me." Deni held him tighter. "Besides, there are many men and women who don't want absolute power. There are many who don't want any power at all. They don't want the responsibility."

"You won't find many people like that in the officer corps. Not only did they ask for their jobs, they had to work very hard to earn their positions, positions of responsibility. No, people who don't want responsibility don't become military officers."

Deni looked toward the others sleeping under a tarp, though she could not see them in the dark. "But military officers do tend to be men and women of a higher moral fiber than the average person. They may not be saints, but I would trust the worst of them more than the best politician."

Nate chuckled under his breath to keep the noise down. "Yeah, but some of them become politicians."

~~~

Mid-afternoon the next day, Nate and Deni approached Mrs. MacKay's horse farm with extreme caution. They left the others several miles back where they would be safe.

"We might be close enough I can see something with binoculars if I climb that big oak over there," Nate said.

Deni slipped out of her pack and laid her rifle across it. "You're too big to be climbing trees. Give me the binoculars."

"I won't have any trouble climbing this one. There are plenty of handy limbs." Nate shed his pack and rifle and then his load-bearing harness, with its pouches that held 20-round magazines for his rifle. "Keep an eye out for trouble while I'm up there."

A few minutes later, Nate was able to peer over the tops of distant trees well enough he could see part of the horse farm. Scanning with his binoculars, he could make out people, looking like little ants, working in the fields. Everything appeared normal and peaceful. He still wasn't satisfied, but that's all he could see from his position.

Nate climbed down and put on his load bearing harness and then slipped his pack on.

Deni regarded him from ten yards away. "Well, what did you see?"

Nate grabbed his rifle and checked the safety on it again. "Looks normal from here. People are working in the fields. The house is still there and the horse stalls. I couldn't see the other buildings. We'll have to move closer to get a better look."

Deni raised an eyebrow. "That's encouraging." She smiled. "Nice of you to finally let me in on it."

He acted as if he hadn't heard a thing she said. "Let's get moving. Real easy and slow."

She looked up at the sky for a second and had a strange smile on her face. "When you're worried, you become really hard to get through to."

He had already taken several steps. After stopping and looking over his shoulder, he grunted, "Huh?"

She tilted her head and regarded him for a few seconds. "I said you shouldn't talk so much. We're trying to be tactical and stealthy here."

Nate looked at her like she was crazy for a second, shook his head, and started walking again.

~~~

Children played on the front porch and under the wide oaks in the front yard. From his hiding position 300 yards away, Nate scanned the scene through his binoculars. "I can't believe it, but everything looks normal." He handed Deni the binoculars. "Take a look."

"I can hear children laughing and playing." Deni took the binoculars and saw exactly what Nate had just described. She swung her attention back to the front porch and froze for two seconds as she peered through the binoculars. "Mrs. MacKay just walked out of the house onto the porch. She's alive."

"Injured?" Nate asked.

"I can't see any wound dressings. She seems a little stiff when she moves, but it could be mostly her advanced age and the ordeal she's been through." Deni handed Nate the binoculars.

Nate didn't bother to look again. "We'll move on in, slow."

Deni grabbed him by the shoulder. "Wait a minute. I would like to know what's going on with you. Are you angry with me about something?"

His eyebrows knitted in puzzlement. "Angry with you? No. I'm worried. I'm also pissed that some asshole in Washington, or some group of assholes, is taking advantage of the weakened state of the country and the people, adding to their miseries.

I'm not sure if someone wants to be a total dictator or what. But it damn sure looks like that might be what's going on. And it's also obvious that there's a power struggle going on, and the people are the ones suffering for it."

"What about the military?" Deni asked. "Donovan isn't the only decent officer in the Army or the other branches. I'm guessing the military is between Washington and the people. That doesn't mean every individual officer and noncom is going to do the right thing, but the great majority of them will stand with the people. If Washington keeps pushing, there's going to be a standoff."

Nate regarded her with a grim face. "If not enough in the military stand with the people and say hell no, there's going to be a civil war. Factions of the military will be fighting each other. Political cabals in Washington will be fighting each other. Civilians will choose their side and join in the bloodbath. When the smoke settles, every town or county could be ruled by a warlord. Or if Washington wins, America could look like Nazi Germany in ten years. I'm not sure which would be worse."

She swallowed and looked back at him as a shadow fell across her face. "Damn Nate, you sure know how to conjure up a nightmare."

"This isn't the America we had before the plague killed most of the human race. It's not the same government, the same people, or the same nation as a whole. Anything could happen now. There are nightmares aplenty, and you don't need an imagination to conjure them up. These nightmares can become reality."

"What do you mean, not the same people?" Deni asked.

"You know what I mean. Everyone has changed. None of us are the same people we were before the plague. Like Brian said, we've been forced to give up a little of our humanity every day, slice by slice. That was part of the price of survival."

Deni nodded. "And in times of struggle like this, when people have been afraid and hungry for so long, they reach out for anything to save them. Right now, millions of Americans would vote another Hitler into power. Fascism, Communism, a Big Brother totally controlling government could easily look like the way out of this nightmare for many. Let the government take care of us. What good is freedom and self-determination when you're starving and forever under the threat of attack from violent brigands roaming a lawless land?"

"Yeah." Nate looked toward the house. "Every time we think things are going to get better, they get worse."

"But you're not giving up."

Nate reached out and lightly touched her face. "That'll be the day. Not as long as people I care about are still alive."

~~~

Thirty-five minutes later, Nate and Deni were only 50 yards from a guard just inside the front gate. Both were behind bullet stopping cover. Nate yelled out, "It's Nate and Deni Williams coming in. Don't shoot."

The Hispanic man got behind a tree. A few seconds later, he responded, "Come on in slow with your empty hands over your head."

A Caucasian man in a sniper's hide heard them. He aimed a rifle in Nate and Deni's direction.

Nate and Deni both knew where the sniper's hide was, since Nate had helped them build it. Deni saw the man aiming their way. "Tell your friend to stop pointing his rifle at us. We're here to see Mrs. MacKay. We heard she has been injured."

The man didn't wait to be told. He pointed the muzzle skyward.

Nate and Deni slowly came out into the open with their hands in the air. They had their rifles slung on their shoulders. The Hispanic man recognized them and smiled, waving them on in. "Welcome! I'll go with you to the house."

Nate and Deni stayed close to their escort. Anyone with a twitchy trigger finger would think twice about taking a shot at them if he might hit one of their own. Nate suspected fear and anger to be prominent emotions on the farm, and many who lost family members would be out for revenge. He was particularly worried about the fact Deni wore military equipment, including Kevlar helmet and body armor, and carried military weapons. For that reason, he made no attempt to hide his efforts to keep Deni between him and the Hispanic man.

She gave him a sideward glance but said nothing.

Two women saw them approaching and soon had all the children corralled into the house. They were not taking any chances.

Armed men and women began to appear from their hiding places behind trees. A few of them recognized Nate and Deni and waved, but a few gave them a cold stare.

The Hispanic man escorting them nodded at Nate and then lifted his worn-out boonie hat to Deni. "I must go back to my post." He turned and headed for the gate at a fast walk, holding his rifle in both hands.

Mrs. MacKay appeared at the door and stepped out onto the porch. Even from 70 yards away, Nate could see the wounds on her arm and face. At that distance they appeared as red lines. Long before the three reached the steps of the porch, he could see the sutures and the puffy red swelling that looked alarmingly like the beginnings of infection.

Deni smiled. "I'm relieved to see you on your feet. Caroline told us you had been injured, and Nate and I were both worried about you."

That old simmering rage boiled Nate's blood.

MacKay noticed. "Have I made you angry already, Nate?"

Nate flinched and tried to soften the features of his face.

Deni glanced his way and then spoke for him. "He's just so angry with those who hurt you he forgot to smile."

"That's about it," Nate said. "I think someone needs to take you to the clinic in town. Those cuts are too red. They're starting to fester."

The old horse farmer rolled her eyes. "Not you too. I've been told that at least five times the last three hours. The fact is there's way too much to do around here for me to be traipsing off to town."

"Do you even know if the clinic is still in operation?" Deni asked. "After what Caroline told us... We have a lot of questions."

MacKay headed for the door. "Come on in and have a seat. We'll fill you in on current events. But then you have to fill us in on what's been happening with you and yours." She stopped and turned back to them. "You mentioned Caroline. Is there anyone with her?"

"Yes," Deni answered, "the little girl Samantha. They're both well."

The old woman put her hands together. "Thank God. We thought they may have been with the group that was murdered." She led them into the living room.

"How many?" Nate asked.

MacKay froze for a second and then went on to the chair she was heading for and sat down. "We're not sure exactly. There are 21 people missing. But some of them are probably just lost or ran away." She blinked tears. "I know Ramiro was murdered. It happened before my eyes. He was never the same after losing his wife, Rita. And now he's gone. They were both good people and old friends."

Nate pressed her with another question, though he could see she was upset. He needed to know what the situation was, and these first questions were just the beginning. "Caroline told us you split into groups when you went into hiding in the woods. She also told us that people in at least one of those groups were slaughtered by CIA operatives. Her estimate was over a dozen."

"Fourteen," MacKay said softly. She spoke her next words louder. "We believe 14 were murdered in that one group."

Nate still hadn't sat down. He leaned his rifle against the wall behind him and slipped out of his pack. After sitting next to Deni on a couch, he asked, "Did anyone with the CIA try to stop these crimes? Or did they all seem to be okay with it?"

MacKay focused her eyes on a different time and place. "One of them killed the man who murdered Ramiro and cut me. He and another one let us go. Kramer was the name of the one who refused to let his partner kill us."

Deni and Nate exchanged glances.

"Brian will want to hear about this," Deni said. "He'll feel a lot better about us letting Kramer go."

Nate nodded. "He's not the only one."

MacKay slumped in her chair. "I'm afraid I have news Brian will take hard. Renee and her father were among those killed."

Nate rubbed his forehead and looked down. "You're right; he'll take it hard. Renee and Brian were becoming friends."

"And Nate and I both considered her and Austin to be our friend," Deni added. "Austin was a good man." She clenched her hands into fists. "Instead of helping the people, Washington's sending killers to murder them." She spoke for MacKay's benefit. "Someone is taking advantage of the chaos to further personal plans, and that someone is our so-called president and whoever is backing him."

"That's the question." Nate's forehead furrowed with worry. "Who's backing him? I mean besides those he selected for Congress and the Supreme Court. We have no idea how big the problem is or if it's limited to America. This may be something that involves crooks in many countries. What's going on in Europe? Who knows? We've been told very little."

"And how much of what we've been told is accurate?" Deni asked.

MacKay waved her hand. "That's all beyond my control. I can only deal with what happens on this farm. Washington's another world as far as I'm concerned."

"Normally I would agree with you," Nate said. "Politics has never been much of an interest of mine. But what's happening in Washington has already cost us dearly and is likely to do so again."

MacKay's irritation came to the surface. "We can't even vote, so what're we going to do? Are you two talking about civil war? I've seen enough good people die needlessly. I won't have any part of going against the military. They'll just slaughter every one of us."

"We might be able to avoid serious bloodshed by spreading the word and organizing the people." Nate noticed that he was upsetting his elderly friend and stopped. "I guess there's no point in discussing this now."

"Yes," Deni agreed. She changed the subject. "We went to the farm and found a note on the door supposedly signed by Col. Donovan. It said we could go home; that we were not being hunted anymore; and that the situation had changed." She looked at MacKay. "Can you verify that?"

MacKay seemed to think for a moment. "There are no guarantees, but you know that. As you can see, we're back home and not hiding anymore. As far as I know, we're safe for now." She shook her head. "Exactly what the hell changed to cause them to suddenly stop hunting us is as much of a mystery to me as their reasoning for hunting us and killing over a dozen of our people in the first place." She glanced at her ticking antique grandfather clock. "The National Guard broadcasts information several times every 24 hours. You might have time to go get the others and bring them back with you before the next broadcast and you can all listen at the same time."

"Uh," Nate hesitated for a second. "The only reason they went after you and your people is because you were known to be friends of ours. They were simply trying to get information from you that could lead them to us. It's part of whatever's going on in Washington." With downcast eyes, he said, "I'm sorry this happened."

MacKay leaned over from her chair and touched his hand. "You don't have to tell me that."

"Well," Nate cleared his throat, "when Brian learns what's happened, he's going to be upset about it. For several reasons." He glanced at Deni. "You might as well stay here while I go get the others. I'll break the bad news to Brian. It'll give him time to simmer down before we arrive." He spoke to MacKay again, "I don't think we should stay long under the circumstances. We'll listen to the broadcast and leave. There's no guarantee our presence here won't still bring trouble to you. Caroline and Samantha will probably want to stay. They'll be more comfortable here than on our little farm and safer away from us."

MacKay made an effort to be stoic but wasn't completely successful. "They're welcome here. All of you are." She wiped her face. "It's not your fault, you know. None of this is your fault. Make sure you tell Brian that."

Nate stood. "I'll try. But sometimes words are weak."

Chapter 17

Nate stood before Tyrone, Atticus, and Brian. Caroline and Samantha kept back from the others and listened. *Perhaps expecting the worst,* Nate thought. "Everything seems to have settled down for the moment. Mrs. MacKay backs up what the sign on the door says. I left Deni back at the farm, since there was no need for both of us to come."

"Let's go then." Brian started for his pack.

"Hold on." Nate stepped closer to his son. "There's more you need to know first."

Brian froze and looked up at him. "Tell us the bad part first. I can tell it's bad. I can see it on your face."

Nate steadied himself. "It seems our old friend Kramer saved a lot of lives." He looked Brian in the eye. "He killed one of his own men when he started cutting on Mrs. MacKay to make her tell them where we were hiding."

"The sons of bitches," Brian blurted. "They had no idea where we were."

Samantha began to cry quietly.

"Anyway," Nate continued, "when the spook shot Ramiro and killed him, Kramer shot his own man and released MacKay and her people."

Atticus swore. "A little too damn late."

"Are you trying to say we did the right thing by letting Kramer go?" Brian asked.

Nate flinched. "Hell, I don't know Brian. We made a decision. If we'd made a different decision, we would've had to live with that one too. Either way we're going to live with it and go on. You understand? We all have to live with our decisions. It just turned out that Kramer saved a lot of lives. He wouldn't have been able to do that if we had killed him. Let's not go through this again."

Brian spit his words. "Well, more than likely he and that other bastard are both dead now. We left them back there in the swamp with bullets in them."

"Probably." Nate lifted his boonie hat and mopped his forehead. "From what Mrs. MacKay told us, they lost something like 14 or 15 people."

"Goddamn massacre." Tyrone fumed. "So that's what kind of government we have now."

Brian swallowed and cleared his throat. He seemed to already know the answer to his question before he uttered the words. "What about Renee and her father?"

The look on his father's face was answer enough.

Brian snatched his pack off the ground where it sat and slammed it on, then reached for his rifle. "Let's go. Talking about it won't change anything."

~~~

Brian said little at the horse farm, but a simmering rage surfaced for a second when he saw MacKay's wounds.

Nate hoped Brian would keep quiet until they left. He was in no mood to be polite company and didn't have the self-control Nate had. Not that Nate and the others were in any better mood. They all felt guilty. Being guests of people who had suffered and lost friends and loved ones because of their actions left them in an awkward position.

MacKay checked the grandfather clock. "Time for the National Guard broadcast. I just hope they have some good news for us. We all need something to light the darkness we've been stumbling around in lately."

The grandfather clock struck 3 o'clock. A woman who had been working in the kitchen walked in and turned on a radio that sat on a fireplace mantle.

"Thank you, Carlene," MacKay said. "I was about to do that. You saved me the trouble."

At first, only static emitted from the speaker, but soon the national anthem came over the airwaves, low at first, and then growing in volume. As the last musical notes faded, a man started to speak.

"Good afternoon. My name is Bob Stone. I don't have to tell you how bad things have been this last year and a half. It's why I'm so happy to have good news for you today. Circumstances beyond Washington's control have hindered government efforts to do more for the American people until now. President Capinos has lost patience and has decided that pleading hasn't worked. So he has stopped pleading and started demanding. A few days ago, he ordered all branches of the military to bring law and order to our nation once again. The order has also been handed down to the head of every department of the federal government: First, protect the American people from lawless brigands. Second, as much as humanly possible, provide medical services, food, and any other assistance they may require."

Brian hissed under his breath, "Bull."

"Yeah," Deni agreed. "Capinos is the one who's been holding the military back and wasting time on bullshit."

The announcer continued, "President Capinos has worked tirelessly with Congress to consolidate what is left of the multitude of federal law enforcement agencies into one. We now have 3,000 federal officers from the former FBI, US Marshals Service, DEA, and many other former agencies, all working under the Department of Homeland Security. At present, they are working on cleaning up Washington, DC. It will take time to hire and train more agents, but over time. DHS will be able to spread its influence of law and order to Maryland, Virginia, etc. But DHS will never be able to provide law and order to the entire nation alone. That's where our military comes in. Keep in mind, though, our military was hit just as hard by the plague as the rest of the population and has been weakened considerably. It will take time to bring law and order to every state, county, parish, town, and hamlet. But President Capinos will not rest until he has accomplished this goal." Silence for a second. "And now we have a word from General Pardee of the National Guard."

Caroline rolled her eyes. "The Department of Homeland Security. We're safe now, people."

"Thank you." The general's voice was as rough as coarse sandpaper and thick with a Southern drawl. "I think Mr. Stone misspoke when he said that President Capinos will not rest until he has accomplished *this goal.* This ain't no damn *goal.* This has got to be done. And the president ain't going to accomplish much by himself. That's a fact. And neither is the National Guard, the Army, the Marines, or any other branch of the military. Every American is going to have to pitch in. That is every decent man, woman, and child. Unfortunately not everyone who survived the plague *is* decent. And they're causing problems for everyone else. I have a warning for those still stuck on dumbass. Hell just might be a place you don't want to go, and your soul may be God's, but your ass is mine if you're caught victimizing people. There won't be any second chances if my soldiers catch you murdering, raping, or robbing. They have orders to administer justice through the barrel of a rifle. We don't have time or resources to be slapping anybody on the ass and letting him go when we catch him victimizing his fellow Americans. Lesser crimes will be dealt with less harshly. But violent crimes carry the death penalty. Listen up on this and let it sink in, because this is the last warning you'll get. We catch you in the act, you die on the spot. Now, anyone listening out there shouldn't get the wrong idea. My soldiers have been ordered to kill only those that need killing. Peaceful civilians will be helped, not abused."

The announcer seemed taken aback. "Uh. What about food and medical supplies? Have stockpiles been warehoused, ready to be shipped out?"

The general's answer was forthright and lacking all diplomatic vagueness or politeness. "I am sickened to admit that too many in government have been sitting on their ass and doing nothing for too many months now. Millions of Americans have starved needlessly because of it. Only recently have plans been drawn up and formalized to help citizens start their own farms locally. This, despite many having begged those in Washington for over a year now to untie our hands and let us do whatever we could to help the people. At first, Washington may have had an excuse for failing the people, as government was so overwhelmed and disorganized for so many months, they just couldn't respond in any orderly and effective fashion. Losing 90 plus percent of your employees from top to bottom will do that. Any military unit would be rendered combat ineffective long before suffering those kinds of casualties. The plague hit so fast and hard, it knocked us all on our ass. But there comes a time, like not long after you're knocked on your ass, that you get up and start fighting back.

That is if you have any kind of a spine at all. Well, Washington has finally decided that it just might be a good idea to save what's left of the American population. It comes way too goddamn late, and I don't understand why it took so long or what mule kicked them in the head and made them change their mind. Anyway, I won't waste time moaning about the past. They've finally gotten out of our way. Now we're going to get busy."

The announcer's nervous voice came over the speaker. "Uh, General, you're not leaving now, are you? You were scheduled to answer questions for another 30 minutes."

The general's voice trailed off as he spoke. "I've got work to do." A door could be heard opening and slamming.

A crowd had gathered in the living room. Several people chuckled.

MacKay raised an eyebrow, a smile on her face. "Those were the most reassuring words I've heard from any government official in a long time."

Music played over the radio, and Nate decided to speak while no useful information could be gleaned by listening to the program. "They might fill the next 30 minutes with music, since the general left early." He turned to Deni. "While I found what I heard interesting, I was hoping to learn something about the local situation. We need to get in touch with Donovan. It's the only way to be sure it's safe to go home."

Deni started to reply, but the music stopped and the announcer came back on. Her eyes flashed to the radio when she heard him mention Col. Donovan's name.

"We have a special message from Col. Donovan in north Florida. He wants to assure his friends there that they are not in any trouble and can go on with their life. The situation has changed for the better, and there is no danger."

The announcer added, "Col. Donovan also wants people in his area of operations to know that he is calling for volunteers to help build a local civilian law enforcement agency of some kind."

The sound of sheets of paper being shuffled could be heard. "Col. Donovan wants to inform people in the area of Glenwood that, while nothing is in abundance, certain vegetables are available at the community farm. They can also be picked up in Glenwood at the town square. Other local farmers are also offering their surplus to the hungry. At the moment, supplies of wild hog meat are holding up, as well as fish caught from local lakes and rivers. All of these food items are available in limited quantities for anyone who shows up at one of the relief centers. He asks that any able-bodied person who receives food volunteer to work on the community farm or one of the private farms in the county as payment. There are many ways to give back. It all depends on what your skills are. Mechanics are needed to maintain the trucks that haul the produce from the farmers to the relief centers, and volunteers are needed at the relief centers themselves.

"A reminder: If you have any law enforcement experience, talk to Col. Donovan. He is trying to start a sheriff's department for the county. If you have any medical experience, please offer your services at the clinic in Glenwood." The announcer stopped talking and ran a recording.

A public service announcement about victory gardens that came straight out of the World War II era played for four minutes.

The announcer's voice came back. "We might not be fighting World War II, but we are fighting famine. A garden in every backyard helped to win World War II, and the same idea can help us defeat hunger. Before the plague hit, only a tiny fraction of American society was involved in the production of food. I don't have to tell you that we now live in a different world. We must adapt or die. I have a garden in my backyard here in Atlanta, as do most of my neighbors. Farming is beneath no man or woman. It is probably one of the most honorable and honest ways to feed yourself and your family. Many of our Founding Fathers were farmers, and some of the best men and women this country has ever produced grew up on a farm.

"Before anyone listening gets the wrong idea, no one is trying to return America to an agrarian society or return us to the 1800s. Think about it for a moment. What are your main needs on a daily basis? If you're like most Americans, you are struggling to feed yourself and your family and you are in constant fear of violent attack or at the very least losing what little food and other needful items you have to armed robbery. If someone in your family is ill or injured, your most pressing needs may be medical services. These basic needs must be met first. Once we have accomplished that, we will start to rebuild society little by little over the years. All levels of government will be reestablished and infrastructure repaired and maintained. No one knows how long this will take. At first, the economy will probably be on a barter basis, but over time it will rebuild as society rebuilds."

Someone turned up the volume in the studio and the Battle Hymn of the Republic blasted out of the radio speaker. A man leaning against the wall nearby turned the volume down a little.

Everyone in the living room seemed to be deep in thought and had nothing to say.

The announcer's voice came back over the radio as the music faded. "This program will be rebroadcasted tonight at 9 PM. I leave you with this thought: We have endured and survived uncounted forms of death. Now it is time we build a new world and enjoy uncounted blessings of life."

Static emitted from the radio speaker, and the man standing nearby clicked it off. "The program didn't last as long as usual this time. I guess the general threw them off schedule."

Excitement crackled in the air, and a murmur rose up in the room. People hungry for any sign that someone besides the local people were actually doing something to make life better drank in an elixir called hope.

A nine-year-old girl looked up at her mother and asked, "What's happening?"

Though infected by the small ray of hope as much is the others, the mother answered, "It could be the beginning of everything, or it could be the beginning of nothing."

Chapter 18

News the government might finally be coming to help sparked excitement that spread fast. People began to gather on the porch outside and in the yard out front, adding to the buzz of voices inside the house.

MacKay stood. "Will you join me in my study where we can hear each other speak?" She motioned with her hands that she meant for all of those in Nate's group to follow her. Samantha refused to leave Caroline's side, so she came with them.

The walls and floor of the study were of polished hardwood. One end of the room consisted of a continuous bookshelf, covering the entire wall. MacKay sat down behind her desk. There were not enough chairs for everyone, so Nate, Brian, and Tyrone stood.

MacKay winced when her wounds pained her, and she shifted in the chair, moving her left arm to a more comfortable position. "What're your plans? I'm asking though I fully understand that you may not believe a word you just heard on the radio."

Nate rubbed his chin and glanced at Deni. "What do you think?"

She bit her lower lip and thought. "I would feel a hell of a lot better if I heard it straight from Donovan. But I don't think we should risk going to town to ask him to his face."

Brian looked up at the ceiling.

"What do you think?" Nate asked, looking at his son.

"She's right as usual," Brian answered. "Not that it matters what I think."

"It matters," Deni interjected. "That's why he asked."

Brian scratched the back of his neck. "Probably should wait to make sure it's safe before we move back into the home and start farming again. Of course we can't stay here either. It might not be safe for us or them. I mean, if they're lying and still want us dead, we're trouble magnets and will just bring more death and misery to these people."

"It wasn't your fault," MacKay insisted.

Nate spoke to MacKay, "It looks like we're going back into hiding until we're sure it's safe."

"I think I'm going to head back to town and chance it," Tyrone said.

"You're not doing this just because you think I'm too old to handle hiding out in the woods, are you?" Atticus asked.

Tyrone tilted his head and looked at the man who raised him. "I was thinking of going back alone. After a week or so, I can get word back to you that it's safe. That is if I'm still alive."

Atticus snorted. "And what the hell am I supposed to do if word comes back that they killed you?"

"Why," Tyrone answered, "stay with the Williams family. Stay alive."

"Bullshit." Atticus nodded to Mrs. MacKay. "Pardon my language. No, I think I'll go on into town with you. The good colonel says he wants volunteer deputies. I suspect that's one thing you have on your mind. You're still thinking of the townspeople. So I might as well go ahead and volunteer too."

Tyrone's chest deflated. "All right then. We'll both go. You're too old to argue with." He turned to the others "It seems Atticus and I are going to be the litmus test. Either they're telling the truth or they're not."

"If they're lying bastards, it's going to cost you," Brian warned. His face turned red for a second. "Of course I realize you know that already."

MacKay nodded and leaned back in her chair as if she had made a decision of her own. "If you two are going into town I might as well go with you."

Everyone stared at her in puzzlement.

"Well," she said "I'm tired of being pestered about these inflamed wounds. If the military is still providing civilians medical care at their clinic, it'll give some credence to the words they just broadcasted over the airwaves."

~~~

First Sergeant Henry Kramer had no idea where he was. Fighting a raging fever and delirious, he stumbled out of heavy woods and onto a dirt road. His entire shoulder had swollen to three times its normal size and had long since stopped hurting much. He suspected it was too dead and rotten for nerves to send pain signals to his brain. The bullet wounds weren't that serious, but days of wading through swamp water and not being able to keep it clean, as well as having little antibiotics, had created a perfect environment for infection. He suspected it was too late for even a fully equipped hospital to save him.

Barely able to stay on his feet, he struggled down the road in a daze. The distant sound of children laughing caught his attention and spurred him on. Approaching a white picket fence that had seen its better days, he saw a white clapboard house, also in disrepair. Six or seven children played ball in the front yard. One five-year-old boy saw him coming and stopped playing. He pointed in surprise. The older children saw what he was pointing at and immediately shepherded every child into the house.

Kramer stopped and nearly fell over. He reached out and held the gate post to steady himself. A man and woman's voice emanated from the open windows. Kramer could tell they were alarmed, even frightened. The thought came to him that they would probably shoot him as he stood there. Surprisingly to him, the thought did not seem so unpleasant.

When the largest German shepherd he had ever seen came charging from around the house, his survival instincts kicked in. Raising the M4 with one hand, he peered through the sight and centered on the bouncing dog's chest.

A woman from inside the house screamed, "Don't shoot my dog!"

He changed his aim, and was about to shoot in front of the German shepherd and frighten it away, when his legs collapsed under him and he fell on his back. Lying there in the dusty clay road, he lost consciousness for a few seconds. He woke again long enough to realize that the dog was not growling or biting, but instead was whimpering and sniffing at his rotting shoulder. Then the dog moved closer and licked at his face. Kramer reached up and petted the dog gently, running his fingers through the gray and black hair. "If I'd known you were friendly, I would never have pointed my rifle at you."

A man wearing worn-out jeans and a faded, torn T-shirt put the muzzle of a double-barreled shotgun to Kramer's head.

Speaking to the woman, he said, "Take his weapons. Make sure you keep out of the line of fire, because if he moves I'm going to blow his head off."

"Don't, Boyd," the woman pleaded. "I don't think he's dangerous. I saw him lower the rifle like he didn't want to shoot the dog."

"Will you just do what I say, Amelia? Please." The man kept his attention on Kramer and held the shotgun to his head.

Amelia carefully maneuvered around Kramer's prone body and took the rifle in one hand and removed his pistol from the holster with the other. Then she stepped back out of the way.

The German shepherd continued to lick at Kramer's face and whimper.

"For God's sake, get that dog out of the way." Boyd motioned with his head. "She won't do anything I tell her. Try to get it to go back to the house. If I have to shoot, it's going to lose its nose."

Amelia spoke to the dog in a gentle tone, "Go back to the house, Juno."

The big German shepherd barked once, jumped over the picket fence, and ran to the house, where a 10-year-old boy was waiting with the door open. As soon as the dog was inside, the boy closed the door.

Still holding the shotgun to Kramer's head, Boyd warned, "Get that big knife on his belt and throw it in the middle of the road."

She did what she was told. "He's more dead than alive." After releasing the waist strap on his backpack, she found the quick release on the shoulder straps and soon had his backpack off. Shaking her head, she said, "I don't know if I can save him. She pulled a small pocketknife from a front pocket of her faded jeans and used it to cut away the filthy jacket and then remove the stinking bandages. "Shot," she said in a matter of fact voice. She looked up at her husband. "Help me get him to the house."

"Oh no," Boyd protested. "We don't know a damn thing about him."

"Okay." She stood and faced her husband. "Let's just go back in the house and pretend he's not out here. He's likely to be dead in our hour or two. We won't even bother to bury him. Wild dogs will probably drag him away tonight anyway. It'll be a good lesson for the children on how to care for our fellow man."

"Oh shit!" Boyd pointed the shotgun skyward for the first time. He turned his head and yelled over his left shoulder, "Somebody bring some rope out here."

The two stood there and looked down at Kramer. Boyd asked, "You sure he's still alive? He looks dead."

The same boy who had held the door open for the dog came running with a few feet of coiled rope in his hand. He started to hand it to Boyd.

"Give it to your mother," Boyd said. "I've got to hold this shotgun on him. We don't know if he's dangerous or not."

Amelia took the rope from the boy. "Clear the dining table and wipe it down. That's where I'm going to work on him."

The boy glanced at Kramer for a second and then ran back to the house without a word.

"Come over here and hold the shotgun," Boyd told his wife. "I'll tie his hands."

A few minutes later they had Kramer on the dining room table and Amelia was cleaning the festering shoulder. "Bullets went all the way through and didn't even hit any bone. Problem is the last wound wasn't taken care of properly and there's too much dead flesh now." She shook her head. "We still have some fish antibiotics, but I'm afraid it would be a waste on him. The dead flesh needs to be cut off. I'd have to cut his entire shoulder off to save him, and his chances of surviving that kind of surgery here are slim to none. I'm a veterinarian, not a surgeon." Anguish contorted her face, as if Kramer were someone she knew and not a perfect stranger. "And this dining room is no ER."

Boyd put his hand on her shoulder. "Well, don't be upset about it. You didn't shoot him. Might as well give him something to put him under. No need for him to suffer."

She gave him a look that would have wilted a lesser man.

"Come on. You just said you can't save him. Does he have a chance or not? If he doesn't, why put him through more suffering?" Boyd could see wheels turning in his wife's head, as she grasped for anything that might save this man who had just appeared out of nowhere and neither one of them knew.

Her eyes lit up. "The National Guard just started a clinic in town. We can take him there." When she noticed that most of the children were standing around gawking at Kramer's shoulder, she shooed them out of the room. "You kids go to your rooms and stay there."

"I'll take him," Boyd said. "If you go, they'll probably ask you to volunteer to help at the clinic, since you're a veterinarian, and that's as close to a doctor most people have seen in over a year."

"They have people doctors there." She started on Kramer's shoulder. "The ride to town in the back of that old dead axle wagon will probably finish him."

"I can tie him across the back of the mule," Boyd quipped.

She didn't bother with another wilting look. "Throw a mattress in the wagon for him to lie on." She looked up. "Hurry. I'll be done in a minute or two, and you might as well be on your way. If you don't linger in town, you can be back by dark. You know how dangerous traveling at night is."

~~~

Tyrone stopped the pickup on the country road 50 yards from the roadblock, keeping his hands on the wheel. A soldier approached their pickup with caution. Atticus and Mrs. MacKay kept their hands in sight and nervously waited.

The soldier stopped in midstride. "I hope you men know you're not wanted anymore. All charges have been lifted. We don't need any unnecessary trouble."

Tyrone stuck his head out the window. "That's what we've been told. We have a woman who needs medical assistance. Is the downtown clinic still open?"

"Yeah." The soldier walked up to the driver side and looked through the window into the cab. "Who did that to her?"

"One of your people," Atticus answered.

"A soldier did that?"

"No. Actually he was CIA or something," Tyrone corrected Atticus.

"Damn sorry thing to do," the soldier commented. "Take her to the clinic. Then go on to see Col. Donovan. I'll radio him and let him know you're coming." He started to walk away, then said, "Don't worry. What you heard is true. Things have changed. I have no idea what Washington's up to, but you're not wanted anymore." He shrugged. "But hey, I'm just a ground pounder; I'm not paid to think."

"I wonder how long it'll last." Atticus didn't expect an answer.

MacKay spoke for the first time. "Do you know if there's going to be an investigation into the murder of my people?"

"Uh," the soldier stuttered, "I don't know, ma'am. They tend to let things go nowadays. If they investigated everything, there wouldn't be time to do anything else. Every bit of it was Washington and the spooks they sent down here. Col. Donovan and we soldiers had nothing to do with it. He even offered to resign and refused to follow what he considered to be illegal and immoral orders. He couldn't see how the people they ordered him to go after had committed any crimes, and he told them so."

"That sounds like him," Tyrone said. "It's reassuring to know he hasn't changed."

A soldier backed a Humvee out of the way, allowing Tyrone to drive on through. They turned left onto Main Street and passed a food distribution center, where food from the farm Nate helped design the irrigation system for was being handed out to the hungry. Signs asking for volunteers to help at the farm or with food distribution were prominent.

Two soldiers met them at the clinic parking lot entrance. One recognized Tyrone and Atticus and waved them on through. "Go on up to the main entrance," the soldier said. "Col. Donovan is waiting for you in the lobby."

Tyrone did as directed. Atticus helped MacKay out of the truck. She seemed to have lost much of her strength and stumbled twice.

Donovan was watching through the large lobby window. He burst out of the front door and ran around to the other side of the truck to help Atticus steady MacKay. Two soldiers armed with M4s tried to keep up, their heads swinging back and forth, scanning for trouble, obviously serious about their duty to protect the colonel.

Tyrone was right behind Donovan. "You all right Mrs. MacKay?"

She attempted a smile. "I guess the long road trip has worn me out."

Donovan saw the red gash on her face, with its fishing line sutures. Then he saw the two lacerations that ran the length of her left arm. "Who did that?" Anger put a hard edge to his face. "Was it one of my soldiers?"

"No," she answered.

Atticus held her by her right arm to steady her. "She told us it was CIA operatives."

Somewhat relieved but still angry, Donovan said, "We'll worry about that later. Let's get her inside."

~~~

Dr. Sheila Brant took one look at MacKay's wounds and barked orders to two nearby nurses. "If I see another laceration sutured with fishing line 100 years from now, it'll be too damn soon."

Atticus couldn't resist. "One hundred years from now? You're rather optimistic, aren't you?"

Dr. Brant flashed him a smile. "I see you're still a smartass." She continued to examine the wounds, pressing on the edges of the red areas with latex-gloved hands. "I think you got here soon enough. We'll know more when we get the blood work back." She looked at MacKay. "This was no accident."

MacKay seemed to be tiring fast. "No, it was done very deliberately. If you don't mind, I would like to lay back and rest."

Concern flashed across Dr. Brant's face for a second. "Sure. Go ahead and lay back. But I'm not through examining you yet." She turned to the others. "Please wait outside."

Donovan's body guards stepped back to give them some privacy when they gathered in the hallway.

"What happened in Washington?" Tyrone asked. "They seem to have done a 180."

Donovan cleared his throat. He appeared to be debating whether or not to answer the question. "The Joint Chiefs of Staff and just about every general officer in every branch of the military threatened to mutiny if Capinos didn't allow a real election soon. Everyone in the military is tired of taking orders from an illegitimate resident who was never really elected by the American people. They're tired of him grabbing power. They're tired of him using the Constitution for toilet paper. And most of all, we're sick of seeing the American people suffer needlessly while our hands are tied and our time and resources are wasted on political bullshit."

Atticus snorted. "About damn time."

"How long before Washington changes their shitsoid minds and they come after us again?" Tyrone asked.

Donovan cringed. "Who knows? I'm hoping we have five or six months."

"Hoping?" Tyrone asked. "Doesn't sound too reassuring."

Donovan nodded. "Your ears aren't lying. I suspect Capinos and his cohorts will try to sabotage our efforts. If we get results that the people can see and experience in their own lives and taste the food we help them produce in their own mouths, Capinos and those he placed in Congress and the Supreme Court aren't going to stand for an election. They'll lose in a landslide, and they know it. Capinos is setting himself up for total power and permanent residence in the White House. He's worked hard to get to this point and he's not going to give up without a fight."

"So this is just a reprieve, a postponement," Tyrone observed. "There's still going to be some kind of confrontation, perhaps even a military coup."

"More like a civil war," Atticus added. "I don't think the American people are going tolerate Capinos or the military taking over and destroying our Constitution. The shit's going to hit the fan."

Donovan's two bodyguards turned white and glanced over their shoulders.

"We're trying to avoid that." Donovan lowered his voice. "The best thing we can do now is work as hard as we can to help the people and show them how much better things could be without Capinos and his gang in power. You two can help by building a viable local law enforcement agency and providing the people in this town protection. It'll look a hell of a lot better if the Army isn't the only source of law in this county. Whether we have six months or two, we should take full advantage of it. By the time Capinos decides to rein us in, we must have the people's trust. They must understand the military's on their side and will give power back to the civilian government as soon as fair elections can be arranged. No one in the military wants a damn coup, and the last thing they want is to see our country turned into a banana republic."

Atticus snorted. "But that's exactly what it'll be if you soldiers take over. The people ain't going to like it."

Donovan exhaled a load from his lungs. "I won't like it either, but it may come to that. It depends on how sane Capinos is. So far, he's cagey and conniving, but reasonable? No."

Tyrone glanced at Atticus. "Well, we'll take up where we left off and try to find more volunteers. The Williams family has had enough of town life and I doubt they'll be coming back. They just want to work their farm and be left alone."

"I expected that," Donovan said. "And I don't blame them. They've done more than their fair share. Besides, if they get their farm going again they can feed a lot of people. Right now that's Job One for every American. Job Two will be protecting the people."

Dr. Brant emerged from the examination room. "She's resting. Of course she's a lot sicker than she's letting on, and exhausted. The blood work won't be back for a while, but I think she'll be okay once we get antibiotics in her. I've already removed the fishing line."

"She's a tough old bird," Atticus said. He scratched the back of his neck. "Uh, don't tell her I said that."

Chapter 19

A week later, Tyrone drove up to the front gate of the horse farm in the old pickup. Mrs. MacKay sat on the passenger side. Her wounds, no longer inflamed, were healing well. Atticus followed in a patrol car.

The guards at the gate greeted them with smiles. Tyrone had used a HAM radio to inform them of their arrival the day before and a warm welcome had been prepared. Though spring had come late, warmer days had brought with them an early crop, and a few of the faster-growing vegetables were already being harvested, in some cases before they were completely ripe. A wild hog had been slaughtered to add to the banquet. Everyone ate outside in front of the big house, under the shade of oak trees.

Tyrone noticed Caroline and Samantha eating at another table. As soon as he finished his meal, he walked over to them and asked Caroline, "Have you seen any of the Williams family lately?"

Caroline answered, "I haven't seen them since the last time I saw you and Atticus. As far as I know they're still in hiding."

Tyrone checked his wristwatch. "There's still time for Atticus and me to drive down to their farm and maybe leave a note on the door and still get back to town before dark. We've been trying to raise them by HAM radio for several days now. They won't respond."

"Could be their radio is down," Caroline suggested. "If they're hiding out in the woods, they won't be near any radio, anyway. I'll go with you if you want."

Samantha pulled at her arm. "No. Don't leave me here alone."

Atticus had finished his meal and was standing by listening. "Nice of you to offer. But there's really no reason for you to go." He glanced down at Samantha's anguished face. "You two young ladies might as well stay here. Tyrone and I can take care of ourselves well enough I think."

Caroline stood. "They're all good friends. And I feel like I should go." Something caught her attention out of the periphery of her vision, and she looked down the driveway. "Speak of the devil. Here come three of his henchmen."

Tyrone and Atticus turned to look, and Samantha stood on her chair the see over the sea of heads. Escorted by one of the gate guards, Nate, Deni, and Brian strode toward them, looking as if they were out for a stroll in a park.

A woman whispered in MacKay's ear and pointed. She smiled and immediately rushed to meet the new visitors. As soon as she was close enough they could hear above the clamor of the crowd, she gave them the good news. "Col. Donovan has assured us it's safe for you to go home. You're not wanted by the government anymore. In their hunt for you, they've caused a lot more problems for themselves than if they had just left you alone."

"Yeah," Nate said, "the cover-up is usually worse than the original crime."

Tyrone and Atticus, as well as Caroline and Samantha, caught up with MacKay. Atticus nodded. "Yep, you guys can go home, but keep your ears tuned to the radio, because there's no telling how long it'll last. Donovan says six months, maybe less."

The three members of the Williams family gave each other confused glances. Deni said, "We saw you go by on the road and noticed you were taking Mrs. MacKay back home. That was obvious proof you three were not locked in a cell as soon as you arrived in town. We thought it would be safe enough to come on in and have a talk."

"Six months or less." Nate raised a brow. "What the hell? Either we're in trouble or we're not."

"Most likely the former," Tyrone said. "The idiots in Washington are shitsoid. Who knows when they'll have a relapse and change their minds? Take their reprieve with a grain of salt."

"What's that all about, really?" Deni asked.

"Well." Tyrone hesitated while he thought. "The way Col. Donovan explained it, Capinos has decided to give the military a free hand in handling the crisis, but not because he hopes they'll get it right and actually help the people. No, he hopes the military will fall on their face, so he can step in and say he warned the people they couldn't handle things and now it's his turn."

Nate finished for him. "So Capinos has given the military six months to perform a miracle, but he might cut that short if he thinks the military's doing too good of a job."

"That's about it," Atticus said. "Our illustrious president intends to cut the military's legs out from under them no matter how it turns out, even if he has to cut the American peoples' throat in the process. He wants to consolidate power. To hell with who gets hurt."

Brian broke in, confusion showing on his face. "So why are the high-ranking officers falling for it? They know they're damned if they succeed and damned if they fail."

"You can feed a lot of people in six months," Tyrone answered, "if you work night and day."

"Six months would allow me to get a good crop in, and that would make a lot of difference for the Williams family," Nate said, his voice trailing off in thought.

McKay raised her hands. "Enough talk. You three may be late to the party, but not too late. Come and join us. There's plenty left for three more friends."

Atticus and Tyrone talked while the three ate. They gave the others as much information about what was going on in town and the rest of the county as possible. "We already have seven volunteer deputies and one radio operator," Tyrone announced with some pride.

Nate set a spoon full of lima beans down. "Are they working for free or food?"

"They get an allotment of food from the farm by the lake, but, hell, everyone's getting food, whether they volunteer for anything or not," Tyrone answered. "Also, the Army is giving us some rations and providing fuel for the vehicles."

"They also got a dozen radios working and scrounged up some batteries for them and a solar charger that can handle a dozen batteries at a time," Atticus added. He winked at Tyrone. "Of course, we can always use more deputies. Uh, you can catch a ride back to town with us."

"No thanks," Deni said, before Nate or Brian had a chance to speak. "If we go anywhere other than back into the woods to hide, it'll be the farm."

"Dad wants to go home… if we can," Brian said. "I have to admit I miss that place myself." His eyes flashed to Deni and Nate to judge their reaction. "I'm tired, and I'm sure they are too." He looked down. "And I'm really sick of losing friends."

~~~

The pain woke Kramer. His entire body shook and jolted, sending bolts of fiery lightning from his left shoulder down his arm and the up left side of his neck and into his skull. He tried to open his eyes and look around, but bright sunlight forced him to immediately close them again. He reached with his right hand to grab his left shoulder and noticed his jacket had been cut away and his wounds freshly dressed. Holding his right hand up to provide shade from the sun, he dared open his eyes again, mere slits, but enough to allow him to see that he was lying inside of a wooden box with an open top, where he could see the blue sky above. The wooden box he lay in abruptly dropped three inches on his left side, causing his shoulder pain enough to prompt him to moan.

He heard a man say, "Whoa!" Tilting his head back and looking in the direction the voice came from, allowed him to see a man sitting on a bench seat and holding reins in his hands.

The man turned and looked back at him. "Sorry about that. I can't miss every pothole. There are too many of them. This old dead axle wagon will rattle your fillings out of your mouth. Even up here where I have the advantage of the seat being on springs."

Kramer tried to sit up, but found he didn't have the strength for it and the pain was too much.

Boyd set the break and jumped down from the wagon. "Don't get too rambunctious back there. You have nothing to fear from me. It's that rotting shoulder that's going to do you in." He reached into the wagon and held up a plastic bottle. "If you're thirsty, here's some water for you." He set the bottle back down.

"Where am I?" Kramer moaned.

"You're in my wagon on a dirt road in the middle of nowhere," he answered. "My name's Boyd. Just as soon not give you my last name. Fact is I'm glad to get you away from my family. It's obvious you're a dangerous man. You're not wearing a uniform or carrying any kind of identification, but I'd say you're military or ex-military." He leaned over and looked down at Kramer, a rusty old .44 special revolver in his right hand. "Somebody has damn near killed you. I'd say you're at least 90% dead. I'd also say you probably killed the one that almost killed you. Point is you're dangerous, and I don't want you around my family."

Kramer looked away. "You going to shoot me or talk me to death?"

Boyd smiled. "Neither. I told my wife I'd take you to the clinic in town. And that's what I'm going to do." He held the rusty revolver up again and then stuffed it under his belt. "This little talk is just to let you know that as long as you just lie there and don't move, you'll be in the hands of the National Guard in about an hour. Give me any trouble and I'll just shoot you."

Kramer looked up at him and spoke with a weak voice. "Why would I give you any trouble? If you're taking me to the National Guard to get medical care, that's exactly where I want to go."

Boyd shrugged. "You might be wanted. It's obvious you've been raising hell somewhere with someone."

Kramer tried for the water bottle with his right hand but couldn't reach it because it was on his left side. Boyd reached it over to him cautiously, then unscrewed the lid while Kramer rested the bottle on his chest. Kramer took a long drink. "Thanks." He coughed. "You might be right about me being wanted. Maybe, maybe not. I'll take my chances. Without medical help, I'll be dead by tomorrow anyway."

"True enough," Boyd said. "But why the hell wouldn't you know whether or not you're wanted?"

Kramer held the bottle up for Boyd to screw the lid back on. "It's a long story full of intrigue and other bullshit that you wouldn't believe. It even involves the President of the United States."

Boyd snorted. "You're right. I don't believe it already. Just go back to sleep and we'll be in town before you know it."

~~~

Nate made his way back to Deni and Brian, who were hiding in the woods a safe distance from the house and barn but were close enough they could overwatch while Nate searched the buildings for booby traps. He dropped to his knees beside them. "All clear in and around the buildings."

"How do the buildings look inside?" Brian asked.

"Pretty much the way we left them," Nate answered. "The soldiers didn't bother anything, and it doesn't look like anyone else has been inside lately."

Deni continued to scan the area with Nate's binoculars. "That's encouraging. About time we had some good luck."

"Well," Brian said dryly, "there wasn't much left after the raiders cleaned us out."

"Might as well go on in." Nate stood. "I've circled the whole area three times and haven't found so much as a boot print."

Deni handed Nate his binoculars. "If we get started on the house right away, we might have it in livable condition by this time tomorrow."

They left the safety of the woods, heading for the front door of the house. "Feels strange, boldly walking out into the open like this," Brian commented. "If I didn't know we had just checked the entire area out thoroughly, I wouldn't do it." He held his rifle tight in both hands and scanned the tree line.

"That feeling will be with you the rest of your life." Nate looked over at Brian as they walked. "A lot of things will. There just wasn't any way to protect you from it all. Not if you were going to survive."

"Don't worry about me. I'm all right," Brian said. "And if I wasn't, it wouldn't be your fault. Besides, I think the worst just might be over."

In an effort to change the subject somewhat, Deni added, "About all that's hanging over our heads at the moment is that mess in Washington. And that's for someone else to clean up, not us."

They approached the front of the house. "That's the way I feel about it too," Nate said. He stopped at the hand pump that was only 20 feet from the front door. "I tried pumping it when I was here, but I get couldn't get any water to come up. The leather in the plunger's probably dry rotted. This'll be the first thing I'll work on."

Brian walked past them and stepped up on the porch. "I'll bet every piece of leather in the barn has been chewed up by rats."

Nate had left the door open when he checked the place out. Deni timidly stepped into the house. "Wow. What a mess." A few seconds later she asked, "Where the hell's the broom?"

Nate took his pack off and put it next to the wall near the front door and then he slung his rifle across his back. "I expect she's going to want at least one bedroom and the bathroom clean before we go to sleep tonight, so help her inside. I'll be in the barn looking for tools to get this pump going. We're going to need water ASAP."

Brian nodded and disappeared into the house. He reappeared a few minutes later and headed for the barn, minus his pack but his rifle was hanging across his back out of the way. Nate looked up from a dusty workbench strewed with parts from the water pump. "I thought you were going to help Deni in the house."

Brian grabbed an aluminum stepladder hanging on the back wall. "She wants me to get the stove working, so I'm going to clean the smoke pipe out and make sure there's no rat's nest in it or anything." As he walked by Nate he added, "You better damn sure get that pump working, because she says she wants to take a warm bath tonight."

Nate chuckled. "We can all use a bath, and that well water will taste as sweet as soda after drinking boiled river water for so long."

~~~

Kramer woke in a room that was dimly lit. A young man he instantly recognized as a soldier slept in a bed on his right. His left arm was bandaged. Kramer turned to his left to check his own left arm and saw that it was gone, as well as much of his shoulder. It looked strange to him, and he felt like a freak, but it didn't hurt much. His faced turned an even lighter shade of white and he grimaced, muttering, "Shit." It was then he noticed the soldier in a bed to his left who had lost both legs. *Must be some serious fighting going on around here. They have so many wounded, they're short on rooms. Have the people risen up against Capinos?*

Kramer was about to doze off again when a soldier walked in. The man stood at the foot of his bed and gave him a thorough going over, obviously taking an interest in him for some reason. He held an M4 in both hands and wore full body armor and a combat vest bulging with spare magazines of ammo. Finally, the soldier spoke, "Relax and rest. My orders are to keep you alive until you're well enough to travel, and those orders come straight from Col. Greene." He motioned slightly with his head. "There are plenty of others backing me up out there. You might prove valuable in the future, and Col. Greene wants to make sure you can testify, if it ever comes to that."

Kramer flinched. When he tried to speak, he found his throat too dry. Only a croak came out.

The soldier filled a paper cup with water and held it to Kramer's mouth. While he drank, the soldier said, "I'm one of the few who know who you are. Most of the others guarding you have no clue what's going on. Better that way. Your testimony could hurt some powerful people. Best if they don't even know you're alive, much less where you are." He put the empty cup on a nearby table and turned as if to walk away, but stopped and said, "I know some of the people you saved." He took a breath. "And a lot of those you didn't, or couldn't. Another soldier out there's in the same boat. We both figure we owe you. If someone gets to you, don't bother checking; we'll be dead." He pulled his M4 close to his chest. "From now on you have amnesia. You don't remember who the hell you are. You understand? Word gets out the Guard has you, we're likely to all die in this hospital from an air strike ordered by

Capinos. Politically, you're radioactive. Keep your mouth shut, and we'll keep you alive."

Kramer nodded, but he wasn't so sure he *wanted* to live at that moment. He wasn't just missing an arm; he was a lopsided freak. To hell with Capinos, and to hell with the country. The drugs made him drowsy. In seconds, he returned to a place where there was no pain, physical or emotional.

Mel waited outside, keeping his attention down the hallway, his rifle in both hands, his thumb on the safety lever. He turned to glance behind him and noticed the soldier who just talked to Kramer was back on post. They communicated by hand signal. Mel nodded and resumed keeping a lookout for trouble.

~~~

Nate watched the sun rise over his newly plowed and planted field. Fog lifted from the river down in the valley on the lower end of the farm, and a gentle breeze came to life with the rising sun, blowing thin clouds of mist uphill and across the field. He turned to Deni and Brian with a smile. "We've accomplished a lot in two weeks. Now we have to keep those seeds moist until the summer rains come."

Deni's smile was as broad as Nate's. "Atticus and Tyrone hauling that tractor and 100 gallons of diesel fuel out here from town made it possible."

"We had a good tractor, but the damn raiders –" Brian stopped himself. "No use going over that now. We have to get that pump hooked to the tractor's power take off and lay out some irrigation pipes down to the river before those seeds dry out." He walked toward the barn, his rifle slung across his back, out of the way while he worked, but within reach at all times.

Deni laughed. "He's getting more like his father every day."

Nate pulled her to him. "This is the happiest I've been in a long, long time. These last weeks have been great therapy for all three of us." They watched Brian work on the pump. "Maybe someday, in a year or two, we can stop carrying rifles with us wherever we go."

Deni's expression changed. "We both know it's not over yet. It could very likely get worse than it's ever been, and it could happen any day now. It all depends on when those in Washington decide to make their move and clamp down on the country." Hate turned her face hard. "Damn men who value power more than people. Most of the human population dead and the survivors suffering, but what are those assholes thinking of? Why, let's take advantage of the situation and create our own little dictatorship. It's probably happening all over the world. Little men with big egos and not an ounce of decency in them."

"I know the shit might hit the fan soon, but it's not a *fait accompli."* Nate swallowed. "And Brian knows that as well as we do. He wants to put this land to work one last time before – well, before whatever happens happens. It's the first time he's taken any real interest in farming. Just maybe we'll be able to raise this crop, harvest it, and process some of it for storage before it all goes to hell again. What we can't keep from spoiling, we'll give away or maybe trade for things we need."

"And then what?" Deni asked. "We take it into the woods and hide it in strategic areas, so we can live on it while hiding from the government?"

Nate nodded in Brian's direction. "If you're asking am I willing to give my son to the cause and let him die in a civil war, the answer is hell no. Nor do I want you to be a part of it. The chances of any of us surviving a civil war are so small –" He shook his head. "No. He has done more than his share in helping this country get back on its feet. We all have."

She raised her chin. "Brian is underage, but I'm not. I think I'll decide whether or not I fight."

Nate softened the tone of his voice. "In the end, yes, it's your decision, but that doesn't mean I have to agree with it or I won't beg you to stay with us. Unless the entire military sides with the people, many civilians who go to war will not be coming back." As he walked away, he asked, "How much do you think I can take?"

She took two steps to catch up with him, but stopped when she saw that he was heading for the river to be alone.

~~~

High pressure steam hissed as it escaped from the release valve on the lid of the pressure canner. Nate had spent most of the day canning vegetables and explaining to Deni how it was done, reminding her many times how dangerous steam can be and to always make sure the release valve never got plugged up. "Let's get out of this hot kitchen while the water cools off a little."

Brian set a five-gallon bucket full of lima beans he had just harvested from the field on the front porch. He walked between piles of cucumbers, green onions, and tomatoes. Farther from the house, a pickup that was overloaded with freshly harvested corn stood ready for a trip into town. He flipped an empty five-gallon bucket over and sat on it. "You guys do know we're almost out of Mason jars?"

"Yep," Deni answered, "we'll be done with canning by sundown."

Nate stepped over to the water pump, worked the handle five times, and then stuck his head under the water flow. He stood and let it drip on his shoulders and his already sweat-soaked shirt. "Summer's with us full-bore. It's almost as hot out here as it is in the kitchen."

Brian looked down the driveway and pointed. "We better get what we can harvested and taken care of. Who knows how much time we have before trouble comes rolling toward us from that direction."

"Might not ever happen," Nate countered. "But then again, it could happen while we sit here talking about it."

"Donovan said six months at the outset," Deni said, her voice carrying with it a sharp edge of anger. "I doubt we have much longer." She clenched her jaw for a second and then looked at the others. "Yeah, we better work fast and get this last batch of canned food cached in the woods. I expect we'll be forced to go back into hiding anytime now."

"I guess this isn't exactly heaven," Brian said, "but the last few months have given us the most peace we've known in damn near two years. It's depressing to know that assholes we never even met are about to take that away from us." He stood, obviously ready to go back to work. "I'll hook the trailer to the truck and start loading it. We'll be ready to head for town in the morning."

Nate yelled after him, "Five or six of those watermelons you planted are ripe enough to take with us."

Brian stopped walking for a second and turned to look back. "Good idea. The kids at the horse farm would enjoy those."

Deni started to say something, but she noticed that Nate seemed to be thinking. "What?"

"We don't have time to allow the beans to dry on the vine, so we'll have to oven dry. That'll also pasteurize them. It's going to be a real challenge to keep that wood stove at the right temperature long enough."

"We're out of Mason jars. What're we going to put them in?" Deni wanted to know.

"Mylar bags," Nate answered. "If we had enough jars, we could just can all of it, but drying's easier. If you're going to eat it within a year, that is. You keep dried beans too long and you have to boil the hell out of them to soften them. The raiders didn't find the bags, or maybe they didn't think they had any use for them. Anyway, we have about 40 or 50 six-gallon bags we can seal the beans in."

"Well." Deni rubbed her aching shoulders. "That'll have to wait until we get back from town tomorrow. Right now we have some more canning to do."

Nate sighed. "Yeah. Let's get it done before dark."

Chapter 20

The Williams family overslept and got a late start, leaving two hours after sunrise, instead of first light, as they had planned. Nevertheless, they grabbed their packs and rifles and piled into the pickup. It was almost 10 o'clock by the time they pulled up to the front gate at the horse farm. They were greeted by the guards, who ushered them through the gate.

"They look worried," Deni commented.

Nate nodded. "Yep. Something's wrong."

Brian cleared his throat. "We never listened to the radio all day yesterday or last night. We're kind of out of the loop. No telling what's going on. Guess we were so busy being farmers we were too busy to be diligent citizen soldiers."

Nate pulled up to the main house. "You got that right. I just hope it doesn't cost us this time."

No one needed to inform Mrs. MacKay they had arrived. She met them before they got halfway to the front porch.

Nate saw the look on her face. "Has it begun already?"

MacKay answered, "HAM operators report that a purge of generals has begun. Last report said over a dozen have been relieved of duty and arrested for treason. The usual Guard and Army reports were broadcasted yesterday, last night, and this morning. None of them mentioned the purge."

"What about the code?" Deni asked. "Has it been broadcasted?"

MacKay shook her head. "No."

Deni referred to a code that would warn the people the civil war had begun. It was a passage written by Hemingway in a personal letter. *Why oh bright beam of an August moon have you not written me?*

"If Capinos is purging generals, for all practical purposes the civil war has started." Nate looked to his left and saw a gathering crowd of nervous faces. "You probably should think about initiating your evacuation plans."

Caroline pushed through the crowd, her rifle slung on her shoulder and Samantha in tow. "It's the military Washington will be concerned with at first, not some horse farm. For God's sake, it's a big country, and we're just little people, no threat to them now that everyone already knows about their shenanigans with the so-called anarchists."

"True," Nate said. "Right now the military is the only thing between us and tyranny, and Capinos will have to deal with them first – if he can. But I guarantee you this farm and mine are on some kind of a list. We don't want to be where they can find us. What I'm saying is it'll take you days to evacuate, unless you leave all the food you just harvested behind. You probably should start the process now."

A tall, 30-something-year-old man with big tattoos on big arms pushed forward through the crowd and asked, "What do you mean if he can? When has the U.S. military ever gone against Washington? Do you have reason to believe it'll be different this time?"

"Yes I do," Nate answered. "But there are no guarantees."

The man moved closer. "Why would it be different this time?"

Nate turned to face the man squarely. "Because Capinos and most of Congress were not legitimately elected, and the Justices they appointed to the Supreme Court are therefore also illegitimate and carry no real constitutional power. On top of that, Capinos and his cohorts have proven they do not give a damn about the American people's welfare. Their actions and inactions have caused the deaths of millions more than had to die in the aftermath of the plague."

Deni broke in. "Keep in mind that soldiers, Marines, sailors, airmen, and Coast Guardsmen are sworn to support and defend the Constitution against all enemies foreign and *domestic* and bear true faith and allegiance to the same. It's true that the oath includes obeying the orders of the President of the United States and the orders of the officers, *according to regulations and the Uniform Code of Military Justice.* No one in the military has to obey illegal or immoral orders. Their oath is not to any illegitimate president or Congress that were never elected by the American people. No one here voted for those in power now and no one in the military did either."

Nate added, "Yes, every military officer rightly believes the President of the United States has constitutional authority over the military as Commander in Chief, but, as already stated, Capinos was not legitimately elected by the American people. He was a very wealthy man before the plague and has somehow managed to scheme and buy his way into power. Even though money has basically no worth at the moment, I guess some think it will someday and are willing to sell out the country for wealth. But the fact remains Capinos wasn't elected president by the people. That is a big difference. To the military, it's *the* difference."

A woman from somewhere back in the crowd yelled out at them, "And why should we trust the military to allow free elections and turn power back over to civilian authority?"

Deni became angry. "That's a good question, but you better pray the military sides with the people. If we have a real civil war, it'll last a decade and finish off what's left of us. That's assuming today's Americans have the spine to fight for the freedom so many past generations have handed over to their children." She threw her hands up. "Who knows? It could all be over in a month. But that doesn't mean the killing will stop. When has capitulating to tyrants done anything other than encourage more killing? In the 1900s, over one hundred million people were murdered by their own governments."

Brian edged closer to his father. "Has there been any effort to organize a resistance? I mean, have they started militias or anything? We never talked about that."

The look on Nate's face took Deni's breath away for a second.

Caroline answered the question for him. "Oh, there are organizations out there all right. Some of them even call themselves militias. But they can't seem to get together and decide on just the right way to hate other Americans. Then you got the raiders, who are equal opportunity haters. Or maybe they don't hate you at all. Mostly they just want to rob, rape, and pillage. Hate may or may not have a thing to do with it. Either way, they're not interested in fighting for any cause."

Nate sighed. "Well…" He had run out of words. He wasn't exactly jumping at a chance to fight in a bloody civil war and didn't want Deni or Brian to either.

Brian glanced up at his father and then looked at the crowd. "Those of us who are left have survived because we're tough. The weak have been weeded out by nature and violence. We'll fight through this just like we have everything else."

Deni whispered in Nate's ear. "You and Susan should've named him Nate Junior."

Caroline smiled at Brian. "I didn't say it was hopeless. Just don't expect more than maybe ten percent of the people to fight. Unfortunately, not all Americans are givers. Many are not even give-a-damners."

Mrs. MacKay said, "Okay. Everyone be quiet for a minute. We've made it this far, and I don't believe this country is going to come apart like an Alka-Seltzer tablet under Niagara Falls just because of some little Hitler in Washington. The safest thing to do is for everyone to go to their assigned retreats now. We'll leave a few people here to guard the farm tonight and every retreat will send a convoy of trucks back in the morning to load up with food and other needful items. We'll keep the convoys at work until we have everything of value to our survival removed from the farm or it becomes too dangerous to continue."

"Chances are, we have plenty of time to get everything out," Caroline said. "I still say we're too insignificant for Washington to bother with."

The crowd seemed to have accepted MacKay's decision, as there were no objections. No one even had anything more so say. The people rushed to their assigned duties and proceeded to carry out their preplanned emergency evacuation.

"Do you think Caroline is right?" MacKay asked.

"It's logical," Deni answered. "We're no threat to Washington."

"Logical yes," Nate said. "But you're assuming our little Hitler is different from Germany's version."

Deni looked puzzled. "What do you mean?"

"Hitler did a lot of things that were not logical, out of hatred, ego, and insanity."

"Oh shit!" Deni nodded. "You're right. A lot of what Hitler did was illogical. It cost Germany any chance of a victory. He seemed to be more interested in slaughtering Jews than winning the war, and sacrificed whole divisions out of false pride, ordering them not to retreat when they could've escaped to fight another day."

Noticing the sinking mood of the adults, Samantha reached for Caroline's hand. Caroline smiled down at her and winked. "Everything is okay."

~~~

Kramer tried to get comfortable in the bed, but his shoulder wouldn't give him any peace. Nurses had put something on his neck so he couldn't see the results of the surgery. It just made him want to look that much more and it hurt when he pushed against it. For the tenth time, he yanked at the handcuff that constrained his good arm and prevented him from removing the neck torture device. "Why don't they take pity on me and put me under? I'm a freak."

The door to his room opened and a full bird colonel walked in, followed by Mel. He noticed the colonel was wearing a 1911 pistol at his side and Mel was loaded up for battle, a rifle in his hands.

"Can I borrow your pistol, Colonel?" Kramer asked.

Col. Joe Greene scowled. "I wouldn't expect a high-speed operator like you to choose that route out of this world. You lost your left arm, not your balls."

Kramer glared back. "I lost more than my arm. I'm a freak. Women will run screaming from me."

Col. Greene's scowl softened somewhat. "Join the club. Women have been reacting to me that way for the last 20 years. My wife had a stroke the last time she saw me coming out of a shower."

Life came to Kramer's eyes for a second. "Okay, Colonel, what do you want? I know you want something. You wouldn't be here otherwise."

Col. Greene turned to Mel and back to Kramer. "Have you forgotten your short conversation with the best damn sergeant in the Guard?"

"Sure, I remember." Kramer's expression made it apparent he didn't like being a pawn. "Look, I'm not some kind of a secret weapon that'll take Capinos down. Everybody in the military has known for over a year he's poison for America, yet they all follow his orders." He glared at Greene. "It's you higher-ranking officers who've lost your balls. And as long as that's the case, Capinos is going to be wreaking havoc on what's left of the people."

Greene's brow furrowed. "Some of what you say is true, but don't doubt the courage of the officer corps or their will to do the right thing, no matter the personal cost. I expect future events will prove you wrong." He stood silent for a second to allow his blood pressure to lower. "And do not underestimate the effect your testimony will have on the political situation." He slammed his right fist into his open left hand. "That SOB has the blood of millions of Americans on his hands. Hell, we'd be back on our feet by now if President Thomson hadn't died in the plague. Might be anyway, if most of Congress hadn't been taken also."

"You got that right, Colonel," Mel said. "I'll stop there, because a soldier shouldn't be speaking ill of his Commander in Chief." He noticed the colonel's reaction. "But, uh, an officer has earned the right, especially under these extreme circumstances."

Greene laughed. "I'll bet you're not so restrained when you're with the enlisted men. Capinos is no president; he was never elected."

Mel nodded. "Yes sir."

Greene directed his attention at Kramer. "I have nothing but respect for you. I'm told you stopped a massacre of innocent civilians and defied direct orders from Capinos in the process." He pointed a finger. "But don't ever disparage the courage and commitment of the officer corps of any branch again. If you do, I'll wait until you're completely healed and whip your ass. Oh, I'll tie my left hand behind my back to make it fair, but there's nothing I can do about the fact I have many years on you and am more experienced in the art of ass-kicking." He shrugged. "I'll try not to take advantage of your youthful inexperience too much, but I *will* kick your ass!"

Kramer laughed. "Yes sir. I mean I won't disparage the officers of the U.S. military again."

Greene cleared his throat. "I wonder if you know that Capinos and the CIA have accused you and one of your team members, Kenneth Rittleman, of murdering civilians."

Kramer blurted, "That's bullshit. We stopped it!" He forgot his wound in his anger and found himself grimacing in pain after jerking around on the bed. "Rittleman proved he was a standup operator. He backed me when things got hairy. Now those bastards are spitting on his memory."

"So he's dead." Greene nodded knowingly. "Maybe I should also mention that Capinos has ordered dozens of general officers arrested for treason. They may have already been secretly executed for all we know."

Kramer turned white. "Judging by his past actions, I think you should assume those generals are dead."

Greene froze, his eyes looking inward and anger coming to the surface. "If that's true… God damn him!"

~~~

Capinos looked up from his desk. CIA Director William Shekel walked into the Oval Office at exactly 3 PM. "On time to the minute," Capinos said. "I don't know how you do it, Bill. Never late and almost never early."

Shekel tried to smile but just couldn't. "Do you realize the shitstorm you've started? Arresting those generals makes it look like some kind a purge. You and I have already talked about how the military is on the verge of revolt. And now you pull this? Also, I thought we had agreed to give the military six months before pulling the rug out from under them. The idea was to give them enough rope to hang themselves. Well, they haven't hanged themselves. In fact they've been helping the people organize and start farms over much of the country. And they've been protecting the people for the first time since it all went to hell." He pointed out the window. "Have you been out in the city lately? The DC no longer looks like some kind of a zombie movie. The streets are safe, and commerce is even starting up again. Hell, there are a few grammar schools open in DC now. And it's not just DC. About 20% of the country has been stabilized. Give them another six months and at least half of the country will be relatively safe and free from hunger. Do you understand what that means? If you don't, the people damn sure do. Pulling this shit now is absolutely the worst mistake I've seen you make so far."

Capinos jumped up from his chair behind the desk, red-faced. "How dare you come in here and bark at me like that! I have a habit of kicking in the front teeth of anyone who snaps at my ankles like a little Chihuahua." He huffed for several seconds and rubbed his hands together. "If we weren't lifelong friends, Bill…"

"Sorry, neither of us have time to hug and kiss. You have put your presidency at stake, and that means my ass is at stake. This was the very worst time for you to pull this. The idea was for us to wait until the military fell on its face. You have chosen exactly the wrong time, while the military is still being very successful and gaining the support of the American people. If you had just waited a few months longer, they were bound to have screwed up bad. That's when you should've stepped in. That was the whole idea."

"Uh, yeah, well," Capinos' strange expression alone could have inspired a psychiatrist to write volumes about a new type of megalomania, "Quit the act, Bill. I see right through it. You're not on my side at all."

"And whose side am I on?" Shekel asked.

"Why, yours of course," Capinos answered.

"What, you think I want your job?"

"Maybe." Capinos smiled. "But I suppose you're going to tell me it's the country you care about."

Shekel seemed to be losing patience. "I've been trying to help both you and the American people."

The laughter that emanated from Capinos was sickening. "It was your men who killed those civilians in Florida."

"Under direct orders from you, it seems," Shekel added. "I would have had anyone involved in a massacre put up on charges."

Capinos laughed again. "It was your idea to blame the massacre on those two missing operators, though I doubt they did it. It was this Kramer guy who seemed to be having qualms about doing his duty."

Shekel examined the Oval Office carpet. "That's true. I was willing to sacrifice two good men for the sake of the country. Now I'm glad they've escaped. Two deaths not on my conscience."

Relaxing, Capinos sat on the edge of his desk and crossed his arms. "Then what's your problem with sacrificing a few generals? I need to make examples of them. Too many high-ranking officers signed that damn petition. I can't arrest them all, not and have enough to run the military. I haven't touched those on the Joint Chiefs of Staff, for the very reason I need them. But a few examples can speak as loud as a thousand."

Shekel turned white. "You're *not* going to have them executed? Don't you know what that will mean?"

"Already have." Capinos' face turned to cold stone. "Just the ones I had arrested. Most of them were brigadier generals."

His jaw hanging slack, Shekel turned white. "Oh my God!"

Confused, Capinos asked, "What, did you know one of them?"

Shekel didn't answer. "My God. It's inevitable now."

"What the hell are you muttering about, Bill?"

"Civil war. That's what I'm muttering about."

~~~

The next morning at Mrs. MacKay's farm.

"The last truck will be leaving soon." Caroline's dilemma brought tears to her eyes. "You three could use an extra rifle, and I would like to go with you. But I have Samantha to think about."

Nate stood by the truck, still loaded with corn, and the trailer also packed with produce. "Samantha is welcome too."

Deni and Brian spoke simultaneously, "You're both welcome."

Nate looked at the little girl, who had little resemblance to his own daughter, but still reminded him of her. "I suppose she would be safer with a larger group. It's your decision. But you're both welcome."

Caroline asked, "You're not still going into town, are you?"

Deni glanced at Nate before answering. "No. It's too dangerous now."

"We're heading home," Nate added. "I'm not sure what we'll do with all this produce once we get there. We won't have much time to prepare it for storage before going into hiding. I don't think we have long before it hits the fan. Not that anyone will come after us specifically, not yet anyway, but we don't want to get in their way while the different factions are going at each other."

Brian watched half a dozen men feverishly load a two-ton truck with sacks of dried beans and canned produce. "We sure can't can it. We're out of Mason jars."

Nate walked over to a group of men loading another truck. He pointed at the trailer loaded with produce. "You think you could hook that up and take it with you? We were going to take it into town, but it's too dangerous for that now."

The man nodded. "Yes, we could do that. Thank you."

"How about the corn?" Nate asked. "We need the truck though. We're in too much of a hurry to get home to walk."

"Uh, we need to get out of here too." The man looked at the pile of corn. "If you give us 20 minutes, we might have time to take some of it off your hands. God knows we have a lot of people to feed, despite all our work harvesting the fields." He shook Nate's hand. "You've been a good friend to us. We all hope you fare well."

Nate nodded. "We'll hang around another 30 minutes then." He returned to the others. "Guess we just solved that problem."

"If they'd give us some baskets or buckets, we could start loading the corn on their truck for them while we wait," Brian offered.

A pale-faced woman ran out of the main house and onto the front steps. She screamed at the top of her voice, "Why oh bright beam of an August moon have you not written me? They just broadcast the code! Why oh bright beam of an August moon have you not written me?"

MacKay joined her on the porch. "Orderly, people! Orderly! There's no need for panic. We have plenty of time."

Everyone froze for a second. Then the yard was a flurry of action.

"Get in the truck!" Nate yelled. "Caroline, if you're coming with us, take Samantha and get in." He ran back to the trailer and unhooked it.

Brian jumped up on the pile of corn in the back of the truck. He waved at Mrs. MacKay. "Good luck!"

She waved back, struggling to smile.

When Nate jumped behind the wheel, he saw that Caroline was sitting next to Deni, Samantha on her knee. He cranked the engine and took off, speeding down the drive and through the open gate. Two guards waved as they passed.

"Is there need for this kind of a rush?" Deni asked. "It's not like there's a drone circling above."

The poor condition of the road forced Nate to slow down. "Maybe not. How can we tell?" He glanced in the rearview mirror and saw Brian struggling to not be bounced off the pile of corn. "What little I know about our new president and Congress tells me not to put anything past them. There are still things we have to do at home before we disappear. It'll be dark by the time we're through."

Chapter 21

Col. Greene read the message handed to him by a lieutenant. His rage obvious, he handed the paper back. "You might want to keep that. Some day it'll be an historical artifact." He looked at the gathering of stunned officers and noncoms in the room. "Capinos just sent us a message. He had most of the generals he relieved of duty executed by firing squad." A few men lost control and yelled expletives. Greene raised his voice. "Don't jump to any conclusions. No one knows how this'll play out or how bloody it'll get. We'll continue to serve the American people." He grit his teeth. "But I for one will no longer take orders from a tinhorn dictator."

The soldiers erupted in a roar of support.

~~~

Capinos expected a little trouble, but he was stunned by the military's reaction and shocked by the people's outrage. *I'll have to stop playing with them.* Decision made, he called for a meeting with the entire Joint Chiefs of Staff. It was late, so he scheduled the meeting for 11 AM the next morning. *My teams will have all night to do their thing before I lower the hammer on the top generals.*

~~~

Nate stopped the truck and pulled over to the side one quarter mile from the farm and got out to check the dirt road for tire tracks.

Brian searched from his perch on the pile of green corn. "I don't see any sign anyone came through here since we did."

Nate scanned down the road to the driveway with binoculars. Satisfied, he said, "We'll walk through the woods the rest of the way, swinging around to the north side."

"Yeah." Brian checked for trouble coming up behind them. "We better hurry if we're going to get the place closed up and be out of there by dark."

Nate looked into the cab through the open door at Deni and Caroline. "Keep your voice down. Don't slam the door." He grabbed his pack off of the pile of corn and slipped the straps over his shoulders. Grabbing his rifle, he said, "I'm going to leave the key in the truck in case someone from the horse farm comes by and wants to take the corn with them. Maybe we can get the truck back later."

Deni nodded. "Okay. We won't be needing the truck for a while."

They slipped into the woods and never looked back.

As they walked through the darkening woods in the dying sunless afternoon, Nate began to grow ever more wary. When he could see the roof of the barn and they were not far from the clearing, he stopped and signaled for the others to get down. Whispering in Deni's ear, he said, "I have a bad feeling about this."

Deni looked back at him with worried eyes. "Knowing you and your ability to smell trouble, I think maybe we should bypass the farm and go on into hiding."

Brian's shoulders slumped, but he said nothing.

Caroline held Samantha with one hand and her rifle with the other, while she constantly scanned the woods for danger. Suddenly she froze and hissed, "Listen!"

Dull percussions shook the ground beneath them. An overpressure wave and then two more followed. The pressure waves were weakened by distance but noticeable.

Brian tried to peer through the treetops at the sky. "What the hell was that?"

"People dying," Nate answered, his voice sounding almost like a moan.

Deni exhaled deeply. "Bombs, missiles, artillery. Hard to say which."

"It damn sure wasn't any deer rifle." Brian continued to look at the sky, searching for danger. He froze. "It couldn't be the horse farm, could it? We couldn't hear it that far away, could we?"

"Sounded like 500-pounders to me," Nate answered. "Could've been 1,000-pounders from farther away." He was the only one there who had seen and heard heavy bombs used in warfare. "I have no idea what they would be using that kind of ordnance on out here. Any asshole who ordered that should be shot."

"What about the farm?" Brian asked again.

Nate looked at his son. "They couldn't have been that far away. We wouldn't have felt any overpressure at all and no ground vibrations if they were. They must've been a long ways off but nowhere near as far as the horse farm." He didn't mention they could have been used against vehicles on the road.

Deni shook her head. "I can't believe it's already started in this backwoods area. So soon?"

"I guess someone's pissed off at the people in this county," Caroline said.

Nate's jaw set. "Maybe Capinos doesn't like us."

It had grown cooler with the sunset, but everyone there was sweating and breathing hard.

Brian pointed. "I saw movement near the barn!"

Nate scanned with binoculars. They were just close enough to the edge of the clearing he could see through the brush. "Armed men. All young and in good shape. No uniforms. But the way they're maneuvering says military."

He watched as a man shouldered an anti-armor weapon and fired it at the front door of the house. A fiery explosion left most of the house burning under a billowing cloud of black smoke.

Everyone but Nate hit the ground and laid flat. Barely controlling his temper, he thought, *these assholes believe in overkill.*

Nate slipped his binoculars under his shirt. "Follow me and stay low!"

They hadn't gone three yards when automatic gunfire forced them to hit the ground again. Bullets chewed at trees just over their backs. Yelling from the direction of the house and barn, intermixed with more gunfire, motivated them to crawl fast until they were far enough back in the trees they thought it safe to run, keeping bent over and low, heading for the river.

Nate ran 50 yards and stopped just long enough to look back and make sure no one had been left behind. He saw all four of them looking at him with wide, scared eyes and sweaty pale faces, gasping for air. Caroline had Samantha in her arms.

She had been carrying her. Nate stepped closer. "Give her to me. We have to move fast, and you have only one leg."

Samantha began to cry but didn't make much noise. Nate held her with one hand and his rifle with the other. "We don't want to even try to outfight them, so we better outrun them. Stay low and on my heels." He took off at top speed and prayed they didn't run into an ambush.

Running downhill through the swamp, Nate came to the river, knowing they would have to swim it. He could hear the killers shouting, coming at them. They needed to put more distance between them and their pursuers before crossing the river or chance being caught midstream and helpless. Loaded down with their packs and weapons, it wouldn't be easy. He pushed himself mercilessly and hoped the others could keep up. It was Caroline, slowed by her artificial leg, he worried about being left behind most. But in the past, she had proven herself capable, artificial leg or no. He noticed Samantha kept looking over his shoulder, keeping her eyes on Caroline, and he hoped she would warn him if Caroline stumbled and was being left behind.

After 40 minutes of pushing through brush, Nate stopped to catch his breath and check on the others. They struggled to catch up and were soaked in sweat, gagging for air. *They look like I feel.* He let Samantha down to rest his arm and looked past them in the direction of their farm – out of sight because of the trees blocking his view – where he saw a column of smoke – his burning house. As he looked and panted for air, another black column rose straight up, insulting the clear sky with its violent message of destruction. They had set the barn on fire, too. Most of the house was concrete and stone, the roof tin, but the inside was mostly wood and the barn nearly all wood. Both seemed to be burning fast.

Deni reached out and hooked a palm tree with her left arm and held on as if she would collapse without its support. Gasping, she looked back. "The bastards are burning the barn too."

Brian turned to look. His chest heaving, he snapped his head around and looked up at his father with eyes full of rage.

Before he had time to speak, Nate cut him off. "Be more afraid than mad. There must be three dozen of them, and they're outfitted like an army. Now let's get across. We don't want them to catch us in the water."

"We'll be sitting ducks," Deni added.

They scrambled down to the water's edge and waded in. Nate scanned the bank quickly with his eyes, finding no logs suitable for helping them across. "You two have your waterproof pack liners sealed well?" He asked Deni and Brian.

They both answered yes.

"Good. You'll need the floatation. The river's not more than five feet deep until just before you reach the far bank. I'll take Samantha across." He hung his rifle on his neck, so he would they have both hands. "Wait there until I'm on dry land. I'll throw you a rope – Caroline first – and pull you across fast. You can hold your breath that long, if you go under."

Deni checked behind them. "Let Brian go first."

Nate heard no sounds of pursuit, but he knew the men who hunted them were all young and in good shape and couldn't be far behind. "Don't argue. I'll need your rifle to shoot them off him if they catch us before we're all across." Not wasting time, he waded in, creating a wave in front, as he pushed forward against the water's resistance. He noticed the river was low and the current weak. It hadn't rained much lately. The tea-colored water felt cold at first, then warm. Heavy with ammunition, his pack had many pounds of negative flotation and tried to drag him under when it got too deep to wade. He sidestroked the rest of the way, his mouth below water some of the time, but Samantha's head always above water. After lifting Samantha onto the bank, he crawled onto dry land and yanked his pack off. A coil of 3/8-inch nylon rope was tucked under the pack's top flap, where he could get to it fast. After Caroline threw him her M4 rifle, he cast the rope to her. She looped it around her, and he began to pull. For two yards, she was under, but he soon had her on the bank, gasping for air.

Caroline scrambled to grab her rifle and get into shooting position. She would be ready to kill anyone she saw on the far bank and keep them off Deni and Brian. When Samantha ran to her, she pushed the little girl down behind a log.

The process worked just as well for Deni. She rushed to get into position to fire across the river.

Nate had Brian across even faster, since he was smaller. They left the river's edge and ran into a 20,000-acre swamp they knew well, the sound of pursuit on the far bank urging them on.

"Why didn't we fight at the river?" Brian asked between gasps for air. "We could've gotten some of them."

Nate didn't answer for several minutes, concentrating instead on running. Finally, he slowed down but didn't stop. "We could kill a few of them, but there are too many. They would just pin us down and cross the river out of our sight, then outflank us and finish us off. There's no point in killing a few of them when it gets us killed in the end. There's nothing left back there to fight over."

"They burned our home," Brian protested. "We took on that gang a year and a half ago."

Nate shook his head, saving his breath. When he came to a large log and had to slow down, he said, "We'll talk later. Run."

~~~

Just after midnight, the exhausted fugitives dragged themselves into thick brush. Nate prayed the canopy of pine trees above would make it difficult for FLIR, or forward looking infrared, to detect them from the air.

Samantha was fast asleep, her head lying on Nate's shoulder. He waited until Caroline had laid out her sleeping bag before handing Samantha to her. "I'll take first watch," he whispered.

Brian grabbed his shoulder. "Do you think there're still hunting us?"

"Someone wants us dead," Nate answered. "Yes, I think they're still hunting us."

Deni already had her pack off and her sleeping bag laid out. "We have to get some rest, Brian. We'll eat something before daylight and push on." She took a much-needed drink from her canteen.

"Then what?" Brian asked.

Nate slipped his pack off, making an effort not to make any noise. He whispered, "After making certain we've shaken them off our trail, we'll go to one of our hiding places and stay there. We lost some of our supplies that we hadn't cached in the woods yet when they burned the house and barn, but we still have more than enough to last a year, on top of what's left at Mel's place."

Brian wasn't finished. "I don't mean to be a complainer, but it seems like every time things are looking up it gets worse than ever. I'm tired of living like this."

"Damn it." Nate put his hand on Brian's shoulder. "I know. We're all tired. Right now we have to get these killers off our trail. How long we end up hiding out here depends on what the military and others in Washington do. There's simply no way to know what's going to happen now. It could all be over in a few weeks. Or… well, it could get a lot worse and last years."

Deni quickly added, "I think generals are formulating a coup right now. Whatever happened must be a big deal, and the military was already losing patience with Washington."

"Maybe," was all Nate said on the matter. "Everyone get some rest. I'm tired myself, and will be waking one of you to pull security in about two hours."

~~~

Samantha cried when Caroline woke her 45 minutes before sunrise. "Shhh," Caroline said. "If you have to cry, be quiet about it."

Each of them ate the first thing they could grab out of their packs, and Caroline finally got Samantha to eat some crackers with blackberry jam smeared on them.

"Let's go," Nate whispered. "I'm sure they're still hunting us."

Two hours later, they came to a small opening in the swamp and Nate turned to his right to skirt around the edge. The sun was over the horizon, casting tall shadows from their side of the clearing and penetrating into the tree line on the far side. A flash of sunlight reflecting off of glass or bright metal caught Nate's attention. "Down!" He landed on his belly, as did the others a split second later.

A staccato of gunshots assaulted their ears, and bullets ripped at the trees just above them.

"Belly crawl," Nate yelled. The others followed him, dragging their bellies on the leaf-strewn swamp floor. Caroline had to crawl on her hands and knees because she had Samantha hanging from her neck, but she managed, despite her backpack being grazed twice by bullets and her prosthetic leg hindering her.

By the time they had crawled 20 yards, the shooting had stopped. Nate yelled, "Stay on my ass and stay low." He jumped up and ran.

~~~

Capinos listened to the ex-CIA operative on the satellite phone. He was part of a team of killers Capinos had hired, mostly soldier-of-fortune types that would kill for money and work for anyone, but the leaders of the teams were ex-CIA. Since money wasn't of much value at the moment, they were paid with lots of gold that might have value again someday, and food, clothing, shelter, ammo, fuel, and other items needed to survive the current conditions of the post-plague collapse.

Capinos scowled. "So you failed to complete your mission." The man on the other end started to speak. "Oh shut up! I don't need excuses about how they're hiding in thick woods or any other bullshit. You men are supposed to be the best. They're just hicks. I'm on a schedule here. And you're running out of time. *I'm* running out of time. I have an important meeting in a few minutes and I expected this little matter to have been taken care of by now." He jerked his head back in reaction to what the other man said. "Huh? Never mind why I want them dead! They may not be a threat to national security but they've pissed me off. Look. I want them dead. If you want to keep your job, you will get this done, and soon."

He terminated the communication and dropped into his chair behind the desk. Mentally switching gears, he regained his composure in preparation for the arrival of the entire Joint

Chiefs of Staff. His request to see them all in the Oval Office was so unusual it certainly alerted the generals that the execution of a few BGs who had signed that damned petition was just the beginning and that the waiting was over. He purposely gave them all night to sweat it out and worry about what was coming. If they all showed up, he was in trouble. If none of them showed up, he was in trouble. If half showed and half were no-shows, he had a chance. It would mean they were not in solidarity. He prayed for discord among the generals.

At exactly 11 AM, his secretary announced that Army General Carl Strovenov, Chairman of the Joint Chiefs of Staff, had arrived. "Alone?" Capinos asked.

The secretary answered, "Yes."

Capinos smiled just a little but seemed to be puzzled. "Send him in."

General Strovenov walked in wearing civilian clothes.

Capinos furrowed his brow. "This is not an informal meeting, General."

Strovenov stood in front of the desk. "The government I swore an oath to serve no longer exists. Why should I be wearing its military's uniform?"

Shocked by his words, Capinos cleared his throat and tried to speak but nothing intelligible came out.

Strovenov looked him in the eye. "The others will not be coming. They are busy preparing."

"Preparing?" Capinos asked. "Preparing for what?"

"To clean up the mess you made," was Strovenov's answer. "There won't be any more executions of military officers, or civilians." He glared at Capinos. "But if your bloodlust still consumes your soul, I'm here to offer my life. Kill me or don't kill me. Either way, elections will take place in less than six months and you will resign your office, effective noon today." He looked at his watch. "You have 50 minutes to have me executed. After that, you will have lost your chance."

Capinos dropped his jaw. "Do you really think you have the power to –"

Strovenov interrupted him. "I have no power at all. I expect to be dead in a few minutes. It's the American people who have the power, *and* the backing of every branch of the military. You went too far and squandered your chance to be the president that led America out of its worst nightmare. You could've been a great icon in world history and respected above our Founding Fathers, but your ego rotted your mind and your soul. Now you'll be despised for eternity." He raised his empty hands in anguish. "We were doing it! In just a few short months, we were making a difference, starting the process to recovery. But you wouldn't have it. To hell with the people and the nation, you wanted power."

Capinos slapped a panic button, alerting Secret Service agents. His hands shook as he lifted a phone off the hook and then he dropped it when he realized it was the red phone that connected him to the Joint Chiefs of Staff. His desperate eyes lit up as he snatched the satellite phone off the desk. Two Secret Service agents burst in, Glock pistols pointing at Strovenov. Capinos motioned with his head. "Arrest him. Hold him in a room somewhere nearby."

Strovenov made no attempt to resist. "Calling your private army will do you no good. You'll just get more people killed needlessly. It's over. You're finished."

The agents forced Strovenov out the door.

~~~

As early morning became mid-afternoon, Nate and the others lost the strength to run, and then the strength to walk fast. Still, they pushed on at three miles per hour, led only by Nate's compass and woodsmanship skills.

Exhausted, Nate found a windfall to sit on. "Take five and have a drink." He slipped out of his pack and reached for a canteen. "We're paralleling the river, heading north. We'll keep going a few miles farther and turn east to cross back over to the east side about sundown, when we still have enough light to see the moccasins and gators."

Brian wiped at his sweaty forehead with an already sweat-soaked handkerchief. "I almost wish it was winter and cold as hell again."

Deni tried to smile. "It's late summer. What do you expect?"

Nate put his canteen away. "If it was winter, the trees would be bare of leaves and they could see us easier from the air."

Deni swallowed a mouth full of water from her canteen, eyes wide. "Those hunting us on the ground could see us easier too."

Samantha cried. She had been crying most of the day. Caroline held a canteen to her mouth. "Drink. You're getting dehydrated." She looked at Nate and Deni, anger creasing her face. "She's too young for this. There's no strength left in her little arms to hold onto my neck while I run. I'm not going to torture her any longer. I'd rather go back and kill some of the bastards while you take her out of here."

Nate cast a glance at their back trail and mopped sweat from his forehead. "One of them is a tracker. That's why we haven't shaken them off our ass. Most likely it's a two-man team. You need at least one man to stay alert for danger while the tracker keeps his eyes on the ground. They switch off every hour or so. Could be a three-man team, but I only need to kill two of them."

Deni gripped her rifle with both hands. "Why does it always have to be you? I was a soldier only a few months ago."

Nate coughed. "Yeah, that's what good husbands do. Run away while their wives fight."

Deni rolled her eyes. "That's sexist bullshit."

"No," Nate said, "it's doing the right thing." He looked at Brian. "I want you to take them to the two islands just before the river turns sharply to the east. On the south end of the first island, the water is shallower except for the first eight feet or so. It'll be easier for you to cross there."

The expression on Brian's face spoke louder than words. "I'll get them across. But you better meet us on the other side sometime tonight. We're not going to survive this without you."

His determination coming to the surface, Nate said, "I'll be there. I expect it's spooks on our trail. I'm not going to let any CIA spooks get the best of me."

"Is that Army pride or something?" Deni asked.

Nate looked around, trying to penetrate the wall of green that encircled them. "More like rage. They shot at us and burned us out. They're trying to kill my wife, my son, and my friend, not to mention a little girl." He stood and slipped into his pack. "Take off. Sunlight's burning."

Thunder rumbled in the distance. Brian looked at the western sky. "That rain comes our way, they won't be tracking us anymore until tomorrow. We'll be on the other side of the river by then." He looked at his father with hope in his eyes. "Maybe you don't have to go back and fight them."

Nate saw Deni's reaction and froze for a second. "Oh hell, I'm not exactly jumping at a chance to get shot at. We'll go on a few miles farther. But if rain doesn't wash away our trail soon, you'll be going on to the river without me."

~~~

The slight breeze that had been too weak to cool them, invigorated by the coming thunderstorm, gradually shook off its lethargy, setting the woods to motion and making it more difficult to spot movement. Nate worried they were moving too fast and could walk into an ambush, but they were being pressed by their pursuers to push on. Each second, each step torturous, Nate balanced the need for speed with the need for caution and tried to ignore the crawling of his skin from nervous tension. He wished he had sent them on without him, but realized if the killers had split up and sent a group ahead to set up an ambush, the results would be worse if he were not with them. They would want to take him out first, and that might give the others a chance to get out of the kill zone, where life expectancy would be measured in seconds. He shivered in the heat and pressed on, turning more to the east. He thought it best not to travel in the same direction too long, to make it more difficult for the killers to set up that ambush he feared so much.

By noon, clouds that had rolled in earlier grew high and deep under the energy of the sun. The humid air was so heavy with moisture rain became inevitable. When it finally came, it arrived with full force, in a torrent, but stopped after a few minutes. A surge of wind, mixing hot air with cool, came down from the blue-black sky and swept down on them without warning. The roar of a soaking downpour rolled across the swampland in an advancing wall of rain. In seconds, they were soaked. The crack of lightning bolts and thunder added to the violence of the tempest.

Bullfrogs croaked in the swamp. More thunder from distant storms hung in the heavy air for a moment before being overwhelmed by the clap of thunder from jagged bolts of lightning above them.

Samantha's cries grew louder with each lightning strike. Nate stopped and motioned for them to gather around him. He yanked his pack off and produced a poncho from a side pocket. While he unrolled it, he said, "Deni. Brian. Help me hold this over Caroline and Samantha so Caroline can get her into something dry before she chills too much. Afterwards, she can use the poncho to keep Samantha from getting wet and cold again."

After Caroline and Samantha were finished and the little girl was warm and dry in the poncho, her little face almost invisible in the shade of the hood and several times too long for her, they moved on. None of the adults wanted to don their ponchos, preferring to enjoy the cold rain and wind, as well as the shower. It felt good not to be soaked with sweat and swamp filth. Besides, a poncho would hinder their ability to run and get at their weapons and ammo magazines.

Nate carried Samantha a while. She was too big for carrying and too small to keep up with them. There was no way she could walk with the oversize poncho on, anyway. Not long after the first storm passed another one hit with equal force. The heavy overcast made the swamp under the canopy of trees almost as dark as night. The closer they got to the river, the wetter it was, and they were forced to go around flooded low areas. It was then Nate realized the rain was coming so fast, the river would be rising by the time they got to the islands. A windfall was nearby. So he walked to it and sat down. The log was soggy but hadn't rotted yet and was still solid. He motioned for the others to sit beside him.

They sat down on the log, grasping their rifles and peering through the rain, alert to the danger they knew was out there.

Nate was about to speak but was interrupted by a crashing in the brush uphill from them. In a blur of motion, they all slid off the log and got behind it.

Noticing fear on the face of the others, Samantha was wide-eyed but silent for once. Caroline whispered in her ear, "Be very quiet and just lay here behind this log." She sat up and shouldered her rifle, clicking the safety off.

Somewhere out there hidden in the green gloom of the jungle, under the shade of heavy rain clouds and the canopy of tree tops above, a killer had just made a fatal mistake.

Nate got down low and peered over the log. He hand signaled for the others to do the same and then mouthed the words, *don't fire until I do.* His skin tingled with nervous tension, all senses on high-volume intensity, eyes funneling in and focusing the images before him in minute detail. He pulled his M14 tight against his shoulder and clicked the safety off with the back of his trigger finger, thinking in a minute or two he just might get a chance to end the hunt by killing the hunters. That is if it was the two or three man team of trackers coming at them and not an entire platoon of trained killers. He hoped the tracking team was far enough ahead of the main force he and the others could kill them and then flee the area before the others arrived. He looked over at Deni, Brian, Caroline, and Samantha and wondered if he was about to get them killed. The only thing that had kept them alive so far was their success at preventing the highly trained killers from locating them and fixing their position so they couldn't sneak off before being annihilated. He gripped his rifle tighter with sweaty hands and resolved to not let that happen.

Chapter 22

A slight movement in the brush uphill and to his right warned Nate. He waited for the man to come into view. The first thing he noticed was the man was looking for tracks. He had lost their trail in the rain, and his efforts were on striking the trail again, not so much on being alert to danger. Nate found it ironic that the man probably entered the river swamp to search for tracks where they would be protected to some degree by the canopy of treetops above and that had brought him and his team directly to their targets, rather than actually tracking them. It was a matter of utter bad luck, and Nate resolved it would be the men who died and not he or those with him.

More movement caught Nate's eye. Another man followed 15 yards behind the tracker and a little to the side. Nate desperately searched for a third man. He had no idea if there was one, but he damn sure wanted to locate him before firing the first shot if there was.

There! Nate aimed his rifle. Glancing at the others, he held up three fingers. He signaled for Deni to take out the tracker and Brian and Caroline to take out the one behind him.

The third man froze when he happened to look in Nate's direction and saw Nate aiming at him from behind the log. Their eyes locked for a fraction of a second, each man seeing death staring back. The bark of Nate's M14 reverberated among the trees. Deni fired. Brian and Caroline fired at the same time, just a hundredth of a second behind Deni. Nate took enough time to make sure all three men were down and that they were alone. "We have to run like hell! Stay on my ass."

Caroline swept up Samantha and they took off at top speed, crashing through the brush. Automatic gunfire spurred them on. They didn't slow down for 15 minutes and then continued on at a jog for another half hour.

Exhausted, Nate sat down on a large root that at least kept him out of the mud and motioned for the others to do the same. He wanted a drink but was too busy catching his breath to stop sucking air.

Deni kept her eyes working, scanning the swamp for danger. "We can't rest now." She caught her breath. "They're not far behind."

Nate nodded. "They're in good shape and a lot younger than me. They'll run me into the ground. You three go on. I can slow them enough to give you a chance. Turn uphill onto drier land and get into the thick stuff."

Brian's jaw dropped.

Deni gave Nate a look that could kill. "Bullshit!"

Caroline stood, Samantha hanging onto her neck. "Let's stop arguing and start running. If I can make it with one leg, you can make it with two."

Nate pulled his tired body to his feet. "Okay. I have a little left in me." He took off, heading for drier land.

A tremendous fireball erupted 100 yards down their back trail. And then another explosion, closer this time. Terror banished all weariness as they took off at a run. More explosions followed. The explosions continued as they ran at a right angle to the river and climbed out of the swamp onto drier land, where tall pines grew. They didn't stop running until Nate fell. By that time, it seemed they were safe, and they stopped to rest for a moment.

"Rockets," Deni managed to say between gasps, "from a chopper. I don't think they were guided bombs or missiles. Not large enough for that." She took in a breath. "We would've heard them coming if they were arty or mortars."

Brian couldn't believe it. "Why do they want us dead so much they use millions of dollars' worth of weapons on us? What did we do?"

Caroline laughed out of nervousness. "It's not their money."

Thunder shook the ground. Another storm was coming in.

Nate seemed to be catching his second wind. He stood, but was unsteady on his feet for a second. "Two things in our favor. Those chasing us can't be that close, or they never would've chanced that air strike. The other thing is that new storm coming this way. It'll keep the choppers away for a while." He looked around and then checked his compass. "Let's get out of here."

They had run less than half a mile when a sound alerted Nate. "Hit the ground!" he yelled.

An explosion took them off their feet before they had a chance to react. Spurting soil erupted 70 yards to their left and another where they had just been a moment before, exploding up from the ground and out, into an ever-widening circle of high-velocity earth. And from the center of each geyser of earth came a red ball of fire, expanding, rising, boiling, and climbing into the sky. And then the shock wave hit them, hurling them bodily up from the ground. The roar so loud their ears overloaded and ceased to hear. Some circuit breaker inside their head switched off, leaving them deaf.

Nate tried to stand, but fell over on his face, his balance failing him. Another explosion, closer still, and the ground came up and slapped his whole body where he lay. He found himself off the ground and in midair. For what seemed to him to be many seconds, but was only a fraction of one, he hung suspended, levitating above the forest floor. Just as he started to fall back to earth, another explosion on the other side of him caused the earth to rise up and slap his underside again. And once more, he felt himself suspended in midair, inches above the ground. In reality, it was only a fraction of an inch, but sufficient enough to create the feeling he was levitating in thin air.

The next explosion was farther away, and then the next farther toward the river. The last one seemed to land in the river itself. Nate knew for certain the others were dead. He frantically crawled along the ground, still not able to stand. "Deni! Brian!"

Nate saw a bloody hand protruding from the fresh earth, quivering and reaching up. He pulled on it and the rest of her emerged from the soft dirt. It was Caroline, still holding onto Samantha, who was conscious but too stunned to cry. Both were alive. Once he saw their mouths were clear and they were breathing and not bleeding too much, he crawled on.

"Deni! Brian!" Nate saw movement to his left and rushed to it on his hands and knees. He thought he heard Deni cough, but couldn't be sure because of the loud ringing in his ears. He found she wasn't completely buried the way the others were, but she seemed to be struggling with something next to her.

Deni yanked on something and it came up from under the fresh earth. It was Brian's rifle. She clawed at the dirt, digging frantically. "Brian!"

Nate rushed to her side and dug with both hands. Then he moved a few feet and dug again. "There should be something. A hand. A boot. Something."

Deni screamed, "There he is!" She tried to stand but fell on her face, so she crawled. Nate couldn't hear her words but saw what she was looking at and followed her.

Brian lay at an odd angle between two large pine trees that had been cut nearly in half by the explosions or metal fragments from the guided bombs. Nate reached him first. Checking his breathing and finding no sign of life, he opened his mouth and pulled out dirt.

Deni crawled up and bent Brian's head back to clear his air passage then blew air into his mouth while holding his nose closed. Nate pressed on his chest. After three cycles, Brian coughed. Deni turned him on his side so he could spit up more dirt.

Nate reached for his pack strap to take the pack off and get at a first-aid kit, but he discovered that his pack had been blown off him. Deni still had hers, so he reached over and took her canteen out of a side pocket. "Brian, can you hear me?"

Brian opened his eyes. He saw the canteen and snatched it out of her hand.

"Wash your mouth and throat out first," Nate warned. He had no idea if Brian could hear him.

Deni checked Brian's legs and arms, then pulled his jacket and shirt up. After checking him for wounds and finding nothing serious that could be detected, her face was no longer rigid with near panic. "I can't find any broken bones or serious bleeding on the surface." Nate and Deni's eyes met. "But there's no way to tell about internal injuries," she added.

Nate thought he understood what she said by reading her lips. He looked over at Caroline and Samantha. "There's no way to tell how seriously any of us are hurt."

Deni noticed the others for the first time. "I'll check on them."

Nate pulled her to him before she had a chance to move. Holding her, he said, "Who's going to check on you?"

She blinked tears. "I can hear you now, above the ringing, and I think I'm okay. You better look yourself over. You're too pumped right now to feel much." She pulled away and crawled to Caroline and Samantha, not even trying to stand and walk.

By the time Deni reached Caroline, Brian had sat up on his own. "Where's my rifle?"

"Can you walk?" Nate asked, not sure he could walk himself. "We still have to get out of here."

Brian tilted his head to aim his right ear at his father. "I can't hear anything but ringing." He took another swallow of water. "What about..." He turned and saw Caroline and Samantha were alive. "Thank God. We're all alive. Let's get moving." He started to stand, but pain stopped him. He tried again and managed, gritting his teeth, but making no sound. Holding his hands out, the canteen still in one, he staggered along and fell to his knees beside Caroline.

Caroline took the canteen and gave Samantha a drink. Deni busied herself checking them both for wounds and broken bones. "Your little finger on your left hand is broken," she warned. "And you have a cut on your right arm that needs stitches."

"Neither is worth worrying about right now." Still holding Samantha, Caroline reached her bloody hand out. "Help me up. We stay here, we're dead."

Nate found Deni and Brian's rifles and carried them over. "Clear the chambers and check the bores for obstructions." He scanned the ground around them for his rifle. Not finding it, he staggered off, searching the area where he thought the rifle might be. He found his backpack 20 feet away, pinned to a pine tree six feet above ground. A limb had gone all the way through, and the pack was hanging there against the trunk. He pulled it off and found the pack damaged to the point he would have to carry it in his hands. One shoulder strap was broken and the other damaged. He heard Brian make a noise and looked up to see him with the M14 in his hand. A quick check confirmed the rifle was not damaged, but the magazine was dented and the rounds inside jammed. He removed it from the receiver, dropping it. Opening the chamber and catching the round inside in his hand, he checked the bore, blew through it, and checked again. Satisfied, he slammed another magazine in. *I would rather not shoot it like that, because the dirt will play hell with the rifling, but if I have to, so be it.*

Caroline limped up to him. "Lead us out of here."

Nate understood what he couldn't hear. He nodded. "Everyone ready to travel?" They seemed to know what he meant, whether they could hear him or not. They all nodded. He pulled his compass out from under his shirt and discovered its plastic casing and baseplate was smashed. Since he didn't want to travel blind under an overcast sky with no sun to guide him, he took the time to fish a spare out of his pack before starting.

At first they traveled only a mile per hour. Their bruised bodies protested every step and resisted their desire to move fast. As their legs limbered up, they managed to walk faster, traveling at two miles per hour the rest of the afternoon. By sundown, they were many miles from the river and in heavy forest. Nate couldn't believe none of the others had asked for a chance to rest. He was dead on his feet and amazed the others were still keeping up with him. *Proves I'm too old for this shit.* He saw three large pines growing close together and turned to them. Though still raining, there had been no nearby lightning lately, and he felt it safe to use the trees for concealment from the air. Thunderstorms, not just in their area but all over the county, had probably forced any helicopter gunships to head for base, wherever that was. The last air strike could've been guided bombs from a plane 20 miles away and modern helicopters could kill from many miles away, also. *I think they were bombs, not missiles. Five-hundred-pounders,* he thought. *Or it could've been arty.* There was a sound just before the explosions, but he couldn't be sure. He knew no artillery or planes came from Glenwood and Donovan's base. There was no landing field, and he hadn't seen any heavy artillery there.

Why would they need such weapons of war? For all he knew, Col. Donovan could be dead or at least relieved of his command. *If the air strike originated from his base, Donovan better be dead or no longer in command. There simply was no excuse for using such weapons of war on civilians.* He looked at his wife and son, Samantha and Caroline, and grew so enraged he could barely keep it inside. *You assholes want a war with the American people? You have it!*

Nate pointed at the space between the three large pines and turned to the others so they could see him speak and maybe read his lips. "We'll rest there a while."

Deni sighed. "I thought you would never stop, and I was afraid to ask you to."

Brian limped along. "I can hear both of you. Been hearing the rain for the last 30 minutes now. Can you hear yet?"

Deni managed a smile. "Yes. I heard your father and you both."

Caroline put Samantha down by one of the large pines. "Can you hear okay?" she asked Samantha.

The little girl nodded, her face all but covered by the hood on Nate's poncho. "I'm tired, and I hurt all over."

"Just lie on these pine needles. We're going to rest now." Caroline offered her a drink, but the little girl just wanted to sleep.

Everyone but Nate dropped to the wet ground and shed their packs. They lay on their back, their rifle in their hands. Nate looked around for trouble. "We shouldn't stay long if we're going to travel anymore today. Our bodies will be so stiff in a few minutes we probably won't be able to move at all. Best to get going soon." He was answered by the sound of snoring from Brian and Samantha.

Deni spoke while she lay flat on the ground. "Give me a minute and I'll take first watch. I think we've gone as far as we can for a few hours."

Taking everything into consideration, Nate relented. "Okay. We have a small child with us, and she's been through too much already. We'll stay here awhile… if they let us."

To Nate's surprise, it was Brian who relieved him and took the next watch.

Brian said, "Fix your pack if you're not going to rest. I'll stand watch."

Shunning sleep, Nate cleaned his rifle first. Afterwards, he got out a sail needle and twine. In 15 minutes, he had both straps on his pack repaired.

While Nate and Brian kept watch, Deni cleaned her rifle. Caroline took the clue and cleaned hers, using Deni's cleaning kit.

Deni saw Caroline's wound and did her best to clean it and close it with sutures. She put a bandage on it that wouldn't come off.

A series of booms in the distance, in the direction of the river, caused temporary alarm, until they realized how far away it was. Samantha slept through it all.

"What does that mean?" Brian asked. "They have no idea where we are?"

Nate and Deni looked at each other, puzzled.

"Don't know," Nate answered. "Maybe they found someone else to kill. What's the difference? We're no threat to anyone. They might as well go after the next person as us."

Deni rubbed a sore shoulder. "I guess we should be on our way before we stiffen up." She sighed and stood. "Samantha's asleep. If she's carried gently, she might not wake up."

Nate slipped his pack on. "I'll carry her. Caroline's arm must be about to fall off. Someone will have to take point, though."

Deni reached over and touched Samantha's forehead. "She's a real trooper. Been through hell. What a world she's growing up in."

The miserable group forced themselves to start again, with Deni in the lead, using a compass to follow a course Nate told her to stay on.

Samantha slept, her head on Nate's shoulder.

The rain-heavy trees drooped, and the very air seemed to weep. They went on, inching their way through the streaming black night, wet and chilled to the bone. And scared. More scared than they had ever been in their lives.

Nate thought about how this little skirmish might be insignificant and would remain hidden in the shadows of history, never to be recorded or recognized as playing any part in the coming civil war, but he was proud to be married to a woman such as Deni and have a son the caliber of Brian. Caroline, he thought, was as good as they come.

It could have been the 1700s all over again. It seemed that once more, a pigmy militia of untrained civilians would soon stand against an army of professional killers and look tyranny in the eye. The weeks and months ahead would determine the fate of the nation and whether freedom would die or live on. He tried to penetrate the blackness around them with his eyes, and he felt the great gloom of the tall forest of ancient trees that were alive when squirrel hunters fought the Brits to defeat. It was an appropriate setting.

Chapter 23

Col. Greene walked into Kramer's room. "It's not safe here any longer. We have to move you."

Before Kramer had a chance to speak, a nurse was disconnecting monitoring instruments.

"We'll take good care of you," Mel said. "You just might help to prevent a civil war."

Kramer turned paler than he already was. "So you've gone against Capinos? The whole Guard? What about the Army and other branches?"

Greene checked his watch. "No time to answer questions. The longer we stay here, the shorter our life expectancy is."

Kramer persisted. "What made you decide to mutiny?" He groaned when Mel and another soldier lifted him and put him on a gurney.

Greene stepped back so the soldiers could push Kramer past him. "I'm a sloppy sentimentalist. I believe in doing the right thing as I see it. The puzzle is knowing what the right thing is." He gave Kramer a hard stare. "That's what took me so long, in case you wanted to know."

Mel and the other soldier pushed Kramer into the hall and disappeared with him around a corner.

~~~

Col. Donovan kept his composure, but he stressed his need for air support. In satellite phone contact with General Bernard Myers at Fort Benning, he yelled, "God damn it. The Air Force reports several missing rotorcraft and planes, and half a dozen drones. I'm not worried about Capinos' private army, but one air strike could wipe us out. We're not setup for air defense. My Apaches and Black Hawks can't stop a JDAM or missile coming in from 20 miles away."

Myers answered, "You will just have to disperse your assets and deny them such a juicy target."

Donovan was incredulous. "Sir, I've already done that as much as possible. Any more dispersing and I won't have a base."

"It's your decision," Myers said. "But you're not going to get air support for a while, so use your judgment. I have to go." He terminated the call.

Donovan shook his head. "He must think I'm a damn fool."

Sergeant First Class Quint Bartow smiled. "It's a hell of a revolution, ain't it?"

Donovan's blood pressure dropped, and he slapped Bartow on the shoulder. He raised his voice so all of the officers and noncoms around him could hear. "Spread them out all over town. Set up individual defense perimeters and camouflage the positions as best you can. Remember, we're under threat of an air strike."

Sergeant Dean Sullivan spoke up. "We don't have enough radios for that many separate teams."

Donovan rubbed the back of his neck and nodded. "I know. The fact is, though, a small team can handle a ground attack long enough for help to arrive. You hear shooting, be ready to join the team that's under attack."

Sullivan responded, "Yes sir. We'll be ready for trouble. It's the confusion at the top that bothers me. We don't know what the hell's going on."

A noncom quipped, "Will someone in Washington please just shoot that bastard Capinos and his cronies in Congress before America starts bleeding?"

~~~

Mrs. MacKay listened to the Apache gunships fly over. She looked around at all the frightened faces. "We better get the people fed." The shack they were in had been turned into a temporary kitchen. It was surrounded by other shacks, spread out under trees. Most of the children and older adults, as well as the sick, were assigned a shack to be shared with as many others that could be fitted in. Everyone else would sleep in tents. Only 25 of her people were with this group. The others were in similar-sized groups, spread out in hiding places as much as ten miles apart from each other. All of their vehicles had been driven away, hidden under trees. Stocks of food and other supplies were piled under tarps, also hidden under trees.

The large wood stove they were cooking on had the shack scorching hot inside. An elderly woman collapsed to the floor. "Get her out of here," MacKay ordered. "Anyone else feels faint, go on outside and cool off."

A man sitting in front of the shack scraping corn off the cob looked up from his work and yelled through the open door, "You might take your own advice. I can feel the heat in there from here. Besides, someone's got the radio working and there's a general talking about what's going on in Washington."

MacKay rushed out the door. "Where?"

The man pointed to an old oak tree. "Radio's over there where the crowd is."

She got to the tree as fast as her old legs would allow and listened in.

A man she later learned was a general was finishing up his message to the people. "The situation is fluid and developing fast, but I can tell you that most of the military has joined in an effort to force President Capinos out of office. He was never elected by the people and has proven himself a would-be dictator, ordering the summary execution of innocent officers, as well as the outright murder of many civilians. We can no longer tolerate the deteriorating conditions in Washington. The American people need and deserve a real leader to help us out of this hell we have all endured for so long.

"Please do not fear a long, bloody civil war. Almost the entire U.S. military is united in this effort, and we are not going to go to war against each other or the American people. We are part of the American people, no different from civilians except for the responsibilities we have sworn an oath to carry out. There will probably be some sporadic, limited fighting, because Capinos has hired a private army. It is small in number and weak in weapons, so all they can do is cause trouble for a few individuals. The handwriting is on the wall; they will be much better off if they quit now and walk away with their lives. Any murders they commit from now on will be punished when they are captured. If any of them are listening, they need to think long and hard about their futures and stop taking orders from Capinos, a man who will not be in power much longer."

He stopped for a few seconds to think about what he was going to say next. "Another worry I'm sure is keeping people awake at night is the question of what next. Are we going to have a nation under martial law? Will we ever have free elections again? We are at this moment working with local and national leaders to formulate plans for elections ASAP. Anyone interested in running for president or Congress should file the paperwork and start building their campaign committee. Let's get a new Congress and president elected in less than six months!"

People around the radio cheered.

MacKay rubbed her chin. "We'll see. I pray he's telling us the truth and it all comes to reality. Some men don't like giving up power once they have a taste of it."

A woman standing nearby who had a baby boy in her arms asked, "Can we go back to the farm now?"

MacKay shook her head. "No way. For all we know, there's no farm left to go back to. We've been hearing explosions. Those weren't leftover 4th of July firecrackers."

~~~

Nate heard a slight sound to his left. He rushed to catch Deni and tapped her on the shoulder. Caroline stepped up to them, with Brian taking up the rear. He pushed them all down. Whispering, Nate said, "I heard something. Form a tight 360 and keep your eyes and ears working."

A light rain had the dark night woods dripping and made it difficult to hear much else. Despite the rain, Nate heard a radio squelch. The others' heavy breathing told him they had heard it too. Samantha slept on his left shoulder, and he didn't dare put her down, she might wake and start crying. His mind raced. What would be the best course of action if shooting started? Should he put her down and shoot back? Or should he just run? If he ran, he would lose the others in the dark.

The killers passed them only yards away. Nate never saw or heard anything distinct, but he sensed their presence and knew they were close. It was then he knew they would never give up the hunt, never relent. He had no idea why these men wanted him and the others dead so much, and he almost didn't care. All he knew was he had to stop them, to get them off their trail. Some way. Somehow. They had all the advantages. Training, equipment, numbers. They could even call in air support. With those odds, he would not willingly take them on directly. First, he had to leave the others in a safe place. Then he would begin his personal war.

He looked at the others, barely seeing them in the dark and rain. Standing before him, holding their rifles tight in the weeping woods, their wet clothes clinging to their skin, mosquitoes clouding around them, he could've thought of them as soldiers, like the ones he served with so many years ago in a different life. But only Deni was a soldier. The rest were civilians, a woman, a teen boy, and a little girl. *It's not right,* he thought, *soldiers waging war on these people. Someone has to stop them.*

After waiting ten minutes to give their pursuers plenty of time to put distance between them, Nate tapped Deni on the shoulder and whispered in her ear, "We'll move out now. Head northeast."

"What's northeast," Deni asked.

"Distance," Nate answered. "It was sheer luck on their part that they got so close in the dark and rain. They're certainly not tracking us at the moment. Besides, we killed their tracking team."

Only two hours later, Nate realized they had to stop and rest. All of them were so tired they were stumbling in the dark and making too much noise. They rested until first light and then ate a quick meal. Samantha was in a poor mood and had every right to be. Unfortunately, her crying and complaining could get them all killed.

Mosquitoes feasted on Nate while he looked over a map. The day had broken clear and it looked like the rain was over. It meant their enemies could track them again. It also meant Nate's poncho could come off of Samantha, which seemed to please her enough she stopped crying for a while. By three in the afternoon Nate's poncho was back on her. Heavy thunderstorms moved in and drenched the woods once again.

"Well," Brian commented, "It'll wash away the tracks we left behind us this morning."

Nate consulted his compass and checked his bearings. "The rain could not have come at a better time. We're almost there."

They had been making their way deeper into rougher country for over an hour, and Nate had led them to a place he knew well.

"Almost where?" Deni asked.

"You'll see," was all Nate would give her for an answer.

An hour and a half later Deni lost patience. "Will you please tell us where the hell we're going?"

Nate pointed. "Up that hill about 50 yards. That's where we're going."

Deni looked where he was pointing. "All I see is a rocky ledge and a patch of trees about half way up."

"Behind those trees is a good place to hide." Nate stopped walking and motioned for everyone to gather close. "It's a little steep climbing up. Try not to kick any rocks loose or leave any other sign we've been on that hill."

Deni gave Nate a strange look. "There's no retreat. If they discover us up there, we're trapped."

Nate feigned hurt. "You have no faith in my abilities, do you? It's got a back door. Come on. We don't need to be standing here." He took Samantha from Caroline. She would have trouble enough with her artificial leg, without carrying Samantha too. Samantha couldn't walk while wearing his poncho; it was twice as long as her. "It's not raining much now, so we'll take this off." After helping Samantha remove the poncho, he allowed her to walk most of the way, until the trail became steep and Nate feared she might slip. It was getting to be a long way down by then. A slip could mean a long fall and roll downhill.

In the lead, Deni approached the stand of trees. She pushed limbs aside and disappeared. Twenty seconds later, the others heard her say something, but couldn't make it out. She reappeared with a smile on her face. "Okay. Why didn't you tell us about this place before? It would be a good spot for a cache."

Nate climbed the last ten yards. "I didn't think we would ever be this far north. The fact is I had forgotten about it. Haven't been here since I was Brian's age."

Samantha grabbed Deni's hand for support. Her eyes were wide as she watched Caroline climb. "She might fall."

Caroline heard. "Nope. I'm not about to fall, just taking my time." She nearly lost her balance when a blue jay fluttered out of the stand of trees. The pretense she wasn't on edge and worried they could be under attack at any moment shattered, she smiled at Samantha. "I need to get some rest. I'm jumpy."

Nate took Caroline's rifle when she came within reach. "We'll all be resting and out of the rain soon. Come on. Let's get into the trees and out of sight."

Making their way between close-growing trees, they found themselves on a level ledge and facing an enclave on the side of the hill that seemed to be the opening to a shallow cave with a 15-foot-high ceiling.

Samantha looked around, her mouth open in amazement. "It's dark in here, and it's not raining."

Nate set his backpack down. "Anyone have a flashlight that still works? I want to look for rattlers back there before we settle down and get some sleep."

"I have one, but I'm coming with it," Deni said. "I want to see that back door you promised."

Nate gave her a weary smile. "I think I'm going to start calling you Tactical Deni."

"Just call me wise." Deni pushed by him and aimed the flashlight at the back of the limestone enclave, keeping it low and partially covered with her hand to reduce the chance someone could see it through the stand of trees from a distance. "I don't see any snakes and I don't see any back door." She turned the light off.

"What were you expecting to find back here?" Nate asked.

"Well," Deni gave him a puzzled look, "I thought there was a cave leading to the far side of the hill. Or something."

"No cave. So I guess it's or something." Nate took the flashlight. "Follow me." He led her around a rock outcropping on one end of the ledge and turned left, going around to the back of the outcropping, and lowered himself into a narrow ravine that curved more to the left, skirting the hill. He nodded. "Keep following this little ravine and it'll take you to the other side of the hill and into thick forest. That's your retreat if attacked."

Deni wrapped her left arm around his waist. "Maybe we should check the whole route. Might be a rock or landslide blocking our escape. If there is, we don't want to find out when it's too late to move to another position."

He held her close to him. "Yep. Your name is Tactical." His face changed, and he looked her in the eye. "When I leave, I'll go that way, so I can check it out then."

"Leave? What are you planning?"

"I can't go to war dragging my son and a little girl with me."

She reacted as if he had just slapped her.

"They're not going to quit and leave us alone, Deni. They have to be stopped. I don't know who they are or why they want us so much, but they won't stop until they're dead."

"You're crazy! How many are there? You don't know. But there are plenty more than enough to kill you."

Nate put a finger to his lips. "Not so loud. There are ways to avoid taking them all on at once, but it can't be done if I'm slowed down by a little girl."

She rolled her eyes. "Yeah. Well, why haven't you said a thing about me coming with you?"

"I would like that. But they'll need you if I don't come back."

"Why don't you just admit that you're pissed at these bastards?"

"I am pissed at them. But that's not why I'm going to leave you here and turn the hunters into the hunted." Nate touched her face, him feeling her soft skin, her feeling his calloused, rough hand. "They won't stop. I don't know why, but they'll keep hunting us until they kill us all. Maybe they were ordered not to come back without our heads."

The look on her face changed, and she seemed to have made a decision. "I guess why doesn't matter. We pissed the nut in the White House off. That's enough of a reason."

"Well, are you finished arguing with me about it?" Nate asked.

She looked at him like he was crazy. "It's obvious you're going no matter what I say. I'd rather you have a clear mind while you're fighting for your life. Might help you come back to me in one piece."

He held her. "Good. Let's check out the rest of the retreat route, so you'll know it, and get back to the others. I need to get some food in me and some sleep before I go hunting."

~~~

Before eating or resting, Nate removed almost everything from his backpack except for water, a little food, and all of his ammo. He kept his meager first-aid kit, though he doubted it would do him much good. While cleaning all of his weapons, he suggested that the others do the same, one at a time.

Deni had ensconced herself in the stand of trees in a position where she could look downhill for any trouble. Brian had just gone off security duty and sat down beside his father to clean his rifle. Caroline and Samantha were sleeping, so Brian spoke softly. "You're going to leave us here, aren't you?"

"Deni told you?" Nate asked.

Brian looked down at his disassembled rifle. "No. But I could tell by the way she's acting. And it's obvious you took us here so we'll be safe while you're gone."

"All of you will be safer here, and I'll be safer with you here." The few feet between father and son disappeared for a few seconds while they looked at each other. "Every one of you is as tough as they come, even Samantha. You, Deni, and Caroline are all survivors. You're still alive because of what you're made of. But what I'm about to do is a one-man operation. It's actually safer for me to be alone the way I'm going to fight them."

"Well, just come back," Brian said. "Do you know how long you're going to be gone?"

"Probably three or four days. There's no way to know. Might be longer."

~~~

Nate woke in the night and tried without success to not disturb Deni. She didn't say anything until he had grabbed his rifle and was about to leave. "Just come back," she said.

Nate stopped and stood in the dark. "I will." He inched his way along the ravine and into the forest.

~~~

The first thing Nate had to do was hunt down those who hunted him. Then he had to wait for the right time and place to kill one of them quietly. By the time he came across their trail, it was less than two hours before dark on the second day. He moved in for the kill. No thunderstorms had showed up in the afternoon, and the heat was oppressive. They must've been pushing themselves pretty hard, because they stopped in a thick stand of pine trees to rest a few minutes. One of the men walked away from the others a few yards to pull his pants down and squat behind a tree. It was a mistake that proved fatal. The others found him five minutes later with his throat cut.

Their efforts to track Nate down failed. When they spread out in a line to reacquire his trail, Nate shot one in the face at a range of just over 100 yards.

For some reason, Nate had found his second wind and felt like he had shed 10 or 15 years. It seemed easy to travel fast with his four-decade-old body. Knowing that they were behind him and had not the time to get ahead and set up an ambush meant he did not have to travel slow and carefully. He swung around to an area they had already been through, where he knew the brush grew so thick you couldn't see more than 20 yards. There were times when he purposely left sign to make sure they would not lose his trail. But he did not want to make it obvious.

That night when it grew too dark for them to track him, he swung around and waited for a chance to kill another one. He estimated where they would be by dead reckoning and guessing when they gave up because it was too got too dark to see tracks. For whatever reason, he missed his mark and gave up after two hours inching his way through the dark woods. He decided that would be a good time to get some rest. They had no more idea where he was than he did them, and he needed the sleep. He had no idea what would come in a few hours.

~~~

Nate woke and realized his face was covered with mosquitoes. He rubbed them off, not slapping at them so as to not make any noise. He sat up. Looking around, he guessed it to be about one hour before false dawn. Only normal woods sounds came to his ears, and when a buck slinked by only 20 yards away, seemingly unalarmed and casually stopping to eat every few yards, he was assured no human being had been through the area recently. He took a quick drink and restarted the hunt.

Nate found them a little more than an hour after daylight. Almost immediately, he realized they were on his trail again. He took advantage of the fact that told him what direction they would be traveling and ran ahead to set up an ambush. Since he was alone, he planned to kill one of them and run. Staying long enough to kill any more than one would be a fatal mistake. He waited in the forest gloom, indifferent to time, as if it were something he breathed in and exhaled like the air, taken for granted and ignored. Nothing else mattered but his survival. His eyes and ears gathered in all data as he constantly scanned the area until he knew every tree, bush, and clump of grass, his eyes penetrating the wall of green as much as 40 yards at times, but in most areas that wall of green was too thick to allow him to see more than 20 yards.

He had been moving nothing but his eyes for 45 minutes, but even they froze when he saw something that had not been there before, and when that something materialized and he could see that it was the camo-painted face of a man, he slowly shouldered his rifle and pushed the safety off with his trigger finger. It was an easy shot, but he waited. He needed to have an idea where the others were before he let them know he was there. Someone's boots scraped against a palmetto frond some yards behind the face Nate had just seen. When he located a third man farther back that told him what patrol formation the team was using and where the others probably were. A quick check to relocate the first man took several seconds, squeezing off a shot and running away at top speed took only one.

Bursts of automatic gunfire from several weapons spurred him on. Staying bent over, he cut to the left and ran 50 yards and then, no longer bent over, cut to the right, running 100 yards before changing direction again. He realized it was only luck that had allowed him to make it the first 20 yards. At least one of the killers had seen him running off and tried his best to shoot him in the back.

The day wore on, and Nate couldn't seem to shake them off his trail. The fact he was no longer a young man soon became the deciding factor in the chase. Exhausted, Nate pushed himself, fully realizing his heart was no longer the heart of a twenty-year-old soldier. He vowed that he wouldn't let them kill him and resisted the urge to stop running and shoot it out.

He liked to think it was his stubborn resolve to deny them the satisfaction of taking his life that spurred him on, but in his pounding heart, he knew it was Deni and Brian that gave him such a will to live. If he could shake them off his trail, he could rest and fight again the next day.

Chapter 24

Sometime in the afternoon, summer thunderstorms rolled in and changed everything. Nate changed course a few more times to throw them off, covering three or four miles, and then he pushed into the thickest brush he could find. There, he dropped to the ground and gasped for air, exhausted. The rain came down hard and heavy, feeling ice-cold on his skin. Steam misted up from his back and shoulders and his head. His eyes kept scanning the woods around him and carried the frightening qualities of a wild animal. But he was still alive.

Do I want to go through that again? he asked himself. *I haven't finished the job. I can't leave any of them alive.* He slipped his backpack off and lay on the wet ground, heavy rain pounding on his face. He opened his mouth and waited until it was half full before swallowing. *Right now I have to rest. If I don't, they're going to kill me without firing a shot.*

~~~

Capinos sat behind his desk and looked the three-star general over. "The Secretary of Defense and I have decided to promote you to Chairman of the Joint Chiefs of Staff." He leaned back in his leather chair. "Uh, the Secretary wanted to be here but is indisposed at the moment." In reality, Secretary Hackleman was dead, executed for refusing to follow orders. "Senate approval will just be a formality. You understand how busy we are in Washington with all this craziness going on. The last CJCS was Army too, and I know people like to rotate that position among the branches, but I believe it best to have a good Army man in charge."

Lieutenant General Jack Silva's wide shoulders extended beyond the back of the chair he sat in. He may have been a general, but he kept in shape. As a young soldier in combat, he had killed with his bare hands more than once, and had done so again in another war, when he was a lieutenant colonel and 40 years old. "And how am I qualified?" He waved his hand. "Forget that. What makes you think I'm interested?"

Capinos gave him a cold smile. "As for qualifications, we're running short of generals. To answer your question why I think you're interested in the position, well, you're the youngest three-star general in the Army. You have moved up fast. That tells me you're ambitious. Also, my people tell me you believe strongly in civilian command over the military and want no part of the mutiny that's going on at the moment."

General Silva shook his head. "I'm not that ambitious."

Capinos flinched. "I understand. You're a true warrior and don't want to give up your combat command. Too much paper pushing for you in the JCS."

Silva leaned forward. "Let's cut the shit. I was hoping you had summoned me to discuss your resignation and handover of power to the people. Don't you know which side I'm on?"

All color drained from Capinos. Talking through his teeth, he said, "Obviously, there has been a mistake. One that will be remedied as soon as you're taken away and shot."

"In that case, I have a right to defend myself," Silva said. He jumped over the desk and punched Capinos twice, knocking him out, then lifted him from behind and put both arms around his neck and head. Applying pressure, he forced his head down and then twisted, producing a distinct snap. He let Capinos fall to the carpet, dead.

Standing straight, General Silva adjusted his uniform and took a few breaths. He looked down at Capinos. "Gutless little weasel. You think you can murder Americans and shit all over the Constitution so many have fought, killed, suffered and died for? With you dead, most of the shitstorm will be averted, and a lot less blood will be spilled."

He stepped out of the Oval Office, where Vice President Piers Trant waited. "The presidency is yours for the next six months as agreed." He made eye contact with Trant. "Keep the people's welfare first in all things and you'll get to be president for six months and then go home a free man. No charges. No trial. No prison." He pulled a shoulder back slightly. "Neither I nor anyone else can promise what the new civilian government will do with you after that, but those are the chances you take. Hell, I might be charged with murdering Capinos. Whatever comes, I know I did the right thing and am willing to pay for it."

The new president swallowed and nodded. "I gave my word. As far as I'm concerned I'll just be a figurehead. Maybe

I can calm the people's worries of the military coup being permanent. They need assurances that there will be free elections soon. In the mean time, you in the military please keep doing what you were before Capinos got in your way. It was working. Over the last months, people were less hungry and suffered a lot less at the hands of the barbarians." He started to turn away, but stopped. "As I explained to the others last night, I had no idea how far Capinos was willing to go. He caused so much suffering and death. Obviously, he was mentally ill."

"Well," General Silva said, "he's not worth thinking about anymore. Let's get to work serving the American people and rebuilding this country." He walked out of the room and disappeared down a hall.

Trant held his hands up and watched them shake. After closing the Oval Office door behind him, he nervously paced back and forth in front of the president's desk, thinking. He had to give General Silva time to get away before calling in the Secret Service.

~~~

Nate woke after two hours and began the hunt anew. He had traveled less than a mile when an unnatural noise prompted him to stop and freeze in his tracks. He thought he had heard someone cough. Getting down low behind cover, he waited, but heard nothing else. Moving on with caution, he came to the edge of a little clearing. The rain fell thin, the color of worn gun metal in the slanting afternoon sun. Men squatted there on their heels, beneath the drizzle.

Immediately, he realized they were not soldiers or part of Capinos' private army. They were of mixed age from their late teens to middle-age. Many of them wore rags and carried shotguns and other civilian weapons. A quick scan with his binoculars told Nate he had seen some of the men in Glenwood, a few of them, he had met. He noticed a big black man on the edge of the crowd and recognized him. He was Tyrone.

Not wanting to get shot, Nate stayed back in the trees and worked his way to the side of the clearing where Tyrone was.

When he was only 30 yards away, he squatted down behind a tree and yelled Tyrone's name. Everyone in the group hit the ground and pointed their rifles in Nate's direction. "Tyrone," Nate yelled. "It's Nate Williams."

Tyrone told the others not to shoot.

Nate wasn't about to go into the meadow where he would make an easy target. "Tyrone, you should know better than to have those men out there in the open like that. There's a team of professionals out here and if they catch you in the open they'll kill you all in about ten seconds. Come to my voice and be quick about it. Stay low."

Tyrone had his men do as Nate said. Not bothering to greet Tyrone or waste any time, Nate led them deeper into the brush. He then showed them how to set up a defense perimeter. "Keep your eyes open. Men are hunting me, and if they find you out here they'll kill you too."

Nate felt things were finally under control well enough that he turned to Tyrone and shook his hand. "What the hell are you doing out here? Is this your militia?"

"More like my posse," Tyrone answered. "As to what we're doing out here, we got word from Mrs. MacKay by radio that your house and barn had been burned to the ground. We came out here to look for you in case you needed help."

"I need help all right," Nate said. "Who told MacKay about the raid on my farm?"

"One of her people saw the smoke, checked it out, and then delivered the message by foot. She radioed us in town."

"Well that was a hell of a lot of trouble to go through for me and my family." Nate looked around at the crowd. "I owe thanks to a lot of people. How long have you been out here?"

"Since yesterday morning. We traveled by boat. We're not far from the river, you know." He rubbed his sweaty face. "We've been chasing gunfire all day. All we found so far are tracks, spent casings, and a couple dead men."

"There are more dead men than that out here in these woods. Anyway, I'm grateful you didn't meet up with any of the live ones, because if you had it wouldn't have been pretty."

Tyrone smiled. "You don't have much faith in our abilities, do you?"

Nate didn't have time to worry about hurting egos. "Actually, I think you might just be the answer to my problems." Nate kicked and scraped a three-foot area clear of pine needles so he would have bare soil to draw a diagram on. "Let's tighten the perimeter up so everyone can hear what I'm saying. I'm going to be the bait and lead those bastards straight to you. It shouldn't be too dangerous because they'll not be expecting you out here. They think they're after one man at the moment, so I should be able to trick them into running right into an ambush. That should give you enough of an edge to counter their training. But everyone must follow the plan exactly. Otherwise it could get real bad real quick."

"I understand." A dark thought came to Tyrone. "Where are the others?"

"They're safe," Nate answered. "If everything goes well, I may be back with them tonight."

Tyrone looked up at the overcast sky. "Thank God. I was worried for a second."

Nate flattened a mosquito on his nose. "Where's Atticus?"

"He's holding the fort in town." Tyrone anticipated Nate's next question. "Donovan and the Army seem to be worried about an attack from other soldiers, or the Air Force, or the Marines. Hell I don't know. I'm not sure what's going on in Washington, but it seems most of the military's on the people's side."

Nate nodded. "Right now our immediate problem is surviving this day. I'm hoping that by working together we can do just that."

~~~

The thunderstorms passed on and the sky cleared, but the sun had fallen to an hour's height above the western horizon by then. Nate finally located those who hunted him only a quarter mile from the river, just where the downward slope to the river valley swamp started. Evidently they had no clue where he was. He intended to give them a deadly hint by putting a bullet in one of them. And then he would run like hell just as he had done before. Only this time he would be leading them into a trap. The fact they hadn't called in another air strike recently told Nate they probably no longer had that option. He prayed he was right. The lives of a lot of people depended on it.

Nate hid in woods so thick with undergrowth his vision was limited to less than twenty yards. He knew they were coming and expected them to be in view any minute. There! Nate saw movement. No form or shape, just movement swimming in the wall of green. Coming closer now. Nothing. Now a movement of shadow in shadow. Dim sunlight reflected off something moving, then disappeared. Twenty yards. Fifteen. A man stepped out of dark freckles of shadow and into a death zone of sunlight. Nate could make out twenty percent of his upper body. He fired and saw an image of the man's head coming apart just before he turned and ran, keeping low as bullets ripped the jungle-like growth up all around him. He felt a tug on his left sleeve and felt a sharp, burning sting. He drove on with all the speed his legs were capable of, digging into the rain-softened soil and leaving a trail his pursuers couldn't miss.

The sounds of pursuit only yards behind, he ran past Tyrone's men and kept running until he came to the place he had previously chosen and dropped behind a hickory log. His danger-heightened senses allowed him to hear the hunters-turned-prey coming for what seemed like an eternity. *Don't anyone shoot too soon!*

Nate almost smiled when he saw the first one come into view. It told him they were all in the kill zone and he could shoot the one in the lead, signaling Tyrone's men to start the killing. Fear something could still go wrong ate at him as he aimed and fired.

A roar of gunfire that had its own distinct sound, different from the times when full auto fire encouraged Nate to run faster, told him the slaughter had begun. Shotguns and rifles of various calibers created a sound like popcorn on a fire, trailing off to individual pops as the kernels of popcorn were exhausted. If everything went as planned, it would be over in seconds.

It was.

Tyrone's men began to come out of hiding and advance on the dead and dying. One thirty-something-year-old man in coveralls aimed his shotgun at a wounded man. Nate rushed to him, yelling, "Don't kill him!"

The man raised his shotgun. "I thought you needed them all dead."

"I'd like to talk to at least one of them if possible." Nate checked the wounded man for weapons and then examined his wounds. The man died before Nate was finished. "Damn it. I wanted to find out who sent them and why."

Tyrone looked down at the body. "The president or one of his cronies."

Someone yelled from the other end of the ambush site, "You want a live one? Here's one."

Nate ran up to the prisoner and saw that he only had a hand wound. He glared at the man, hate in his eyes. "I'm all out of patience. And I'm all out of mercy. You bastards have been trying to kill me and my family, as well as a friend and a little girl for days now, even calling in air strikes on us. You destroyed my home and left me with nothing but hate. If you answer my questions, no one will touch you. But if you hesitate or I think you're lying to me, I'll show you just how much I hate your guts."

The man looked Nate in the eye. "I'll answer your questions."

Two men came up behind him and tied his hands behind his back.

Nate checked his wound. He got out his first-aid kit, cleaned the hand, and bandaged it. "Okay. Now let's see if you meant what you said. Who do you take orders from?"

The prisoner didn't hesitate. "Directly from the president. We're contractors, soldiers for hire. Capinos offered us work with good pay and good food. That's our part in this mess. Nothing else. The politics aren't my concern."

"Pay?" Tyrone asked. "Money's not worth anything now."

"It will be someday." The man grimaced from pain. "He pays in gold. Gold will always have value."

Nate wanted to get to the point. "I think you're telling the truth about working for Capinos, so you're on the right track so far. Why does Capinos want me and my family dead so much he sent you?"

"Capinos is after a man named Kramer and he thinks Kramer is with you. Kramer has information that could get Capinos and many others executed for the murder of most of the human population." He looked up at Nate, sweat running down his face. "You, you're wife and son, as well as your friends, aren't exactly his favorite people either. But it's Kramer he wants." He swallowed and looked at Nate. "Personally, I have nothing against you. And after what you just did and the trouble you've caused us over the last days – well – I have a lot of respect for you."

Tyrone reached over and snatched the man by the collar. He put both hands around his neck. "You mean to tell me Capinos was involved in causing the plague? And you knew and did nothing?" He shook the man violently. "Answer me!"

Nate tried to pry Tyrone's hands off the man's neck. "Damn it, Tyrone, you can wring his neck later. I still need more info from this bastard!"

Tyrone let the man drop to the ground, where he gasped for air, his face already turning blue. He pointed a finger at the prone, gasping man. "You damn well better have some reeeeaaally good information for Nate! I'm thinking of roasting you on a slow fire, just so you can get an idea of what's waiting for you in hell."

A combination of stunned silence and loud outrage shot through the other men. *The plague wasn't an act of nature? Some asshole caused it?*

Nate jerked the man up and sat him down on a log. "Ever hear of a get out of jail free card? Call this your chance to get out of hell free. You tell me what you know about the plague and who caused it."

"Kramer knows a lot more than I do." The man still hadn't caught his breath. "I mean, I can testify in court against Capinos, but Kramer's the one you want. I and everyone you killed here today were hired after the plague had played out and done its killing. Kramer's the one who knows a lot about Capinos."

Nate became sick. Disgusted, he turned away.

"What is it?" Tyrone asked.

Nate ran his hand over the top of his aching head. "I'll tell you later." He turned around. "Strip the bodies of weapons, ammo, radios, and any papers. Bring the papers to me. They might be carrying something that could be evidence against Capinos and who the hell ever else is involved in the worst crimes since the Holocaust."

The man in coveralls walked up to the prisoner. "What's your name?"

The contractor asked, "Why, so you will know the name of the man you're about to execute?"

"Nate and Tyrone don't want you dead yet," the man in coveralls answered. "I just wanted to know the name of pure evil."

"My name is Paul Russell. I had nothing to do with the plague and learned of Capinos' involvement after I went to work for him. I lost my entire family to the disease like most people. I'm just a contractor."

Worried the man in coveralls would kill an important prisoner, Tyrone stepped between them. "We have to keep him alive. He may just help to prevent a civil war."

"I know. That's why he ain't dead already." The man in coveralls walked away.

Tyrone noticed that Nate still looked sick. "We might as well go pick up your family, Caroline, and the little girl."

Nate took a deep breath. "Discovering that Susan and Beth were murdered, that some group of monsters purposely murdered most of the human population…" He shook his head.

Tyrone glanced at Russell for a second and put his hand on Nate's shoulder. "I know. Feel the same way. Like a mule kicked me in the gut."

Nate motioned for Tyrone to follow him. They walked far enough no one could hear. "I'm almost certain this Kramer is dead."

Tyrone furrowed his brow. "How do you know?"

"Brian tangled with him and another CIA operative in the swamp not far from the farm. We think Deni got a bullet into him. We didn't want to chance making sure and left him for dead." Nate shrugged. "There's a chance he radioed for a pickup, but by that time he had helped Mrs. MacKay and her people out. He may have been wanted by Capinos by then. If he was, he probably wouldn't radio for help. Chances are he's dead."

"Damn it." Tyrone looked at Nate, showing compassion. "You had no way of knowing. Hell, if this asshole shot at you right now, knowing what you know, you'd have to shoot back. You're always the guy who keeps his head when the world's turning to shit. Don't change your ways now." He took a step. "Come on. Let's go get your family. You might as well catch a boat ride to town with us."

Nate nodded. "Okay." They walked back to the others.

Tyrone checked the items the men had taken off the contractors and examined two radios.

Nate stood in front of Russell, looking him in the eye. "Stand up. You're going for a boat ride."

Russell stood.

Nate glared at him for a second.

Russell stared back, not knowing what to expect.

Nate finally said, "Forget it. I was going to knock the hell out of you, but if I get started I'll probably kill you, and we need you to testify. Maybe later." He started to walk away and then turned and knocked Russell down.

Tyrone ran up. "Did he try something?"

Rage overtook Nate for several seconds. "He knew what Capinos had done and he still worked for him. My wife and little girl… millions and millions of people… He's an asshole. And I have asshole proximity intolerance. I can't stand to have assholes like him around me. The SOB gives Nazis a bad name." Nate started for him again.

Tyrone braced to stop him. "Hold on! I lost family too. He'll get his."

"He's spitting teeth now, but he needs to die." Nate stepped away.

Someone turned on a radio he had taken off a dead contractor and changed frequencies until he heard something. Donovan's voice came over the airwaves. "Capinos is dead. Pass the word that the president is dead. Anyone siding with Capinos and his cronies in Congress needs to know that it's over. A new government will be elected by the American people sometime within the next few months. Give it up. You lost. The people won!"

A low murmur of confused voices rose to a roar, everyone demanding from no one in particular what the hell that meant and whether or not they could believe it.

"I believe Col. Donovan," Tyrone answered.

"I'm pretty certain you can believe what Donovan tells you," Nate said. "Whether or not it's over and there'll be no civil war, well, your guess is as good as mine."

~~~

When they reached the river, Nate saw the armada of mostly jon boats and realized he just couldn't take the chance of traveling that way. He told Tyrone, "I'll ride a few miles with you. That'll bring me closer to my family, but I'm not going to ride the rest of the way. It's too dangerous. You're an easy target on the river, and we don't know if there are more search and destroy teams out here. And if there is another kill team, we have no idea how much air support they have."

They traveled by starlight. Just able to see well enough to keep the boats between the banks, they were forced to go no more than five miles per hour. After a few miles, Nate told Tyrone he wanted to be let off.

Tyrone found a place where the brush wasn't too thick and headed for shore. "But you're going on into town, aren't you?"

"Town might not be safe. Until any chance of a civil war has passed, we're staying hid in these woods."

"Here." Tyrone handed Nate a radio they had taken off one of the contractors. "I don't know if it'll do you any good or not, but there it is."

Nate took the radio. "Might be able to learn something listening in." He shook Tyrone's hand. "Thanks for helping me. You and your men went through a lot of trouble and risk."

He tried one more time. "I think you should leave the boats here and come with me. I'll help you get back on foot. Traveling by boat is too dangerous right now."

Tyrone smiled in the dark. "You saw how these guys are in the woods. I think we're better off chancing it and using the speed of the boats to get out of here before daylight than we would be trying to walk out, even with you leading us."

Nate nodded. "You made it here, so I guess the risk might not be that high. Good luck."

Chapter 25

Nate traveled in the dark until he was several miles from the river. After a quick meal, he went to sleep, expecting to start out before false dawn and make it to Deni and the others early the next day. As he fell asleep, he wondered if the worst might be over. Could a real shooting war be avoided?

~~~

Instead of approaching the ledge from below, Nate decided to come in the way he left, through the ravine. He stopped just within hearing distance to listen. The first thing he heard was Samantha laughing. He moved in closer and could hear Caroline and Deni having a conversation about when one of them should go looking for Nate and who should go.

Nate spoke just loud enough they could here. "No need for that."

Deni rushed to him. After they held each other, she looked him over and saw blood on his sleeve.

Checking what she was looking at, he noticed for the first time his left arm had been grazed by a bullet halfway between his elbow and hand. Surprised, he took his jacket off and looked at the minor wound. "I hadn't even noticed that."

"Uh huh," she said.

He knew Brian must've been on watch, hiding in the stand of trees, looking downhill at the area bellow them. "Well, speaking of not noticing things, I managed to come right up on you. Who's on security? Anyone? Who was watching the back door?"

"Don't change the subject," Deni said. "Sit down and let me clean that. You can tell us what happened while I work."

Nate spoke to Caroline, "Might as well call Brian over so I don't have to tell the story twice."

She raised an eyebrow. "Something must have changed if you feel comfortable with not having anyone on watch. Did you get all of them?"

Nate nodded. "I had help. Go get Brian. Then I'll tell all of you what happened."

~~~

Fifteen minutes later, everyone sat around soaking in what Nate had told them. He pulled the radio Tyrone gave him out of his pack and turned it on. "Let's see what we can learn."

All they got was a small amount of traffic between soldiers, nothing about the situation in Washington.

Brian sat on his rolled sleeping bag. "We shouldn't be thinking it's over. Some other asshole could step in and take Capinos' place."

Nate turned the radio off to save the batteries. "At least we know nothing is going on at the moment. If they were fighting a battle, the traffic would've made it obvious." He looked at the others. "All's quiet on the southern front at the moment."

"Okay, but what now?" Deni asked. Just stay here a little longer?"

Caroline butted in, "But how quiet is it on the northern front? Meaning Washington."

"Well," Nate pulled his pack to him so he could get out more rifle ammo to replace what he had shot and reload a magazine, "we can make it to that hunting shack before dark. It'll be a good place to wait out a civil war."

"Sounds good to me," Brian said. "Let's pack up and get a roof over our heads."

The others seemed to agree, as they began to gather up their belongings and prepare to leave.

~~~

'Free body piercing by Smith & Wesson.' That's what the sign said above the door of abandoned hunting shack. It was one of the hiding places Nate and the others had previously chosen and stocked with supplies. Nate had no idea who the owner was. Most likely, he had died in the plague.

Brian kicked mud off his boots before stepping up on the small porch, his rifle in his hands. "Lots of free body piercing going on nowadays."

Caroline stood watch 30 yards off in the brush, where she could see the front of the shack and keep an eye on Samantha, who was half asleep on a bench near the front door. Deni stood watch 50 yards behind the shack.

Nate worked on his backpack, completing repairs he started days before, when they were being chased by Capinos' private army. He looked up, put a finger to his lips, and pointed at Samantha.

Brian sat down beside him. Keeping his voice low, he asked, "How long are we going to stay here, not knowing what's going on in the world?"

"We're resting." Nate pulled the sewing twine tight and tied it off. "I don't know about you, but I was damn near dead by the time we dragged our asses up here."

Brian jerked his head and looked away. "It was you that nearly killed us. We had to keep up." He turned and looked at his father, smiling, respect showing on his face. "You don't ever quit."

"Nobody quit, not even Samantha."

"Well." Brian looked at the little girl. "She didn't have much choice. But she sure is a tough little girl. I guess that's the main reason she's alive. That and Caroline."

Nate nodded. "Our band of survivors has stuck together. That's what pulled us through so far."

"Yep," Brian said, "we don't quit on each other, and we don't quit on our friends. You taught me that. I guess before it all went to hell I didn't realize how important people are." A thought came to him. "You think we could just stay here and wait out whatever happens? You said many times that we're not going to make any difference if there's a civil war."

"We're not. A civil war's too big of a thing for a few people like us to influence at all. I'm thinking about going for a radio, though. We need to find out what's going on. Hell, it could all be over."

"Mel's place?" Brian asked.

"No," Nate answered. "Best to stay away from there. Might not be anything left but a crater by now, anyway."

"Where then?"

"I think I'll try to find MacKay's people." Nate took a stone from his pack and began to sharpen his knife.

"Alone?"

Nate stopped for a second and looked at his son.

"You told Deni?" Brian asked.

"Not yet."

Brian pretended to mop sweat from his forehead. "You had me worried for a second. Now I doubt you'll be going alone."

Nate coughed. "You think so, huh?"

"I expect she'll lay down the law and that'll be the end of it."

Nate laughed. "Maybe you're right."

"You should listen to that military radio one more time before you leave. Might learn something."

Nate put his knife back in the sheath. "Why don't you turn it on and we'll listen right now?"

At first all they heard was an unusual amount of static. Brian switched frequencies and a man's voice emanated from the speaker. "Continuity of government in Washington has been secured and things are stabilizing. All branches of the military are untied in America's efforts to bring back full enforcement of the Constitution. Vice President Piers Trant has agreed to step down as soon as elections are held four months from now and is cooperating fully. Junior officers and noncoms in the field report great strides in the reduction of violence, and law and order has been restored to over half the country. Local people have cooperated with this effort and we are certain more people will volunteer to help out in this matter. Anyone with prior law enforcement experience should be sought out and asked to volunteer to serve their communities. In recent weeks, we have managed to pick up where we left off in our struggle to end famine, and progress in that area continues to amaze and please commanders, as well as those who enjoy full stomachs for the first time since the plague."

"Sounds good anyway," Brian said, a definite tone of doubt in his voice.

The batteries drained to the point the radio would no longer work.

"No more info by radio," Nate said. "There's only one way to find out what's going on locally. As for Washington and the rest of the country, we may not know for months." He got up from the porch, his rifle in hand. "I'll go talk it over with Deni. It's time for me to take over security in the front, anyway."

~~~

Caroline slipped into the shoulder straps on her backpack and tightened the waist strap. "I'm glad we had a chance to rest up and eat regularly for a while. It's going to be a long trip for Samantha."

Brian patted Samantha on the head. "Don't you worry. This trip will be easy compared to what we went through coming out here. There won't be any mean men chasing us this time."

Nate raised an eyebrow, but said nothing.

Deni gave Samantha a hug in an effort to calm her fears. "There won't be any big rush this time either. You'll probably be able to walk most of the way, unless you get tired. We've all been so busy we haven't had time to give you the attention we should have. But we all think a lot of you."

Nate looked around to make sure they hadn't left anything. Closing the door to the cabin he said, "Let's go. Keep five-yard spacing with Deni in the rear. Stay alert."

As the day progressed and the miles passed under their feet, Nate worried that the others were being a little too lax. He had to admit to himself, though, that the woods did seem less menacing than they had since all the way back to the day Brian was shot in the leg almost two years before. Long ago, fighting some needless jungle war some politician had sent Americans to fight, Nate had developed the ability to tell when he was being hunted. He didn't have that feeling on this day. Nevertheless, he refused to let his guard down and took every precaution.

Despite Nate's precautions, they made good time and found themselves less than a half a mile from the MacKay farm two days later.

"You know the routine," Nate said. "Deni and I'll check out the farm, and if everything's okay we'll come back to get you."

Deni and Nate had not gone 200 yards when movement in the woods ahead sent them ducking behind trees for cover. They shouldered their rifles and clicked the safety off, ready for trouble. They both flinched when a rifle shot boomed. A terrified squealing wild hog crashed through the brush and into a small clearing, where it turned a tight circle and then fell over dead, blood pouring from his chest.

A teenage boy crept along, following the blood trail and torn up soil that the fleeing hog had left behind. He carried a lever action 30/30 in his hands.

Nate and Deni smiled at each other.

"Hey, Pedro," Nate yelled. He waved at the teenage boy.

Pedro froze in his tracks for a second, but then recognized Nate's voice even before he saw him. He walked on up to the hog and waved when he finally saw Nate step out from behind a tree.

Nate walked up and shook Pedro's hand. "Good shooting. You've got a lot of pork there." Nate motioned with his head towards the farm. "How are things? Is it safe for us to come on in?"

Pedro nodded and smiled. "Yes everything is fine. No trouble lately. You are welcome to come there with me. Everyone will be happy to see you."

Nate spoke to Deni, "Why don't you go get the others while I help Pedro field dress the hog?"

She nodded and disappeared into the woods.

~~~

A man ran into the house and informed Mrs. MacKay of the arrival of Nate and company. A crowd of more than 20 smiling men, women, and children met them. Pedro and Nate had tied the gutted hog to a pole and were carrying it between them, with the pole on their shoulders. Nate noticed the crowd was in a good mood. Everyone laughed and joked. Some of the children said hello to Samantha and told her they missed her.

MacKay approached them with a smile on her face. She looked them over, perhaps for injuries or signs of illness. "I'm so happy to see all of you alive and well. Dinner will be served just before sundown. I hope you'll join us."

Caroline hugged several of the women and children. "I was so worried. We heard explosions and feared they had bombed the farm."

"Can you tell us anything about what's going on?" Nate asked. "We've been in the dark for days."

MacKay raised her brows, wrinkling her forehead. "The short answer is things seem to be getting better at the moment. So far the military has been doing exactly what they promised they would do. And it does look like we'll have national elections soon. As for the long answer, we'll talk it over on the porch where it's cooler."

Most of the crowd left to go back to work, but a few stayed to listen. MacKay settled into a chair and invited her visitors to find a chair also. "I'm afraid what I'm about to say will turn your stomach and make you angry. Evidently things are coming to light about the source of the plague."

Nate and the others glanced at each other, but remained quiet, waiting to hear what she had to say.

A look of total repugnance darkened her face. "It appears there was a group of wealthy, powerful, and soulless men and women, including scientists, who took it upon themselves to design a terrible disease. They planned to release it after they had inoculated parts of the human race they, in their infinite wisdom and egos, had decided were not useless eaters and therefore were necessary to carry on the human race." She gave them a strange look of repulsion. "Mind you, most of those they deemed fit to live were just common working people. I guess even elitists understand that all societies need people who do all the work. But most of the third world and the less affluent areas of the developed world, well, they just had no use for them. So their plan was to inoculate those they wanted to live and kill off the rest." She held her stomach and took several seconds to regain her composure before she went on. "Something happened before they had a chance to inoculate very many people. Even most of the elite, the first on their list to be protected, hadn't been inoculated when someone at one of their disease production centers made a mistake and Pandora's Box was opened before they were ready." She closed her eyes. Tears ran down her face. "You know the results."

Caroline commented, "I'm sure the leaders of the scheme were all men."

Ignoring her, Nate said, "We discovered some of what you just told us ourselves. A prisoner Tyrone and his men took to town told the part he was willing to admit to knowing. Of course he claimed he started working for Capinos after the plague had done its work and had nothing to do with murdering over 90% of the human population."

Deni leaned forward in her chair. "I guess he's the one the military got the rest of the story from."

MacKay wiped her face. "No. They have another witness. They won't say who he is or where he is. Evidently the National Guard has him."

Brian froze for a second, his mind racing. "You don't suppose Kramer made it out of that swamp and lived, do you?"

"Now that's an idea," Deni said. "But it could be anyone."

"Oh yes." MacKay seemed to remember something. "Your friend Mel was here yesterday looking for you. He had flown over your farm in a helicopter and saw you had been burned out. Anyway, he said to tell you he was formulating a plan to help you get another home built. I guess his friends in the Guard were offering to help. He also said to tell you he had met a friend of yours and to tell you that Henry had lost his left arm but had recovered and was talking like a canary." She shook her head. "I have no idea what he meant by all that. He was being very obscure about it."

Brian laughed. "I have no idea what he was trying to say."

"Neither do I," Deni said, a smile on her face.

Caroline quipped, "Ignorance is much safer for all concerned. I don't know nothin'."

MacKay leaned back in her chair, a twinkle in her eye. "Now that you've jogged my memory with your coyness, I seem to remember a Henry." She rubbed the scars on her arm. "But let's change the subject."

Chapter 26

Nate and the others stayed at the horse farm that night. The next morning, Nate sat on the front porch and talked with Deni and Brian about going into town with a truck borrowed from MacKay to look for building materials. They had to build something to live in out on the farm, even if it was just temporary.

While they were talking, a Black Hawk flew by, following the dirt road.

"Now what?" Brian wondered.

As dozens of people gathered in the front yard to watch, a second helicopter circled the farm and then landed in the road near the gate.

"Should we run into the woods?" a man standing nearby asked.

Three soldiers appeared, walking down the drive and escorted by one of the men guarding the gate. Nate grabbed his binoculars from his pack. He smiled. "It's Mel!"

"Great!" Brian put his rifle down.

"Do you recognize who is with him?" Deni asked.

"Col. Greene," Nate answered. "I don't recognize the other soldier."

Caroline had come out of the house with Samantha. "Mel and Greene are two of the dozen men in the world I have respect for. He made sure I was taken care of when I lost my leg. Him and Mel both."

Deni gave her a sideways glance. "Most men wouldn't think of hurting you. Way too many would, but most wouldn't."

Caroline came back with, "You can't tell until you get to know them."

"Let's discuss the darker side of men some other time," Nate said. "Something's up or they wouldn't be here." He raised his right hand and waved.

Col. Greene approached them. He got straight to the point. "We're delivering two prebuilt sheds to your farm. Not exactly comparable to this place, but they'll do for now. Trucks will be going by sometime within the hour with the sheds on trailers. The road's kind of rough and it's slow going, but they'll be here."

"Huh?" Nate asked. "What're you talking about?"

Greene looked around at the gathering crowd and noticed that not all of them seemed pleased to see him. "Don't worry, ladies and gentlemen, this is a friendly visit."

"Yeah," Mel added, "Colonels don't walk around in hostile country with just two sergeants for security. We thought we would be welcome here, especially since we're bearing gifts and good news."

Nate tilted his head. "Why are you giving us those sheds?"

Greene rested his left hand on his pistol belt, hooking it with his thumb, and rested his right hand on the butt of his pistol. "It was Capinos who ordered the air strike on your home. The way I see it, that makes the U.S. Government responsible for the damages. The sheds are just for you to use until we can get enough men over there to start work on a new home and barn."

"I expect the well and hand pump are gone too," Brian said. "Probably even the septic system got blown up."

Greene pulled a notepad out of a pocket and scribbled on it. "Mel, you should've told me about the well. You've been to the farm."

"Sorry, sir." Mel winked at Nate. "If you want, I'll make a list."

"You do that," Greene said.

A shadow of anger fell on Nate's face. "Was it Capinos who authorized the air strike on my family and friends while his private army was hunting us in the woods?"

Greene looked back at him. "I understand how you feel, but Capinos is dead. No need to waste time hating the bastard. Yes, he authorized the air strikes, but the one in the woods happened after he was dead. His killers who were hunting you had the plug pulled on them soon after that and lost all support. I guess they continued to hunt you anyway, not knowing what else to do. We didn't know anything about much of this until later. Since then, we've found witnesses who've helped authorities make arrests all over the world. Got about three dozen locked up here in the U.S." He cleared his throat. "We made the mistake of naming a few people in the less civilized countries.

Well, they didn't bother with a trial. Some of the poor bastards died slow, even a few women."

"Maybe they're not as uncivilized as you think," Caroline offered. "Maybe we could learn from them."

Greene gave her a strange but understanding smile. "Well, I guess our ways are different from theirs."

Something caught Deni's attention.

Greene noticed and turned to look up the driveway to see a Humvee coming. "That'll be your ride." He turned back to those on the porch. "That is, if you're ready to go home. We need you to tell us where to put the sheds. I'm sure you'll want them out of the way of the area where you want the new home built."

"Well," Nate said, "we were thinking of going into town to scrounge up building materials. But I guess we could go on to the farm first."

"Don't worry about building materials." Greene checked his watch. "I've got to get back to the base. Mel can go with you in the Humvee."

Deni shook Col. Greene's hand. "Thanks for helping us out."

Greene smiled. "We haven't started yet. This country owes you more than we could ever repay."

Mel spread his arms. "Well, grab your stuff if you're going."

Samantha pulled at Caroline's arm. She bent down and listened as the little girl spoke in her ear. Caroline stood. "I guess Samantha and I'll stay here for a while. I would like to help you with the house, but Samantha wants to stay where she feels safer and there are children her age."

Deni hugged them both. "Probably the best for her. You're both welcome anytime. Visit or stay forever. You're part of the family."

Nate held Caroline and patted Samantha on the head. "Deni's right. You're both part of the family."

"Yep," Brian added, "we've been through too much together not to be friends for life."

After saying quick good-byes to Mrs. MacKay and the others, they grabbed their packs and rifles and jumped into the Humvee.

Colonel Greene got out at the road and transferred to the waiting Black Hawk. Mel took his place on the passenger side in the front to make more room for the others, and the driver started for Nate's farm.

Halfway there, they rounded a curve in the pothole-filled dirt road. The driver had to slam on the brakes when a 12-year-old boy ran out of the woods. He was bleeding from the nose and mouth and had obviously been beaten. His eyes were wild with terror as he scrambled to the driver side of the Humvee, yelling something unintelligible and pointing into the woods. Mel jumped out with his rifle at the same time Nate did. Deni and Brian were not far behind. The driver remained seated behind the wheel in case they had to leave in a hurry.

"He's one of Mrs. MacKay's people." Brian said to the boy, "Slow down. We can't understand you."

The boy pointed. "Down that Jeep trial. Men are hurting my mother." He caught his breath. "They killed my father."

A woman screamed in the distance.

Deni took several steps on the run, her M4 in both hands.

"Hold on!" Nate caught up with her. "We can't rush into this."

Mel pointed down the road. "That looks like the turnoff to the Jeep trail." He looked at Nate. "How do you want to do this?"

"We sure won't use the trail. Could be an ambush." Nate looked at the boy. "If it is, he's a damn good actor. No matter, we'll come in careful."

The driver grabbed the boy and threw him in the Humvee, then backed down the road 100 yards and waited.

The woman continued to scream.

"Let's go," Deni said. "Damn it."

Nate led them into the woods. They paralleled the Jeep trail 30 yards back, using the woman's screaming as a beacon. They found two vehicles on the trail, a flatbed truck mired in sand and a four-wheel-drive pickup stopped just behind it. All of the doors on the vehicles were open. It appeared the occupants exited in a hurry.

The scene they came to next was something Nate wished Brian wasn't there to witness. Before he knew it, Deni had killed two of the men, putting a bullet in their heads. The third one ran into the woods, obviously unarmed, since he had no pants on. Nate yelled, "Stay here and stay alert." He took off after the man, but not in a direct way. Instead, he circled around the scene of carnage and didn't go near the screaming woman.

The woman seemed to be too dazed to do anything but stare at her dead husband and cry.

Brian held his rifle with sweaty hands. "It's been forever. Why didn't he let us go with him?"

"Five minutes or so," Mel corrected him. "Just enough time for Nate to break every bone in his body." He looked around again, trying to penetrate the wall of green and search out any danger, seeing no sign of anyone. "I'll go, but I expect to find little left of that SOB, just a bloody mud puddle."

"Oh, forget what Nate said." Deni started across the trail. "Stay here my ass. He's always going off to fight alone." She stopped when Nate appeared, dragging the bloody and unconscious man by the feet.

Nate stopped in the middle of the trail. "I think he tripped on a root and hurt himself."

Deni barely looked at the rapist, looking instead at the crying woman. "Yep. That's what happened. He must've fallen down about 20 times. I'll go help her. You better put some pants on that asshole before I shoot him." She ran down the trail.

Mel and Brian walked up. Looking down at the prone rapist, Mel said, "I'm not giving him my pants, only have what I'm wearing. Why don't you just let Deni shoot him?"

Nate half-smiled, still catching his breath. "So you heard that, did you?"

"Why didn't you shoot him?" Brian asked. "He deserves it."

"I thought I would hand him over to the Guard and see what the new official brand of justice looks like. We've had plenty of unofficial street justice lately." Nate kicked the rapist over on his stomach. "Anyone have something to tie him up with?"

Mel produced handcuffs. "This should work."

Nate put them on the man's wrists. "I wonder what Col. Greene would say we should do with him."

Mel laughed. "He would've shot him before he got into the woods."

"Hmm," Nate said, "I guess official justice isn't much different from the do-it-yourself kind."

Mel laughed. "He calls it apocalypse law. We get back to the Humvee, I'll radio it in and get the victims some help and this asshole off our hands." He grinned. "Then we'll see about building you a home. I think things are going to get better now. After the election, we'll have a real government in Washington, and in time, we'll have local and state government back and civilian law enforcement. The military will still be needed for awhile, but over time, we'll pull back and let the civilian government take over like it should be."

"Sounds good," Brian said. "But I think Dad'll still be kicking ass when it's called for. He can't help himself."

Also by John Grit

Feathers on the Wings of Love and Hate:

Let the Gun Speak

(Volume 1 in the series)

Feathers on the Wings of Love and Hate 2:

Call Me Timucua

(Volume 2 in the series)

Apocalypse Law

(Volume 1 in the series)

Apocalypse Law 2

(Volume 2 in the series)

Apocalypse Law 3

(Volume 3 in the series)

Apocalypse Law 4

Raw Justice

(Volume 4 in the series)

Patriots Betrayed

Short Stories
To Kill a Cop Killer
Fierce Blood
Old Hate

14909481R00166

Made in the USA
San Bernardino, CA
08 September 2014